# CALLUM'S MISSION

A LOGAN FAMILY WESTERN - BOOK 3

DONALD L. ROBERTSON

CM Publishing

# COPYRIGHT

**Callum's Mission**


CM Publishing





Don@DonaldLRobertson.com

❀ Created with Vellum

to remove the loop. "Get up."

He gathered his rope, hung it back on his saddle, and led the animals to the hitching rail. Once the animals were tied, he turned back to the four men. "Now, all of you, on your feet."

When they were up and standing together, Callum said, "All right, what's going on here?"

No one answered, but three of the men looked at the man wearing the bloody red-and-white checkered shirt with the badge almost torn off. Callum stepped up to him. "Philo, what in the world are you doing attacking Bret?"

He said nothing.

"He's been bullying the town, along with his brother Noah," Jenkins, the storekeeper said. "Since his pa took over as marshal, nobody's safe."

Philo turned toward Jenkins. With his right eye swollen shut, and his left puffed and red, he gave Jenkins what evidently was supposed to be a hard look. Unfortunately for him, it was only comical. Some in the crowd laughed.

"Don't worry about Mr. Jenkins, Philo," Callum said. "I'm the man you should be concerned about. Why did you attack my brother?"

Philo looked down, moved some dirt around with the toe of his boot, and mumbled something.

"What?" Callum snapped. "Speak up."

This time Philo looked up at Callum. "I said, he started it."

Callum hit him, a short, powerful right. The blow landed directly on his left eye. The man grabbed his face and fell to his knees, moaning.

Leaning near Philo's ear, Callum said, "I know Bret didn't start it. You can tell your pa, the marshal, to stay away from my family. This is your only warning."

He straightened and looked at each of the battered men. "Did all of you hear what I just told Philo?"

Each one nodded.

# 1

The tall man sat erect on the back of the big roan appaloosa, leading a buckskin mule. Sweat rolled down from under his gray hat and across a broad forehead, eventually reaching the wrinkles at the corners of his light blue eyes. A warbler intoned his intermittent song, while a mockingbird, sitting on a limb above the rider's head, joined in.

Callum Jeremiah Logan was excited. His stern face didn't reflect it, but he felt it in his heart. He was nearing home. The thick hardwood forest thinned, suddenly opening to a small town with a wide main street. Oak and hickory trees surrounded the little town of Limerick, Tennessee. Not much happened here, as Callum could attest, since he had grown up no more than ten miles away.

Today, though, people crowded the opposite end of the normally calm street. Callum walked the appaloosa toward the crowd. He heard someone yell, "Leave the boy alone!" The sound of blows being hammered home carried to him.

As he reached the edge of the crowd, he saw what the spectators were watching.

Four grown men were attacking a boy of sixteen, though he

did look older. The boy's knuckles were bloody, along with his shirt, but none of the other four had gone unscathed. Each was bleeding from the battle. Callum knew the boy was sixteen because he was his younger brother Bret. Blood streamed from his nose, but he was still on his feet, serving whoever came within range.

Callum loosed his lariat from the piggin' string on his saddle, making a loop while walking Shoshone, his appaloosa, toward the fight. He dropped the mule's lead rope and rode into the crowd. The spectators separated, giving the rider on the big horse ample room. He rode to the nearest man, slipped his boot out of the stirrup, and kicked him with the heel of his boot, striking him in the back of his head. He dropped like someone had hit him with an axe handle. Callum tossed the loop over another of the men and jerked hard, yanking him off his feet and into the dirt. After dallying the rope around his saddle horn and dropping to the ground, he disregarded the man—he knew his horse. Shoshone would maintain a tight rope, keeping the man on the ground.

The remaining two men, shocked, stood with their hands hanging to their sides. Bret walked up to the older man, in the bloody red-and-white checkered shirt and drove his left hand deep into the man's stomach.

Callum recognized him, Philo Pickering. A quick thought flashed through his mind. *What are the Pickerings doing jumping Bret?*

From the force of Bret's blow, Philo doubled over. As his head jerked down, the sixteen-year-old grabbed the man by both ears and drove his head into his rising knee. Philo collapsed, unconscious. Bret turned, looking for the next assailant, and saw his big brother grinning at him, the other man lying on his back, toes pointing to the sky. The crow cheered.

"You shore know how to welcome a brother, boy."

Bret grinned back and stuck out his hand. Callum walked up,



knocked the hand away, and gave him a big bear hug. He broke the embrace, stepped back, and surveyed the young man. The four men had landed some damaging blows. The boy's lips were smashed, it looked like his nose was broken, he had a big welt on his right cheek, and a deep, bleeding cut arced over his left eye.

"I'm really glad you're back, Callum."

"Why is Philo jumping you, and who are these other yahoos?" Callum asked.

"It's a long story."

The man Callum had kicked was on his knees, starting to get up.

"Stay down, Mister," Callum said.

"I ain't staying down. I'm gettin' up."

Callum walked over to the man, placed his boot, none too gently, on the man's rear and gave a hard shove. The man sprawled, facedown, back in the dirt. Callum then turned to the crowd, recognizing some familiar faces.

Mr. Jenkins, the storekeeper, was standing to the rear of the crowd. "Mr. Jenkins, would you mind getting Marshal Stevens? These boys oughta cool their heels in jail for a while."

"Welcome back, Callum," Jenkins said. "Stevens is no longer our marshal. The fine people of Limerick have voted in a new one —a Pickering. He won't do nothing to his kin. In fact, two of them are deputies."

"Let me outa this rope. That danged horse keeps pulling m down when I try to get up."

Callum turned to Bret. "You have a gun?"

"Not with me. It's in the wagon."

Callum pulled one of his Remington Beals from the hol and handed it to his brother. "Keep an eye on 'em. If they tr leave, shoot 'em. I've got to tie up my horse and mule."

Callum walked over to the man, turned to Shoshone, said, "Easy."

The horse relaxed the tension on the rope, allowing C

"Good. That applies to all of you. Now, git!"

Philo had regained his feet but was still holding his face. The four men hurried up the street, disappearing into the marshal's office.

Mr. Jenkins approached Callum as the crowd dissipated. He stuck out his hand. "It's sure good to see you, boy. If I was younger, Bret, here, would've had some help. Although, I must say, he was holding his own pretty good, for a young fellow."

"How are you, Mr. Jenkins? It's been a while."

"Fine, fine. What's it been, a year, since you and Josh pulled out for the West? There's been some almighty drastic changes since you boys left. Before I start, let me say I'm truly sorry for what has happened to your folks."

Callum was watching his bleeding brother, half-listening until Jenkins mentioned his parents. He whipped back around. "What do you mean? What's happened?"

"I'm sure Bret will fill you in, but your folks were burned out over a month ago. Seven of your pa's best horses died in the barn fire. On top of that, a proclamation came in that collaborators with rebel forces would be subject to confiscation of all property."

"That's crazy. It was a war, and two of their sons fought for the North."

"Makes no never mind. The state government is made up of the Radicals, most from Eastern Tennessee. They were in unconditional agreement with the North, and have completely taken over the government. If a family had anyone fighting for the South, they're considered collaborators. Why, I'd—"

"I'd like to stay and talk, Mr. Jenkins, but Bret needs to head home. He needs some tending to."

"Yes, yes, I understand," Jenkins said, glancing at Bret's swollen and bloody face. "You best be on your way." He turned and started for his store.

"Let's get home," Callum said.

Bret lurched toward the wagon, while Callum untied

Shoshone and Buck. After mounting, he followed the younger Logan. By the time he got there, a man with a shotgun had approached his brother.

Callum recognized Old Man Pickering. The frock coat did little to hide Pickering's belly overhanging his trousers. It was obvious the two were arguing. Bret's height, already crowding six feet, forced the pudgy marshal to look up at him as he shook his finger in Bret's face.

Pickering turned his head and locked Callum in a gaze from his little, beady eyes. "You should've stayed gone, but since you're back, I'm placing you under arrest."

"What's the charge, Marshal, spanking your deputies?"

Pickering pulled the hammers back and started to swing the weapon to cover Callum. The barrels had barely begun to move, when he found himself staring into the muzzle of Callum's Remington.

"You keep turning that shotgun toward me, Pickering, and your boys'll be hauling your fat carcass to the cemetery. Now, hand it to Bret, and do it nice and easy."

Pickering stopped his swing and cautiously handed Bret the double-barreled ten-gauge. Bret shucked the two caps from the nipples. He then closed it and started to lean it against the store front, noticing the faces staring through the glass, watching the confrontation.

"Wait, Bret," Callum said. "Reach down and break off a couple of good-size splinters and stuff 'em in the nipples. We don't want the marshal, here, popping a couple of caps on that greener and blasting us before we get out of range."

Bret reached down to the rough wood of the boardwalk and ripped away two thick splinters.

Pickering stood, watching, red-faced and frowning. "You got no right to do that. I'll have to take those nipples off and clean 'em out."

Bret gave the shotgun back to the marshal.

"You finished what you come for, Bret?" Callum asked.

The boy nodded, his eyes on the marshal.

"Then why don't you climb back into that wagon, and we'll take our leave of this fine town," Callum said.

"I'm coming after you boys. You can't treat the law like this and get away with it."

Callum slid the Remington back into its holster. "Don't make that mistake, Pickering."

Bret popped the reins, turned the horses in the street, and headed them out of town. Callum held Pickering's gaze a moment longer, then, turning in the saddle, so he could watch Pickering, followed Bret.

They rode for a mile without saying anything, watching their back trail. Finally, Callum said, "Pull up, and I'll ride with you." He dismounted, tied Shoshone and Buck to the back of the wagon, and slid his Spencer from the boot. Then he lifted his canteen from around the horn and walked to Bret's side of the wagon. "You need a little tending."

"I'm fine. We need to git on to the house."

"First things first. Lean over here." Callum pulled his neckerchief from his neck and doused it good with water. He went to work cleaning his brother's face, starting with the cut over his eye. "That's a pretty bad cut. Ma may need to sew it up when we get home." Callum went on cleaning until most of the blood was gone. He poured more water on the cloth to rinse it, then wrung it out and retied it around his neck. As soon as he had climbed up onto the seat next to Bret, the boy started the team.

"Thanks."

Callum, an anxious frown on his face, said, "Is everyone all right?"

Bret nodded. "Yeah, but it's bad, Callum, real bad. They burned down the house and the barn. If it hadn't been for Frank, we might've died trapped in the house."

Callum turned to watch for anyone following them, but the

road was clear. Bret had stopped talking. "Go ahead, the road's clear."

Bret again nodded and slid his flop hat to the back of his head. "Whoever set the fires meant to kill us and the horses. I don't understand that kind of meanness. They could've had the place by auction if they'd just waited. The state had already delivered a letter to Pa saying because of his collaboration with the South, they were taking the land and the property. It was brought out by Marshal Pickering."

"Pickering doesn't have jurisdiction outside the town," Callum said.

"He does now. He's been given special authority to deliver these papers all over the county."

"Mr. Jenkins said we lost seven horses in the fire."

"It was a terrible thing. That lumber in the house and barn was old and dry, went up like kindling. Even with Frank's warning, we just barely got out of the house, and you should have heard the horses in the barn." Bret stopped for a moment, fighting to control his emotions. The lives of all the family members were tied up in the horses, and this type of grisly loss struck deep in each one.

Callum squeezed his brother's shoulder.

Bret continued. "As if that wasn't enough, they even managed to shoot our other horses. The only reason these two survived, was Pa and Colin had taken them up Short Mountain to get a deer. They were going to camp out and be back the next day. Course, when they saw the flames they charged on back, but they was too late."

Callum couldn't believe it. All the Morgans gone except for these two mares. It took a pretty low-life brute to set a person's home on fire and kill their stock. "So, this is all the riding stock you have left?"

"Yes, sir. This is it. All them years Pa worked with the Morgan line, gone, except for these two."

"Don't forget Chancy," Callum said. "He's still in fine shape."

"Speakin' of Chancy, how's Josh doing?"

Callum grinned. "He's good. I'll tell everyone about his escapades when we get together. How's Ma and Pa?"

"They're both fine. You know them. They don't worry about yesterday. Course, if Pa finds the men that done this, he'll kill 'em. He's not long on patience for bad folks."

Callum nodded in agreement. Though Ma believed in it, Pa wasn't long on forgiveness either, once he or his had been wronged. Come to think of it, forgiveness wasn't one of Callum's top traits either.

Bret guided the horses off the road and onto a narrow path. Callum, noticing the turnoff, said, "You living at the old place?"

"Yeah. It's pretty crowded. The men sleep outside, leaving the house to Ma and Kate. We helped Pa throw up an open shed for Ma to cook under—keeps the sun and rain off."

They continued through the forest for several miles. A small white-tail fawn stepped into the trail ahead of them. The sunlight that slipped through the thick canopy glistened on the young deer's spots. The doe walked into the opening, looked at them, flicked her tail, and leaped into the thicket, the fawn following.

Callum gazed at his brother. The boy looked tired and dejected. It was hard enough on the adults when a tragedy like this struck, but the young folks' hurt went deep. Callum knew how close the family was with the animals that died. He felt sure his sister, Kate, was struck the worst from this despicable act. She loved every one of those horses, and had been instrumental in their care through their growing years.

"You ready to head for Colorado?" Callum asked.

At the mention of Colorado, Bret's face brightened. "Danged right I am."

"Boy, you're not too old for Ma's lye soap. If she hears you swearing like that, she's liable to stuff a whole bar in your mouth."

Bret turned to his brother and grinned. “I’ve heard you. You’re no angel. She’d have to wash both our mouths out.”

“You’ve got a point.” Callum was about to continue when they broke out into the small clearing.

Less than fifty yards away sat the old homeplace. Pa and Frank worked on the house, while Kate helped Ma with the cooking. Callum looked around. He didn’t see Colin, his youngest brother. Everyone turned to look at the wagon. Kate started to wave, stopped, stared for a moment, then broke into a run, her long blonde hair glistening in the sun. Pa shaded his eyes from the bright sunlight, turned and said something to Ma, and then Frank. The three of them started toward the wagon.

Bret pulled up when Kate reached them. Callum stepped down and picked up his sister in his big arms, swinging her around like a little girl. She hugged him, laughing. He stopped and held her away from him. “My, my, I reckon in the past year, you’ve turned into about the prettiest girl in all of Tennessee.”

She slapped him on the chest. “You’re just as big a liar as you’ve always been.” Her blue eyes flashed with laughter, then suddenly became sad.

“Did Bret tell you?” she asked, just now looking at Bret. Seeing his swollen nose and the cut over his eye, along with dried blood that Callum had missed, her eyes grew large. “Oh my goodness, Bret, what happened to you?”

Ma moved directly to Bret, looked his face over quickly, and turned to Frank and Pa. “Matthew,” she said to Pa, “you’ve got enough help. I’m taking this boy. He needs that eyebrow sewn up.” She turned back and said, “Come on, son.”

“Oh, Ma,” Bret said, “I’m fine.”

Without another word, she stepped to the side of the wagon, grasped her son’s arm and yanked him off the seat. With Bret in tow, she marched to the house. Looking over her right shoulder, she said to Callum, “It’s good to see you, son. We’ll talk later.”

# 2

Callum watched his youngest brother come dashing from behind the house. Colin slid to a stop in front of him. “What happened to Bret’s face? Do we have a place in Colorado? Are the mountains taller than Short Mountain? Did you see any Indians? When—”

“Whoa, little brother. There’ll be plenty of time to answer all of your questions,” Callum said, removing his left arm from around his sister, then grasping and squeezing Colin’s shoulder. “You’ve grown like a horseweed, and I can feel some real muscle there. You’re almost as tall as Kate, but not near as pretty.”

Colin grinned his satisfaction with his brother’s compliment.

Kate gazed up at her older brother. Though sad, she glowed with excitement. “You’ve been gone so long. Where’s Josh? What happened to Bret?”

He watched his father and Frank stride toward him. “That’ll wait, Kate.” His worry over his father’s appearance caused the short answer. The patriarch was looking old, and slightly stooped. But what could you expect—his Pa was seventy-one. Glancing down, he could see the hurt in his sister’s face. He grabbed her up in another hug, and whispered in her ear, "Sorry, I was just worried about Pa."

She flashed him a look of understanding as their pa and Frank reached them.

"Welcome home, son. It's good to have you back," Matthew Logan said, extending his large hand to his son.

Callum felt the strong, firm handshake of his father and knew some relief when he felt the strength still in that hand. "Thanks, Pa. It's good to be back. How's your leg?"

Matthew Logan looked down at it and swung it around. "Seems to be working mighty well. Don't think it'll slow me down on our way West. We are going West, aren't we?"

"Yes, sir, we sure are."

Frank had been holding back while the family had their say. Callum stepped over to the hired hand and extended his hand. "Good to see you, Frank. Pa's not working you too hard, is he?"

Frank grinned as he shook Callum's hand. "Of course he is, boy. He don't stop."

"Believe me, Frank, I know how you feel."

"Let's get these things unloaded, and, Colin, you can put the wagon up and take care of the horses."

"But, Pa, I wanted to hear what Callum has to say."

"You'll hear everything, Colin," Callum said. "I've got to unload my horse and mule, and give them a rubdown. I'll be right there with you."

"We'll all be there, except Kate," Pa said. "Kate, honey, why don't you go help your Ma? We'll be in shortly."

Kate was patting Shoshone on the neck. The big stallion seemed to enjoy her attention. "This is a beautiful horse, Callum. I don't think I've ever seen one like him."

Callum rubbed Shoshone's nose. "He's a fine animal. He's lost some weight with our trip, but it won't take long for him to put it back on. Now, you'd better do what Pa says. I'll tell you all about him when we come in."

She gave the spotted horse one more rub and ran for the house.

"When'd she start wearing pants, Pa?"

"Right after you and Josh headed West. What'll surprise you is that Ma suggested it. She said that since Kate was doing so much man's work, it would be easier if she wore pants. Her dresses were getting filthy, and occasionally, her feet got caught up in the hem. We didn't want her falling when she was working stock."

Colin had jumped in the wagon, driven it next to the old lean-to, and started unhooking the two horses. The men followed, and with all three working, leaving Callum to take care of his animals, they had the wagon unloaded, the tack hanging, and the horses watered, fed, and rubbed down in rapid fashion. With Callum finished, the four men grabbed the supplies that were meant for the house and headed across the yard.

They set the supplies on the rough table, outside the house. Callum looked around, then turned to his pa. "Bret filled me in on what happened, but I'd like to hear it from you."

"First, I want a hug from my boy," his ma said, walking out of the house with Bret, the cut over his left eye now sewn closed.

Callum enclosed his ma in his big arms. Her smell of lilacs and biscuits, tinged with a hint of bacon, brought back many happy memories. After the hug, she stepped away, and Callum smiled down at her. "I'm glad you're all right, Ma. You do smell good."

She laughed as she stepped past Callum to get to the cooking stand over the outside fire, pushing her son in the chest. "You were always full of the blarney, but it's good to have you home."

At the mention of home, a momentary pall hung over the family. "Here, now," Pa said, "we'll have none of that. We'll be headed for our new home in Colorado soon. We have an adventure ahead of us, and a lot of hard work."

Kate piped up. "Hard work's nothing new around here."

Ma turned from the big iron pot she had been stirring and popped Kate on the bottom with the wooden spoon. "Keep a civil tongue, young lady."

Everyone laughed, including Kate, but she moved out of range of her ma.

"I'd like to know what happened here, Pa," Callum said.

"We'll talk about that later. Right now, I think we all need to hear the good news you bring. Rebecca, if supper is about ready, why don't we all settle around the table, and Callum can bring us glad tidings while we eat."

Rebecca smiled at her husband. She, Kate, and Colin started moving food to the table.

The roughed-out table, where everyone had their place, had been built by Pa years ago, when he and Ma with their new baby, William Wallace Logan, the oldest of the brood, had first moved here. Over the years and after they had moved into the big house, they would come back up to the mountain home to picnic. Pa had built chairs, as the need demanded, and today, everyone had one.

The outside cooking fire was more than just a fire. Pa and Frank had dug a shallow, eight-foot long pit that was now full of hot coals. The blacksmith in Limerick had built the supports from Pa's drawings. A steel rod, about three feet above the hot coals, ran the length of the pit, and was supported by metal tripods at each end, with a bipod in the middle. An assortment of pots hung from long metal hooks. About three feet of the pit had no pots hanging over it. This was where Ma did her baking.

Once the food was distributed on the table, the family sat. Pa was at one end with Ma on his right, with the children seated on opposite sides of the table. Frank sat at the other end.

"Sit here by me," Pa said to Callum.

Once everyone was seated, Pa bowed his head. "Lord, we thank you for Callum returning safe and ask you to watch over Josh, and also William, wherever he might be. We're grateful for this here food we have before us, though it was by our own sweat it was growed. Amen."

Callum smiled inwardly. Pa believed in God, but he couldn't stand the rigid, organized religions. However, he loved Ma, who was a devout Presbyterian, and, for the most part, at least, respected her beliefs. She looked at her husband, after the prayer. "The food wouldn't have grown, Matthew, without the Lord's rain."

Callum watched the other kids. They were all trying to hide their grins. It had been like this since he was a boy.

Their father patted his wife's hand. "I know, Becky. We can use all the help the Lord wants to pass on to us." He then shot a stern look at their not-so-young kids. "Quit your grinnin' and get to eatin'."

"Yes, Pa," echoed from around the table.

After they had finished, Callum leaned back in his chair. "Ma, I haven't tasted ham gravy that good since last I was here, and I can't believe those biscuits just didn't float right up off the plate."

Becky smiled at her son. "I'm glad you liked it, Callum. It's so good to have you back. Now, we want to hear about Colorado, but first, tell us about Josh. How's he doing?"

"Ma, you and Pa ain't gonna believe this." Callum was a good story teller, like his Pa and his Uncle Floyd. He reached for a biscuit, broke it open, and spread some fresh-churned butter on it.

"I sure missed your fresh butter, Ma," he said, adding a glob of homemade blackberry jelly, before taking a big bite. "Mmm. That is really good."

Kate could take it no longer. "Callum, tell us about Josh!"

The big man looked up from his biscuit with feigned surprise, "Oh yes, Josh. He's married."

Pa and Ma looked at each other, smiles on their faces. The boys shook their heads in disgust, and Kate clapped, her even, white teeth exposed in a grand smile.

"When?" Ma asked.

Callum thought for a moment. "Reckon it must be almost two years ago." He looked directly into his mother's blue eyes. "You're a grandma."

Ma grabbed Pa's arm and squeezed. "The child's a boy, and doing well, isn't he?"

Callum shook his head. "Ma, I still don't know how you do that, but you're exactly right."

Pa nodded. "She's got the gift, son. Just like your brother Josh, and Kate, here. Over the years, I've come to listen to her."

Callum nodded and continued. "Yes, sir, Ma sure does."

"What's his name?" Bret asked.

Callum looked at his pa. "Matthew Conner Logan."

His mother turned to her husband, putting her hand back on his arm. "Oh, Matthew, our first grandson is named after you."

Callum watched his pa. The older man's blue eyes filled. He ducked his head and cleared his throat. When he looked up, his eyes were clear.

"That was mighty nice of Josh and . . . what's his wife's name?"

"Her name," Callum said, "is Fianna Caitlin Logan. She was an O'Reilly. She is a well-educated young Irish woman from Massachusetts."

"Oh good," Ma said. "But how in the world did they meet?"

"Ma, that's another story in itself. I've got so much to tell you, it might take a week."

"Son," she said, "I'm glad you don't exaggerate like your Pa. Let's finish eating, then we'll get the dishes cleaned. We can sit around the table. I never thought I would say thank goodness for no rain, but I am now. Without the rain the mosquitoes aren't bad, so we can sit here and listen to your long tale." She smiled at her son in the growing darkness.

"Let's finish up, while we still have some light. I'll light the lamps," Pa said. He stood, went into the house, and returned with three glass whale oil lamps, distributing them along the table.

The rest of the family, including the boys, helped with the dishes, everyone anxious to hear Callum's stories.

After all of the family returned to the table, Callum began. He told of Josh's trip to Texas, of his brother being saved by the Indians, and about Fianna. He glossed over his troubles in Colorado and told of the ranch and gold mine. Everyone hung on his every word.

"Do we own a gold mine?" Colin asked.

Callum shook his head. "No, Colin, we don't. However, the lady that did, believed we saved her from killers, and she gave us a portion of what she received when she sold it to a mining company. So we have quite a bit of money to help build our ranch."

Pa finally said, "It's getting late. I'm sure Callum has a lot more to tell us, but it'll have to wait until morning. We've got a lot of work to do around here, if we're planning on pulling out anytime soon. You know where you're sleeping. Callum, why don't you and Frank, and Bret, join me? I want to check the animals before we go to bed." He looked over at his wife. "Becky, would you make sure beds get laid out? Callum and I need to do some talking."

She rubbed her hand along her husband's bony shoulder. "You go ahead, Matthew. I'll get the beds ready and get Colin and Kate taken care of."

Colin kicked a clod from between the chairs. "Can't I go, Pa?"

"Not this time, son. You listen to your ma. We'll be back shortly."

"You're gonna talk about the raid, aren't you? I want to hear!"

Matthew Logan stopped and turned to his youngest son. Speaking in a firm voice, he said, "Boy, you've been a big help today, but tomorrow's gonna be hard. Do as your ma says."

Callum winked at Colin. "Maybe I'll let you ride Shoshone tomorrow."

Colin's eyes lit up. "Good night, Pa. Good night, Callum. Good night, Frank." He turned and ran to his ma. "I'm ready, Ma."

She patted him on the shoulder, and the three of them went into the house to move the men's bedding outside.

The walk to the lean-to was done in silence. Upon reaching the animals, Callum said, "How bad is it, Pa?"

His father sounded tired. "It's bad, son. If it hadn't been for Frank,"—he nodded to Frank, in the thickening darkness—"the whole family could've died, except for Colin and me, in the fire. Why don't you tell what happened, Frank.?"

Frank cleared his throat, paused, and began. "It were a night like this. Darker than the inside of a powder horn. I was sleepin' in my shack over at the edge of the woods. Reckon those fellers didn't want to waste time burning it. Anyway, I don't sleep well no more, what with the rheumatis'."

"Frank, get on with it," Pa said.

Frank stopped and spit. He glared at the older man. The only things clearly visible, in the dark, were the whites of his eyes. "Don't you go tellin' me to get on with it. I may work for you, but don't git bossy on me. I ain't so old I cain't git anuther job."

Callum heard his pa chuckle, "All right, Frank, go ahead with your story."

"I aim to. Now, where was I before I was interrupted? Oh, yeah. As I was saying, my rheumatis' keeps me awake. I saw a little glow through my shack's window. For a moment there, I was thinkin' it was comin' daylight. Then I come to my senses and opened the door.

"Five scalawags were settin' the house on fire. They had already lit off the barn. It was startin' to blaze. I grabbed my Harper's Ferry 1841, picked out one of that trash what was setting fire to the house, and cut loose. That fifty-four caliber ball clean knocked him over. At the shot, them other rats got out of there fast. They grabbed the one I shot and took off for the tree line. As they passed Thunder and Amigo, they gut-shot those boys. You wouldn't find a more even-tempered stallion than Amigo, and those dirty dogs shot 'em. They was just standin' there, watchin', Callum. They'd do no harm to no one."

Frank shook his head. When he looked up, his eyes glistened in the light from the far away lamp, sitting on the table. "I raced to the house, though I don't move too fast anymore, slammed open the door, and started yelling. It was then I heard the first horse scream from the barn. Lordy, I'll never get that sound out of my head."

He looked at Callum, and with an almost pleading voice, said, "I had to warn the folks. If I'd tried to get the horses out of the barn, folks mighta died. I loved them mares. They was sweet as morning honeysuckle, but the folks came first."

Callum placed his hand on Frank's shoulder. "You did right, Frank. You had to save the family. And we're mighty appreciative."

"Yep, I did." He took a deep breath. "We managed to get everyone out, but that old dried-out timber went up fast. Didn't have a chance to save anything. Every gun yore pa owns, went up in that fiery Hell. Even that fine set of dueling pistols he was given."

Frank gave a long sigh. "Lordy, those poor horses. They all burned. They was all screamin' before they died. You ain't never heard such a bone-chillin' sound."

Callum could feel the anger boiling within him. All he could think of was getting his hands on the men who did this. *What kind of animal would set a house and barn on fire with people and horses inside, and then gut-shoot two innocent horses?*

"Did you recognize anyone, Frank?"

"Nary a soul. They left their horses down the road, and where they left 'em was in that sandy dry creek bed—no tracks to speak of. But I'll tell you one thing, if he ain't dead, that feller I shot is bad off."

"I'll do some checking," Callum said. "We need to take care of this trash, and then pull out of here.

"Pa, Bret here filled me in on the way from town, but could you go over what was lost in the barn?"

"Son, fortunately, we were able to get everyone out of the house alive, but didn't save much. Then we had to listen to the horses in the barn die. I thought it was going to kill Kate. She tried to rescue them, but I had to hold her back. You know, Goldy was her favorite. Then we had to put down Thunder and Amigo. That was almighty hard. This has been a terrible month."

Callum's right hand massaged the grip of his .44 Remington. "Pa, do you have any idea who could hate you so much as to kill all those horses and try to kill the family?"

"I've been doing some hard thinking, but I'm at a loss to come up with anyone who would be so vengeful."

"What about Noah, Pa?" Bret said.

Callum spun to Bret. "Noah Pickering? Why would he want to do this?"

"He was mad at Pa. He tried to come courting Kate, and Pa ran him off our property, told him if he ever came back, he'd horsewhip him within an inch of his life."

# 3

"Callum," Pa said, "you remember Noah Pickering?"

"Sure. He was like all of the Pickerings, shy of work and a troublemaker."

"You nailed it. After the old man managed to get elected marshal of Limerick, Noah started lording it around the countryside, He and his cronies making trouble for folks. He's read some of them dime novels that are coming out, and he fancies himself a gunfighter. He's wearing a holstered handgun low on his right hip. Figures everyone's afraid of him. Guess he felt that nothing could be done to him with his old man marshal and him a gunhand. Reckon he made a little mistake with Bret."

Callum turned to his little brother, though he was little only in age. He could look Callum almost in the eye. "What happened, Bret?"

"Wasn't much. I ran into him in town. He made a comment about Kate, and as you used to say, I read to him from the Good Book."

Frank chuckled. "I'll say he did, chapter and verse. Noah made a big mistake when he popped off to Bret about Kate. This here boy just rightly cleaned that feller's plow for him. Noah tried to pull his gun, but Bret, here, danged near broke his hand."

Callum squeezed his brother's shoulder. "Good for you, brother. How old is this Noah?"

Pa stepped in. "He's about twenty-one or two, but I can't feature even him stooping so low. The whole family could've died."

"One more question. How many does he have in his little posse?"

Bret said, "Not many, maybe three or four."

"How old are they?"

Bret thought for a moment. "The youngest is at least twenty, and the oldest is pushing twenty-five."

Callum nodded. "You know them, then."

"Yep, know 'em all."

Callum turned back to his Pa. "That's where we should start. If one of them is dead or recovering from a gunshot, we've got our horse-killers."

"It doesn't make sense, son. Old Man Pickering stood to take everything, the farm, equipment, horses, everything under this new confiscation act. It'll all go to auction, but no one will bid against Pickering. Why would his son kill what would eventually end up as his property?"

"Noah has a bad temper, Pa. I beat him up, and you really ate into him when he came here to court Kate. I hadn't thought much about it, but he could've done it." Bret was quiet for a moment, thinking. "He did it, Pa. I know he did. Let me get my rifle, and we can get after that polecat."

"Hold on, Bret," Callum said. "We can't go off half-cocked. Maybe he didn't do it. First, we need to find out who's needed a doctor recently. We've got to be careful about how we do it. Now that Pickering is the law, we don't want him coming down on our family before we get out of here. I think it best we wait until we're headed West. Then a couple of us will come back and find the killers."

Callum turned to his pa. "How long would it take for you and the family to be ready to leave?"

"Pretty fast, son. Most everything burned up in the fire. If we had the rolling stock and teams, we could be out of here in a couple of days."

"Do you know where to get them?" Callum asked.

"What do you think, oxen or mules."

Callum didn't hesitate. "Mules. If we were going to cross the mountains, I'd go with oxen, but we'll be following pretty close to the Arkansas all the way. Water won't be a problem. We'll have some rough terrain through the Indian Territory, but then we'll see it level out."

Frank spoke up. "Old Ezra Mason has all those mules. The marshal's gonna be confiscating 'em any time, since Mason's sons fought for the Confederacy. I bet he'd sell 'em to you for a good price and be happy to mess with Pickering's plans."

"That's a good thought," Pa said. "How many wagons and mules do you think, Callum?"

"Two wagons. At least twelve mules with three or four spares, so say sixteen. Does Mr. Mason have that many?"

"Oh, yeah," Frank said. "He's got at least twenty or so."

"But, son, I don't know if we have enough money for wagons, mules, and supplies."

Callum grinned, his white teeth reflecting from the lamp at the house. "We don't need to worry about money, Pa. I've a passel of gold in my bags from the sale of the gold mine. But right now, I'm dead on my feet. How about we hit the sack for tonight?"

The older man put his arm around Callum. "Sorry. I didn't consider you'd been riding all day, and you and Bret had that scuffle in town. I imagine you're both tired. Let's head for the house."

. . .

Callum rolled out of his bedroll to the early morning call of bobwhite quail. He could see his ma by the kitchen fire preparing breakfast. She, Pa, and Frank were the only ones up. He slapped his hat on, pulled up his boots, and fastened his gunbelt. Releasing the leather thongs holding the Remingtons in their holsters, he drew each and checked the loads. The big handguns slid smoothly back into their holsters.

Callum looked up and saw his ma watching him. "They're tools, Ma. To keep us alive."

"No need for you to justify guns to me, son. The Logans and my folks, the Dohertys have been protecting their families longer than you've been on this earth. Now, sit down over here with your pa and Frank, and have some breakfast."

Callum pulled up a chair next to his pa. "Mornin', Pa, Frank."

"Mornin', son."

"How do, Callum," Frank said.

"What's the plan, Pa?" Callum asked.

"I reckon gettin' those mules should be first on our list. Then we need to get a couple of wagons, and I think I know just the place."

Frank looked up at the older man, just as Colin and Bret sat down. Kate was stepping from the house. Good mornings were said all around, and Kate moved quickly to help her ma.

After the boys were seated, Frank said, "You talking about Ansel Smith?"

"I am."

"You think he'll sell to us?"

"Maybe.

"Callum," his pa said, "Ansel Smith just moved here from Vermont. He's been here goin' on six months. Says he was tired of the winters. Since the confiscation order has been published, I'm guessing it'll be touch and go whether he'll sell to us. Being from Vermont, of course he supported the North. He even lost a son, so he's not keen on supporting anyone he sees as a Southern sympathizer.

"Plus, there's another problem. The order prohibits me from purchasing any type of goods, other than what's needed for personal survival."

"All right," Callum said. "I'm gettin' a little tired of this." He got up from the table and walked over to his saddlebags. Opening one side, he rummaged in the bag for a moment, then pulled out a letter-size leather packet. From the packet, he extracted a paper. He strode back to the table, sat, and handed the letter to his pa.

Pa unfolded the letter and began to read. A smile drifted across his face. Once he finished the letter, he handed it back to Callum and said, "Why don't you tell everyone what this contains?"

After eggs, ham, biscuits, and gravy had been placed on the table, Ma and Kate sat.

Ma said, "Why don't you bless the food first, Matthew? Then everyone can eat while Callum tells us about the letter."

Everyone bowed their heads and Pa said, "Lord, we're grateful, Amen."

The short prayer drew a look from his wife, but he elected not to see it and said to his son, "Tell 'em."

Callum cleared his throat and held up the letter. "This is a statement from Josh, that I'm to act as his agent in all legal transactions and all purchases. He signed it as Major Josh Logan, United States Army, and it's been witnessed, signed, and has a seal stamped on it by the federal judge in Colorado City. Now, how about that?" He looked around the table as the kids and his ma clapped.

"Don't get too excited. This should make it easier, but Pickering and others could still muddy the water." He grinned at Kate. "But this'll make it mighty tough for 'em." Growing serious, he looked back at his pa. "What this does mean is that if it belongs to Josh, they can't take it. So, you need to sell everything to him. That way, Pickering can't confiscate anything. That includes the farm. Then, if you've got a buyer, I'll sell it to 'em. By doing that, Pickering is up a creek."

"Yes," his pa said. "That makes sense." He turned to his wife. "Is that all right with you, Becky?"

His wife smiled at him. "Thank you for asking me, Matthew. Yes, I think this is a great idea, and when Mr. Smith sees Josh's letter, I don't think he'll hesitate to sell the wagons. You know," she said, pausing to think for a moment, "he might be interested in buying this farmland, though Frank's house and this one are the only buildings still on the property."

"That's a good idea, Becky. We'll make the offer," Pa said. "Kate, get a pen and some paper from the house."

"Yes, Pa," Kate said. She jumped up and ran inside, her blonde hair flying behind her. Moments later, she returned.

Pa wrote out a bill of sale, signed it, and though it wasn't necessary, slid the paper to his wife. While handing her the quill pen, he said, "You sign it too, Becky."

The respect he showed for his wife wasn't missed by those at the table. Ma signed it, gave her husband a radiant smile, and slid the paper back to him.

"You got a dollar, son?"

"Reckon I do." Callum reached into a vest pocket and handed a dollar to his pa. The two men reached across the table and shook hands while the ink dried. Then Callum folded up the contract and put it into the leather packet with Josh's statement.

"Callum," Pa said, "I want to tell you, we had some gold money at the house that burned. It was buried under the house. After the remains died down, we went back and got it. There's about five thousand dollars in double eagles. That's what we've been saving and what we made in the horse sale a couple of months ago."

"I'm so glad we sold most of them," Kate said. "No telling how many more would be dead like Goldy." Her eyes teared up for a moment, then she regained control.

"I am too, Katy," Pa said, as all the others nodded their agreement.

There were a few moments of silence, then Pa continued. "What I was going to tell you, Callum, is that money is now yours."

"When we're out of Tennessee, I'll give it back. That money belongs to you and Ma. Besides, I've brought more than enough to take care of all the expenses. Now, one more thing. Everyone here is armed well enough to get by in Tennessee, but not on the trip or in Colorado. We have a good chance of facing hostiles, both Indian and white. So we need more weapons.

"I'd like to see everyone with at least two sidearms, including Ma and Kate. That'll give you ten fast shots when you need them. Also, we should have a repeating rifle for everyone, and a couple of extras in each wagon."

"Good gracious," Pa said, "you're talking at least five hundred dollars and that's not counting powder and ball."

"You're right, Pa, but we could need every one of them. What I recommend," Callum said, "is, first thing, we go to town and pick up those weapons."

"I hate to say it, son, but we have only two horses. We'll need to buy some more."

Bret spoke up. "Pa, you sold seventeen horses to Mr. Wright. I'd bet he'd be willing to sell some back to you, at a profit, of course." He grinned at his last comment.

Pa nodded. "I bet you're right." He thought for a moment. "Those driving the wagons will also need a mount, and we should have at least one extra, per person, for the trip." He looked at Callum. "We should buy ten, and we'll need tack for six. All of it was lost in the fire. Can we afford that much?"

"Absolutely. How about if we get a move on? I'd say the first stop is town. We'll pick up the guns, ammo, and tack. Then we'll head over to your Mr. Wright's, and see if we can cut a deal."

At his statement, Ma jumped up. "Kate, Colin, give me a hand washing these dishes. With all of us working, we'll be done quickly."

Frank stood. "I'll lend a hand, Rebecca. Reckon I still know how to wash a pan."

Thirty minutes later, Callum rode out ahead of the wagon. His pa was driving, with Ma and Kate, sitting next to him. The two boys and Frank tried to get comfortable in the wagon bed.

Mr. Jenkins had just opened his store, when they pulled up in front. Before dismounting, Callum looked around and removed the thongs from the Remingtons' hammers. He checked they were both loose, and stepped down from his saddle. He figured Shoshone must be a striking horse, because the few folks who were on the early-morning streets were looking at them. He tied Shoshone at the hitching rail, and followed his folks into the store, walking up to the counter where Jenkins stood.

He had greeted everyone as they came in, and now spoke to Callum. "Morning. How can I help you?"

"Mr. Jenkins, we need some supplies. We'll be needin' more later, but this is our business, and I'd like to know that it will stay between us."

"Certainly. I've no reason to prattle to anyone. Now, what can I do for you?"

"How many handguns do you have in stock?"

Jenkins glanced down at Callum's Remington Beals riding in his holsters. "I'm sure I have enough for your needs. Are you replacing your Remingtons?"

Callum laughed. "No, reckon not. With the attack on our

home, I just felt it would be smart for everyone to be better armed. I'm looking for two handguns and a long gun for everyone except me, and powder and lead."

Jenkins' eyebrows went up. "My, my. That will be quite a purchase." He looked at Callum, turned his head slightly, and gave an almost imperceptible nod.

"Mr. Jenkins, I can pay for it." He pulled a heavy sack from the bottom pocket of his vest and dropped it on the counter.

Jenkins eyed the sack for a moment. Gold was not seen in Limerick very often these days. "Of course you can. My apologies. Come with me."

He led Callum to the glass counter. On the wall, behind the counter, was an assortment of rifles, and under the glass sat three revolvers. Callum looked down at the handguns. "Is this all you have?"

"Oh, no, of course I have more." He slid two cartons from under the counter, picked one up, and, using the box, pushed clothing to the end of a table it was displayed on, and set it on the table. He left enough room for the second crate and retrieved it. With a small pry bar, he worked the tops off, to display a number of Colt and Remington handguns, resting in cradles.

Kate and the two boys had crowded around the crates.

"I ain't never seen this many guns before," Colin said.

Unfortunately for him, his mother was standing nearby.

"Do not say ain't, Colin, or you'll be sitting in the wagon."

Colin turned his head to look up at Callum and whispered, "Pa uses it."

"I heard that," his ma said. "One more word, Colin, and you're gone."

"I'd slack off, brother," Callum said. "You ain't winning this one."

"Callum Jeremiah Logan, you're not too old to get your ear pulled."

Callum turned and walked over to his ma. He kissed her on the check, and said, "Yes, ma'am."

She turned her twinkling blue eyes toward him. "Now, get along with you."

He laughed, walked back to the weapons, and started taking them out of the box. His pa and Frank each took one out and, while holding the hammer, tried the trigger.

"You including me in this?" Frank asked.

"Only if you're going with us."

"I don't reckon your pa could get along without me, but I'd travel to Californy for a new handgun. I don't need a rifle. I can give a grasshopper a haircut at five hundred yards with that old fifty-four."

"Frank, I know you're good with that rifle, but if a bunch of Indians are charging you, what are you going to do after that first shot?"

Frank shoved his slouch hat to the back of his head and scratched his full head of gray hair. "Well, boy, I reckon you got a point. I'll git one of these here new lead chunkers, but I'll hang on to that old Harper's Ferry 1841. When I need to reach out and touch a-body, it'll do it."

Callum nodded in agreement. "You're right there. These Winchesters fire a lot of lead, but they don't have the range your Harper's Ferry has. That's why I keep my Spencer. It fires a little slower, but it'll reach out quite a ways."

"What about me and Ma?" Kate called to Callum.

He walked back to the table with the handguns, placed one hand on his sister's shoulder, and looked at his pa. "What do you think, Pa? You reckon we should get a couple of the Remington New Model Police in thirty-six caliber for Ma and Kate? They'd be easier to carry."

"Good idea, son, but I recommend one pocket pistol each, and a full-size revolver for the second gun. They could keep the pocket pistol in a dress pocket or, where Kate's concerned, in a smaller holster, and the other could be holstered in the wagon next to them or on the saddle, if they're on horseback."

Callum was about to answer, when the bell over the door jingled, and Marshal Pickering, along with a deputy, walked in.

# 4

"Here, what's goin' on?" Pickering shouted when he saw all the guns on the table.

Callum, pointedly, turned and stared at Pickering, while Frank worked the action on the Winchester Yellow Boy he was holding, even though it wasn't loaded. He started to speak, but his pa lightly pushed him back and stepped forward.

"You caught those murderers that burned down my house and barn, Marshal?"

"Well, uh, now see here, Logan. What are you doing with all these guns?"

Callum watched his pa's cool presence. The older man stood well over six feet, though now, with his age, he was slightly stooped. However, he still towered over the fat man who faced him. His gray eyes were the color of flint, as he stared down the Marshal?

"It's Mr. Logan, when you address me, Marshal. I asked you a question, and I don't like repeating myself."

"Well, no. I ain't."

"See, Ma, the marshal says it," Colin said.

All eyes, except for Callum, his pa, and Frank, turned toward the boy, and his ma gave him a look that bode nothing good.

"What kind of leads do you have?"

"Why, I ain't got nothin' yet. But I'm just startin'."

Pa's eyes narrowed and he almost hissed, "You're just starting? It's been over a month, and my family was almost killed."

The marshal had started sweating. His yellowed detachable collar strained to keep his fleshy neck in place. He took a handkerchief from his black roundabout coat and wiped his forehead.

"Mr. Logan, I am working as quickly as I can. I—"

"Do you have any suspects?"

It was obvious, Marshal Pickering was not enjoying himself. As any observer could tell, he had originally entered the general store because he had seen the Logans' buckboard and planned on running them out of town, maybe even putting the old man in jail. Now he was on the defensive.

"Mr. Logan, if I may finish. I'm working hard to find those folks what burned your barn. Why, I—"

"Marshal Pickering," Pa said, contempt edging the title, as he interrupted the lawman, "Frank was able to get a slug into one of the varmints. You know of anyone shot around here, like anyone in your son Noah's gang?"

The marshal hesitated, then finally said, "Noah don't have no gang. He just has some friends, and no, I ain't heared of anyone gettin' shot lately."

Callum spoke up. "When I find the cowards that almost killed my family, you'll hear about it then."

The marshal shook his short little finger toward Callum. "You listen here, Callum Logan. This ain't the Wild West. We're civilized folks around here. You go off shooting any innocent folks and I'll see you hang."

Callum took a deep breath. "We're busy, Pickering." Ignoring the marshal, he turned to his family and said, "Let's get this wrapped up. We've got a lot to do today."

But Pickering wouldn't leave it alone. "Callum, you tell me now, what do you need with all those guns?"

Callum turned toward the marshal again. "Afraid that's my fault, Marshal. After getting home and finding someone had tried to kill my family, I felt they needed a little more firepower for protection. Who knows, maybe those horse-killers and attempted murderers might come back before I find 'em." Callum waved his arm toward the table where all the guns rested. "You think we got enough, or should we get more?"

The marshal examined the weapons lying on the counter. "Why, looks like you got plenty here."

The deputy leaned over to the marshal and said, "He's hurrahing you."

Pickering's face, even though it was already red from the heat, turned even redder. He addressed Matthew Logan. "You can't be buying guns. The order says only for survival."

Callum spoke up. "Oh, Pa's not buying them, Marshal, I am, and you might spread the word, if anyone else comes sneaking around our place, all they'll get for their trouble is a bellyful of lead."

"You fought for the South. You got no more right to buy these guns than your pa."

Callum moved toward the marshal and deputy. "Do you have a writ for me? Cause until you serve me with a writ, I intend to buy whatever I please. Now, if you've got business here, take care of it, and leave us alone. If you've got none, head out!"

The marshal looked at his deputy, then at Pa Logan, and finally at Callum. "Don't push me too far, Callum. You'll find I don't make a very good enemy, and you best not go shootin' anybody." He spun on his heels and, followed by his deputy, started for the door.

"Have a good day, Marshal," Jenkins called, as the two men pushed through the door, slamming it behind them.

The storekeeper turned back to Callum. "He's right about one thing, Callum. He doesn't make a good enemy. Your folks live here. I'd go easy."

"I've seen his kind all across this country, Mr. Jenkins," Callum said. "Now that the South is down, they're going to tromp on it more to get all they can out of it. I wasn't partial to Lincoln, but I thought him an honorable man. If he had lived, I don't think we'd be seeing families losing their homes to confiscation."

Jenkins nodded his head. With a dejected look on his face, he said, "You may be right."

"But enough of that," Callum said. "We need to buy guns. Pa, I've explained the difference between the Colt and the Remington. I prefer the Remington, even though it's a little heavier, because of the strap over the cylinder, which makes it stronger. But it's up to each of you."

Colin spoke up. "You mean Bret and me can have two and a rifle?"

"That's up to Pa. But I recommend it, and Kate also. We don't know what we might run into on—" Callum caught himself before mentioning the trip, even though he thought Mr. Jenkins was an honest man—". . . .the farm."

"We'll buy you weapons, boys," Pa said. "You'll not get the handguns until I know you can safely load and shoot. Understand?"

"Yes, Pa," came from both boys.

"All right, Mr. Jenkins," Callum said. "Looks like we've got a passel of guns here. We'll need leather for all of them, and three twenty-five-pound kegs of powder, also patching material and lead. I want five hundred rounds of rifle ammunition for each rifle selected, whether it's Winchester or Spencer, and an extra five hundred rounds of .56 Spencer for me."

Jenkins was methodically figuring each rifle and handgun, making sure that all accessories were included. Everyone had tried on holsters and made their choices.

Callum waited for the grand total. At the last moment, he

said, "Mr. Jenkins, how about including three ten-gauge shotguns with twenty-five pounds of double ought and twenty-five pounds of number six shot."

Jenkins laid three double-barrel shotguns on the counter alongside the other weapons, and computed the total. He looked up at Callum, and slowly turned the tablet around to face him.

Callum ran his finger down the numbers, looked at the total of seven hundred sixty-five dollars and pulled out his bag of double eagles. He slowly counted out three stacks of ten, and one stack of nine. Jenkins picked them up and placed them in a separate box from the cash register.

"Mr. Jenkins, how about a sarsaparilla and candy for everyone."

"This is just like Christmas!" Colin shouted.

Everyone laughed, as Jenkins dispensed the drinks and the hard candy. He handed Callum the change, then turned to Pa. "I know you're leaving. It's obvious. Matthew, you've been a good friend to me and this town. I just want you all to know"—with this he looked at Ma, Frank, and then Callum—"that I wish you Godspeed to wherever you go. Your secret is safe with me, and, Callum your gold will help me assist those who need help, for a long time."

Pa stepped forward and shook Elijah Jenkins's hand. "You've been a friend to danged near every person in this here county, including us. I wish you good fortune, Elijah."

Everyone shook the storekeeper's hand, Callum waiting for last. Finally, when he grasped the man's small hand in his, he said, "We won't leave for a while, Mr. Jenkins, and we'll be back to make more purchases before we go."

Most of the weapons were in boxes. Mr. Jenkins helped load the wagon. With all the people plus the guns, powder, and ammunition, the wagon had gained a great deal of weight. The horses strained to get it moving.

"Callum," Bret said, "we still need saddles. Why didn't we get them at the general store?"

"That's a good question, Bret. From the time we cross the Mississippi River, we're going to be in Indian country. The last thing you want is a new squeaky saddle. Old, oiled, worn-in saddles are bad enough. New ones can be heard in the next county."

"Oh," Bret said, "I hadn't thought of that."

The family drove the short distance to the livery. Marshal Pickering stood in front of his office and watched them pass. Callum kept an eye on him until they pulled up in front of the stable. He turned Shoshone where he could watch Pickering as he dismounted. The marshal stood in place for a moment longer, spit on the boardwalk, and walked back into his office.

Daniel Ivers had lived in the small town of Limerick as far back as Callum could remember and was another good friend of the Logan family. In fact, he had sold Callum his first saddle. He didn't look the part of a blacksmith. He had short-cropped gray hair and brown eyes set in a friendly, wrinkled face. Though he stood a little over six feet tall, he had never weighed over one hundred sixty pounds, but he had wide, strong shoulders. He had won many an arm-wrestling match from men outweighing him by forty pounds or more.

He walked from the stable up to Callum and extended his calloused hand. "Boy, it's good to see you. You're looking mighty fine, 'cept maybe you could use a mite more of your ma's cooking." Everyone laughed, and he nodded to Ma. "Becky, it's a pleasure to see you."

"You too, Daniel. I do hope Dora is well. Please give her my best, and thank her for those delicious pies she brought by after the fire. That was so sweet, and they were delicious."

"Yes, ma'am, I sure will." He then winked at the kids and turned to Pa and Frank. "Matthew, Frank, what can I do for you?"

As Frank touched the brim of his hat with his forefinger in

acknowledgment to Daniel, Pa said, "Need some saddles."

The blacksmith nodded and said, "I can fix you up. Come on in."

Bret watered the horses while the men bargained. After a good forty-five minutes of dickering between Pa and Daniel, the two men came to a deal, and Callum paid for their purchase.

Fortunately, they had found everything they needed. With the wagon packed with gear and people, they started for Ansel Smith's farm.

The heavy wagon made for a smoother ride, but harder pull for the horses. Because of the weight, everyone, except for Pa, who was driving, climbed down and walked alongside. Callum had tried to get his ma to ride Shoshone, but she would have nothing of that. She insisted she could and would walk. Fortunately, Wright and Smith's farms were between the Logan farm and Limerick.

On the left, the north side of the road, the thick timber of hickory, sugar maple, and sassafras, gave way to a beautiful green, rolling pasture, surrounded, and divided, by a meticulously built four-rail post and rail fence. A road running up to the house turned north from the main road, and paralleled the horse pasture to the left. Just as they made their turn, a red fox dashed from left to right, almost under the horses' feet. The animals jerked back, but Pa tightened the reins and spoke calmly to the pair. They immediately settled down and continued up the scenic road to the house.

"Look, Pa," Colin said. "That fox has a baby rabbit in his mouth."

"Oh, that poor little rabbit," Kate muttered.

"That's life, Katy," Pa said. "Animals have to kill, just like we do, to eat. Why, if we stayed here, we could very possibly be eating some of that rabbit's brothers or sisters, when they're grown."

"I know, Pa. It just seems so harsh."

The fox continued to run, until it cleared the grass area, and ran into the timber on the other side of the road.

"Life is harsh, Kate," Ma said. "However, it's also beautiful. That little baby rabbit could be feeding baby foxes, who will grow up for you to admire in the wild, or trap for fur."

"You and Pa are right, Ma. Sometimes it's just hard to see." Kate was watching the horse pasture. "Stop, Pa!" she shouted, and, after running to the fence, climbed to the top rung. Leaning forward, her feet were hooked behind the middle rail, while her thighs rested on the top.

Callum had to pull up when Kate dashed in front of him. He watched her climb the fence, put a finger to each side of her mouth, and emit a loud, shrill whistle.

Most of the horses on the west side of the pasture were the Morgans they had sold to Samuel Wright. The horses had been watching the wagon make its way up the road. When Kate whistled, their bodies went rigid. She whistled again, and seven or eight of them broke into a gallop, racing toward her, the others following. When they stopped, they all stretched their necks to reach her.

Kate rubbed each one between the ears and on the upper neck while she talked in low tones to them.

Callum shook his head. "She sure has a way with horses."

"Yes, she does," Ma said. "That's one reason I have a hard time keeping our sugar and apple supply intact."

Pa laughed. "She does spoil them horses, but she also has a connection with them. I've never seen the like. It breaks her heart when we have an auction, and they leave. But she knows that's their life, and she handles it. I swear, she's the best horse trainer I've ever seen.

"Come on, Katy. We got to get going," Pa called.

She gave one last rub and, laughing, her long blonde hair bouncing loose and blue eyes flashing, dashed back to the wagon. "Sorry, Pa. I couldn't help myself. It was so good to see them."

The large, white house, set about five hundred yards from the road, was positioned so it looked out over the entrance and horse pastures.

"Katy, if things go well, I want you to pick the horses out for me. I'll be talking to Sam. Pick out three mares, and make the rest geldings. We need the mares for breeding when we get to Colorado, right, Callum?"

Callum, riding close alongside, said, "That's right, Pa. Josh has Chancy, and I have Shoshone here. I'm real curious about what kind of stock will come from this horse."

"I'm bettin' good," Pa said, then started to turn to Katy.

"Pa?" Callum said.

The older man turned back to Callum.

"You know Wright doesn't like me. I'll take care of these horses, while you make a deal. Just get a signed contract stating they are being sold to Josh in Colorado and delivered by me." Callum handed him the refilled bag of double eagles. "That should cover it."

"That's smart, son. He hasn't cared for you since you walloped his boy, Herbert, right out in front of the church steps, with the preacher and everyone watching, for being rude to Charlotte in church."

At the mention of Callum's dead fiancée's name, his ma gave a sharp intake of breath and said, "Matthew!"

Callum responded quickly. "Ma, it's all right. It's a long time ago."

For a moment longer, Pa looked at his son through sad eyes, then, as they were now close to the house, he leaned over to Kate and spoke in almost a whisper. "All right, Katy. One of the mares will be yours. So pick out your favorite. But make sure all you choose are strong and fast." He gave his daughter a direct look. "You understand me, Katy girl?"

"Yes, Pa," she whispered back. "I'll do my very best."

As they had finished speaking, Samuel Wright, who had been

standing on the house's high, wide front porch, started down the steps, his eyes glued to Callum's horse. His wife, Maybell, followed him.

Pa helped Ma and Katy down from the wagon, as the boys leaped over the side, and Callum stepped down from the appaloosa.

"Matthew, Becky, Kate, it's good to see all of you," Samuel Wright said. He turned to Callum, appraised his Western dress, and said, in a much cooler voice, "Callum, how are you? I heard about your altercation in town."

"I'm fine, Mr. Wright, and it wasn't my altercation, as you put it. Four of Pickering's deputies had jumped Bret. It looked like he was doing mighty good, but I jumped in because I like a good fight."

"Yes, I seem to remember that about you."

He turned back to the family. "Please, come in, and we'll have something to drink."

"Pa, I'll take care of the wagon and horses."

"Good idea, Callum. Thanks, son."

"Pa, can I help Callum?" Colin said.

"That'd be fine."

Frank, nodding at the barn, said, "I'll give 'em a hand," and started walking in that direction.

Callum, followed Frank, leading Shoshone to the watering trough, and, while the appaloosa was drinking, he started shortening the stirrups. Colin had jumped into the wagon, driven it to the trough, and jumped down, all the time watching Callum. The two Morgans joined Shoshone in quenching their thirst.

Once Callum finished with the stirrups, he looked over at Colin's shiny face.

"Climb up there on Shoshone, brother. See how you like him."

"You mean it?"

"Wouldn't of said it if I didn't."

# 5

Callum watched to see if Colin could reach the stirrups from the ground, to get on the big horse, but his brother had it figured out. He grasped the reins in his left hand, then rested it on the saddle horn for balance, and smoothly leaped up, thrusting his left foot into the stirrup, while swinging his right over the horse's back in one fluid motion. After settling into the saddle, he turned a proud face toward his big brother and Frank.

"Well, you just gonna sit there?" Callum said.

Colin grinned and rode the horse sedately around the barnyard, and to the house and back. Returning, he was about to get off, when Callum said, "Looks like he likes you. Why don't you take him down the road a ways, give him his head. With all this walking, he needs to burn off some energy. Now, go have some fun."

Callum watched as Colin turned Shoshone around and started him off at a trot. *Lordy,* Callum thought, *that is one pretty horse.*

Colin was no stranger to the saddle. He let Shoshone trot for a short distance, then put his heels to him.

Watching from the wagon, Callum felt a brief moment of fear. Shoshone accelerated so fast, it looked like Colin would lose the saddle, but he hung on, flexed his knees, stood a little in the stirrups, and leaned over Shoshone's neck. *My gosh, that horse can run. It looks like he ain't hardly touching the ground.*

Frank spoke in awe. "I'll be double-dawg-danged. I ain't never in my life seen a horse get that fast, so quick, from a trot."

Callum watched intently as the two neared the main road. Fortunately, the turnoff to the Wrights' farm had been built at an angle, and Colin leaned just a little as the big horse turned the corner, and raced away, back in the direction of town. Finally, passing the open area of the pasture, Shoshone and Colin disappeared behind the trees. Callum continued to watch. Five minutes or so had passed before they reappeared, racing back. Shoshone seemed to be going even faster.

Nearing the turnoff, Colin slowed Shoshone to a lope and then, turning onto the private road, he eased the big horse to a walk.

Callum could see the boy's grin when he turned toward the barn.

Colin was breathless. "Callum, that's the fastest horse I've ever been on. I can't believe it. He took that turn so smooth I almost didn't even know it was there, and when I leaned forward and talked to him, we started flying. There for a minute I didn't know if I could hang—"

"Slow down, fella. I was watching it all. Why don't you climb down, walk him a bit more, and let him have a little water. You did good."

In one smooth motion, Colin brought his right leg back over the saddle, kicked his left foot out of the stirrup, and, holding on to the saddle horn and cantle, jumped to the ground. "I'll do it right now, Callum. Thanks for letting me ride him."

"Glad you like him, little brother," Callum said, while walking to the horse. He rapidly readjusted the stirrups for his long legs. "Never know when you might need to leave quick."

Finishing, he patted Shoshone's sweaty neck, and Colin led the horse along a shady, tree-covered path.

Callum watched his brother walking the horse, and his thoughts drifted back to the thoroughbred farm that used to be just down the road to the east. It was Charlotte's home. She had fine folks.

Honest, that was the main requirement for the Logan clan. A man could be a lot of things, but if he lied or cheated his fellow man, as far as they were concerned, he wasn't worth shooting.

He could picture her standing on the tall veranda, the afternoon breeze drifting up from the creek, moving wisps of her long blonde hair, much like Kate's looked now. She always seemed to be happy when he saw her. Always, except when he had ridden by on that warm June day in 1861. He had come to tell her goodbye. He was on his way to join the provisional army that Governor Harris had formed for the protection of Tennessee. His other brothers, Josh and Will, had left weeks earlier to fight for the North.

He still remembered the taste of her soft, salty cheeks, on his lips, tears sliding down her face. That was the only time he'd ever seen those brilliant green eyes release tears of anything but happiness.

One of the hardest things he had ever done was leave her. But even harder was to come back, after the war, and find that cholera had claimed the lives of his sweet Charlotte and her family. What would life be like if he hadn't left? If he had taken her West before the war? They could have found a place where the war couldn't touch them.

"Callum? Callum, are you all right?" Colin asked, pulling on his sleeve.

He took his hat off, removed his bandanna, and wiped his forehead. Pushing the thick, brown curly hair back, he captured it with his hat. After retying his bandanna around his neck, he looked down at his little brother and ruffled his hair. "Yeah, Colin, I'm great. So you liked your ride?"

"I loved it. I've never, ever gone that fast. It felt like Shoshone had wings."

Callum looked down at the excited boy. His flesh and blood, the last of Ma and Pa's brood. Even the ravages of war and the loss of home and horses hadn't taken away Colin's enthusiasm.

"Callum," Kate called as she bounced down the porch. "Get Shoshone. Colin, bring the wagon with the saddles. We need to collect the horses. Pa's made a deal with Mr. Wright for seven geldings and three mares. He said I could pick them out from the ones Pa sold him."

Callum swung into the saddle, while Frank, Colin and Kate jumped into the wagon. The four rode to the horse pasture gate and Kate whistled. The Morgans again galloped up to her, stopping just short of the entry. This end of the pasture had smaller holding pens, that opened into the larger pastures. Kate's skill and knowledge of these horses quickly became evident. Colin had parked the wagon at the pen, jumped out, crawled through the fence, and run to the entry that opened from the pasture. When Kate would pick out a horse, he would open the gate and Kate would lead the animal in.

After only a short time, Kate had selected ten good horses. Callum had dismounted, and he and Frank were busy moving saddles and additional tack to the upper rail of the holding pen. While the crew was busy picking horses, the others walked up.

"Thank you, Sam," Pa said. "You've been a big help."

"You've always been a friend, Matthew. I wish you luck."

Frank had chosen one of the bigger geldings. It was saddled, and stirrups adjusted. Frank led it over to the exterior gate, tied it to the upper rail, and caught Pa's eye. "This one's yores." Without another word, he turned and grabbed another saddle and blanket, along with the rest of the tack, and headed over to another gelding. He talked to the horse for a moment, rubbed its neck, and tossed the blanket over the horse's back, smoothed it out, and followed with the saddle.

Everyone else was saddling their horse of choice, and in only a few minutes, everyone was mounted, except for Ma. She had been talking with Maybell Wright. The two women gave each other a long embrace, and Ma stepped back. "Take care, Maybell," she said. "These are tough times, and there are many desperadoes in the country."

Maybell smiled back. "It's just like you to be thinking of someone else when you have such a challenge ahead. Thank you, but you're the one that must take care."

Callum had tied Shoshone to the back of the wagon and was standing at the side to help his ma up and onto the front seat. "Ma, could you ride with me?"

"I'd love to, son. Are we ready?"

Pa, who was mounted, nodded. "I believe we are. Sam, would you open the gate, and we'll be on our way."

Callum stepped around to the other side of the wagon. He climbed to the seat and picked up the reins, clucked a couple of times to start the Morgans, and led the way out, leaving everyone else behind to say their goodbyes.

Upon reaching the main road, he stopped and waited for Pa to join them. When Pa and the others had pulled up with the horses, Callum said, "Pa, I've been thinkin'."

"Wait," Ma said. "We need to eat. Kate and I brought some dinner."

"Yes, ma'am," Callum said, "but we're burning daylight."

Ma laughed and slapped her son on the shoulder. "You sound just like your pa, and you'll no more get by with that statement than he does. Now, turn left. There's a nice clear little pasture, with a fresh spring on the right, less than half a mile."

Callum tossed a frustrated look to his pa. Pa just shrugged his shoulders.

"Callum," Ma continued, "it won't take but a few minutes. The horses can graze, and so can we." She smiled at her son. "Let's go, we're burning daylight."

Callum laughed, snapped the reins, made a left turn, and, headed down the road.

"Ma, you're a tough cookie, but a mighty pretty one."

She laughed, in her happy way. "Son, it is so good to have you home."

They had been driving only for a few minutes when a circular clearing appeared on the right.

"Pull in here," Ma said. "You remember this spot? We used to picnic here quite often when returning from church."

Callum pulled the wagon into the pasture and headed to the southwest corner, where a patch of pawpaw grew. He knew the spring was located behind the pawpaws and flowed into a small creek.

Pulling up the horses, Callum jumped from the wagon, walked around to the opposite side, and helped Ma down. Kate had joined them and was helping get the baskets out. Callum grabbed one and carried it over to where his ma had spread her homemade quilt. She took out metal plates and utensils and set them on the edge of the quilt.

Frank looked around. "What about coffee?"

Ma gave him a sharp look. "There's water at the spring. We don't have time to make coffee."

Frank mumbled something under his breath about the importance of coffee, picked up a metal plate, and served himself. He moved back by a tree, sat down with his back against it, and started eating.

Everyone quickly devoured the fresh smoked ham, green beans, and cornbread. Once finished, Ma called Colin, Kate, and Bret. "Run these back to the spring and rinse them off, so we can be on our way."

The kids picked up the utensils and dashed behind the

pawpaw thicket. Moments later they were back, putting them into the basket.

"That was mighty good, Becky," Pa said.

"Yes, it was, Ma, thank you," Callum said.

"So, it was worth the stop?" Ma asked, addressing Callum.

He grinned back at her, knowing there was only one thing to say. "Yes, ma'am, it sure was."

"Let's go buy some wagons," Pa said, "and sell the homeplace. Although, I believe Mr. Ansel Smith will try to steal it."

"Matthew," Ma said, "that is a harsh thing to say about neighbors. They've been very nice. Look at the food they brought us after the fire."

"You may be right, Becky, but I know how I feel."

"Pa," Callum said, "the sheriff is goin' to take everything you have, if he gets the chance. Obviously, he won't be able to get it from the Smiths. There's no doubt they were with the North. So, if you sell him the land, have him deduct the cost of the wagons, and hopefully any spares and harness. You'll have more money to take with you."

"Yep," Pa said. "That's a good idea. The reason I know it's a good idea, is because that's exactly what I planned on doing."

Everyone laughed.

Callum continued to his pa. "How about you, Frank, and Ma go purchase the wagons and make a deal on the land. I'll take everyone else and get the mules. We'll keep the horses with us, even though we'll pass our place. That should make the mules easier to handle, since they just naturally like horses. Once we've made our purchase, we'll head back to meet up with you. How's that sound?"

While they had been talking, the boys had loaded up the wagon.

"Sounds like a plan." Pa tied his horse behind the wagon, helped Ma up, and sat waiting while everyone mounted.

"You don't have to drive the horses, Callum," Kate said. "Just let me ride up front, and they'll follow me."

"Sounds good. Colin, why don't you ride up front with Kate? Bret and I'll ride drag."

"Sure thing," Colin said.

"Yeah, he's happy," Bret said. "He don't have to ride back here in the dust, like we do."

"Brother, you better get used to dust," Callum said, alongside Bret. Turning in the saddle, he glanced back at the wagon with Pa and Ma, and Frank riding along behind. "If the weather stays dry, you'll be eating dust all the way to Colorado, and then you'll be stuck in it working cattle. That's one of the things you put up with as a cowhand."

"I was just joking, Callum. I'm glad to be back here with you."

"I had a reason for having you ride back here. I have some questions for you about Pa. Looks like his leg has healed pretty good, but he's not looking or sounding like himself. Have you been noticin' anything?"

"Yeah, Ma's worried too. Pa's slower now, and he's forgetting things. Before you came back, he told Frank to ride over to the homeplace and check on it. It wasn't fifteen minutes later, he was looking for Frank, so as to send him over to the homeplace. Stuff like that has been happening a lot. I'm really glad you're back."

"I am too, Bret." They glanced to the left as they passed the Wright home, where they had just purchased the horses. Callum watched the animals that were following Kate. They didn't pay the place any mind at all.

Bret went on. "It seems like it's gotten worse, since the fire. Pa took to those horses mighty strong. He hurt mighty bad with their loss. It looks like, since you've showed up, he's just turned everything over to you."

Callum was surprised at his younger brother's insight. He had noticed that about Pa. He was more inclined to let someone else make a decision. He just wasn't himself. Callum glanced over at Bret. The boy looked like he was filled with dark thoughts.

"Tell you what, when we get back to the place and after we've got the stock taken care of, we'll clean up the new guns and do a little loadin' and shootin'. How's that sound to you?"

Bret immediately cheered up. "That sounds great, but don't you think it might be too late?"

"Never too late. That Injun's not gonna wait until it's daylight to try to lift your hair, so we won't wait to shoot these new guns. Then we'll get some more practice in tomorrow."

"Can I practice fast-draw? I'd like to know how to do that."

"No. We won't be practicin' any fast-draw tonight. I want you to get used to these guns, both cleanin' and shootin'. I know all three of you are good with rifles, so you know how to shoot. But a handgun is a different beast. You'll first learn to hit with it, and then you can start working on speed. But you've got to remember, hittin' what you shoot at is the most important, not how fast you get that pistol out of the holster."

"I remember Josh saying the same thing. Callum, do you like the new ranch?"

"It's mighty nice, set in between mountains that reach nearly to the sky. Majestic pine trees scratch the bellies of the clouds, and wait until you see the quaking aspen. In the fall they cover the mountainsides in flashing gold. I never seen the like."

The two men rode behind the horses, dust from the dry road covering them with a fine, white powder, but neither noticed, both were focused on the description of the ranch. They watched as Pa turned the wagon down the Smith lane, with Frank following.

Callum continued. "You can see the valley from the front porch of the ranch house. The grass is up to the cows' bellies, and the flowers will take your breath away. There's purple Columbine, and pink shootin' star, purple fireweed, and yellow blanket flower.

"Bret, you never seen such cactus flowers too. You'd never think such thorny devils could be so pretty, but they put on flowers that are all yellow and red and pink. I'm telling you, brother. It's mighty pretty."

"It sounds terrific."

Callum pondered for a moment. Then gave an emphatic nod. "Yep, it is, but you've got to remember, it ain't just pretty, it's deadly as a rattler in the outhouse. First, there's Indians. Some are friendly, and some will lift your hair at the first chance they get. Then there's snakes. They got more types of rattlesnakes than I thought existed. And insects. They've got scorpions you could throw your saddle on. That's why you learn real quick, to knock out your boots in the morning, before you put them on. If that ain't bad enough, you've got your run-of-the-mill bad hombre. There's folks that go West to get away from the law. Like I said, bad hombres. Them you just naturally have to kill, like a rabid dog."

Bret nodded. "Like Noah Pickering. He ain't never done anything good."

"Yep, if he was the one. If he was, we'll settle up after we get the family on their way." Callum watched Kate and Colin turn right into the lane that led to a nice barn and a rundown shed.

"Well, I'll be," he said. "You got me talkin'. I don't think I've talked that much since..." His mind slipped to Charlotte and the long talks they'd had under the big sweetgum tree. He shook it off and grinned at Bret. "Why, since I got into a talkin' contest with your Uncle Floyd. You know how he is."

A grizzled-looking old-timer, his dirty shirt unable to hide the powerful shoulders, came walking out of the barn. Callum and Bret joined Kate and Colin.

# 6

"Well, looky here. If it ain't Miss Kate and a whole passel of Logans." He touched his hat to Kate, and walked straight to Callum. "Been nigh-on to a year since I seen you and Josh around these parts, boy. Welcome back. Git down, all of ya, and come on in. You can tell me all about what's happening with that blue-belly brother of yours, while I git us some coffee going."

Callum laughed and dismounted to shake the man's hand. "It's good to see you, Mr. Mason. I'd take it easy with that blue-belly talk. You wouldn't want Josh riled at you."

"Shaw, he'd know I'm only hurrahing him. I think the world of that boy. I reckon he spent more time here than any of you, besides Kate. Now, you call me Ezra, boy. You've earned the right.

"I'm mighty sorry about what happened to yore folks. Any lowdown cuss that'd kill a horse like that oughta be gut-shot and left to die." He glanced over at Kate, just climbing down from the saddle. "Sorry, Miss Kate. Reckon I get carried away sometime."

"No need to apologize," Kate said. "I feel the same way. I'd do it myself, if I could find the culprits."

Mason chuckled as he motioned them toward the house. "I

imagine you would, girl. Not many ladies I know have the grit you do. Shoot, not many men I know with your grit."

Kate flashed a brilliant smile at the old man. "Thank you, Mr. Mason."

"Ezra, thanks for the offer," Callum said, "but we just had dinner a ways back. We're actually here on business."

"Shore nuff? Well, you just fire away."

"We'd like to buy some of your mules."

"If you'd ask me a couple of months ago, I'd of said, not no, but he—uh...heck, no."

He glanced at Kate, and she gave him another radiant smile.

Chuckling, he said, "Guess I'm not used to being around ladies since Liza's been gone." His face changed as he glanced at the gravestone set at the base of the big red oak that shaded the house. He cleared his throat. "I reckon I wouldn't have sold 'em 'fore this danged writ come out. Now that good-for-nothin' Pickering." He stopped and, in disgust, shot a long stream of tobacco at a grasshopper that was sitting innocently by the barn. The tobacco juice almost drowned him. The grasshopper tried to fly, but his wings were so loaded they could only flutter. To escape, he started jumping and fluttering. Finally, on the third try, wings working, he launched and escaped the barnyard and Ezra's tobacco juice.

"What I was saying, I don't often sell my babies, but since the state, or Pickering, is gonna take 'em, I'd rather you have 'em. How many you thinkin', two, four?"

Callum slid his hat back, and gave Ezra a little grin. "Would sixteen be too many?"

Ezra yanked his hat from his head, bent over laughing, and slapped his leg. Then he stopped and looked at Callum. "You're bein' serious, ain't you?"

Callum nodded. "Yes, sir. I sure am. I've got the gold to pay you right now."

He started laughing again. "Boy, I ain't much of a prayin' man, but I got to fess up. I been prayin' for a way to save my babies from Pickering, and now you come along. Heck yeah, I'll sell 'em to you." He turned to Kate. "Miss Kate, you already know all my mules. Why don't you go pick out the ones you want. He stopped and looked at Callum. That all right with you?"

Callum laughed. "She's about the best in the family, when it comes to animals. You bet."

"Smart move, young feller. That girl knows her riding stock. Miss Kate, pick out the ones you want. Callum and I'll dicker on the details."

"Come on," Kate said to the boys, "we'll herd the horses into the corral, and then pick out the mules we want." She looked back at Mason. "Is that all right with you, Mr. Mason?"

"That's fine, girl. You just do whatever you need to." Turning back to Callum, he said, "Tie that horse of yours up by the house, and we'll go in and talk. I need a cup of coffee."

While they were near the barn, Callum let Shoshone drink, then followed Mason to the kitchen door, where he tied the horse.

Once inside, the kitchen looked just like he remembered it. When they were boys, Will, he, and Josh were good friends with the Mason boys. They'd come inside to enjoy Mrs. Mason's wonderful pawpaw jam and biscuits. Unfortunately, she had died —the doctor called it consumption—a year before the Fort Sumter, followed by all four of their sons in the war. Callum watched the back of Mr. Mason as he set the pot on the indoor stove. *You're a strong man, Mr. Mason,* Callum thought. *I had a hard enough time with losing Charlotte. What would I have done if I had lost my whole family?*

"Sit, boy." Mason indicated the long table. He pulled out a chair across from Callum, and the two men sat facing each other. "That's a mighty fine horse you have. I seen a mountain man come through Nashville with one a them, maybe twenty year ago. He sure looks like a runner."

"He is that. He's an Indian pony that was given to me by a Shoshone. That's what I named him. Don't tell Pa, but he's probably the best horse I've ever had."

Mason chuckled. "Yes, sir, yore pa raises some fine horses." Then his face clouded over. "I swear, Callum, if I ever find out who did your family dirty, his breathin' days are over. Who ever heard of gut-shootin' a horse? That man begs for killin'."

"Thanks, Ezra. Pa and I intend on taking care of that before we leave."

"So, it's true. Yore pa told me that you and Josh were joining up with your Uncle Floyd to start a ranch in Colorado. Reckon you must've got it done."

"Yes, sir, we sure have. That's why we need your mules. They'll be pullin' two wagons. We figure with sixteen, that gives us some spares, if something happens." Callum watched the old man momentarily wince at the thought of something happening to one of his mules.

"That's smart, son. If I was younger, I'd go with you. There ain't nothin' left for me here. The marshal will be taking everything as soon as he finds the time. He's going all over the county, confiscating poor peoples' property, and just because they supported the South. That weasel and his brood fought for nobody. Bootleggers, that's all they've ever been, and bad hootch at that. But that's beside the point. You want to buy some mules."

Callum looked out the door. Kate and the boys were herding the mules into the corral with the horses. As expected, the mules walked right over to the horses and started smelling. There would be no problem. He turned back. "Mr. Mason, how much do you want for your animals?"

The older man leaned back in his chair and stroked his thick beard. The beard had once been black, but now the gray was taking over. No matter what color, though, it effectively stored crumbs. He felt a crumb as he stroked, stopped, picked it out, looked at it, and popped it into his mouth, then grinned at

Callum. "Never know where the next meal's coming from. Callum, I'm not dickering with you folks. You can have the whole lot for fifty dollars a head."

Callum sat back, stunned. "Ezra, that's not even half what those animals are worth."

"I reckon, but that's your price. Take it or leave it."

"Ezra, I'm not going to take part in stealing a man's livelihood. I'll give you one hundred dollars a head."

"Boy, you Logan's were always honest people. Why don't you go ahead and take fifty a head. I'm pleased to sell 'em, and you folks just lost your home and horses. I'm glad to do it."

Callum shook his head in frustration. He was good at bargaining, but he had never been in a situation like this, where he was trying to pay a man *more* than what was asked. "Pa would be disappointed in me if I didn't pay you at least a hundred dollars a head for those animals. We won't find better anywhere, and they'll cost more."

"Nope, boy, you ain't payin' me no hundred dollars a head. Fifty. Not a dime more." At the last statement, Mason crossed his arms and leaned back in the rough-cut chair, now worn smooth with time.

Callum had an idea. He leaned forward and placed his thick forearms on the table. "You mentioned you'd like to go to Colorado, but you're too old. Pa's going, and you're at least fifteen, twenty years younger than him. Come West with us. How would you feel about raising mules in Colorado? They need 'em out there. There's all sorts of mining going on. Those mines and prospectors are looking for good mules. Consider this hundred dollars a head a stake.

"You could live close to us, and make use of the ranch facilities to breed and raise the stock. If it'll make you feel better, you could pay us a little something for each sale you make on the mules."

"You serious, boy?"

"Mr. Mason, I've never been more serious."

The older man looked around the kitchen and through the door into the rest of the house. "I ain't lived nowhere but here for forty years. My Liza girl is buried right there by that big ole red oak." He paused for a moment, a far-seeing look in his eyes. "Don't know where my boys are buried."

Callum knew the man was wrapped in the past, the happy days, the cheer, the laughter. He waited.

Finally, Mason slammed his big fist on the table. "I'll do it! Crazy though I may be, but I'll danged sure do it. I ain't been no farther west than Nashville, but if you're serious, count me in."

Callum took out a pouch. He opened it and started counting out double eagles. After a moment he paused in the counting and looked up at Mason. "Ezra, do you have anyone interested in buying your property?"

"No. I guess I'll just leave it to the danged carpetbaggers."

"That may not be necessary. Ansel Smith has indicated to Pa that he's interested in buying more land. Pa is selling our place. You might try him."

Mason thought for a moment. "Even if that Yankee gave me pennies on the dollar, that'd be more than what I'd get if I just left it. I'll try him tomorrow."

Callum nodded, and continued counting. He made four stacks of twenty. Neither man said a word until he finished. Then Callum said, "Ezra, how many mules do you have, and do you have any other stock you'd like to take with you?"

"I reckon I got twenty-two mules, and two donkeys. I bought both them boys when they was just weaned. Them little suckers are mighty cute. If I sit down anywhere they can get to me, they'll come over and try to lay down in my lap. I also got three mares for breedin'. They've got about the best disposition you could ask for. That's what you need when you're raisin' mules. If their momma has a bad attitude, they'll train it into their foal. Mules is smart, and they just don't forget. I also got me two milk cows and my old blue tick hound, Blue."

"Pickering's going to take everything, right?"

"Yep, except what the state's decided I need to live on."

"Do you think the donkeys can make the trip?"

"Shaw, them donkeys'll still be going when that big horse of yours is done give out."

Callum chuckled and then said, "All right, if you trust me, why don't we do this. I'll buy all your stock, except Blue. You might need him."

Mason laughed. "Reckon he wouldn't be too happy with me sellin' him. He might not hunt anymore, not that he hunts much now. He just lays around in the shade, watching me work."

The two men laughed, and Callum went on. "When we get out of Tennessee, you can buy them back. I'll buy all of them for one dollar."

Mason shook his head again. "That Pickering is goin' to be fit to be tied. That'll be a beautiful picture.

"Boy, I'd trust my life with your family. Why, I guess that's what I'm doin'. I'll do it, by gum. Let me get a paper."

When Mason had returned, Callum said, "This needs to be legal. I need you to make the bill of sale out to Joshua Matthew Logan, Major, Army of the United States."

It took a few minutes for Mason to list all of the stock and the amount. Finally, he signed the document and slid it across to Callum. Callum signed it as agent, and let it sit for a moment to dry.

"Make one more," Callum said, "so you'll have it."

After the paperwork was finished, the two men shook hands and stood. "Ezra, I know Pa and Ma will be happy you're coming. Ma has worried about you being down here by yourself for a long time."

"Well, that's might nice. I've always considered your pa a

friend. Your ma is a fine woman. She helped my Liza a right smart amount when she was sick."

"I want to mention one more thing," Callum said. "I'm going after the Pickerings. Like I mentioned, once the family is well on their way, I'll do what needs to be done, but the point is, there could be blowback. I just want you to be aware of it, since we're traveling together."

Ezra's face turned hard. "Boy, don't you be concerned about me. If'n I had a chance, I'd be sendin' those scalawags where they deserve. Now, when you plannin' on leavin'?"

"As soon as we're ready. Hopefully no later than the end of the week. You need some help packing and loading?"

"Reckon not. I'll just be using pack mules, no wagon, and I got everything I need for them."

Callum had folded up the bill of sale, and nodded at the gold. "Best not leave that sitting out. You wouldn't want the wrong people to see it."

"Son, I been taking care of money longer than you've been suckin' air. Reckon I know what's needed. Now, let's go see what's happenin' with them mules."

Callum, a barely visible grin on his face, led the way to the corral. It wasn't large, and it was getting full. They walked up to the post and rail fence and leaned their forearms on the top rail.

"Miss Kate shore knows my animals. She left out my pets, Betsy and Janice. Those two are about the sweetest mules I think I ever knowed."

"Good," Callum said. He called across the corral to Kate. "Is this all of them?"

"Yes, they're all ready to go, and they get along fine with the horses."

"Yes, sir," Ezra said, "A horse is what brought 'em into this world and took care of 'em. Them mules like horses."

"Ezra, I should have asked earlier, but are your mules broke to harness? It's not a problem if they're not. It'll just take us a little more time to get 'em used to it."

"Son, them mules is broke to just about whatever you have planned. You want to plow, they're good. They're good with a pack saddle and in harness. You just want to ride 'em, they're fine trail mules."

Ezra got a conspiratorial look on his face and leaned closer to Callum. "See that gray on the other side of the corral? If you want to make a little money, run him against a horse. Unless that horse is mighty swift, he'll beat him every time. I don't know what happened—he came out of the same mare as several of the others—but he is fast."

Callum grinned back at him. "I'll remember that. Unless we need him, we'll keep him out of harness."

Ezra nodded. "Good idea. One more thing: These mules have been raised gentle. They've had human attention from the time they come out of their momma. They like people. You treat 'em right, and they'll do what you ask, unless they feel they'll get hurt doing it. You treat 'em mean, and they'll never forget, never."

"Thanks, Ezra, I'll remember that and pass the word to everyone. What about a touch of the whip, when you're needin' a little bit more pull?"

Ezra shook his head. "Never! You touch him with a whip, and he'll hate people for the rest of his life. You need more pull, just ask him. He'll do it."

Kate, Colin, and Bret had ridden around the corral. They pulled up next to Callum and Ezra. "We're ready," Kate said.

"Well, I've got some news for all of you," Callum said to his brothers and sister. "Ezra, here, has decided to go to Colorado with us and raise mules on the ranch."

The Logan children had always liked the Masons. All three of them grinned, jumped to the ground, and ran to the older man. Kate gave him a big hug. "Mr. Mason, I'm so glad you're going with us. It'll be so much fun."

The old man turned red. "Why, if'n I'd knowed I'd get a hug out of it, I'd decided when yore pa told me." Everyone laughed.

Colin and Bret stepped up and put out their hands.

"Mr. Mason," Colin said, "I'm glad you're going with us."

Ezra's sun-baked hand, the color of dried leather, closed around the young boy's. "Thank ya, Colin. I'm lookin' forward to bein' with ya."

Bret stuck his hand out. The boy was taller than the older man. "Welcome, Mr. Mason."

Mason put his hand on Bret's shoulder. "You just keep growing, boy, you surely do. Thank you. I'm looking forward to seeing Colorado."

"Guess we'd better get this stock moving," Callum said. "Pa's busy trying to buy Mr. Smith's Studebaker wagons."

"That'll cost him," Ezra said. "Smith has the first penny he ever earned. In fact, he's so tight I can here him squeak all the way down here. Yes, sir, I surely can."

Kate and Colin giggled. Callum and Bret grinned, and then Callum said, "Be that as it may, we've got to get these mules there to pull those wagons." Callum glanced at the sun in the west. "We only have about three hours of daylight left."

He walked back over to Shoshone, swung up into the saddle, and rode back to the corral. "Ezra, if you'll let those animals out, we'll be on our way. Kate, you ride point, so the Morgans will follow you."

Kate, Bret, and Colin mounted and waited for Ezra to open the gate. The Morgans came out first and trotted after Kate. She turned and waved to Ezra. "Bye, Mr. Mason. See you soon."

Reaching the road, she turned right, followed by the Morgans and the mules. Colin waved to Ezra and followed behind the last mule.

Callum leaned forward, his forearm resting on the saddle horn, and extended his right hand to Ezra. "We'll let you know when we're leaving. I'm thinking this week. The sooner the better.

Let us know if you need any help, or any space in one of the wagons for some of your things. If we don't hear from you, we'll swing by to let you know the exact day."

The old man took Callum's hand, his grip firm and confident. "You take care, boy, and many thanks. You've been a lifesaver for an old man."

Callum tipped his hat and was gone, disappearing behind the thick brush along the road.

# 7

The herd arrived at the Smiths' place in a cloud of dust. Callum rode past Kate. "Keep them well away from the house."

He could see two men, one wearing a black, round-brimmed hat, with a short, flat crown, walking toward them, along with Pa and Frank.

Turning to Colin, Callum said, "Stay back here, and don't let any of the stock try to dash for the road. Bret, come with me. We may need your help hooking up the mules." They reached the front of the column, just as the four men got there.

Smith, his round, black hat almost blocking his eyes, looked over Callum and Bret, then, without greeting, said, "The wagons are behind the barn. We've already loaded the extra wheels and axles. The harnesses are laid out. Bring your mules around there."

Callum signaled to Kate, who walked her Morgan behind Callum and Bret. The horses, and then the mules, followed. Pa walked up to Callum. "Everything go all right?"

"Yes, sir. Ezra wants to come with us. I told him we'd love to have him."

Pa nodded emphatically. "Good. Ezra will be a big help on the trip, and he knows his mules."

"Yes, sir. That's what I figured. He also wants to sell his land. You think Mr. Smith might have an interest?"

Pa patted Shoshone on the neck. "I don't have to think. He told me he was still looking for land."

"Good. I told Ezra to come on down and talk to him."

Pa stepped back, while Callum loosened his rope and tossed a loop over the first mule's head. He was a little apprehensive how the mule would act with a rope settling around his neck. He shouldn't have worried. The mule was docile and walked right up to the wagon. Frank took the first one, backing him up to the wagon while speaking softly to him. The mule remained calm, backing and then standing in place while the harness was fastened.

After Callum released the first mule to Frank, he watched Bret leading the gray up next. Riding to Bret, he said, "Don't hook the gray up. We'll use him for a backup. I've other plans for him."

Bret nodded, released the gray, and rode back to the mules to get another. Kate rode over to Callum. "Mr. Mason told you about how fast the gray is, didn't he?"

Callum grinned at his sister. "He did. I don't know if it will ever be necessary to use him, but I want to keep him out of harness, if possible."

The hookup went quickly for both wagons. The mules were calm and tractable, each following the gentle commands of the men. In only a few minutes the wagons were ready.

Pa called Bret. "Son, would you mind driving our wagon?"

It was more a command than a request. Bret said, "Yes, sir," and rode to the wagon, tying his horse to the rear, and climbing to the seat. He picked up the reins and waited.

The Smiths said their goodbyes, and Pa helped Ma climb onto the seat of the first Studebaker. Walking around the wagon, he motioned to Callum and Kate. They rode over, and he said, "The wagons will lead out, followed by the stock. When we get there, put the animals in the west pasture. That little creek will give them water. See you at the house."

The procession left the yard, with Callum and Colin bringing up the rear. Colin coughed. "It sure gets dusty back here, don't it?"

Callum nodded, his bandanna over his nose and face. "Yep. It comes with the job."

Colin nodded in acceptance, following Callum's example and fastening his bandanna around his face. Callum could see the boy's eyes wrinkle and knew he was grinning. "What you grinnin' about, boy?"

Colin turned his twinkling brown eyes to Callum. "I feel like an outlaw with my mask on."

Callum grinned back at him, then grew serious, thinking of the outlaws he'd had to deal with in Colorado. They were either dead from lead poisoning or from stretching a rope. "I just hope this is the closest you ever come to being one."

The two of them rode on in dusty silence.

Shadows were lengthening when they turned onto the lane to the house. Callum rode through the mules and horses to get to Kate.

She looked at Callum and grinned at his dust-covered face. "Glad I wasn't riding back there. Looks like it was a little dusty."

Callum pulled down the bandanna. "Yep, but not bad. Nothing like what you're gonna see on the way to Colorado, missy. At times, you'll be so caked with dust you can't scrape it off with a fingernail." He grinned back at her. "Think on that." He turned Shoshone west and galloped to the gate. Leaning over, he pulled the latch and swung the gate open as the mules and horses arrived.

The Morgans immediately recognized the pasture, and went galloping off to the creek, with the mules hard on their heels, the gray easily catching them. Callum watched them go. *That mule can really run,* he thought. *I think he just might beat a better-than-average horse.*

He turned Shoshone, and rode back to help with the unhitching. By the time he got there, all of the mules had been unhitched. They had been watching the other mules and horses, so it took little urging to get them moving to the gate. Once inside the pasture, the mules ran in the direction the others had gone.

Callum dismounted and led Shoshone to the wagon Pa was unloading. Pa handed the sack containing the remaining gold coins to Callum. "He bought the land," Pa said. "We've got to be out of here no later than this weekend. That's when he wants to be over here to start plowing. He's turning these horse pastures into cornfields."

Callum looked across the green pastures. They had dug and strained and cut and pulled to get all the trees, stumps, and brush cleared from the pastures. They were now perfect for horses, and they were going under the plow. He shook his head. *I'm glad I'm headed back out West,* Callum thought. *I never realized how much I don't like civilization until I arrived in those empty mountains. The sooner we're out of here, the better.*

"The worst part," Pa continued, "what with the confiscation order, he got it for a song. He knew he had us where he wanted. It's a shame, but we're not coming back, so it doesn't matter." Pa stopped and, turning, gazed first at the pastures, then the mountain. "This land has been good to us."

"Pa, you did good. We needed those wagons, and we're losing this land and everything on it, anyway. If you hadn't sold it, Pickering would have just taken it, and the fact you sold it to Smith, there's no chance Pickering can take it from him. Smith's a dyed-in-the-wool Yankee. The court will never allow it."

Callum glanced to the west. "Did you notice the high clouds?"

"Oh, yeah," Pa said. "I was hoping we'd at least get out of here before rain set in, but it looks like we're in for it. I'm guessing either tomorrow evening, or the next morning."

"If we're goin' to get everyone practicing, at least with the handguns, while there's any daylight left, we better get started." Callum turned to call everyone in, when, out of the dusk came the sound of gunshots. He leaped back into the saddle. "That sounds like Ezra's place. Bret, Frank, let's ride."

The two men swung into the saddle and chased after Callum who was disappearing in the twilight. They rode hard, pushing the horses, until they neared the Mason turnoff. Sporadic gunfire snapped through the trees.

Callum pulled up and waited. Frank and Bret joined him. All three horses were breathing hard. "Leave the horses here. Stick with me until we locate the shooters."

About that time, a roar came from the house, and a man's scream split the night, fading quickly. The shot was followed by rapid fire from the woods.

Frank said, "Sounds like Old Ez is well enough to shoot. He don't miss with that Sharps."

Callum nodded. "We'll slip through this thicket. When we reach the edge, we should be able to make out the shooters from their muzzle flashes. Then we'll spread out, and when I shoot, pour it on them, and then move, quick. You don't want to be there when they fire at your muzzle flash." Callum turned to his brother. "Bret, you never shot a man. Don't let that stop you. They'll be wantin' to kill you, so you've got to get them first. Just pretend you're squirrel huntin', and don't shoot until I do."

The men slipped through the thicket until they were near enough to the edge to see two muzzle flashes coming from the tree line across from Mason's house.

"All right, spread out, and wait for me. When I shoot, you shoot, then don't forget to move."

They separated and took up positions. Callum was behind a thick hickory. He looked both ways, barely able to see the faint outline of his brother and Frank. Again, the Sharps boomed. *Couldn't of been better timing if I was prompting you, Ezra,* Callum thought. For after Ezra's shot, two repeating muzzle flashes could be seen. Callum took aim with his Spencer, moving his aim point about six inches to the right, and pulled the trigger. Frank's Spencer and Bret's Henry cracked, as soon as Callum shot. He fired two more times, moving the aim point to the left and right.

"Let's get out of here!" someone yelled.

Callum and Frank fired at the voice. Then they heard scrambling and a horse racing down Mason's lane.

Bret called to Callum, "That was Noah. I'd recognize his voice anywhere."

Callum shouted to the house. "Ezra, this is Callum Logan, with Frank and Bret. Are you all right?"

They heard a cackle of laughter from the house. "Danged sight better than those fellers layin' in them trees. Come on in, and I'll put the pot on."

"Don't assume those bushwhackers are dead," Callum said to Bret. "Run to the house. We'll be right behind you. Ready, Frank?"

"Let 'er rip, boys."

Bret lead the way, with the other two men running behind them. They jumped the steps, landing on the porch, and flew through the door. Frank slammed the door behind them. Mason's gold was still sitting on the table, in neat stacks.

"Ez, you old codger," Frank said. "What kinda hornet's nest did you stir up?"

Ezra had pulled a chair away from the door and was leaning against the wall, sipping on a steaming hot cup of coffee. He pointed to the pot on the stove. "Hep yoreself and grab a chair."

After each of the three men had gotten a cup and joined him against the wall, he gave Callum a sheepish glance. "Reckon I made the mistake you wuz talkin' about. I left that gold sitting right there on the table, and went out to feed the stock. I no more than made it to the barn, than I heard horses coming down the lane. At first, I thought it was you." He nodded at Callum.

"When I could finally see 'em through the trees, I could tell it weren't you, so remembering the gold on the table, I ran back to the house. I just made it into the kitchen, when up rode the devil himself—Noah Pickering and three of his gang."

He took another sip of coffee and waited a moment. "I was standin' in the door, but I reckon one of them boys could see the gold on the table behind me. He yelled, 'He's got gold.' Once he done that, Pickering snatched that Colt out of its scabbard and shot at me. I reckon he nicked me." They could see a bloody spot near Mason's waist.

Callum said, "You better let us take a look at that, Ezra."

"Not necessary. Ain't nothin' but a scratch. I'll doctor it up after you're gone. Anyway, they started to dismount. Knowin' the type of people that are around here now, I keep my Sharps with me most of the time. It was leanin' against the wall, next to the door. I just rightly swung it up and blasted one them fellers clean out of the saddle. That was him you passed when you was runnin' in. He ain't goin' nowhere. Well, you ain't never heard such a ruckus. Yellin' and screamin', they spun them horses around and took out for the trees. They made it while I was reloadin', lucky for them. Then we traded lead, until you showed. I'm shore beholdin' you did. I'm thinkin' Pickering is the only one to make it out of here."

All three sat thinking of the last few minutes. Then their reverie was broken by a faint call. "Help me."

Mason reached for his Sharps and, standing, said ominously, "I'll help him."

Callum stood quickly and walked to the door, opening it slowly. "How bad are you hurt?" he called.

"I think I'm dying, Mister. It hurts something terrible."

"You have a gun?"

"Yes, sir, but I'm throwing it away—listen."

Callum could hear the weapon hit the brush. "Is there anyone else out there?"

"Yes, sir, but he's dead. I heard him."

"All right, I'm coming out, but if you try to shoot me, I'll fill you so full of lead it'll double your weight."

"I ain't got a gun, Mister. I truly ain't."

"Stay in here," Callum said. "I'll go check on him."

"That varmint could be lying," Mason said.

"I know, but I don't think he is. I'm not going to leave a boy out there to die, no matter how bad he is."

Callum walked past the dead body in the yard and out to the trees, stopped, and reached down. He grasped the man under his arms, and dragged him to the porch, where Bret helped him stretch the man out.

Bret shook his head. "Orville, I told you a long time ago to stay away from Noah. He's bad news." Bret looked up at Callum. "His name's Orville Nelson."

Orville tried to nod but was unsuccessful. It was obvious the boy was bleeding out from a stomach wound. "I know you did, Bret." He gritted his teeth for a moment, as a wave of pain washed over him, and he broke out in a heavy sweat. Once it was past, he continued. "But Noah said it would be easy money. My folks are sure going to be upset. Pa told me to stay away from Noah, but I wouldn't listen." He started coughing, and a small trickle of blood began to flow from the corner of his mouth.

"Orville, who was the boy shot at our farm, when you tried to burn it?"

His eyes traveled quickly to each man on the porch. "I'm sure sorry about that."

He was taken over with a burst of coughing that racked his young body. He finally regained control, took a deep, rattling breath, and said, "Noah was really mad at Bret for whippin' him, and when Mr. Logan run him off, he just kind of lost his head. He told us we'd go burn a haystack. He ain't said nothin' about burnin' the house and barn, specially with them horses in there. Then he shot the other two horses in the pasture. The rest of us just wanted to get out of there, specially after Simon Dinkus got shot. He lived for a couple more days, but he died."

The boy turned his head to look at Ezra. "I'm right sorry, Mr. Mason. Pa always said you were a good shot."

"Ezra stepped to the boy's side. "Your ma and pa are good people. It's too bad you brought this on 'em. They're gonna be hurt mighty bad."

Tears started to flow from the young man's eyes. "I don't want to die."

Bret turned away, and walked back into the house.

"Boy," Mason said, "it's out of yore hands. You was dead when you rode up to this house. You just hain't got shot yet. I don't miss with this here Sharps."

The boy looked at each man on the porch. He took several shallow breaths, then a deep one that turned into a long sigh. His head lolled to the right, and he was gone.

"Pickering has caused a lot of suffering," Callum said. "There's going to be some sad folks tomorrow when we take these bodies in. There's two more out there, both dead. We'll drag 'em onto the porch, and take all of them to town in the morning.

"Ezra, you want to come over to our place tonight?"

"Why for? They ain't comin' back. Even if they did, those donkeys and ole Blue will raise a ruckus. I'll stay here tonight, and get everything ready tomorrow. When you figure to leave?"

"Today's Wednesday. We'll load up tomorrow. Seeing as we don't have much, it won't take long, so I'll say be at our place early Friday and we'll put this country behind us."

"Fine with me," Mason said. "Thanks for the help."

Callum nodded. "Come on, Bret, let's get the other bodies." They dragged the other boy from the woods, and the one in the yard, and laid them both next to Orville.

Bret identified the additional two bodies. "These two are

Payton Lee and Elvis Wilson. They've been running with Noah since we were little."

"Guess they ain't gonna do no more runnin'," Mason said. He spit his chaw of tobacco off the end of the porch. "You boys want some more coffee?"

"If you're good, Ezra, we'll be getting back," Callum said.

"Head on out, boys. You takin' these bodies in, or am I?"

"We'll be by with the wagon in the morning to take them off your hands."

"Good 'nuff. See you boys tomorrow."

"Reload, if you haven't already," Callum said to Bret.

"Oh," Brett said. He took out a handful of cartridges from his pocket, slid the follower almost to the muzzle, turned it to the locked position, and started dropping forty-fours down the magazine. Once loaded, he reversed the steps and turned a sheepish look to Callum. "I'm done."

Callum nodded, looked at Frank, and said, "You ready?"

To answer, Frank stepped off the porch and headed for the horses. They mounted and headed for home. They had ridden halfway back to the farm, when Bret pulled up. He leaned out over the side of his horse and threw up, waited a second, and threw up again. He looked toward his brother. "Sorry."

Callum shook his head. "Killing a man should never be easy, Bret. Sometimes we have to do it to enforce justice or defend ourselves. Ma has taught us that every man's our brother. I think, in the spiritual sense, that may be true, but what we've just done is sometimes necessary, even if Ma is right. We do what we must to protect family and friends. Just don't ever get to liking it.

Bret wiped his mouth on his sleeve. "Thanks, Callum."

The three men continued in silence.

Callum knew that everyone at the house would have heard the shooting, and would want to know what had happened. He had no desire to go over it, because, even though he had done it during the war, and several times since, it still sickened him. But now, he was the oldest son. Time was catching up with Pa. It would be up to him to get this family through to Colorado. *It would be nice if I could do it without taking another life.* Then he thought of Noah Pickering, and felt the cold anger boiling up inside.

# 8

Callum rolled out of his soogan early. Today would be a busy day. Early as he was, Ma and Pa were up ahead of him. He beat out his boots, pulled them on, and stomped them into place. After putting his hat on, he slung his gunbelt with the two Remingtons, and checked each weapon. Satisfied, he slid them back into their holsters, fastening the thongs to keep them secure.

"Morning Ma, Pa," he said, walking to the table.

"Morning, son," Ma said, stirring the gravy. She stopped, moved to the huge dutch oven, and brushed the coals off.

Callum jumped to her side. "I'll get that, Ma." He slid his gloves on and lifted the dutch oven by the heavy wire handle, moving it off the coals. Next, he removed the lid, allowing the smell of fresh biscuits to waft through the air. The aroma of fresh-cooked sausage and gravy, combined with the smell of the hot biscuits caused his mouth to immediately began salivating. Frank was up, with Colin and Bret following closely behind Callum as the smells also tantalized their olfactory nerves.

Colin rubbed his eyes, then, after pulling his boots on and while still in a sleep stupor, stumbled over to the table and dropped into a chair. Bret, wide awake, tossed back his blanket and joined the group. Kate arrived with fresh-churned butter, placing it next to the jam and jelly already on the table. Within minutes, everyone was seated, Pa had said grace, and food was disappearing rapidly.

Callum finished, leaned back, and looked at his ma. "I've said it before, but I think this will be the only westward wagon trip where everyone gains weight."

They all laughed. Colin looked at his brother. "Callum, when do we practice shooting?"

"Frank glanced at Callum. "I think he's got ants in his pants."

"As soon as we finish eating, son," Pa said. "But I'm thinking you'll be doing more than just shooting."

"Pa's right," Callum said. "You need to know your weapon—not only how to shoot it, but how to load and clean it. After we finish with breakfast, we can get all the weapons out here on the table. We'll take 'em apart until you're comfortable, then we'll do some dry firing, and then we'll shoot."

"Callum," Ma said, "we need to get everything loaded, if we're leaving tomorrow."

"Becky," Pa said, "we'll get it all done, but everyone, including you, needs to know how to clean, load, and shoot these guns."

"But, Matthew, we need to get out of here."

Pa walked over to his wife and put his arm around her. "No one's gonna attack us, not here. There's just too many people. With all the help we have,"—he gave Colin and Bret a pointed look—"we'll get it done before dark. Now let's get you working on your Navy Colts."

Callum had chosen the .36-caliber Navy Colt for his ma, Kate, and Colin. They were some lighter, with a shorter barrel and less recoil. Plus, the Navy had a little better balance and pointed well. Colin had complained a little, until he picked up one of them. It fit his hand better than the forty-fours, and he was immediately in love.

Frank, Pa, and Callum were all familiar with the handguns, so they worked quickly, familiarizing the others with the new weapons. Once they knew how to clean them, it came time for dry firing. Callum never liked to snap a weapon on an empty chamber, but it might come down to life or death. He wanted everyone ready.

The sun was just peeking over the horizon when they loaded their two handguns. It was time for firing. Callum had set up the targets. He and Pa had decided Bret would go first. When he started firing, it was obvious his skill with the rifle carried over to the revolvers. With his first try, he put all of the .44-caliber balls in a three-inch circle. Ma was next. She eared back the hammer and squeezed the trigger, hitting dead center. Callum looked at Pa.

"Your ma has always been a good shot," Pa said.

When she finished, it was Kate's turn. She watched her little brother switch from one foot to the other. "Pa, would it be all right if Colin goes next?"

"Can I, Pa?"

Pa looked to Callum, and Callum nodded.

"Sure, son, go ahead, but you be careful, and do like Callum showed you."

Colin stepped up, his right hand dropping to the revolver resting in its holster and drew the Colt in one easy motion, bringing it up to eye level. It had no more than leveled when he squeezed the trigger. He reached up with the thumb of his left hand and eared the hammer back, while keeping the revolver leveled at his target. He fired again. After repeating this action two more times, he lowered the Colt, dropping it unerringly back into the holster without a single glance down.

The silence sounded as loud as the earlier gunshots.

"Did I do all right, Callum?"

Callum had walked out to the shingle he had set up for Colin's target. There was a single hole in the center, with scalloped edges. He counted three scallops. Pulling the shingle out from between the two tree limbs, he carried it back to Pa, who examined it and handed it to Frank. Frank looked at it, looked at Colin, and then back at the hole. "Reckon we all oughta be shootin' them Navy Colts, if that's how they shoot."

"Callum?" Colin asked again.

Callum put his hand on his brother's shoulder. "Colin, I've got to tell you, I don't think I've ever seen anyone shoot like that the first time." He handed Colin the shingle.

The boy looked at it, basking in the high praise from his brother, then looked up, a huge grin splitting his face. "I guess that's pretty good?"

Pa clapped his youngest son on the shoulder. "Colin, that's a lot more than pretty good. You may just have the knack. Which is also a little scary, but you done really good."

Next Kate stepped up and did an excellent job.

"She takes after her mother," Pa said.

Callum put his arm around his sister's shoulder and squeezed. "You and Ma are deadly. I wouldn't want to be a bad guy trying to get to you."

She laughed. "If any outlaws come around, Colin, me, and Ma will protect you men."

"Now, I feel safe." He released his sister and turned to Pa. "I need to go pick up those bodies at Ezra's. They need to go into town. I'd be much obliged if you and Bret would ride in with me. Both of you need to be wearing your handguns."

"Do you need to take Bret, Callum?" Ma asked.

"I do, Ma. I might need some help, and Frank needs to stay and work with you on shooting the rifles and the handguns. We'll be back soon."

She nodded. "Just be careful, and watch for Noah Pickering and his gang."

"I'll watch for Noah, Ma, but I'm thinking there ain't no more gang." He turned back to Kate. "Would you mind whistling up those horses again? I want to give Shoshone a rest. He should have had more, but this'll have to do." Then he looked at Bret. "I'm going to need you to drive the wagon. Be sure and bring your handguns and rifle."

Bret nodded. He was already carrying one .44 Remington in its holster. Now, he slid the second one behind his waistband, and picked up his Henry and some cartridges. He checked the loads in the revolvers, took a moment to load the Henry, and followed Kate to the gate. Like Bret, Kate had one revolver riding in its holster on her hip and the other stuck behind her waistband. She whistled, and the Morgans came trotting over. She grabbed the mane of one of the chestnut geldings and walked it to Callum's tack. While she was doing that, Bret tossed a lead over two of the other geldings.

"You remember Spirit, don't you, Callum? He's such a sweet horse, strong and fast."

Callum saddled and bridled Spirit and stepped into the saddle. "Thanks, Kate. We'll be back before you miss us."

Ma walked out to Pa as they were about to depart and, placing her arms around his neck, looked into his eyes. "Matthew Christopher Logan, you are a good man. Thank you for marrying me."

He grinned back at her. Then, catching her seriousness, the grin faded and he stood quietly looking into his wife's eyes. "You've been my sunshine, Becky."

"You be careful, Matthew. I'm not having a good feeling."

He leaned forward to kiss his wife. Her arms tightened around his neck and she pulled him close. After a few moments, he released her, she stepped back, and he swung up into the saddle. He sat there looking into her soft blue eyes, then grinned at her. "Get that shootin' done, Becky. Don't beat those kids too fierce."

The family had been stunned into silence at the open display of affection, but Pa's comment broke the quiet. They all began chattering with disclaimers, each one claiming to be the best.

Callum had watched in surprise, but cleared his thoughts and said, "Frank, if you'd keep an eye on things, I'd be much obliged."

Frank and Pa exchanged looks, and Frank gave a small nod, then turned back to the table, where Colin anxiously waited with Kate. "All right, let's get these rifles shot so's we can load the wagons up 'fore that rain gets here."

Bret, driving the wagon, led the procession out of the yard and turned toward Ezra's place.

EZRA WAS NOWHERE to be seen when they arrived. Inside the barn, pack saddles were laid out with supplies sitting alongside. Callum figured he was over at Ansel Smith's place.

They loaded up the bodies and covered them with a tarp to keep the flies off. It was nearing eleven o'clock when the wagon, bracketed by Callum and Pa, rode into town.

Bret drove the team straight to the marshal's office. Callum and Pa tied up their horses next to the wagon. Nearing town, Callum had released the thongs securing the two Remingtons to their respective holsters and checked they slid smoothly. Stepping down from his horse, he glanced at Pa's and Bret's holsters to ensure they had done the same. Both had freed their weapons.

Followed by Pa and then Bret, Callum opened the door and walked into the marshal's office. The stench was overpowering, a mixture of man-sweat, soured food, tobacco, and moldering slop jars. The smell fit right in with the appearance of the office. Newspapers were scattered about the small room, empty coffee cups dried out on the desk, and tobacco stains discolored the floor near the spittoon.

Pickering reclined in his chair, feet propped up on his desk, reading the newspaper. When Callum entered, he dropped his feet to the floor and reached for the ten-gauge against the wall behind him.

Callum shook his head. "Don't do that, Marshal. We wouldn't want you to have to explain how the marshal of Limerick was relieved of his shotgun—again."

Pickering scanned each of them. Eyes filled with hate drifted to the holsters filled with Remingtons, and finally came to rest on Pa. "I'll be out to see you early next week, to serve you with a writ of confiscation. We'll see how that settles in yore craw."

Pa said nothing.

"Get up," Callum said, "and come outside. We've got something for you."

"What?"

"Just get out here, or we'll leave 'em on your porch."

Now, curiosity and concern got the best of him. He stood, shoving the chair against the wall, almost knocking the shotgun over, and stomped to the door.

Flies buzzed around the three bodies under the canvas, and they were starting to get ripe. A few people had gathered around the wagon. Callum walked to the side, picked up a corner of the canvas, and flung it from the bodies. The people nearest the wagon jumped back and gasped. Across the wagon from Callum, a big man, rough-dressed, said, "Had to happen. Those boys was just too mean." He stared across the wagon at the marshal. "Pickering, you could have stopped it, since your boy was the leader."

Pickering ripped his gaze from the boys and stared at the man speaking. "Hush yore mouth, Jim Bob. My boy's honest as the day is long."

Jim Bob held the marshal's gaze. "By your definition that may be right, but by our'n, they're all thieves."

Pickering spun to face Callum. "How'd this happen?"

"Well, Marshal, we heard shots last night," Callum began. "Upon arriving at Mr. Mason's farm, we opened up on the bushwhackers that were trying to kill him. When we started firing, we heard a horse take off. These three collected lead for their trouble. Orville was alive long enough to talk to all of us, Frank Tyler,

Ezra Mason, Bret, and myself. He confessed to the attack on our farm, and said that the man Frank shot, Simon Dinkus, died a couple of days later."

Pickering listened to Callum's story, concern written all over his face. Everyone knew that his son Noah had been the leader of this gang since he was a kid. "How do I know you ain't lyin'?"

The crowd had grown larger. Little happened in Limerick. This was the most excitement they'd had since the war. Those at the back of the crowd strained to hear the conversation.

"Marshal," Callum said, "I'm a reasonable man. I could understand your concern if it was just me. But I've given you the names of the men that saw this and heard Orville's statement. You can interview each one, or just take my word for it."

The words had hardly left Callum's mouth, when the atmosphere was ripped apart by a woman's piercing scream. She was being held up by an average-sized man, dressed in homespun pants and shirt, wearing a flop hat. His gaze was going between the bodies in the wagon and Callum.

Callum groaned inwardly. He recognized the couple. It was the parents of Orville Nelson. They were good folks, but their son had gone astray. "Mr. Nelson, Mrs. Nelson, I'm mighty sorry you have to see your son like this. We'll get them up to Mr. Thompson's place as soon as the marshal lets us go."

"You killed my son?"

Callum shook his head. "I don't rightly know. We were all shooting. I'm just mighty sorry we had to do it."

Nelson looked down at his son, lying in the wagon, flies crawling all over his face and body. Then he looked up at Callum. "I'm coming for you. I hold you responsible. If you hadn't come back, this wouldn't have happened."

Before Callum could respond, the storekeeper, Mr. Jenkins, who was standing next to Nelson, said, "Ira, don't do that. I hate to speak harshly of your son, but he rode with Noah Pickering, and he's caused great harm throughout our valley."

At the mention of Noah, the crowd looked back at the marshal. He had to say something. "Nobody's claimed Noah's been in any trouble, lately. He's cleaned up his life. He wasn't with these bushwhackers."

"You call them bushwhackers, Marshal?" Callum said.

"Yes, I do, because that's what they are."

Callum looked at Bret and Pa, then back at Pickering. "Well, I'd say you are right, and what I didn't tell you, when Orville was dying, he said that Noah had led them to Mr. Mason's, and he was the one we heard riding out of there."

The marshal swallowed hard. "I reckon he was gettin' out of there because these other fellers started a fight, and he didn't want to be involved." Pickering nodded, obviously pleased with the straw he had grasped. "Yes, sir. That's what happened."

"Pickering," Callum continued, "Orville also said that your son was the leader of the group that set the fires at our place. Both of them. One at the barn, where five horses died, and the other at the house, where everyone in the family, except for Pa and Colin, who were out camping, was asleep inside. As if that wasn't enough, he shot the two studs that were quietly grazing in the pasture. Now, that's from his dying gang member, Orville Nelson, not from me. So, I'm asking you to swear out a warrant for your son, for attempted murder, and wanton destruction of property."

The marshal's forehead dripped with sweat. He looked nervously left and right, as if looking for an escape route. His beady little eyes darted through the crowd, then settled back on Callum. "I can't swear out a warrant on my own son."

"Folks," Callum addressed the crowd, "you heard him. Is this the marshal you want for your town?"

"No!" the crowd shouted in unison. "Take his badge," someone yelled. "Yeah," someone else yelled. "If these boys had been arrested younger, they might still be alive."

Jim Bob had moved around the wagon, and was now standing

next to Marshal Pickering. With the speed of a striking snake, he hand flashed out, ripping the badge from Pickering's vest. "You're done. Pack up your stuff and get out of that office." He turned to Mr. Jenkins. "You think the city council will go along with this?"

Several business owners from the crowd shouted, "Yes!"

Jenkins said to the man now holding the badge, "Jim Bob, how about you taking the marshal's job? You're an honest man, and that's what we're looking for." He looked at the other city council members in the crowd, and they all nodded.

Jim Bob looked down at the tin star in his big hand, then back up at Jenkins. "I ain't never been no lawman, wouldn't know where to start or what to do."

Callum put his hand on the man's shoulder. "You're a good man, Jim Bob. Just continue to be honest and fair to all people. You're big enough to enforce what you say. Back here in the East, you don't need to be a fast gun. Carry a shotgun. That works in all cases, but Jim Bob, it's time this town had a decent marshal."

Jim Bob looked directly at Jenkins while pinning the badge on his vest. The crowd gave a rousing cheer.

Pickering had been forgotten. His head kept turning like an owl, his eyes traveling to all the people who had gathered around the wagon. He looked down at the tiny holes in his vest where the badge had been pinned. He turned to slip out of the crowd, and Jim Bob's big hand clamped down on his shoulder so hard he winced. He tried to squirm out of the man's grip, but the grip only tightened. Finally, he stopped squirming.

"Where's your two boys, Pickering?"

"Jim Bob," Pickering responded in a quivering voice, "I honestly don't know."

"Two things. You ain't never been honest, and call me Marshal."

# 9

"Marshal," Callum said, "we need to get these bodies to the undertaker."

Jim Bob nodded. "You go ahead and take 'em to Phineas. When you're done, come back over to the office and leave a statement."

Callum and Pa untied their horses, while Bret climbed back up to the driver's seat, and drove the wagon to Phineas Thompson's office. Phineas was the town barber, dentist, undertaker, and furniture maker. With the combined income from the four professions, he made a decent living, although it was said, he was a better furniture maker than he was a dentist. Phineas was standing outside his barbershop when Bret drove up. The Nelsons, along with several other of the townspeople, had followed the wagon.

Bret stopped the wagon and Callum, stepping down from Spirit, said, "Mr. Thompson, we've some business for you."

Phineas gazed into the wagon bed at the three bodies. "You payin' for the burial, Callum?"

Pa and Bret had dismounted and were standing on each side of Callum.

"Yep," Callum said. "Figure that's the least we can do."

Orville Nelson's father spoke up. "I'll not have you payin' for the funeral of my son." He turned to Phineas. "We'll be paying for our boy."

"How much?" Callum asked.

"I'm guessing you are inquiring about the basic funeral?" Phineas said.

"Yep."

"Then that'll be twenty dollars for the two."

"We'll be unloading all three," Callum replied. "We need to be getting back to the farm."

"That'll be five dollars extra for storage, for the Nelson boy."

Callum gave Phineas a hard look, then counted out twenty-five dollars. He and Bret carried the dead men through the barbershop, or dentist's office, depending on what a person needed, and on to the back, where they laid the boys, one at a time, on top of different coffins.

Pa had been standing by the horses, talking to the Nelsons.

"You boys look like you could use a haircut," Phineas, always the enterprising entrepreneur, said.

"No, thanks," Callum said.

"How's your teeth, need some dental work? I can fix you right now, no waiting. I have some folks coming in, but you're already here." He gave a quick little chuckle that turned into a dry cough. Once stopped, he gave Callum a questioning look.

Callum shook his head and said to Bret, "Let's get out of here. We have a lot to do today."

"Have a fine day," Phineas said as they stepped outside.

The Nelsons had disappeared, and Pa turned at their arrival. Callum could see Pa's eyes widen, and his right hand flash for his gun. Callum, reacting, grabbed for his Remington, but as Pa continued turning, he shoved Bret hard against Callum, causing both men to lose their footing. Callum's heel caught on the rough boardwalk, and in falling, Bret jammed him against the office wall. Callum, now wedged between Bret, the wall, and the boardwalk, watched with horrified eyes, as guns exploded.

Pa had managed to get his Remington into action, but the way Callum had fallen, all he could see was Pa and Bret's thick shoulder. He heaved Bret from him, his right hand again driving for his revolver. To his horror, with the roar of guns, a bright red spot blossomed on Pa's chest. Callum, frantic to get his gun into action, watched Pa fire again, just moments before a second spot blossomed in his neck. With the second bullet, the patriarch of the family collapsed, his gun falling from his lifeless hand.

Callum had cleared Bret and pushing himself erect, turned at the same time. Everything seemed to be happening in half-time. He saw the liver-spotted hound that had been lying in the doorway of the general store, now on his feet. People who had still been gathered around the wagon, giving their opinion, were scattering, but seemed to be moving slowly. While he was turning, his Remington was coming up, and Noah and Philo Pickering slid into view.

Both held smoking Colt revolvers. A third round snapped near Callum's head. It had come from Noah's gun. He could see the killer's face, a grimace of hate and pain. Blood covered his left shoulder. The hammer on Callum's Remington finally reached full cock. Instantly, he pulled the trigger, and, through the heavy white smoke from the burning black powder, he saw another hole appear in Noah's body, his time high in the right chest. He watched Noah stagger back, lower his Colt, then start to bring it up again.

A gun blasted, almost in his ear, and Philo staggered to his side. Callum had eared the hammer back again and pulled the trigger. This time the bullet traveled unerringly, straight through Noah's heart. *If he has one,* Callum thought, as the blast from his side came again. *It must be Bret.* Philo staggered back, his arm dropped, and then he started raising it again. Callum fired into Philo. With the third shot, Philo dropped his gun and sat down in the street. Noah had fallen, straight back, off the boardwalk, into the dust of the alleyway, his arms flung wide.

Silence cloaked the country town. Both of the attackers were in the dirt, out of action. Callum dropped his revolver back into the holster while turning to Bret. "You all right?"

Bret nodded, and said one word, "Pa."

The two brothers dropped simultaneously to their knees alongside their father. Callum ripped the older man's collar away and tore the shirt open, exposing the gaping hole in his neck.

"Pa?" Bret called, kneeling over his father, his face filled with shock.

Callum looked into his father's open eyes and knew. The steel-gray eyes that had twinkled with happiness, and had more than once caused men to step back, were dull and lifeless. Callum looked at the lines of his pa's face. *You got old, Pa, but the age never took the fight out of you.* He picked up the hand that still clung to the Remington and slowly opened the fingers, not realizing what he was doing.

In the distance, he could hear Bret sobbing. With dazed eyes, he looked to his left, and saw Bret, smoothing back Pa's white hair. Callum put his arm around his younger brother, shoved Pa's Remington behind his waistband, and stood. Bret stood with him.

"Are you hurt?" Callum asked.

Bret shook his head, tears cutting muddy channels through the caked dust on his face. Callum looked at his brother. *He looks so young, and now he's taken part in killing at least two men, maybe more.* Callum took a deep breath and looked around. People were gathering around the Pickering brothers, talking and pointing at him and Bret.

He tightened his grip around his brother's shoulders. "Bret, pull it together!"

Bret looked into Callum's face, his eyes lost. "Pa's dead, Callum."

"I know, brother." Callum had turned Bret to face him and stood with a hand on each arm. "We're now the oldest here. We've got to take care of Ma and the family. The two of us. You understand?"

Bret stared at him with a blank look on his face. Then, gradually, he started to focus. Callum watched his brother age before his eyes.

The younger man pulled himself together, wiping his face on his sleeves. He sniffed, then, with eyes focused and hard, he looked at Callum and nodded. "I'm ready."

"Good," Callum said. "Let's get Pa in the wagon. You grab his feet."

The two sons lifted the lifeless body of their pa into the wagon, and covered him with the canvas that had previously covered the three boys. Bret tied Pa's gelding to the back of the wagon. Callum glanced at the two men on the ground just long enough to ensure that neither the dead one nor the one dying could lift a weapon, then swung into the saddle.The horses turned to head back home.

Bret turned the wagon as the new marshal walked up to Callum.

"My gosh, that happened fast," Jim Bob said. "I'm right sorry about your pa, Callum. Reckon he was the finest man I've ever known. I had no idea Noah and Philo were anywhere around."

Callum shook his head. "We didn't either. They might of killed all of us, if Pa hadn't shoved us out of the way. It took me too long to get my guns into action. If I had just been faster, Pa might still be alive."

"Nothin' you coulda done, Callum. I was watching from the window, when they stepped out. They had their guns drawn. They had the drop on you. Your pa was a hell of a man. After he'd pushed you two down, he stood there, knowing he was a dead man, and managed to get a bullet into both of them. I couldn't believe how fast you and Bret got untangled and into action. I never seen such shootin'. I'm surely glad those two are gone, because I could've never handled 'em."

Bret, in the wagon, said, "Can we go, Callum?"

Jim Bob stepped back. "You two go ahead. I seen it all. There'll probably be an inquest, but there's enough witnesses, you ain't gonna have to appear."

"One last thing," Callum said. "Could you ask Mr. Jenkins to have the store open early in the morning? We'll be coming in."

"I'll be glad to."

Callum touched the brim of his hat with his left pointer finger and clucked to his horse. "Much obliged, Jim Bob."

THE SHORT TRIP back to the ranch seemed to go on for hours. Callum's mind wandered through his growing years. He thought of hunting and fishing with his pa, all the outdoor and fighting skills he had taught them. He and Will, and Josh had been lucky. Pa was still in his prime as they were growing up. He could remember Pa stepping into the middle of a fracas when he and his two brothers had gone from sparring to out-and-out fighting. Pa had grabbed each one of them—and they were big boys—by the collar and threw them to the ground. Then, with both fists on his hips, he'd explained to them the importance of blood kin. They'd never forgotten.

Now, he was gone. He'd never get to see the Rocky Mountains. Then Callum's thoughts slammed to a stop. *What about Ma? She's going to be heartbroken.* Unconsciously, he shook his head. Coming out of his thoughts, he looked around. The horses had turned up the lane to the house without him realizing it. Only minutes separated the family's happiness and despair. He looked around. Bret followed with the wagon, quiet and solemn. That was so unlike him, but Callum didn't blame him. If he could make this trip last all day, he would. The last thing he wanted to do was break the news to the family.

They broke out into the clearing and rode down the edge of the pasture. He could see everyone working feverishly, loading the wagons. The first to look up was Colin. He stopped for a moment, then started running toward the wagon. Ma came from behind a wagon and saw Pa's empty saddle. Her hands shot up to her mouth for only a moment. Then, taking them down, she yelled at Colin, calling him back.

Kate stepped from behind a wagon with Frank. She watched them ride up. Callum could see the confused look on her face as she turned and said something to Frank, then looked back. He moved closer and put his arm around her. She looked up at him and then back to the empty saddle. Tears began to flow.

Bret pulled the wagon up in front of the house and brought the team to a stop. Ma looked at his young face, walked to the back of the wagon, and slowly lifted the canvas edge. Tears streamed down her cheeks as she stood silently looking at her husband. She reached out and caressed his cold cheek with the back of her hand, then unconsciously combed his hair back with her fingers.

Callum had moved to the rear of the wagon, next to his mother. He made room as Kate, Colin, and Frank slowly gathered around. Kate and Colin were crying. Ma put her arms around them, then motioned for Bret and Callum to join. They stood like that for a few moments, then Ma said, "Callum, you and Frank move the table inside. Then bring your pa in the house and lay him on the table. Bret, son, take care of the horses, wash out the wagon, and clean the canvas."

Frank stepped up and clasped Pa's feet, slowly sliding him toward the end of the wagon. Callum grasped the tall man's shoulders and lovingly lifted him. Once inside the small house Pa was laid on the table.

Ma said, "Thank you, Frank. Would you build a large fire outside, and keep it burning through the night?"

"Ma," Callum said, "we need to bury Pa as soon as possible. I can't believe it hasn't started raining. It's looked like rain all day. If we wait, the grave will turn to mud."

"I'll prepare your pa, and we'll have a wake tonight. In the morning, we will bury him. That will allow most of his folks to be here. It will not rain until we're done."

Surprised, Callum replied, "Ma, no one will be here. Nobody knows."

"They'll come, Callum. Now, leave me be while I prepare your pa, and tell Kate to start a fresh pot of coffee."

He turned for the door, grasped the latch, stopped, and looked back. "It was Noah and Philo Pickering—they were waiting. When we came out of the barbershop, Pa saw them. They were behind us. We had no idea. He pushed us out of the line of fire. The bystanders said that Noah and Philo walked out of the alley with guns drawn. He didn't have a chance, but he pushed us out of the way."

His ma looked at him for a long moment. Then she gave him the sweetest smile as she caressed her husband's face. "That was your pa. His family always came first." She had looked down at her husband, then raised her head and gazed at her son. "You and Will and Josh, you're just like him." Then she looked back down and started cleaning her husband's face.

Callum watched for a moment, then pulled the latch and stepped outside. After closing the door, he gazed up at the sky. It looked like it could rain at any moment. He looked inside the wagons, and to his surprise, they were almost completely loaded.

"Went pretty fast," Frank said. He had been building the fire bed and had just lit the kindling. The firepit was in front and to the side of the house. The day dwindling now, with the cloud cover, was growing dark and glum. Wind had picked up and moaned through the sweet gum trees.

Callum walked over to Kate. "Ma wants you to make a fresh pot of coffee. We're having a wake for Pa, and she seems to think a lot of people are coming."

Kate sniffed, pulled a rag from her pants pocket, and wiped her eyes. "If she says so, then they'll be here."

Callum thought for a moment, and then nodded. Kate was right. Ma had the sixth-sense. Too bad it didn't work this morning. But did it? What was the hug and kiss between the two of them? Could she have known, or suspected?

He went back to the wagons to see if there was anything he needed to rearrange. Everything was in its place. They'd need to stop at the general store tomorrow, on their way out of town, and load up on food and feed. But that was all that was needed. Fortunately, Mr. Smith had had extra tires, axles, tools, and grease. He had sold it all to them. The weapons and powder had been dispersed and everyone had practiced. All that was left was Pa. At the thought, he paused, thinking about his pa's last seconds, standing tall with a smoking gun in his hand. He wasn't a man who would've done well dying from some sickness.

As he considered that, he heard the sound of a rider coming up the lane from the road. It was Mr. Mason, closely followed by the Smiths. Behind them came Mr. Jenkins and his wife. As soon as they stopped, Mrs. Jenkins and Mrs. Smith nodded to him and the others and went straight into the house, closing the door behind them. Callum looked over at Kate. She looked back with that I-told-you-so look. He nodded, and walked to the two men.

"Sorry about your father," Ansel Smith said, as he shook Callum's hand, followed by Bret and Colin. Kate was at the fire, whipping up a stew.

"He was a right good man," Ezra chimed in.

While they were talking, other people started arriving, neighbors who had just heard. Callum was being told how his pa had helped neighbor after neighbor. They all had a story of how he had come to their aid.

The sunset, barely visible through the thickening clouds, was striking when it slid low between earth and cloud, sending bright red and orange beams onto the old home, then disappearing quickly behind the trees, leaving the clouds momentarily lit with gold, then pink, and finally a somber gray.

Frank kept the fire stoked, and now it blazed high into the sky. People continued to come. Callum, often through the night, shook his head with amazement.

THE RAIN HELD OFF, as Ma had predicted. Callum looked around at the mass of people. Friends had heard and ridden through the darkness, and were still arriving. Everyone had brought food; many of the men had brought liquor. Glasses were raised to Matthew Christopher Logan. The children were shocked at the turnout, but Frank and Ma acted as if they expected it.

As daylight arrived, a big man rode in on a lathered midnight-black thoroughbred. He climbed down and went straight to Callum. "Has he been interred yet?"

"No, can I help you?"

The other men stood around, looking at the well-dressed man who had arrived on the lathered horse. He looked at Callum in surprise. "You don't know me?"

"No, sir, I don't reckon I do."

"I'm your second cousin, Ethan Bryce Logan, from Virginia."

"I have heard of you. It is a pleasure to meet you."

"And to see you again, Will. Why, when your father brought you to Arniston, you were a little tyke."

The men standing around Callum grew quiet.

"I'm Callum, Cousin Ethan. Will has not returned from the war."

A stricken look crossed Ethan's face. "I am so sorry. I didn't know. Have you heard any news at all?"

"Nothing. He was fighting for the North, so no one was around him that might have known to bring us a message, but Ma swears he is still alive."

Ethan brightened. "We will hope. Let me say, I am deeply sorry to hear of Matthew's passing. I heard that you put an end to the white trash that killed him."

"We did."

Bret had come out of the house and walked straight to Callum. "Ma says Pa's ready."

# 10

"Thanks, Bret," Callum said. Then, with his hand on his brother's shoulder, he turned to Ethan. "Bret, I'd like you to meet your cousin Ethan from Virginia. Ethan, this is Bret. He also was involved in downing the Pickerings."

The two men shook hands, standing almost eye to eye. The resemblance among the three of them was striking.

"I have something," Ethan said, "that might suit your pa, if it's all right with your ma, and I would love to see her."

"Bret, take care of the guests. I see that Colin has already taken care of Ethan's horse."

Ethan turned to look where Callum's gaze rested. The man's horse had been taken to the watering trough, the saddle and blanket stripped, and Colin was busy rubbing him down.

"Thank you, Callum. Midnight carried me all the way from Nashville last night. I'm sure he's tired. Another brother?"

"Yes, the youngest. His name is Colin. The young lady wearing pants and helping the women at the table is our sister, Katherine. She prefers Kate. Now, come with me. It's time Ma knows you're here."

Callum knocked, and at the call from inside, opened the door, stepped back, and followed his cousin inside.

Pa was wrapped from head to foot in the Winding Cloth. The cloth was perfectly clean, with no blood seepage. *I don't know how she did it,* he thought. *Pa was covered with blood.* He then cleared his mind and looked at Ma. She was obviously tired, but her strong spirit showed through.

When she saw Ethan, she immediately stood, hurrying to him and wrapping her arms around him. "Oh, Ethan. I am so glad you are here. I don't know how you made it, but you've made Matthew very happy. I wish you had your bagpipes."

A sad, but caring smile raised his cheeks. "Ah, Rebecca, I am so sorry for the loss of Matthew. This land will not be the same without him. I find my heart full, knowing that I travel nowhere without my beautiful bagpipes. They are in a special case I had made that rests comfortably on my horse. It would be my pleasure to play for the procession."

"Oh, bless you, Ethan. Matthew talked of you often--your determination as a young man, and your success. I don't think he could have been more proud of you if you had been his son. Your father was always dear to his heart."

"Ah, the sweet Irish Becky. Thank you. I take it you'll be leaving for the burial soon?"

"Yes, we're ready here." She turned to her son. "Do you have a stretcher made, son?"

"Yes, Ma. It's made for eight men. Since we'll be carrying it on our shoulders, Colin is not quite tall enough, but I'd like to include him. It won't add much."

"It is a long way up the mountain."

"We'll be fine, Ma. It hasn't started raining yet."

She gave him a knowing look.

"I'll take my leave and get the bagpipes ready," Ethan said. "I'll start playing, and you can come out when you're ready."

Callum went out behind Ethan and gathered the pallbearers,

all big, strong men, men who owed Matthew Logan in many different ways. They came into the small house, dwarfing the inside with their size. Each man, humble and sad, moved to his assigned position. Reverently, they moved Pa's body to the stretcher.

Frank and Callum were in the front, with Bret behind Frank and Colin behind Callum. Callum placed his big hands on the strong limb, one of eight that extended under the stretcher, from side to side. He looked at the others and nodded. Each man lifted the stretcher to his shoulder. At that moment, a massive crash of thunder split the darkened morning, followed immediately by the haunting wail of the bagpipes playing "Amazing Grace."

Callum listened for the sound of rain on the rooftop, but heard nothing. He led the men outside with his pa's body, turned, and started up the path to the family graveyard on Short Mountain. Ma followed with Kate and the other ladies. They were trailed by the men. There was a soft breeze whispering through the hickory and sycamore trees. The quail, warblers, and mockingbirds were silent. Nothing was heard except crunching from the boots and shoes walking along the tree-lined path, and the notes of the bagpipes drifting with the wind.

*Pa would like this,* Callum thought. *He always loved to be in the woods on quiet mornings, and he loved the bagpipes. I just wish Will and Josh could be here.*

The column wound its way slowly up Short Mountain. The clouds seemed to be moving faster, now, and it looked as if the top of the mountain was ripping the belly of the clouds apart. As they neared the graveyard, an area just below the crest, on the south side of the mountain, a couple of drops of rain fell—and then stopped. It was like God had said, "Not yet."

The small graveyard had been leveled many years in the past. Several Logans rested here. Friends who had arrived last night, had been up here through the night, preparing the site and digging the grave. Callum looked around at the work that had been done, grass cut or cleared, logs cut and on end, just the right height for sitting. A frame had been built, over the grave, on which to place the stretcher. All this time, Ethan had continued playing the bagpipes. The men gripped the handles, and softly laid the stretcher to rest on the frame.

Ma had moved in front of one of the logs. Everyone who was going to sit was waiting for her. She seemed to be waiting for something. The song ended. The last mournful note of the bagpipes sailed across the valley on the wind, and Ma sat.

The preacher stood to say a few words. Callum retreated into his thoughts. *It doesn't matter what the minister says. He knew a totally different man. He knew a man that went to a church building with his wife to bring her happiness, but worshiped in the forest.* Callum pictured his many years spent with his pa in the outdoors, communing with God. *Many of the Indians believe a warrior goes to a happy hunting ground. I hope they're right, for Pa's sake. He'll go crazy sittin' on a cloud.* At the last thought, a grin slipped across his face, then disappeared.

The preacher stopped and moved away. The bagpipes started again, and Callum, along with the other pallbearers, stood and stepped to the grave. They lifted the stretcher. Two men moved the frame from the grave. Four more came up with ropes and pulled them around the four corner braces. Slowly, Pa's body was lowered into the earth until it rested on the rocky bottom. The ropes were retrieved, and Ma stepped forward. She picked up the shovel and tossed in the first of dirt, then she handed the shovel to Kate. She did the same thing, followed by Colin, Bret, Callum, and Frank.

Men took up the shovels, and began filling the hole. When it was filled and mounded over, several large boulders were placed to rest over the top. Upon finishing, several things happened. One of the men looked to Ma and nodded, she turned to go back down the mountain, the bagpipes stopped, and a clap of thunder, louder than the first, crashed against the mountainside and echoed across the valley. And the bottom of the clouds opened and poured a torrent of rain over the family and friends as though Heaven itself mourned the earthly passing of a good man.

The wind had picked up, driving the rain. Callum stepped up beside Ma, to help her down the mountain. Many other men were doing the same with their wives. The lane quickly turned from dusty, to muddy, to a rushing stream, cascading down the mountainside.

Finally reaching the bottom, Ma moved through the crowd of people and personally thanked each one. Because of the rain, the mourners hastened to leave, so they could get home before the road became too muddy to travel. Frank and Bret had quickly pulled tight the puckers on the wagon covers, protecting the supplies inside.

The people disappeared almost as magically as they had arrived. Within twenty minutes, the yard was again empty, with the exception of Ethan's horse and Ezra's pack mules, horses, and donkeys. Ezra had brought all of his stock when he came early in the morning, figuring they would be leaving as soon as the funeral was over.

They gathered under the shed, wearing their slickers against the pouring rain. It was time to leave. Callum motioned to Frank, Bret, and Colin.

"Let's finish the loading," Callum said, "and hook up the mules. I'd like to be well on the other side of Limerick by dark."

Ezra walked up. "I'll help with the mules. They know me. We need the rain, but I sure hope it don't last too long. That road will turn to a bog. Even these mules won't be able to pull the wagons through the stuff."

The men loaded the remaining cooking gear and personal items. Callum double-checked the powder to make sure it was remaining dry, then jumped to the ground, closing the back of the wagon, and pulling the pucker tight. The mules stood quietly as they were harnessed. He watched the proceedings. *Good thing we've got Ezra and his mules. They're the calmest I've seen.*

He walked back over to Ma and Ethan. "We're ready."

"Let me check inside again," Ma said.

"It must be hard for her to leave," Ethan said, after she disappeared into the house.

"Hard to leave Pa. She's excited about moving West. She's as much a mover as we are." Callum removed his hat and beat water from his chaps. "You headed back to Arniston?"

"Yeah. I'll spend the night in Nashville and leave in the morning."

Callum watched Ma come out of the house with a few small things, and put them in the back of the wagon she would be driving. He reached under his slicker and into his vest inside pocket, pulling out a map. He pointed out the Greenhorn Mountains, their valley, and the Sangre de Cristo range, then tapped his finger where the ranch house was located. "You ever get out in this country, you'll find Ma and Josh's family right here. You'll always be welcome."

"Won't you be there, Callum?"

"Not ready to drive a stake in the ground just yet. There's too much country out there to see. If I can find him, I'll join up with Uncle Floyd. He knows the country."

Frank stomped up in the mud. "We're ready. Bret and Colin saddled your horse."

Callum nodded. "You driving the lead wagon?"

"Yeah. Figure the kinks will get worked out of those mules pretty quick. Looks like the lane is getting a little dicey."

Callum looked around. Ma was on the seat of the second wagon. Kate, Bret, Colin, and Ezra were mounted, holding the stock. The wind blew out of the west, and the horses and mules wanted to turn their tails to the wind and drift east.

Callum walked over to Shoshone, wiped some of the standing water out of the saddle, and swung up, watching Ethan do the same on Midnight. He looked over to the stock, and everyone nodded. Callum rode past Ma. "You ready?" he called, raising his voice over the steady roar of the rain. She nodded. Without any further conversation, he rode to the front, yelled, "Wagons, ho!" even though no one could hear him, then waved his arm forward, and started out. Ethan had guided Midnight up next to him.

"If it's all right, I'll ride with you as far as Limerick, then I'll be on to Nashville."

"Company's welcome," Callum replied, thinking about the final trip from the homeplace. There had been good times here. *Rest in peace, Pa,* he thought. *I hope you enjoy the view from up there.*

When they turned onto the road, Callum was pleased. It was muddy, but not yet a quagmire. The wagons could make it through without having to stop and connect more mules. He wondered how Ma was taking this quick departure after Pa's burial. He remained deep in thought until they reached Limerick. The rain had not let up.

The wagons stopped in front of Mr. Jenkin's general store. Ma stepped down and, along with Kate, entered the building. Callum was about to turn and hitch Shoshone to the rail when he felt Ethan's presence.

"I'll be leaving. Tell your ma and Kate goodbye for me. I want to get to Nashville before dark."

Callum extended his hand to his cousin. "It was good to see you. Ma'll be disappointed she didn't get to thank you for the music. It meant a lot to her. Be careful."

Ethan shook Callum's extended hand. "You'll always be welcome at Arniston. Give your mother my apologies."

With that, Ethan pulled his hat low over his eyes, and turned Midnight into the wind. Callum sat, watching him disappear behind the thicket of trees surrounding Limerick. He dismounted into the muddy street, tied Shoshone, and walked back to Ezra, Bret, and Colin, where they were keeping the stock bunched behind the wagons. "We'll be out of here as quickly as possible. Do the best you can with the stock."

He turned, and with Frank, who had climbed down from his wagon perch, headed for the general store's front door. After pulling the latch, they followed the door as the wind blew it open. Pushing it closed, Callum looked around. Ma was busy purchasing their supplies. He started to walk over to see how he could help, when the door opened, rain lashing the inside of the store. The man, rapped in a slicker with his hat pulled low over his face, pushed the door closed.

When he turned back to face Callum, he held a gun. It was Ira Nelson, the father of the boy who was killed at the Mason farm.

With an old Walker Colt clutched in his right hand, he said, "I told you I'd kill you, Logan. You killed my boy. He's gone, and his ma is heartbroken."

Callum knew there was nothing he could do. The man was at least ten feet from him, and all he had to do was pull the trigger. Callum's revolvers were under his slicker. Nelson had him cold.

Mr. Jenkins, while helping Ma with the supplies, glanced up when the door opened the second time and saw Nelson holding the big five-pound Colt. Jenkins was well known for loving the game of baseball. Limerick had fielded a team every year for the past ten years. During the war, it was hard to get a game up because all of the men were gone, but occasionally, enough boys and older men could be found. That was when Jenkins shined. He loved the game, and he loved to pitch. Older now, his pitches had slowed down, but his ability to cut the corner of home plate still aggravated his opponents.

Standing at the counter, he could see that Callum had no chance. Once Nelson fired that big forty-four, it would be all over. A full load of sixty grains of powder behind the one hundred forty-eight grain round ball would blow a hole in Callum big enough to drive a wagon through. He had a gun under the counter, but it was at the far end, near the cash register. There was no time. Sitting on the counter before him were cans of vegetables. The closest was a two-quart can of beans weighing close to four pounds. Each can dwarfed the five-ounce baseball he was used to. But he had to act.

Jenkins picked up the can of beans and in one smooth motion, his old arm launched the projectile toward Ira Nelson. Best case, he hoped to hit the gun, but hitting Nelson's arm might do the trick.

The can slowly tumbled in flight. It didn't have far to go, much less than the sixty feet the baseball had to travel, but it was much heavier. He had to adjust for the weight, therefore the can was not going straight to Nelson's hand or arm, but was arcing, to offset gravity.

Mr. Jenkins watched intently, holding his breath. It looked like the can would strike Nelson's hand. The store erupted in smoke, flame, and a tremendous blast. Callum, Nelson, and the can disappeared in the massive smoke cloud from the sixty grains of black powder in the enclosed space of the store.

CALLUM KNEW the man was going to pull the trigger, but there was absolutely nothing he could do. His mind raced, going back to the promise the Shoshone medicine man had made, that his body would never again be struck by a bullet. A moment of morbid humor brought a chuckle. *Guess he was wrong.*

## 11

From the corner of his eye, Callum saw a can appear and, just as it struck Nelson's hand, the big Walker Colt fired. He could smell the singed hair on his left arm, mingled with the acrid smell of burning black powder.

The blast of the Colt, galvanized Callum into action. He leaped forward, grasping Nelson's wrist and thrusting upward. Nelson was trying to cock the gun with his thumb, but couldn't quite reach it, as Callum" right fist slammed into the side of the man's head. His grip relaxed. The gun fell to the floor, and Nelson collapsed into an aisle of sewing equipment, scattering thread and needles everywhere.

Callum picked up the Walker and, holding it in his left hand, yanked Nelson to his feet with his right. He pulled the man with him as he backed up and placed the Walker on the counter, well out of Nelson's reach.

The door to the store burst open. Ezra, Bret, and Colin followed the marshal inside. Colin, the last, slammed the door shut against the wind.

"What's goin' on? Who fired that shot? Is anybody hurt?" Jim Bob said, looking quickly around the room, his shotgun ready.

"Reckon I won't ever be able to hear again," Callum said. "Other than that, everybody's all right. How 'bout you lower them hammers, Marshal, while I catch my breath?"

Jim Bob lowered the hammers of the shotgun to half-cock and looked from Callum to Nelson, now seeing the Walker on the counter and Nelson standing with his head down. "Ira, did you do something stupid?"

Nelson looked up at the marshal, then lowered his head again. "I guess I did."

"All right, what happened?"

Mr. Jenkins spoke up. "Ira, here, tried to shoot Callum with that old cannon." He indicated the Walker Colt.

"Ira," the marshal said, "you know I've got to take you in. Why would you go and do something like that?"

Nelson looked up at the marshal again, his face a picture of haunted misery. "My son's dead, Jim Bob. My wife is beside herself. She won't stop crying. What's a man to do?"

The marshal looked down at the broken man. "I'll tell you what he ought not do. He ought not try to kill a man what was just defending folks from your son's attack. That's what he ought not do. I'll tell you something else. I'll be holding you in the jail until the judge is in town again, and he'll try you and send you to the state pen. Now, who's gonna look after your wife?"

"Marshal?" Callum said.

The marshal looked his way.

"I'm mighty sorry Orville's dead, and I'm sorry Mrs. Nelson is going through so much trouble over it. I sure wouldn't want to add to her misery by sending Ira off to prison. If he can promise me he won't be sneaking around tryin' to do me in, I'll not prefer charges."

Nelson looked straight at Callum. "You got my word. I don't know what got into me. I guess I was blaming you for all the wrong raisin' I did with Orville, but I swear, I'll never try nothin' like this again."

"That's good enough for me, Marshal," Callum said. He turned around to the counter and picked up a can of beans and hefted it, then looked at Mr. Jenkins. "You threw this all the way across the room, and hit his gun?"

Mr. Jenkins looked at everyone with a sheepish grin. "I did." He hefted a can of green beans, similar to the one he threw, while rubbing his shoulder. "It's a mite heavier than what I'm used to."

The marshal wore a confused look, so Kate spoke up and told him the whole story of how Mr. Jenkins had hit Mr. Nelson's gun hand with that can of green beans.

When she was finished, the marshal shook his head. "I've heard everything now." Then he grinned and turned to the storekeeper. "Bet you never thought your love of baseball would save a life, did you?"

Jenkins laughed. "Well, Jim Bob, I've loved baseball for a long time. Reckon it's time for it to love me back a little."

Everyone joined in laughing. Ira had a small, timid grin on his face.

Jim Bob turned back to Ira. "Thank your lucky stars. You get a pass today, but I'm gonna take this old Colt. You can pick it up in a couple of days." He turned to Callum. "Looks like you folks are leaving, so I reckon you'll soon be well down the road?"

"That's our plan, Marshal. Course, with this rain, who knows?"

The marshal took off his hat and spoke to Ma, who had been quiet throughout the proceedings. "Mrs. Logan, I wish you well. I'm right sorry about what happened to your husband. I'm hoping this is a safe trip for all of you."

"Thank you," Ma said. "I'm sure you will be an excellent marshal for Limerick. I wish only the best for you."

The big man acknowledged with a nod.

Nelson spoke up. "If it's all right with you"—He looked at Callum—"I'll be going with the marshal. I'm truly sorry. I have no idea what I was thinkin', but it won't happen again. Have a safe trip."

"You danged right you'll be comin' with me," the marshal said. He reached for the Walker Colt, shoved it behind his gunbelt, and motioned Nelson out ahead of him. When the marshal opened the door, the wind blasted in, driving heavy rain in front of it.

"The horses!" Bret shouted and dashed out the door.

Ezra chuckled, checked his slicker, and pulled his hat down. "We left 'em unattended. They've probably already drifted out of town. If we're not back when you leave, don't worry about us. We'll catch up with you." With that, he motioned Colin ahead of him, and the two of them stepped outside into the driving rain.

"Ma," Callum said, "let's finish with the supplies and be on our way."

"Don't rush me, son. We'll be finished as soon as we can. Now, Mr. Jenkins, let's get that flour and cornmeal."

An hour later, the wagons were loaded and the family headed out of the little village. Callum rode next to his ma's wagon. They couldn't talk, because the rain was so noisy, but he felt just the closeness might comfort her. She was leaving almost everything she had known behind. Even he felt a touch of melancholy, leaving his pa in a grave on Short Mountain, knowing he would never come back this way again. He wondered how the rest of the family felt. He remained near his ma until the road started to narrow, then glanced back toward Limerick. The horses and mules still hadn't caught up with them. He watched for a moment longer—nothing. *Ezra will watch over the younguns,* he thought. He turned Shoshone toward the front and trotted past the two wagons. Frank had his old flop hat pulled down so it was impossible to see his eyes. The rain ran in a steady stream down the back of the hat, following a crease, and continued down the back of his yellow slicker coat.

*Miserable weather to start a trip in*, he thought. He took a quick glance at the sky. His reward was a wet face, and rivulets coursing down his back under his slicker and shirt. He lowered his head and wiped his face with his hand. *We'll have to make the best of it.* Watching the road condition, he hoped it wouldn't get worse, but knew it would. This was Tennessee. This road was only hours away from turning into a swamp even a wagon pulled by all the mules they had couldn't keep from getting stuck in. They had, at best, three more hours of travel, before they'd have to stop. He had a stopping place in mind, only five or six miles down the road. It was a rocky outcropping on the other side of a small creek. Hopefully, the rain hadn't swollen it so much they would be prevented from crossing.

He adjusted his slicker and then his hat, hunched his shoulders, and leaned into the rain. Callum reached down and patted Shoshone on the neck. Softly, he said, "I know you hate this, boy, but we'll have you under some trees before long." The big horse tossed his head and continued into the rain.

They came to the creek sooner than he had expected. It wasn't wide, maybe forty feet at the crossing. Plenty wide enough to keep the wagons from dragging. The creek was up, but not so much it might prevent them from making it across.

He rode back to Frank in the lead wagon, and shouted to be heard above the hard rain. "Should be no problem. Right now, it's only up about a foot. Take it through, then pull in the first clearing on your left. Don't worry about getting stuck. It's all rocky ground."

Frank raised his hand in acknowledgment, and tightened up on the reins as the mules dropped down the sloped bank. Callum watched until he saw them top out on the other side of the creek, pulling the wagon. He waved to his ma as she rolled by. She acknowledged with a nod, concentrating on controlling the mules at the crossing. Once past, Callum eased Shoshone back a little more to allow plenty of room for the remuda as Ezra, Kate, Bret, and Colin pushed them forward in the rain. At their first chance, they'd turn their tails to the rain, and head back to town.

Callum rode over to Ezra. The older man squinted at him from under his hat. "We gonna ride into the night, or—" He stopped when he saw Frank pull his wagon off the road to the left. He looked up at Callum and winked. "You best not be readin' my mind, boy. You danged sure wouldn't like it much. I'm not too keen on gettin' my tail soaked." He looked down and behind himself. "Reckon that's about the only dry place on me."

Callum leaned over to him. "Got a place up ahead. It's pretty rocky, so we shouldn't have to worry about the wagons getting stuck. We might figure on doing a rope corral tonight under the trees. Make it big. I want to give the animals enough freedom where they can graze. When you cross the stream, let 'em water. That'll do for tonight."

Ezra nodded as Kate guided her horse next to Callum. "We're stopping up ahead?" Kate asked, indicating Frank pulling off the road.

Callum explained to Kate what he had just told Ezra. Then he asked her, "How are you doin'?"

She nodded, turning her head so that she could look at him without the rain hitting her face. "I'm doing good. I wish Pa was here. It doesn't seem possible he's gone."

Callum shook his head. "Hard for me to believe, but I can't help thinkin' he's lookin' down on us, and he's probably already seen those mountains we're gonna have to wait several months to see."

A smile tugged at the corners of her mouth, and he could see her brilliant blue eyes light up. "I hadn't thought of that, brother. Thanks." She bumped her Morgan mare with her boot heels, to catch up with the rest of the remuda.

Callum sat watching her trot toward the others. A frown

crossed his face. *I'm gonna have to watch out for her. She's turned into a real beauty.*

THEY HAD BEEN on the trail for almost a month. Much longer than he had hoped. The rain had been unusual for this time of year, falling almost continuously while they traveled west. The roads had turned into small rivers, becoming swamps in lower elevations. Several times it had become necessary to hitch up the remaining mules to pull each wagon out of the mire. But now, the sun was out. It had been that way for the past three days, providing them with hot, sweltering days, but a dry road.

Sweat glued Callum's shirt to his body, a jagged white sweat line indicating the separation between dry and wet cloth. He had stopped on the knoll overlooking Memphis, the wagons, mules, and horses a short distance behind him. The city was a welcome sight. Hopefully they could find a riverboat that would be leaving for Fort Smith soon. He had gone back and forth with himself, trying to decide what would be best. However, now that the first leg had taken so long, he had made the decision that he would look into a riverboat. That would cut close to a month off their trip and keep them off a trail that was fraught with danger. Gangs of thieves and killers roamed freely along the trail to Fort Smith. The law seldom ventured into the thickets for fear they wouldn't return.

He turned in the saddle, and looked back. The mules were pulling the wagons with ease, seeming to enjoy the dry road. A smile drifted across his face. The group had worked well together. Ezra, already a friend, had become a family member, jumping to help at any task. Colin had taken on whatever he was told to do without a complaint. Colin was most like Pa. He had become a quiet boy. Before Pa's death, he had been loud and boisterous, but now he had toned down, and listened closely to what he was told.

Colin seemed most excited when they practiced with the guns, which Callum had tried to do every day. They would have to replenish their supply of powder and ball, and rifle ammunition in Memphis, but the practice had been worth it. Bret took to it easy. He was becoming quick with the handguns, and deadly with the Winchester. Kate also had surprised everyone with her expert shooting. Of course, Kate had always liked to hunt with Pa. He had trained her well. Now, she could get that Colt Navy in business fast and hit what she was shooting. Ma did well too, but again, Pa had trained her.

It was young Colin who surprised everyone. At just thirteen, he could snake that Colt Navy out of his holster almost as fast as Josh. Like Josh, he hit what he was shooting at. The boy's hands were still too small to smoothly reach the hammer with the hand he held the revolver in, so he had started using the palm of his left hand to knock the hammer back. What was really surprising, was that he was able to stay on target. Callum had seen shooters fan their weapons, but they always scattered their shots. Not Colin. He had the unerring ability to keep that muzzle pointed to the same place. He could stack those thirty-six-caliber round balls so tight, you could cover them with a silver dollar.

Callum watched the wagons grow closer, Frank in the lead. Moving Shoshone to the opposite side of the road, Callum allowed them to pass. They moved down the road a ways and stopped.

"Oh, Callum!" Ma called out. "We've made it to Memphis. I was beginning to wonder if we would ever get here. But look at that river. This is the first time I've seen the Mississippi. It's breathtaking. Who would have thought it was so wide?"

After stopping his wagon, Frank sat looking at the sight. He pulled back the brake handle, locked it in place, and stepped down, after securing the reins. He walked to Ma's wagon, leaned against the side, and said, "Been a long time since I been to

Memphis. Wuz a time you had to keep your money close—a pretty rough town."

"Reckon it probably still is," Ezra said, from the back of his mule. He, Bret, Colin, and Kate had pushed the remuda alongside the two wagons, the horses and mules now pulling at the thick grass near the road.

"Look how big the river is," Kate said. "Pa always described it as big, but, without having seen it, you just can't picture it as that wide."

Colin's eyes were huge as he looked at the river, moving from the far north, at its first appearance, to the south, where it snaked behind tall pine trees. Then he looked at Callum and, with a touch of awe in his voice, said, "Callum, I ain't never seen so much water."

Ma smiled at Colin, not even taking the moment to correct him, letting him enjoy his experience.

"Hey! Either move on or get those wagons out of the way. We don't need backwoods gawkers blocking the path."

Callum turned slowly in the saddle to see a covered, two-horse surrey behind the remuda, followed by two armed riders. On the front seat, holding the reins, sat a rough-looking character dressed in a white shirt and a red bowtie, with red garters pushed up his long white sleeves. The garters were stretched tight around massive biceps, and the white shirt did little to hide the bulk in his shoulders. Behind him sat an older man, even bigger, wearing a burgundy frock coat and tie. His hands were stretched forward, resting on the rounded gold knob of his cane. To his left sat a beautiful young lady. The woman immediately grabbed Callum's attention.

She had soft brown hair hanging in ringlets framing her face, beneath an almost flat yellow hat. Her complexion was pure as ivory, and brown eyes gazed out from beneath the thick black eyelashes. However, the beauty of her face was diminished by the high-chinned, haughty look she cast at the travelers. She reached down and grasped a corner of her full, lemon-yellow silk skirt that had slipped outside the carriage. With disdain, she flipped it back into the carriage, and sniffed at the back of her white glove. She leaned over and said something to the older man. He, in turn, spoke to the driver.

The driver gave a single sharp nod and yelled, "I ain't tellin' you again. Make room!"

# 12

The surrey had pushed up to the rear of the remuda, just behind Kate. The driver picked up his whip and, showing no concern for her well-being, slashed at Kate's Morgan, drawing blood. The mare reared and screamed, immediately trying to break away. When she couldn't, she started bucking. Startled, the remuda raced away down the road. As the horses moved out of the way, there was room for the surrey to pass to the left of the wagons. The driver, seeing an opening, popped the whip, and the horses team started to move forward.

Kate maintained control of the mare and raced after the horses, with Bret right behind her to help.

Once Callum saw that Kate was all right, he yanked loose his rope, made a loop, and, as the surrey rolled past, lightly tossed it under the roof and over the driver's head. Fortunately for the man, the rope dropped past his neck and over his forearms. Callum looped his end around the saddle horn and watched the rope grow taut, dragging the driver over the top of the front seat and momentarily into the lap of the startled young lady sitting on the backseat.

Callum soon found she was definitely no lady. For when the driver hit her chest and lap, she gasped, and let out a string of curses that would embarrass a mountain man, violently shoving the driver away from her and over the side of the surrey.

While being dragged from the carriage, the hammer of the driver's gun, thrust behind his waistband at the small of his back, caught in the fragile white lace that ran down each side of a set of buttons on the front of the woman's yellow dress. Ripped in half, part of the lace continued with the man, hanging from the revolver at his back like a tail. The other half hung limply from the woman's collar. She watched the driver as he continued his fall into the rough road.

When he hit the ground, Callum eased Shoshone forward, allowing slack in the rope. As the team of horses passed, Ezra reached out and grabbed the bridle on the one nearest him and brought the team to a halt.

Callum stepped from the saddle as the man stood, now struggling to get the rope up and over his head.

The man's arms were stretched high, the rope just clearing his head, when Callum walked up. He slung the rope to the ground. "It's time you learned a lesson, Cowboy. I'm gonna beat your sorry—"

Callum hit him square in the mouth with a driving left, followed by a powerful right in the same place. Blood shot everywhere. The man's front teeth were visible through the deep cut in his upper lip. He took a step back, and Callum followed with a left uppercut to the solar plexus. The man doubled over, and Callum, gripping his gloved hands together, slammed them into the back of the thick neck.

The big man's legs wobbled for a moment, then collapsed. He sprawled, face-first, into the road. The two men behind the wagon had ridden up and were sitting still, both hands resting on the pommels of their saddles. They were looking past Callum. He turned to see his youngest brother, sitting calmly in his saddle, a Navy Colt in his right hand.

"Mister," the tall man on the left said, "I ain't never seen anyone clear leather as fast as that kid did. I don't know who you are, but you're gonna have to keep an eye on him. I thought for a minute there, he was gonna shoot us."

Beyond Colin, he could see Ma and Frank standing with their rifles leveled at the two men. "If you'd gone for your guns, he would have, and if he didn't, they would. You fellas shuck those weapons and drop 'em in the dirt. You can pick 'em up at the sheriff's office."

Without another word, the two riders dropped their handguns and rifles to the ground.

"Good," Callum said, "now ride on past. I'll ask you to cause no trouble to the folks catching our stock."

The two rode past Callum, keeping their eyes on Colin. They tipped their hats to Ma and kicked their horses in the flanks, disappearing around the bend in the road.

Callum looked over at Colin. The boy was grinning. No fear or concern showed on his face. Callum watched as he holstered his Colt, sliding it unerringly into the holster, while maintaining eye contact with him. A groan issued from the man on the ground.

Callum reached down, grasped the man by one arm, and dragged him to his feet. He pulled the revolver from the man's waistband and shoved him at the surrey.

The woman yelled, "Keep that blood away from my dress, Cooper! You've already done enough damage."

Callum held up the revolver and looked at the big man in the back of the surrey. "This'll be at the sheriff's office with the rest of the six-shooters."

The man watched Callum with eyes that reminded him of a snake. The bloody driver, now slumped against the carriage, turned to face Callum. In a low, guttural tone he said, "You'll regret this, Cowboy. I've killed men with these." He held up his fists.

Callum slid the man's revolver behind his gunbelt. "Mister, you can have a piece of me any time, but if you're through talking, climb back up in that fancy carriage and get out of here."

Callum watched the man climb into the carriage, then turned and mounted Shoshone.

"What's your name, Cowboy?" the woman asked, her words spit out like they were something bitter in her mouth.

He looked at her for a long moment. She was no longer attractive. He could see the hardness in her thin lips, drawn like a line across her face. He touched his hat. "Callum Logan, ma'am. Now you best be on your way."

Her face hardened even more, as she turned it forward, away from him. "Let's go, Cooper. Now!"

The carriage passed the two wagons and disappeared from view. Callum glanced over to Colin, who was sitting quietly, watching where the carriage had been. When he glanced at Ezra, the old man had been watching Colin. He looked at Callum, raised his eyebrows, and said, "Guess we better get that stock," and started off after Kate and Bret.

Ma caught the look and said to Colin, "Go help with the horses, son. Have Kate and Bret hold them near the road, and we'll be along shortly."

"Yes, Ma." He galloped after Ezra.

Frank had walked to Ma's wagon, carrying his Spencer, and helped her up onto the seat. Callum rode up, dismounted, and walked to the water barrel fastened to the driver's side of the wagon. A tin dipper hung next to it. He slipped the dipper from its hook, opened the half-lid, and dipped into the water, then walked to the front of the wagon and offered it to his ma. She took it and drank deeply. When she finished she handed it back to Callum. "Obliged, son."

He moved back to the barrel, drew out another dipperful and

drank the cool water, flipped the remaining drops from it, hung it back by the leather thong, and closed the lid.

Frank spit, and said to Callum, "You whacked that chuckle head pretty fierce. All you boys are just like yore pa. When he got his dander up, he was one curly wolf." Frank kicked a horse apple close to the wagon wheel he was leaning on. "Did you see yore brother?"

Ma spoke up before Callum could comment. "I saw him. Scared me to death. When those two men reached for their guns, you couldn't see his hand move, and his gun was pointing at them, Colin sitting on his horse, grinning."

Callum shook his head. "I've been showing everyone how to shoot, and I'm thinkin' Colin still sees it as a game. I'll have a talk with him." He looked at the sun, now well past its zenith. "It's gettin' late. We best be on our way."

The two wagons, with Callum in the lead, moved down the road to Memphis. Houses lined the roadside, at least one every quarter mile. Dogs barked from yards, while horses and cows watched them pass. The road twisted its way west, with Memphis disappearing behind huge red oak trees and glistening silver maples, their leaves flashing in the breeze.

Still outside of town, Callum came up to the crew and horses, resting in a small park next to a gurgling creek. He rode Shoshone to the stream and stepped down, letting the horse drink. As soon as the wagons pulled up, Callum turned to Bret and Colin. "Why don't you two water the mules. When you're done, we'll be on our way." The two headed for the wagons to get buckets.

Frank and Ma had pulled the wagons to the opposite side of the road, leaving enough room for travelers to pass by. They climbed down and joined the family.

"You still hankerin' to latch on to a riverboat?" Ezra asked of Callum when Frank and Ma had joined them.

"I am." Callum removed his hat and wiped the sweat from his

forehead with his sleeve. "It's late in the year, and they may have already stopped, but if they're still running, we could save near a month of travel."

"That'd suit me fine," Ma said. "What would suit me even more, is a bath. Do they have baths on those riverboats, Callum?"

"Yes, ma'am, they do, but we should be able to get that taken care of here in Memphis. I doubt we'll get out tomorrow, so we might be here several days."

"Good," Kate said. "I'd like to look around."

Callum said, "I'm sure there'll be plenty of time for lookin' around. We'll leave the wagons at a livery, along with the horses and mules."

Frank shot a serious look at Callum. "We'll need to keep a guard on those wagons. No telling what all might be stolen."

"You're right, Frank, but it won't take all of us. I figured to break the guard up between me, you, Ezra, and Bret. But before we do anything, I'd like to get our supplies restocked."

"First thing," Ma said, "is a hotel. I've got a month of Tennessee dirt ground into my skin. We'll get cleaned up, and then restock the wagons."

Callum squatted down and pulled a long stem of Johnson grass. Once he started chewing on it, he looked up at his ma."If you've got something, supplies wise, you want, just tell us. Frank and I'll take you and Kate to the hotel, drop you off, and then go to the store to load up the wagons."

"That sounds good." She turned to watch Bret and Colin finish watering the mules. The boys hung the buckets on the hooks just beneath the dippers, then trotted back across the road to join the rest of the family.

When they arrived, Colin said, "We gonna eat here? I'm gettin' hungry."

"No." Callum stood and stretched his back. "We'll eat in town. Let's get moving. We still have a lot of day left."

MAIN STREET BUSTLED with commercial traffic. People hurried across the busy thoroughfare, rushing between a steady stream of loaded wagons headed to the wharves, and empties returning. Teamsters shouted at each other as they passed. Frank stopped the lead wagon behind the surrey in front of the Overton Hotel. Ma pulled up behind him.

Frank set the brake, looped the reins around the brake handle, and climbed down from the wagon. He looked over to Callum, who was tying Shoshone to a hitching rail. He nodded his head to the surrey and fired a long stream of tobacco into the street. After wiping his mouth on his red-checkered shirt sleeve, he said, "Ain't that buggy the one that feller was drivin' what was in such a dad-blamed hurry?"

Callum nodded as he helped Ma down from her wagon. "Looks like it." He looked up at Kate. "Why don't you come on in. Once we get rooms, we'll take all the animals to the livery. You and Ma can stay here and get cleaned up."

Kate, her neck craned back to gaze at the tall five-story build, finally shook her head. "Never in my life have I seen anything like this." Her head turned as she examined the multiple arches and columns at the hotel's entrance. "Callum, you think they'll let us in here?" She swung down from her horse, looped the mare's reins over the hitching rail, and stared at the two doormen, resplendent in their black top hats, red frock coats, and black cravats.

One saw her looking. He doffed his hat and bowed to her. "May I help you, Miss?"

One hand flew to her face, as she suppressed a giggle. It partially hid the brilliant red of her rosy cheeks, now glowing. Callum, a wide grin on his face, immediately came to her aid. "Yes, I think you can. If you'll step over here to the back of this wagon, I'll hand you the ladies' bags."

"Yes, sir," the doorman said, as he strode to the back of the wagon Ma was driving. "How long will you be staying with us?"

Callum reached into the back of the wagon, and pulled out two carpet bags, handing them to the doorman. "At least one evening, maybe more."

"Please follow me, sir," the man said, and marched toward the line of entry doors. The other bellman opened the door nearest them.

Callum looked toward the still-mounted men. "Ezra, you and the boys going to be all right with the stock, while we get some rooms?"

"We'll be fine, boy. Don't you go and get me nary a room. I'll be sleeping at the livery with my mules."

"You sure? Those beds oughta be feeling mighty good tonight."

"Not fer me. Anyway, they probably ain't lettin' Blue in there no how." The hound sat at the horses' feet staring up at his owner. "You go ahead and get them rooms, and we'll find a livery."

"You're probably right.

"Frank, you mind watching the wagons?"

"Suits me. Wouldn't want to leave them alone on this street. No telling how many sticky fingers would be helping themselves."

Callum turned and quickly joined Ma and Kate just before they walked into the massive lobby of the Overton. Kate immediately stopped in the doorway, gawking. Ma grasped her arm firmly, leading her into the spacious interior away from the doors. The melodic sounds of a piano drifted across the lobby.

"Isn't it beautiful?" Kate exclaimed. "Why, look at that huge staircase, and the curtains. The purple curtains and the dark wood walls are breathtaking. Everyone is dressed so well. Callum, you didn't answer me. Do you think they'll let us stay here?"

They continued to a long counter, where three men worked,

signing in customers. Callum tipped the doorman, removed his hat, and tossed it on the counter. "Kate, we're about to find out." He looked at the young man stepping up to the counter in front of them. He had the reddest hair Callum had ever seen.

"May I help you, sir?"

Callum nodded. "Yep, you sure can. We'll have six folks staying. I'm thinkin' we'll need three rooms with two beds in each."

The man looked at a chart. "Yes, sir. On the third floor, we have two rooms that are connected, and one room directly across the hall. They all have two spacious beds in them."

"Sounds good. How much?"

"How many nights will you be staying, Mister. . . ?"

"Callum Logan, and at least one night. It depends on the riverboat schedule going up the Arkansas to Fort Smith. We have two wagons and several head of horses and mules."

The clerk figured quickly, wrote an amount on a piece of paper, and slid it across to Callum. As soon as he passed the paper over, he reached under the counter and pulled out a schedule. "Mr. Callum, it looks like there are two riverboats leaving tomorrow morning, the Lone Star and the Mary Ann. You're very fortunate. With all of the rain out West, the riverboats have continued to operate. Usually, this time of year, the river is too low for the riverboats to make it as far as Fort Smith."

"I guess we're just livin' right," Callum said. He reached into his vest pocket and pulled out a pouch, counted out six double eagle gold pieces, and slid them across to the clerk. "Will that cover the bill?"

"Yes, sir, indeed it will. I forgot to tell you, breakfast will be included in your room charge. Show your keys to the waiter, and he'll take care of the bill. Now, if I could have you sign in for everyone." He slid a ledger across the counter.

While Callum was signing the register, the clerk leaned over, looked at a board against the back side of the counter, then reached down and removed six keys. "Will six be enough, sir?"

"You bet." Callum looked the young man directly in the eyes. "Which riverboat would you recommend?"

Callum's direct gaze flustered the clerk only for a moment, then, holding Callum's gaze, he said, "Lone Star, sir. By far. The captain is a good man, and he is an excellent river captain. Plus, the food is excellent, and he will have accommodations for the ladies."

Ma, who had been listening to the conversation, said, "How do you know so much about the Lone Star?"

The young man gave her a big grin. "The captain's my Pa. He's been running the Mississippi, Arkansas, and Red River as far back as I can remember, and Ma runs the kitchen. Peaches are in season, so try her peach cobbler. It's about the best you'll ever eat." He paused for a second, realizing what he'd said. "No offense, ma'am. I just mean it's very good."

Ma smiled at the young man and reached across the counter and patted his hand. "No offense taken. I'd be offended if you didn't think your ma was the best cook. I'll tell her we met you. What's your name?"

The clerk smiled back at her, showing even, white teeth. "Name's Austin Hill. Pa's from Texas. He named all the kids after Texicans."

"That's a nice name, Austin," Ma said. "You've been a great help."

"Thank you, ma'am. Enjoy your stay." Austin tapped his hand on the brass bell sitting near the register. The soft ding reverberated through the lobby, and almost immediately a young man, uniformed in the hotel livery, arrived at the counter. "David, please take these fine folks to their rooms." With that, Austin handed the keys to the bellboy.

"Thank you," David said. "Would you follow me, please." He turned and headed for the carpeted staircase.

Suddenly, the air in the lobby was split by a frosty tone that chilled the room. “Father, that’s the ruffian that accosted us and beat Mr. Cooper.”

Callum, recognizing the harsh female voice, turned to see her accompanied by the large man who had been riding with her in the surrey. He was carrying the same knobbed cane. Behind him strode two men, cut from the same pattern as the one he had beaten.

# 13

"Sir," the large man said, "you beat my driver today. I take umbrage with that." The man stared down at Callum.

Callum nodded at the bellboy, grasping his ma's and Kate's arms and giving them a slight push. "Go on to your rooms. When we get the wagons put away, we'll be back." He looked at Kate, and could see her concern. He gave her a small grin. "We'll take you out to see the town when we get back."

"Sir! I am speaking to you."

At the same time, he felt a nudge on his shoulder from the cane tip.

Callum looked at the bellboy. "Go."

"Yes, sir." David nodded quickly, stepping out. "Right this way, ladies."

Reaching the bottom of the burgundy carpeted stairs, Kate glanced back. Callum saw his ma grasp her arm and pull her onto the first step. They continued up the stairs.

He slowly turned back to the man. "Where I come from, Mister, that could get you shot dead."

The two bruisers stepped out from behind the man and started for Callum.

*Great,* he thought. *Here I stand with both my guns latched down. One of these days I'll learn, if I live long enough.*

Thrusting his cane horizontally in front of the two men, the big man stopped them. "Not yet, gentlemen. I'd like to talk to this cowboy before you teach him the lesson he deserves." The word cowboy spilled from the man's mouth like sour milk. "I understand your name is Callum Logan. It is for you to understand that you cannot affront Colonel Chester E. Hughes as you did today, and not expect to be punished."

Patrons in the hotel lobby stopped their conversations and turned toward the loud voice.

Callum noticed the people around them had turned to stare at the door. He glanced that way and, to his relief, Frank stood inside with his Remington Army drawn and hanging easily at his side.

Callum nodded to the door. "I reckon your punishment is gonna have to wait for another day." He turned to the girl. "Ma'am, I can promise you, if you was my sister, my ma would've washed your mouth out with soap a long time ago."

Ignoring the angry look on the girl's face, he tipped his hat to the Hughes group, slipped it to the back of his head, and strolled over to Frank, unfastening the thongs on his holsters as he walked.

Hughes said, in a voice low and barely audible. "This isn't over, Logan."

Callum ignored him and continued toward the door. Once outside, he said to Frank, "That's what I call a timely entrance. I figured I was about to get hammered into that pretty carpet. Why'd you come in?"

Frank had slipped the Remington back into his holster. From about six feet away, he spit a long stream of tobacco juice into a potted plant by the hotel's entrance. "You was gone too long. I thought I'd better check. Glad I did."

They had stopped at the hitching rail. Callum untied

Shoshone and retied him to the back of Ma's wagon. Kate's Morgan had been taken with the rest of the stock. "Let's see if we can find our people," he said, climbing up to the wagon seat.

Frank waved and walked on to his wagon. A few minutes later, Callum watched as Frank's wagon lurched forward into the crazy Memphis traffic. Callum let a buckboard pass and then followed. It didn't take long. Less than three blocks away, they came upon a large livery. The mules and horses were inside the huge corral, along with the donkeys. Frank pulled to the front of the livery, stopping before he reached the tall second-story doors that opened, allowing the lowering or raising of bales of hay or sacks of feed.

Callum halted the mules behind the other wagon, wrapped the reins, swung his legs over the side, and jumped down. As he was straightening up, a rotund man, wearing an apron and a worn and dirty bowler, stepped from the darker interior of the barn.

"How do? Name's Slim." He patted the ample belly his apron did little to hide. "Reckon you can figger how I latched on to that handle. How can I help you men?"

Right behind the man, Ezra, Bret, and Colin stepped out of the huge barn.

Callum tilted his head toward them. "Did they fill you in?"

The man removed the bowler, pulled a dirty rag from the heavy leather apron, and wiped his bald head. He looked at the rag for a moment like he was measuring the amount of perspiration that had soaked the material, then slipped it back into the apron pocket. The hat flopped back onto his head. "Told me some. Hadn't yet got to the wagons."

Callum looked at Slim. "Reckon someone was funning you when they stuck you with Slim."

"My pa. I weighed near to twelve pounds when Ma birthed me. It was said that he took one look at me and said, 'That boy's gonna eat me out of house and home. Maybe if we name him Slim that'll slow down his hunger.'"

Ezra laughed. "Did it work?"

"Well, heck no. Pa had to work twice as hard just to keep enough beans on the table for me, much less my eight brothers and sisters. Now, tell me what I can do you for."

Callum looked at the big barn. "We're gonna need a place to put these wagons for at least a day, maybe more. Depends on how soon we can get up the Arkansas."

"Looks like one night for you, then. There's a boat pulling out tomorrow morning. Was I you, I'd get on down to the wharf and talk to the captain. See if there's room to get those Studebakers on the barge."

"Which one?" Callum asked.

"Why, the onliest one I'd recommend, the Lone Star, but you better get on down there. I hear she's fillin' up."

"Obliged." Callum untied Shoshone from the back of the wagon and mounted. "Frank, make sure everything's ready for a quick departure in the morning. I'll see you in a bit."

Swinging into the traffic, he immediately moved the big horse to a trot, weaving around the many obstacles. It wasn't long before he showed up at the wharf, where the sounds were almost overpowering. Men were yelling, riverboat whistles blasted, wagons rolled on wooden wharves, along with the steps of men either loading or unloading material from the boats, and beneath it all came the low rumble of the steam engines.

The traffic slowed to a near standstill at the wharf, where wagons were parked and men lumbered across the road under heavy burdens. Callum slowed Shoshone, often having to stop him to allow someone to cross in front of the big horse. A well-dressed man ran across the road, carrying a valise. Callum called to him. "Can you tell me where the Lone Star is docked?"

The man stopped, looked up at Callum, then pointed south

along the wharf. "The third boat. The big side-wheeler with the double stack."

"Thanks," Callum said to the back of the man's frock coat, as he hurried on his way toward an office in one of the buildings fronting the street. Callum pulled up to tie Shoshone to a hitching rail, across the street from the wharf, and was immediately accosted by a boy of twelve or thirteen years old, about Colin's size. He was barefoot, dressed in homespun shirt and pants. His pants were clean but had holes in both knees and were held up by a rope around his middle. His tousled blond hair hung almost in his eyes, and he looked like food hadn't passed his lips for days.

"Mister, that's a mighty pretty horse. There's a lot of theft down here on the waterfront. I'll watch him for two bits and make sure nobody bothers him or your stuff."

Callum appraised the young man, noting his shabby but clean appearance and erect stance. "What's your name?"

"Name's Virgil, but everybody calls me Virg."

Callum nodded. "I'm Callum Logan. Tell you what, Virg, I'll hire you to take good care of Shoshone here until I get back, for four bits, not a penny more." He pulled out a quarter and tossed it to the boy. "Here's half now, and I'll give you the other half when I return. If you need me, I'll be at the Lone Star."

The boy frowned, his blond brows drawing together and tossed the quarter back to Callum. "I don't take charity, Mister. Two bits is fair, and two bits is what I asked for."

Callum caught the quarter and gave the boy a hard look. "I give charity to no healthy man. This horse means a lot to me, and I pay a man an honest wage to take care of him. Four bits is honest. Take it or leave it."

The frown disappeared from the boy's face, replaced by a toothy grin. "Gee, Mister. I didn't realize how important this horse is. I'll be takin' good care of him."

"Good." Callum tossed the two bits back to the boy, turned with quarter in air, and crossed the street to the Lone Star.

The loading of the riverboat was proceeding systematically, compared to the other boats. An impressive man, obviously in charge, stood at the gangplank directing the stevedores, as they hauled load after load of wood aboard. He was of average height, but his shoulders and arms were massive. Under his thick red hair, now tinged with white, were wild, flaming-red eyebrows that crashed together above his nose. From under those threatening eyebrows, and set in a deeply tanned and wrinkled face, were the bluest eyes Callum had ever seen. The bowl of a corncob pipe was gripped in his right hand, which between puffs, was being used to direct traffic.

As he approached the man, Callum was careful to stay out of the way of the line of men loading the boat. "Morning. I'm lookin' for Captain Hill."

"You need look no further. I'm Hill. Who might you be?"

Callum stuck out his hand and watched it disappear in the grasp of the captain. "Captain, the name is Callum Logan, and I'd like to get a ride with you to Fort Smith."

The captain looked Callum over, his eyes stopping at the two guns hanging around his waist. "We've got room, but I'll not have trouble on my boat."

"No, sir. I don't blame you. I'm not lookin' for trouble. I won't run from it, but I promise you, I'll start nothing."

"Good. I'd ask no man to run. That'll be twenty dollars, and you can stow your gear aboard. I'll be pulling a barge. You can put your horse there."

"Well, there's the problem, Captain. I'm not the only one."

"As you can see, we're a big boat. Though on this trip, I've got a herd of movers on board, headed for Oregon, but we still have plenty of room. So bring all your people. I've room aplenty."

Callum gave the captain a lopsided grin. "More than just people."

A clang rang out when two of the stevedores dropped a passenger's trunk on the gangway. The captain cast a severe gaze toward the two men and pointed his pipe at them. One of them shook his head, shrugged his shoulders, and held his palms up. The captain looked at him a moment longer, then turned back to his conversation with Callum.

"Maybe you best spell out what you've got that needs to get to Fort Smith." He then pushed the stem of his pipe between his teeth and took a puff, exhaling through his nose, looking much like the smoke issuing from the twin stacks on his riverboat.

Callum explained about the people, wagons, mules, and horses. He watched the dark eyebrows rise as he listed everyone and everything. When he finished, he said, "Austin said to mention him when I was talking to you."

The older man's face brightened. "Fine boy. I would have preferred he join me on the river, but every man has to make his own way. If Austin likes you, then I'll make it work.

"See that big barge just behind my boat?" The captain pointed with the lip of his pipe and continued without waiting for Callum's confirmation. "It's eighty feet long. Notice there's livestock there already. That's from an outfit that's traveling to Oregon. They'll be purchasing their wagons and additional animals at Fort Smith. It'll be crowded, but you should have room for your wagons and livestock. The corrals will hold your mules and horses. I'm planning on pulling out at ten sharp tomorrow morning. You'll need to be here by seven, so that we can get you loaded."

"Thank you, Captain. Riding with you cuts six weeks of pushing through timber and mountains from our trip. Especially the southern edge of the Buffalo Mountains."

Captain Hill watched the smoke from his pipe curl upward, then turned his attention back to Callum. "That country's not only rough but is home to several gangs and river pirates, but because of our size, they'll not be bothering us. You're lucky the

Arkansas is still running deep enough for us to navigate this time of year. You'll be ridin' on what is probably our last run this season."

"Thanks again, Captain. We'll see you in the morning." Callum turned to head back to his horse and stopped. He turned back. "What can you tell me about that young towheaded fella watchin' my horse?"

The captain nodded. "His name's Virgil Brogan. Rest of his family died in a fire near six months ago. Good boy. I try to give him work when I can, a hard worker."

"So you'd say he's trustworthy?"

"Yes, I would. That boy has man-size pride. Right now, he carries a bit of a chip on his shoulder, but with the right guidance, he'll grow to be a good man."

"Thanks." Callum turned and walked across the wharf, dodging his way across the busy street, and approached Virgil.

The boy had been giving Shoshone a good brushing when footsteps crunched behind him. He turned to see Callum approaching. Giving the horse one last pass, Virgil dropped the brush into his bag. "All done, Mr. Logan?"

"I am."

People who knew Callum, were well aware he didn't waste time mulling over decisions. He made up his mind quickly and then pressed forward. Today was no different. "You tied to Memphis, boy?"

Virgil's eyebrows dropped, and he tilted his head as he stared at Callum. "What do you mean, Mr. Logan?"

With the forefinger of his left hand against the underside of his gray, sweat-stained hat brim, Callum pushed the hat to the back of his head, allowing the brown, curly hair, now black from sweat, to fall almost to his thick eyebrows. "Virg, I'm taking my family to Colorado. I've got a ranch out there. I could use some help. It'll be hard work, and I'll accept no complainin'. I'll pay you as I would any hired hand. Once we get there, you can work for my brother punching cattle. You interested?"

While Callum talked, the frown on the boy's face disappeared, replaced with eyes wide and mouth wider.

"Well, don't stand there with your mouth open, boy. Give me an answer."

Virgil's surprise turned to excitement. "Yes. Yes, sir. I'm ready to do whatever's needed. I've always wanted to go West, just never thought I'd have the chance."

"You got it now. You need to go get your stuff, or let anyone know?"

Virg looked down at his shoes. "No, sir. My family's dead. I'm wearing all I've got."

Callum nodded, fished another quarter from his vest and tossed it to Virgil, then untied Shoshone and swung into the saddle. He kicked his left boot out of the stirrup, and reached one arm down. "Let's go."

The boy looked at him for only a moment, then stepped up to the stirrup, grasped Callum's hand, and swung up behind him. The two of them rode in silence for a ways, then Callum said, "You need some clothes if you're going on the trail with us." Callum could feel the boy's body stiffen.

"Mr. Logan, I told you before, I don't take charity."

Callum trotted Shoshone up the street toward the hotel. "Boy, like I told you, life give's you nothing for free, and neither do I, but I need you to be dressed proper, so you don't cast a bad light on me. You're part of this outfit, now, so you've got to look the part. I'll take the cost of the clothes out of your wages."

They came to a clothing store, and Callum guided Shoshone to the hitching rail. Virg slung a leg over and dropped to the ground. Callum followed. Before the two of them walked into the store, Callum handed the boy a twenty-dollar gold piece. "An advance on your first month."

Virgil's eyes grew big as he looked first at the gold piece and then at Callum, who placed his hand on the boy's shoulder and gently shoved him toward the door. "Let's get you some clothes."

A young store clerk looked up from behind the counter and spotted Virgil walking through the door ahead of Callum. "Virgil Brogan, you get your scrawny butt out of this store. I don't need you running off customers."

Virgil, his wide but thin shoulders pulled back, was taking a deep breath to respond, when Callum stepped around him to the clerk. In his boots and with his hat on, he towered over the man. The clerk involuntarily took a step back, his eyes growing large at the hard expression on Callum's face.

"He's with me, boy," Callum said, his gruff voice carrying throughout the store. Other customers stopped what they were doing and turned to see what was happening. "You'll be outfitting him for a trip West. You reckon you can do that, or do we need to take our business elsewhere?"

A middle-aged lady had been helping a customer in the back of the store. She stepped out from behind a rack of clothes. "Nathan, apologize to Virgil. Then come back here and help Mr. Abrams."

The clerk looked at the lady speaking, back at Callum, then at Virgil. He cleared his throat, and mumbled, "Sorry." He then turned and hurried to the back, disappearing around the corner where the lady had been standing.

"Hello, Virgil. I'm sorry for Nathan's attitude. Sometimes I think I've been too easy on him."

"That's all right, Mrs. Jacoby," Virgil said.

She turned to Callum. "I am truly sorry, sir. My name is Eugenia Jacoby. Please call me Jenny. Might I help you and Virgil?"

# 14

Callum smiled down at the petite, older woman. The years had been kind to her. Her white hair was plaited down each side of her head, pulled to the back, and rolled into a soft bun. The plaits and bun were covered and held in place by a sheer silk net. As he looked at her, the word regal came to mind. "Callum Logan, ma'am. I need to outfit this young feller. He's going West with us."

Jenny turned to Virgil and gave a soft clap of her hands. "Oh, good. I am so happy for you, Virgil." She turned back to Callum. "His parents were such good people. It was a shame what happened to them.

"Now," she continued, her voice much more businesslike, "let's see what we can do for you." She turned and marched to the back of the store, motioning them to follow.

Callum pushed Virgil ahead of him. "Go ahead, Virg. Let's get this done as quick as we can. I'm hungry." He could see the boy's eyes light up when he mentioned food.

It didn't take long for Jenny to fit Virgil. The boy stepped from behind one of the changing screens. *All the difference in the world,*

Callum thought. *Clothes can really make a difference.* "How's that feel to you, Virg? Comfortable?"

"Yes, sir, these canvas pants feel mighty good." He held his arm out and rubbed his hand over the sleeve of the red-and-black checked wool shirt. Then he looked down at the brown, high-heeled cowboy boots on his feet. When he looked up, his grin seemed like it would split his face.

Callum looked at the boots and back at Virgil. "You need 'em if you aim to work cattle with us." Then he turned back to Jenny. "He needs a hat and a vest. Without a hat, that Western sun will bake his brain."

"I think I have just the thing." She walked over to a display counter and picked up a wide-brimmed, flat-crowned, black hat. "Do you like this, Virgil?"

Before he said anything, he looked to Callum. After Callum's slight nod, his grin got bigger. "Yes, ma'am, I like that a lot."

She brought it over and he tried it on. It fit him like a glove, but it didn't have a cord to go under his chin. Callum took it and looked it over. "You have any rawhide, ma'am?"

She turned and brought back a long, narrow piece of rawhide. Picking up a hammer and punch, she asked Virgil, "I'm correct in assuming you want this hat?"

At his enthusiastic nod, she set the hat down on the counter, picked up the punch, and about midway, adjacent to the crown, she rapidly punched a hole on each side. With the rawhide string, she ran it up and through one hole, looped it around the crown and down through the opposite hole. Once that was completed, she looked at Virgil for a moment and then cut the rawhide, quickly tying the two ends together.

"There," she said, "that will keep your hat on when you're in a storm."

Another clerk had piled the clothes on top of the counter. Virgil's eyes were as big as silver dollars. He looked at Callum in amazement. "That's a sight of clothes, Mr. Logan."

"You'll need 'em. Why don't you go check on Shoshone? I'll be along shortly."

"Yes, sir." Virgil whirled and ran out the door, his boots making resounding thumps on the wooden floor.

Callum laughed, and then said, "He won't be likin' those boots quite as much in a couple of days. I reckon he'll have blisters all over his feet. How about puttin' his old shoes in with the other clothes? That'll give him something to wear when those boots are painin' him too much."

Jenny smiled. "Yes, it does take a while for that leather to mold to one's feet." She walked over, picked up the old shoes, brought them back, and set them down next to the new clothes.

"How much do I owe you, ma'am?"

"Let's see, three pair of pants, three shirts, boots, long-johns, socks, vest, hat, heavy coat and working gloves. That'll come to thirty-seven dollars and forty cents."

While Callum counted out the money, he said, "I had a feeling that you wanted to say more about the death of Virgil's folks."

Jenny leaned over the counter to look out the front window. She saw Virgil rubbing Shoshone's neck. After looking around the store to ensure no one was near, she leaned over the counter slightly toward Callum. In a low tone, she said, "I believe they were murdered. Men that work for Chester Hughes were seen around their home before it caught fire. Unfortunately, there was not enough evidence to prove they were involved, but the marshal is still investigating the fire. That boy's whole family was killed. Someone needs to pay."

Callum flashed back to the horror he still saw on his family's faces when they talked about the fire at the farm. *I can't imagine what Virgil must be going through,* he thought. *I guess we'll never know if it was Hughes or not.* He shook his head as he was putting the change back in his vest pocket.

Jenny looked up at him. "I sense you are a good man. I'm glad you're taking Virgil away from Memphis. There are only bad memories here for him."

"Thanks, ma'am." Callum looked at the stack of clothes. "You have a carpet bag around here? We need to do something with these things until we can get them packed."

"Of course." She left and returned quickly with a well-worn but usable bag.

He reached for his gold sack. She smiled and shook her head. "No charge. This bag is old. It will handle these things until you find a better place to put them." She stuffed the clothes and shoes into the bag and slid it across to him.

"That's right nice of you, Jenny," Callum said. "I'm obliged."

Picking it up, he touched his hat brim in salute and headed out the door. When the door closed, Virgil looked at Callum. "Mr. Callum, I do have one thing I need to get, if you don't mind."

Callum handed the bag to Virgil, untied Shoshone, swung up, and reached down. Virgil handed up the bag, then joined him on the appaloosa's back."Where is it, Virgil?"

"It's at Mr. Bickham's livery. He lets me stay there."

"That makes it might easy, cause that's where we're headed."

Only minutes had passed when the man and boy pulled up at the livery. Callum left Virgil with Shoshone at the water trough, while he walked to the back of the livery. He found Frank, Ezra, Slim, Colin, and Bret currying the last of the mules.

"Looks like you boys been busy," Callum said as he looked through the window at the remainder of the stock in the corral.

"Yep," Slim said. "These fellers saved me a passel of work by hanging around and helping."

The men talked for a few more minutes, Callum explaining his good fortune at the wharf. At the sound of Virgil leading Shoshone into the barn, everyone looked toward the entrance.

"Who's that?" Colin asked.

"That's our new hand," Callum said. "He was so good at

watching after Shoshone down at the wharf, I offered him a job. He's going West with us."

"Why, that's Virg," Slim said, "and look at them new clothes. He shore needed 'em."

Colin shot a confused look at Callum. "You bought him new clothes?"

Callum, at the sharp tone from Colin, turned to look at his brother. "You got a burr under your saddle, boy?"

Colin stared at Callum, not backing down. "He ain't family!"

"Colin," Bret said, "what's the matter with you? Where's your manners?"

His face red with anger, Colin spun on Bret. "You ain't Ma, so don't try to act like her."

Virgil, having tied Shoshone in the stall, was near enough to hear the conversation. He came walking around the corner of the stall and faced Colin, his hands on his hips. "I aim to pay for these clothes."

Ignoring Virgil, Colin looked up at Callum, who had been taken aback by his brother's harsh response to Virgil. "We don't need him!"

"That's enough," Callum ordered, his voice like flint. "I've hired this boy, and he's going with us to Colorado, and that's the end of it. Now, you go over there and shake his hand."

The muscles in Colin's jaws writhed like snakes. Without another word, he marched over to Virgil. Callum watched his brother approach the new boy. Virgil stuck out his hand, as Colin stepped close. With his hand reaching out, he was off balance when Colin sucker-punched him. It was a jarring blow to Virgil's left cheek, knocking him to the dusty ground.

Virgil had been living on the streets for the past six months. It had been a rough-and-tumble time of survival. He had also worked on many of the riverboats when they were docked. With that money, he managed to average at least one meal a day. But many times, he'd had to fight to keep his wages. The life of an orphan in Memphis was hard and unforgiving. He had learned the folly of running from a fight.

Colin, two years older and with the blessing of a mother who provided him three nutritious meals a day, was taller and at least twenty pounds heavier than Virgil. With his constant working on the farm, he had built young muscle in his chest and shoulders. His blow to Virgil's cheek sounded like a club hitting a melon. As soon as he hit Virgil, his feet spread and his fists went to his hips. He had only a moment to glare at the younger boy, now on the ground.

Virgil wasn't one to be whipped by one blow. He swept his right leg to the left, hooking his new boot behind Colin's left ankle. The leg was jerked out from under him, and he fell hard to the ground, the unexpected fall driving the wind from his chest. Virgil pounced on top of him like an angry cougar. He dropped a knee on each side of Colin's slim waist, and started pounding at the older boy's face. His first blow split Colin's lip, while the followups bruised his eyes and cheeks.

Colin had regained his breath and launched himself from the hay-covered ground. He managed to hit Virgil once, when he a large hand wrapped around the back of his collar so hard that he gasped for air. With one hand, Callum yanked Colin to his feet, holding Virgil in the other. The minute he grabbed Virgil, the boy stopped swinging, but Colin continued, at first trying to hit Virgil, but with the realization he was out of reach, he started kicking at him.

Callum shook Colin like he was a sack of oats until the boy calmed down. The other men stood watching, their faces showing disbelief at what they had just seen.

"You all right?" Callum asked Virgil, still holding Colin in a steel grip.

"Yes, sir," Virgil said. It was obvious the boy could see his future in the West disappearing, but he held his head high. "Mr. Logan, I surely appreciate you trying to help me." He reached into his pocket and pulled out the twenty-dollar gold piece that Callum had given him.

"I ain't worked for this or the clothes. I'll take what I'm wearing and what's in the bag back to Mrs. Jacoby's and get my old clothes. She's a nice lady. She'll be glad to give you your money back."

Callum held Colin off his feet and stared in his face. "You done?"

Colin nodded sullenly, and he was lowered to the ground and released.

"Virgil, put your money back in your pocket. I hired you," Callum said. "I'll decide if you need firin'. This shouldn't of happened. My brother's been taught better. If you want it after this, the job's still yours."

Virgil glanced at Colin, who was still glaring at him, and said defiantly, "Yes, sir, I sure do."

"Good. You go finish with Shoshone, and after that, we'll all go find a place with some good food. How does that sound?"

"Sounds good to me, Mr. Logan." Virgil turned to go back to the stall.

"Wait a second," Callum said. He shoved Colin in the stall's direction, causing his brother to stumble over his first few steps. "You help, and no fighting."

Callum watched the two of them disappear behind the wall of the stall, neither saying anything to the other. He shook his head and walked back to the men, all of them staring at Colin's back with disbelief.

"Bret, do you have any idea what got into your brother? I've never seen him like that."

Slim quickly interrupted. "I got work to do in the office. See you folks later. Remember what I said, Ezra." He turned and marched off, his boots clunking loudly on the small deck surrounding the front of the office.

After Slim had disappeared inside the office, Frank spoke up before Bret could respond. "He's been brooding. First, losing those horses in the fire and hearing their screams as they burned alive hit him mighty hard. I'm tellin' you, he would have run into that fire if your pa hadn't held him back.

"Then your pa gettin' killed really did it. I think he's hurtin' almighty bad. You're the man of this family, now, and you bringin' in another boy younger than him pushed him over the edge. I reckon he thinks he ain't important to you no more." Frank spit a long stream of tobacco that had been building up while he was talking. "That's about all I've got to say."

"He has been awful droopy lately," Bret said.

Callum thought for a moment. "All right, here's what we're going to do. I'll keep him with me most all of the time. In fact, Frank, why don't you and Bret take one room, and Colin and I will take the other. Also, on the trip, he's going to be paired with me, no matter what I do. That way, we'll have plenty of time to talk. I ain't no doctor, but that might help.

"Ezra, you mind keeping Virgil here with you tonight? That'll work out even better. That way there'll be two sets of eyes and ears around the wagons."

"I'll appreciate the company. Slim done invited me to dinner with him. I bet he won't mind having Virgil along."

The men had just finished talking when the two boys walked out of the stall and headed toward them.

"Virgil, I'm gonna ask you to stay here tonight and help Ezra keep an eye on the wagons. He says Slim has invited him to dinner, so you'll be going with him."

Virgil's eyes lit up. "Really? Mrs. Beckham is about the best cook in Memphis. She was a good friend of my ma. Thanks, Mr. Logan. I'll keep a real good eye on these wagons."

"You switch off with Ezra, so you can get some sleep tonight. We'll be pullin' out early in the morning. Now, you haven't officially met everyone here. The feisty one, who welcomed you so graciously, is Colin."

Bret's chuckle drew an angry look from Colin, but Bret just grinned at him.

"This here is Ezra, the best mule breeder in the country. You'll be spending the night with him. I'd make sure I slept as far away as possible. Ezra's snoring will most likely raise the barn's roof."

"It ain't near that bad," Ezra returned, "though it might keep them light sleepin' horses awake."

Virgil grinned at Ezra and shook the grizzled hand. "Pleased to meet ya."

"This other one is another Logan. Reckon he's a mite friendlier. His name's Bret."

Bret nodded and shook the boy's hand.

"Ezra, be sure and let Slim know that we'll be pullin' out early tomorrow morning. I want to be on board that boat by seven. We miss this one and we've got a long trail ahead of us, just gettin' through Arkansas."

"I'll do 'er. We'll be ready."

Callum nodded. "Let's head back to the hotel," he said to Bret, Frank, and Colin.

They left the livery and walked the short distance to the hotel. Nothing was said during the short walk. Colin was still sullen. His left eye was swelling shut and turning blue, and his right cheek was red from the repeated blows.

They entered the hotel and walked up to the counter where Callum had registered. A different clerk was on duty. He took in the rough, dusty attire of the three men, noted Colin's swollen eye, and then looked up at Callum. "How may I help you?"

"We registered earlier, Callum Logan with a party of six."

The clerk checked the register. "Ah, yes, Mr. Logan. Here you are. The ladies are in room three-ten. The other two rooms are three-twelve, which is adjoining, and three-eleven across the hall." He picked up the remaining two keys, handing them to Callum. "Enjoy your stay."

"Thank you. We'll need water to our room for baths, immediately."

"Yes, sir. It will be coming up right behind you." He turned and waved to one of the bellmen.

"We'll also be leaving about six in the morning. Will there be a place open so we can grab some grub before we leave?"

"Oh yes, Mr. Logan. To accommodate many of our early-departing guests, the restaurant"—he emphasized restaurant —"will be open at three a.m."

"Thanks," Callum said, and turned to head up the wide stairs.

Frank eyed the spittoon sitting at the corner of the stairs, and let a long stream loose over the plush carpet, hitting dead center and causing a dull ring. "Well, I want everyone to know that I am indeed privileged to eat at Overton Hotel's fine *restaurant.*"

"If they'll have you," Bret said.

"Show some respect for your betters, young feller, and I'm your better, if you ain't noticed."

Everyone chuckled, including Colin. The four of them arrived at their rooms, and Callum handed the three-eleven key to Frank. "Colin, you're with me. Frank, why don't we figure on headin' out for some grub in about an hour? That should give you and Bret time to look respectable again."

"One hour," Frank said, as he unlocked the door.

Colin started to knock on his ma's room.

"Not yet," Callum said. "You need to get cleaned up before Ma sees you."

Colin grunted and tried to look at his brother through the swollen eye. "All right."

# 15

Ma stood with her hands on her hips. Consternation was written on her face as she stared at her youngest child. Callum had just finished explaining what had happened between the new employee and her son. The boy now stood with his hat off and his eyes examining the intricate weave of the rug beneath his feet.

Kate, clean from her bath and smelling of lilacs, sat in the large wing-backed chair next to the window, her blonde hair braided and resting on her head like a golden crown. Never having seen this side of her brother, she stared at Colin through crystal blue eyes, wide open in disbelief.

Ma's right foot tapped the floor as if she were keeping time with the sound of the tinny, saloon piano slipping through the partially open window. "Can you tell me why you attacked a boy younger than you, with no provocation?"

Colin scuffed at the carpet with his left boot toe and, still looking down, said, "I don't like him."

Her voice sharp, like the edge of butcher knife, Ma said, "You don't like him? Young man, you don't even know him."

Silence reigned in the room. Ma threw Callum a frustrated

look, then turned back to her younger son. "I ask you why you did it. 'I don't like him' is not an answer. Tell me now!"

Callum watched his ma. Two little red spots appeared just below her eyes when she was angry. He had only seen her like this a few times. It was never good to be her target when those spots appeared. And even though his brother had attacked Virgil, he couldn't help but feel sorry for him.

Colin's head came up slowly. His dark brown eyes looked almost black. "Ma, I don't know. When I saw him, I just got mad. He looked so smug in those new clothes that Callum bought him. Pa wouldn't of done that. Here we walk around in homespun, and he gets new clothes. It don't make sense at all. And he's so young. What's he gonna do? Wash dishes?"

Callum rolled his eyes at the last comment. You didn't get sarcastic with Ma when she was mad.

Her index finger came out and leveled at her young son like a weapon. "Don't you get smart with me, young man. I'll tell you what he's going to do. Whatever Callum tells him, and as far as your pa not buying that boy clothes, that is exactly what he would do." Her voice softened somewhat. "I know you're hurting with the loss of your pa and those horses, but stop and think, son. That boy has lost not just his pa, but his ma and his brothers and sisters. And they died in a fire, just like the horses. Don't you think he hears those screams in the dark part of his mind at night? How do you think he feels?"

At his ma's last statement, Colin looked to Callum. "I didn't know that."

"Yep, he did. He's been trying to make a living doing odd jobs around Memphis. That's how I met him. The boat captain told me about him. Said he was a hard worker. I figured we could help him out, since that's what Logans do, and he'd learn to be a good hand. I sure didn't figure you'd go wild on him."

Colin looked back at his ma. "I reckon I made a mistake, Ma. I have to be truthful with you. I really don't know what happened.

Something just snapped and I was hittin' him." A small grin escaped. "I reckon he got even for that." He licked his cut lip and tried to wink his swollen eye.

"Callum," Colin continued, "I'd like to try to make it up to him. I imagine you're going to give him a gun, cause we all need protection on this westerly trip. I'd like to give him my saddle gun, and help him pick out a horse. Would that be all right?"

"Reckon that'd be just fine, Colin. I think Virgil would like that." Callum looked over to his ma and received an almost imperceptible nod. "I hope you've learned that flying off the handle can be a big mistake. This time it was with fists. That can be corrected. But now, you're carrying a gun. When you pull a gun on a man and take his life, you want to be danged sure you're doing what's right. You understand?"

"Yes, sir, I sure do."

Ma spread her arms, and the man-boy ran to her. She wrapped her arms around him, and with sad eyes, gazed at her older son. The hug lasted only moments, and Colin pulled away.

He looked around at everyone. "Looks like Kate's hungry."

His sister jumped to her feet and punched Colin in the shoulder. "We know who's hungry. Fighting always makes men hungry."

Ma tried to generate a stern look through the smile slipping out. "Don't tease your brother, Katherine. You don't want to make me angry."

"That's the truth," Kate said, striding to the door and opening it to find Bret and Frank just leaving their room. The three of them laughed at that remark, and silently agreed, while Bret and Frank looked at each other.

"What'd we miss?" Bret asked.

Taking his arm, Kate gave her brother a big smile, and said, "Nothing you'd want to be involved in."

"Take my arm, Colin," Ma said.

Colin crooked his arm and allowed his ma to hook her arm

through his. Callum and Frank followed them down the hall and the wide stairway to the lobby. Men in the lobby stopped and watched the beautiful blonde and stately, attractive woman behind her glide down the stairs, while some of the women surreptitiously eyed the handsome man following them down.

"Shopping or dinner?" Callum asked, reaching the lobby.

"I think we all need a good, sit-down dinner," Ma said. "It may very well be our last for a while."

"Then dinner it is." Callum turned the group toward the hotel restaurant.

THEY HAD RESTOCKED the wagons after showing the ladies the town. Colin took the opportunity to get to know Virgil. The altercation quickly became a thing of the past as the boys talked about horses, guns, Indians, and the West.

After a sound night's sleep and a filling breakfast, Callum swung up onto Shoshone. Slim stood at the tall doors of the livery, as they rode out. and Callum leaned over and shook hands with the man. "Thanks for your help, Slim. Maybe we'll see you again."

"Mebbe so. Good luck to you."

Callum nodded, clucked to Shoshone, and led the wagons into the already-busy street. Teamsters pulled up as the two wagons, mules, and horses emerged, waiting impatiently in their haste to drop their goods and load up again.

Upon reaching the wharf, Callum rode directly to the Lone Star. He led the wagons to the barge behind the riverboat, and waited as a large man wearing a small straw hat hurried across the wharf. He came to a stop near Callum.

"You be Mr. Logan, I'm guessing."

"Yep, I am, and do I hear a bit of the Scottish?"

"Aye, laddie, and so you do. Hamish Cornyn is me name, and

you can call me Hamish. I be the first mate aboard Captain Hill's Lone Star. 'Tis lucky you are to be sailin' up the river with the captain. He knows what he's about."

"Thank you, Hamish. You can call me Callum, and it is a long list of fine Scottish and Irish folk I be descended of."

Hamish beamed at Callum. "'Tis a blessing, lad, a true blessing. Now, load your animals into the aft corral. There's room for you to put your wagons side by side next to the corral. Rope you'll find aplenty to tie them down. Moving them along would be good, as we've more stock coming soon that will be using the forward corral. I see Virgil be with you, a very fine lad."

Callum turned and called to Bret. "Bring the stock up. We'll load them first, into the back corral."

Bret waved back, and Kate, Colin, and Ezra, carrying Blue over the saddle in front of him, herded the stock on board the barge. Virgil had jumped down from the first wagon, waving at Hamish, as he dashed by to open the gate into the corral.

There was a little hesitation from the mules, but Ezra spoke to them softly and led them across the wide gangway onto the barge. Once all of the herded animals were safely corralled, Callum motioned for Frank to drive the lead wagon on and park it next to the edge of the barge across from the pen.

Frank spoke to the mules, popped the reins, and the animals started for the gangway. The left lead mule balked at the water coursing beneath the gangway, causing the wagon to jerk to a stop. Ezra came jogging over to the animal and started rubbing its nose and talking to it in a soothing tone. After a few minutes, he nodded to Frank, who again popped the reins, and, holding the bridle, Ezra led the team smoothly aboard the barge and into their position.

Ma followed Frank with no problem and pulled up next to his wagon. Frank, like the mules, was staring over the side of the barge at the river water moving quickly down the side. The barge continued to rock with the movement of the animals.

Callum looked around to see how they were doing. It appeared that none of them liked the rocking. He swung down next to Ezra. "You think these animals will settle down?"

Ezra nodded. "Sure they will. You watch 'em. In just a little while they'll be grazing on the hay at the end of the corral, peaceful as can be. We'll have no problem, as long as it stays nice and calm back here." He turned to Ma's wagon. "I'm gonna unhitch these rascals and get them in the corral. They know me. Though they're a mite nervous on this here boat, they'll trust what I say."

Ezra stopped for a moment. "What's that ruckus?" He turned and looked, along with all the mules, horses, donkeys, and milk cows. On the street leading to the wharf, men were hard-driving wild-eyed mules toward the Lone Star's barge. Hamish had run to the barge gangway and was standing on it, waving his arms and yelling at the men, trying to signal them to turn the mules, but it appeared they ignored him.

Callum, seeing the danger Hamish was in, made a snap decision. He yelled at Ezra, "Get ready, I'm turning those mules." Still mounted on Shoshone, he whirled the horse around and leaped from the barge, past Hamish, into the face of the oncoming crazed animals. He pulled a Remington from its holster and let loose with three rapid shots. The lead mule snorted and reared on its hind legs, blowing snot on Callum. He could see the terror in the animal's wide eyes. It turned and plunged back into the mules following.

The other mules, slipping and sliding on the wooden wharf, turned, and, eventually gaining traction, raced up, down, and across the wharf, kicking over boxes stacked for loading. Several charged through shop windows, along the street fronting the wharf. Mules screamed, people screamed, and drovers cussed, but there was no way the mules were going to settle down any time soon. Fortunately, the confusion and danger had moved away from the Lone Star and its barge.

Hamish trotted up to Callum. "You saved my life. If you'd not turned those crazed animals, I'd be fetching up to St. Peter's pearly gates about now."

Callum looked back at Ezra and the crew. They were all calming the horses and mules. Fortunately, they had kept the panic from infecting the animals on the barge. Ezra saw Callum watching and waved. Callum turned back to Hamish. "Who the blazes were those idiots?"

Hamish shook his head. "Those beasts belong to Chester Hughes. He's of a mind to lead a wagon train from Fort Smith to Oregon, and he wanted to bring his muleys along. I'll promise you one thing, lucky he'll be if'n the captain even lets him and his daughter travel with us, now."

Callum could see the captain hurrying toward them from the gangway. He stopped next to Hamish, slightly out of breath. "I saw. . ." He stopped for a moment to catch his breath, then continued. ". . .everything that happened. Hamish, you're lucky Mr. Logan was here, or you would have been a dead man."

He turned to Callum. "Mr. Logan, I normally do not condone gunplay in town, but I definitely make an exception today. Thank you for saving my first mate. I cannot believe those idiots tried to race those mules onto this barge. Why, if the animals had made it on board, the way they were running, they would have gone through the corral and right into the Mississippi."

"Glad to help, Captain," Callum said, as a man dressed as a cowboy, with a low-slung holster on each hip, rode up to them. His boots were polished to a high gloss. The wool shirt he wore was clean, and a crease ran down each arm. The dark gray vest had four front pockets, one of which showed a faint outline of a single-shot Derringer. His black hat looked freshly brushed.

Callum looked him over and decided that to take him for a dude would be a big mistake. The holsters were worn, and bluing was wearing off around the visible portion of the Colt's cylinder where it rode in the holster. The man's rifle scabbard, though oiled and clean, showed signs of long use, as did the Spencer that rested into the well-shaped cavity of the scabbard. The man's steely gray eyes rested calmly on Callum.

"Reckon you're the man that fired those shots, stampeding our stock?"

"That's right."

The man nodded. "You cost us plenty. We lost mules into the river that we'll never recover."

The moment of relief, the calm after what could have amounted to Hamish losing his life and the Logans losing not only their stock, but their wagons, was gone. The air almost crackled with tension.

Captain Hill demanded, "Who are you?"

The man never removed his piercing gray eyes from Callum's face. "People call me George Cassidy."

"Are these mules you tried to drive onto this barge and kill my first mate yours?"

Now, Cassidy slowly moved his head toward the captain, his eyes tracking like gatling guns. "They belong to Colonel Hughes. We'll round them up and bring them back to the barge."

The captain had dealt with many different kinds of men throughout his years on the rivers. Though this man was a deadly killer, he was not fazed. "You'll be loading no mules on this barge." Turning to Hamish, he continued, "Let the folks off that'll not be caring for the animals, and then pull the gangway."

Hamish gave a sharp nod. "Aye, sir."

Cassidy looked over the remaining empty space on the barge, and said, his voice level, "There's room for our stock."

"Not on this barge, there isn't. You can't come driving animals like the devil's after them and expect to load them here. I do not want troublemakers on board my vessel. If you think you can behave, then you can come aboard to Fort Smith. Otherwise"—the captain paused to pointedly look at Cassidy's horse, then looked at the killer directly—"ride."

"What about our riding stock?" Cassidy had, at no time in the conversation, raised his voice. He had remained cool, but threatening. "Colonel Hughes is leading a big wagon train from Fort Smith to Oregon. We should at least have our riding stock aboard."

That statement gave the captain pause. He stood thinking for a moment, then turned to Callum. "You have most of the stock back here. You mind if Cassidy and his men bring their riding stock on board?"

"Nope, not if he thinks his men can control their animals." He and Cassidy locked eyes for a moment. Callum saw the slightest tic at the corner of the gunman's left eye and watched the calm man tense slightly. Then the moment was gone.

Cassidy looked down at the captain, his face expressionless. "There'll be no trouble." Then he looked back at Callum. "Your name?"

"Callum Logan."

Cassidy nodded his head as if recognizing the name. "You get around. Be seeing you, Logan."

Callum watched as the man swung his horse around and trotted off to the men gathering the mules.

"Mr. Logan," Captain Hill said, "you best watch out. That is a dangerous man. It's said he's killed seventeen men in fair fights. No telling how many otherwise. Keep an eye out."

"Thanks, Captain. I'll do just that."

The captain glanced back at the others gathered at the end of the barge. "Fine. We have rooms set up for you and the ladies. Come aboard when you're ready, but don't wait too long. We'll be leaving shortly." With his last statement, the captain hurried back to the gangway, where people were again streaming aboard.

Callum swung down from Shoshone, walking the horse back to the aft corral. Hamish moved alongside him.

"Death, it is that follows men like Cassidy." Hamish said. "You can smell it. No matter how clean the man gets, the smell of death hangs in the air. Watch yourself. No good comes from that man."

"Thanks, Hamish." All of the mules and horses had been loaded in the corral. Everyone was busy tying down the wagons. Callum introduced Hamish around, and Colin spoke up.

"That killer would have never cleared leather if he'd tried to draw on you. Ezra had his Sharps dead center on the man's head."

Callum glanced at Ezra, who was showing a little grin. "Thanks. I kind of expected something like that."

"Weren't just me," Ezra said. "Bret and Frank had beads on that skunk too. He'd been ventilated but good."

Callum looked at his brother and Frank. "Thanks. Now, who's staying on the barge?"

Frank and Ezra finished securing the last rope to the outside wagon. They both stood and stretched their backs. Ezra nodded and said, "That'd be me."

"Good, the mules know you," replied Callum. "But don't get into it with Cassidy's bunch. They'll be bringing their riding stock aboard. The captain said only the animals they're riding, none of the mules. We'll be spelling you when the boat stops for wood." Callum turned to Ma. "Let's get everyone aboard the riverboat."

# 16

As the sun neared its zenith, the Lone Star pulled away from the Memphis dock, towing the barge with animals and wagons behind. When it was well away from the other boats and in the main flow of the Mississippi, Captain Hill began the turn across the wide expanse of water, his expertise coming into play to keep the barge lines taut as the current piled tons of water against the starboard side of the Lone Star and the barge. The force of the mighty river caused the two vessels to heel far over. It lasted for only a moment, as the boat continued its slow turn downriver. But in that moment, a matronly lady, holding the hand of a lad, no more than six years old, lost her balance on the slanting deck. In so doing, she released her hold on the boy's hand. As the two hurtled toward the railing, a heart-wrenching cry for help escaped her lips.

Frank, who was well to Callum's left, grabbed the woman by her left arm, stopping her progress, and allowing her to regain her balance. However, the lad, in a stumbling gait, hurtled toward the churning abyss of the Mississippi. A grown man, thrown from the riverboat into the churning maelstrom, would have little chance of survival. If the river didn't smash the child against the side of the boat, then the side paddle-wheel would crush him.

Callum, anxiously watching the barge follow the riverboat in the maneuver, turned at the shout for help echoing behind him. He immediately took everything in. He saw Frank reacting to the woman. Though her terror-filled eyes followed her son sailing toward the opening and the water below, he registered her as safe and concentrated on the young fellow hurtling toward the rail.

Unfortunately, the safety railing stretching around the riverboat was built to retain adults, not youngsters. The boy's height would allow him to pass below the top horizontal rail and above the lower. The slats, between the two railings, were spaced too far apart to prevent the youngster from plummeting to the water below. Turning, Callum stretched his arm thrust his hand between the boy and the water. With a vise-like grip, he clamped onto the tyke's small hand and jerked him into his arms.

The riverboat stabilized quickly, continuing its turn in the wide Mississippi.

"Oh! Thank you. God bless you. Thank you. Stanley, thank the nice man," the woman gushed, as she reached to take the boy from Callum's hold.

The youngster pushed back against Callum's arms and looked into his face. His blue eyes still larger than normal from the close call, he said, "Thanks, Mister. Now can I get down?"

Callum grinned back at him. "Sure, Button." He stood the boy on the now-stable riverboat deck.

Ma Logan stepped forward and put her arm around the shaking woman. "You poor dear. What a horrid fright, but everything is fine now."

The woman, shorter than Ma, pushed her bonnet back to see her. "Yes, it was frightening. Thank the Lord that these men were handy to save us both." She thrust out her hand to both Frank and Callum.

Callum noticed her grip was firm and her hands calloused.

"Ma'am, just glad we could help."

Frank nodded. "My pleasure, ma'am. Glad we were here."

She continued as the Logan family gathered around her. "My name is Nora Simpson. This young man you just saved is James Avery Simpson."

The boy spoke up quickly. "I go by Stanley, Ma."

She glanced down at the boy. "Yes, we call him Stanley." Smiling at Ma Logan, she said, "Now, may I have your names? My husband, Avery, will be anxious to know the names of the men whose debt he is in."

Ma removed her arm from around Nora's shoulder and began introducing the family. "The man that grabbed you, is a good friend of ours, Frank Tyler."

Frank nodded to Nora. "Ma'am."

Turning slightly toward Callum, Ma continued. "This fine-looking man that saved Stanley is my son, Callum, the next two are also my son's, first Bret, then Colin. The young man next to Colin is our new hired hand, Virgil Brogan."

"Hi, Virg," Stanley said. "You going to Oregon with us?"

"Reckon not, Stanley. I'm working as a cowhand for the Logans."

Nora took Virgil's hand. "I'm so happy for you. These seem like fine people."

Ma turned to Nora. "So you know Virgil?"

"Oh yes, we knew his parents. Our family was heartbroken when we heard about the fire. Virgil stayed with us for a while, but then he stopped coming around." With her last words, she had turned back to the boy, a question in her dark brown eyes.

Virgil looked down at the deck for a moment, then squared his shoulders and met Nora's look. "I'm right sorry, ma'am. I appreciate all the help you and Mr. Simpson were to me, but I felt like I was a becoming a burden. Beggin' your pardon, Mrs. Simpson, but I can take care of myself."

Nora's smile became more tender. "I know you can, Virgil. You are a fine young man. I just want you to know that we are your friends and will always be there for you." Her smile widened. "Having said that, I am very happy for you. I know you will make the Logans a fine cowhand."

He beamed at the last statement.

"Now," Nora continued, "who is this lovely young woman with all of these tough men?"

Ma Logan laughed. "This is my only daughter, and I assure you, she can hold her own with her brothers. This is Katherine. We call her Kate."

Kate stepped forward and took Nora's hand. "Nice to meet you, Mrs. Simpson. I'm glad Callum was there for Stanley."

"Thank you, Kate, as am I. You are a lovely girl, even in those horrid pants. Please, call me Nora."

Kate laughed easily. "These pants make it a lot easier for me to ride with the men and work the stock."

"Thank goodness we have her," Callum said. "She's the best I've ever seen with horses."

"Well, I'll declare. Kate, maybe you can show Stanley sometime? He hasn't done a lot of riding."

"I'd be glad to."

Callum looked around at the people squeezing by their group. "Reckon we ought to be on our way. Looks like we're holdin' up traffic a mite."

"Yes," Nora said. "I'd love for you to meet Avery, my husband. Would you care to join us for dinner at noon in the dining room?"

Callum looked to Ma.

"We'd love to," She said.

Callum watched Nora try to hold Stanley's hand as they walked away. The boy pulled his hand away and marched slightly ahead of her. "Independent little tyke, isn't he?"

"Yes, sir," Virgil said. "He sure is. When I'd let him go with me, back in Memphis, he got me in more fights than I can count. He didn't back down from nothin'."

"Well, he'll need that independent streak out West." He looked back at the barge, throwing up its own bow wave behind them. "Everything looks quiet back there. Guess Ezra kept the stock calmed down in that turn. I'm sure glad he decided to come along."

Frank nodded. "He's got a way with animals. Onlyest other person I've ever seen with that kinda touch is Kate."

She smiled at Frank and gave him a kiss on the cheek.

"Here, now," he said in a deep, gruff voice. "Ain't no call for that." But everyone could see he enjoyed it.

"Let's get to our rooms and drop this gear," Callum said. "It's gettin' close to dinnertime. I'm anxious to try out some of that good cookin' that Austin was talkin' about. This'll give us a chance to get to know the Simpsons. She mentioned Oregon. They must be going with the Hughes outfit."

WHEN THE FAMILY made it down to the dining room, it was starting to get crowded. Callum let his eyes drift over the people. He saw some rough-looking men in buckskin coats and flop hats, their rifles leaning against the table where they were sitting. He could make out several families. A couple of them were obviously farmers, but most appeared fairly well-to-do. Of course, there were the gamblers.

The far end of the dining room had an accordion door that was closed almost all the way, left open only wide enough for a man to get through. From the talk and tinkle of glass that could be heard on the other side, it was obviously the saloon. The door probably opened after the meals were served, to provide more space for the saloon.

At one table, he saw several men with sidearms and Western getup. They, like the gamblers, were in sharp contrast to the affluent travelers that made up the majority of diners.

"There's the Simpsons," Virgil said, pointing to the family waving at them.

Ma took the lead as they moved toward the large table.

The man at the table stood, and, as they approached, Nora said, "Hello, everyone. This is my husband Avery Simpson."

They all introduced themselves and shook hands.

"I am in great debt to you," Avery said. "Nora told me what happened. Mr. Logan, I am extremely glad you were there and alert. You diverted what could have been a stunning disaster at the very beginning of our trip."

"Call me Callum, Mr. Simpson. I'm sure that anyone else would have done the same thing."

Avery Simpson looked around the table. "Please, call me Avery. I am not, sir. From what Nora has told me, it happened so fast, she was amazed at your quick-thinking and reaction." Nora was sitting between Stanley and his father. Avery reached behind and past his wife, to tousle his son's hair. Stanley looked over at his father and shook his head, a scowl on his face.

"Thanks," Callum said. He looked around the table. "Anybody hungry?"

All the boys sounded off in unison, "Yes!"

Laughter followed the emphatic statement.

"Why don't we eat." Callum waved to the waiter, and added, "Frank and I were glad to help."

Avery, recognizing that Callum wanted the subject closed, nodded to the two men and responded, "I think packing and loading whetted everyone's appetite. I'm sure Stanley is ready."

"Yes, sir!" the boy said.

The two families ordered their lunch. The meal was the same for everyone, fried chicken, gravy, biscuits, and green beans with peach cobbler for dessert. The dinner arrived quickly. There was little conversation while the meal was being consumed.

Ma Logan laid her fork down and looked across the table to Nora. "You mentioned that your family is moving to Oregon."

"Yes," Nora replied. "We have a wonderful opportunity." She glanced to her husband.

"Wonderful," Avery concurred. "With the war, and since, life has grown more difficult in Memphis. Colonel Hughes has been a real blessing."

Callum looked down the table at Ma, then across at Avery. "How's that?"

Everyone had finished. Virgil pulled a biscuit from the few remaining in the platter, broke it open, and spread butter on it. The waiters took their plates and replaced them with bowls of cobbler.

"You still eat a lot, Virg," Stanley said.

Unfazed, a grin crossed Virgil's face. Shoving the big bite of biscuit into the corner of his mouth, he mumbled, "I do, Stanley. It's good."

Nora smiled at Virgil. "Of course it is. Mrs. Hill has a reputation for being an excellent cook." She turned to her son. "Stanley, mind your own business."

"But Ma, that's Virg's fourth biscuit, and they're big."

Avery Simpson leaned around Nora so that he could see his young son. "Stanley, listen to your ma. One more word and you'll find it difficult to sit down."

Stanley looked at his pa defiantly for a moment. It appeared that he was about to say something, and thought better of it. He picked up his spoon and lost himself in his cobbler.

Avery Simpson cleared his throat. "Callum, Mr. Hughes came by and offered us an opportunity to go with him on his wagon train to Oregon. It is such great timing. We did pretty well during the war. After I was wounded, I came back and started a small hardware store and gunsmithing business. It did well for a time, but over the last two years, my gun business has declined, and bigger hardware stores have moved into Memphis. They are basically putting us out of business."

Avery paused a moment to take a bite of the peach cobbler,

and a bit stuck to his thin mustache. He reached up with his napkin, wiped the cobbler away, cleared his throat, and continued.

"Colonel Hughes said that if I had enough money to buy our wagon and mules, with sufficient left over to start anew in Oregon, then he would be pleased to invite us on the train with him."

"Wasn't that nice?" Nora added. "We were just about at our wits' end. He is such a nice man." She rolled her eyes. "Of course, he has such a hard time controlling his daughter. She is a wild-child."

She leaned across the table and dropped her voice in a conspiratorial tone. "Can you believe what happened today? I didn't see it, but I understand some wild cowboy fired his pistol at the mules Colonel Hughes's men were trying to drive aboard the barge." She paused a moment for effect. "Isn't that frightening? Some of the others on our journey said they were almost run over by the stampeding animals. Isn't that just atrocious! Colonel Hughes said we must look out for the man. He is dangerous."

Callum leaned forward, and with the same low tone said, "Nora, I'm that wild, dangerous cowboy."

The woman recoiled like Callum had slapped her. Her eyes shot wide open. "You?"

"Yes, ma'am, I was the one, and if I hadn't stopped those mules, they would have run over Mr. Cornyn, and very probably turned over the barge with our mules and wagons on board."

Nora looked to her husband.

Avery stared at Callum in consternation. "That's not the story we heard. Colonel Hughes said that you were angry because his daughter had previously rebuffed you. However, having met you, I find it hard to reconcile the two stories."

Callum was about to respond, when he felt a jab in his shoulder, and a gruff voice from behind him said, "Simpson, what the devil are you doing eating with these people?"

## 17

Callum made a sharp turn in his chair and clamped his left hand solidly on the end of the cane Hughes was poking him with. Rising, completing his turn, while slipping the leather loop from his revolver with his right hand, he yanked hard on the end of the walking stick. Hughes, surprised at the sudden reaction, had no time to tighten his hand on the gold-embossed knob handle and stood, astonished. He could do nothing but watch as Callum, in one smooth motion, placed his other large hand near the handle, lifted his leg until his thigh was parallel with the riverboat deck, and slammed the middle of the walking stick over his thigh. The hickory emitted a sharp crack. Callum snatched the piece from his right hand, and using his left, threw the two shattered pieces at his antagonist's feet.

In a calm voice, Callum said, "Reckon you won't be poking anyone else with that fancy walkin' stick." He then glanced at Cassidy, standing slightly to the left of Hughes.

The man stood relaxed, arms crossed, and mouth stern. His eyes, and the wrinkles at the corners, were the only thing that showed the humor he felt. He watched, appearing to wait to see how his boss would respond, but a discerning man could tell he was enjoying the drama happening before him. Callum dismissed Cassidy as no threat, for now, and turned back to Hughes.

The six-foot-four-inch bulk of the man dwarfed Callum. The man's face was the bright red of a ripe apple. His huge arms were pulled away from his sides, and his hands were clenched into club-like fists. The skin was pulled tight around his hard gray eyes, and Callum waited for the punch. It never came. Callum watched as the man regained control of himself, his arms relaxing.

"That was a dangerous move, Mr. Logan," Hughes said. "I've broken people for less than that."

"Hurt him, Papa. Hurt him, now!" Sabrina shouted, beside herself with rage.

"Now, now, Sabrina. We'll deal with Mr. Logan at a later date." Hughes looked around the large, packed, silent dining room. Only the sound of dishes tinkling in the kitchen could be heard. Every eye was turned on the two men.

Hughes bent over and picked up the two pieces of his broken cane. He looked at it for a moment, then locked his gaze with Callum's.

"This was expensive, Mr. Callum. I expect you to pay for it."

Callum's eyes never wavered. "Chalk it up to education, Hughes. If you don't have anything else for me, go on about your business. We haven't finished eating."

Hughes doffed his hat to the women at the table. "I hope this outburst from Mr. Callum hasn't ruined your meal." He then drilled Avery with his cold gray eyes. "See me later, Simpson." In a lower voice, he said, "Logan, this is twice you've caused me and my family trouble. There won't be a third."

Callum said nothing.

Sabrina called Callum a vile name, and the three turned, walking deeper into the dining room to find a table for dinner.

Many of the people traveling to Oregon with him offered condolences for Callum's offensive manner and invited the trio to sit with them.

Callum turned back and took his seat. Frank leaned forward so that he could see Callum and said, "I don't think most of these people saw him sticking you with that cane. Looks like you didn't make any friends here today."

"Reckon I'm not out to make friends. My job is to get everyone to the ranch safely, and I aim to do it." He went back to his peach cobbler.

The Simpsons were quiet, except for Stanley. "Golly, Mr. Logan, you done broke that cane that Mr. Hughes carries, like a matchstick. I don't blame you. If somebody poked me with it, I'd done the same thing."

Avery leaned around his wife again so that he could see his son. "James, that's two. I told you not to speak. We'll talk about this when we get back to the room."

Stanley hung his head, as if he knew he was in for a licking, but that didn't keep him from looking up at Callum.

Callum was watching the boy. He winked at him. "Thanks, Stanley. I just bet you would."

Nora Simpson took a deep breath and exhaled audibly. "Mr. Logan, please don't encourage him. I'm afraid your subterfuge may have gotten us in trouble. We had no idea you were the one that caused the problem at the barge, until you told us. Now, we could be in trouble with that fine Mr. Hughes."

Kate immediately jumped to Callum's defense. "Nora, you weren't there. All you've heard is rumor colored by lies. You just saw Hughes jab Callum, and it wasn't the first time that—"

Callum held his hand up to Kate, stopping her, and addressed Avery. "I hope I haven't caused you trouble. If you find you need help, let me know." He turned to the rest of the Logans. "Everybody done?"

Nods from down the table indicated the everyone's readiness

to leave. As they stood, Captain Hill strode up to Callum, shook his hand, and touched his cap brim to the ladies.

"Understand there was a bit of a problem?"

Ma Logan stepped up and explained what had happened.

"You needn't worry, ma'am. One of the waiters saw all of it. He said he was surprised that Callum didn't belt Hughes."

At his statement, Nora gasped, and the captain turned to her. "Yes, ma'am, that's what he said." He placed his hand on Callum's shoulder. "If this man hadn't done what he did, my first mate would be dead, and the barge with all of the Logans' animals and wagons would have turned over."

Nora looked at her husband in astonishment.

Captain Hill turned back to Callum. "The waiter said that Hughes was shocked to see his cane broken. I wish I'd seen it, but watch yourself. That man doesn't forget an affront. Now, I've got to get back to the bridge."

The family walked from the dining room, conscious of the many people glaring at them.

Ma looked around, meeting many eyes and making them look away. "I imagine this is not going to be as pleasurable as I had hoped."

"Sorry, Ma," Callum said. "I guess my temper got the best of me."

"Don't apologize, son. I expected it at the hotel, the first time he jabbed you with his cane. I would say you have demonstrated an abundance of patience. Anyway, no matter how disagreeable some of these people might be, this river trip beats riding those wagons. Why, we get to sleep in a bed for the next week." She took his arm, squeezed it, and smiled up at her son. "I can't imagine anything better than that."

They made their way to their three adjoining rooms. Ma and Kate had the first one, Callum and Colin the second, and Bret, Frank, and Virgil had the third.

"Virgil," Callum said, "you'll be in with Bret and Frank. With only two beds, you'll be sleeping on the floor." Callum grinned at the young boy. "Watch for splinters."

"Heck no, he won't," Colin said. "There's plenty of room in those beds for us both. Why, I bet we could put four or five in one."

Callum, surprised, gave Colin a serious look. "Are you sure that's all right with you?"

"Yes, sir." Colin turned to the younger boy. "If it's all right with Virg."

Virgil, his face split with a huge grin, looked at Colin, and then Callum. "You bet. It's fine with me."

The adults looked at each other with relief on their faces, then everyone disappeared into their rooms.

~

HUGHES and his daughter occupied the only large suite on the Lone Star. He sat behind the oak desk, and his daughter stood beside him, her hand resting on his shoulder. In uncomfortable straight-backed chairs, next to each other, sat Cassidy and Cassidy's second-in-command, Jack "Flatnose" Blake. Cassidy had moved his chair to the opposite end of the table to get away from Blake's stench.

Hughes slammed his fist on the desk, making the paper and inkwell jump. "I want something done about the Logans, and I want it done now!"

Cassidy glanced over at Flatnose. "If you don't take a bath today, I'm gonna throw you in the Mississippi."

Blake grinned back at him. "Sure, George. Today. Just as soon as I get a chance." He then rubbed his flattened nose on his sleeve and leered at Sabrina.

She had been watching the younger man with disgust. She

held his stare for a moment, then shouted back at him. "Don't stare at me, you filthy dog!"

Blake turned back to Cassidy, the leer still on his face. "George, I think she likes me."

"All right, kid," Cassidy said, "settle down." Turning back to the angry, red-faced Hughes, he asked, "So, what do you have in mind?"

"What do I have in mind? I want him gone, finished, disappeared. You understand? That's your line of work, not mine. I expect you to take care of it."

Blake leaned toward Cassidy, "You think you can handle that, George?"

Cassidy loved few things, but one of those was Jack "Flatnose" Blake. He had raised Blake as an outlaw and saw the boy as a copy of himself. However, there were times that Blake pushed him too far. This was one of those times. Like a striking snake, Cassidy's hand shot out and gripped the man's forearm, and in a low, threatening voice, he said, "That's enough!"

It looked as if he had slapped the boy. Blake looked down at the floor, and then at Cassidy. "Sure, Boss. I ain't meant no harm." He slumped in the chair, pulled his folding knife from his vest pocket, and attempted to clean the packed dirt from under his fingernails.

"I can handle it, Colonel." Cassidy hated calling the man by that title, but he had plans that would require letting Hughes think he was running things. "All I needed to know was whether you wanted it done now, on the boat, or once we've arrived. There's less chance of anything going wrong if we wait till we get to Fort Smith."

After Cassidy's reprimand of Blake, Hughes had started cooling down. "He needs to go now. We have no idea how much damage he has already done among the movers. If he stays around them till we arrive in Fort Smith, there's no telling how much bad feeling towards us he might stir up. The sooner, the better."

Cassidy nodded. "We sure want those folks to trust us. I've got to hand it to you. Persuading this many businessmen to leave profitable businesses and travel by wagon train to some unknown place is beyond me. I can't see how you've done it."

Sabrina patted her father warmly on the shoulder, and he smiled up at her, patting her hand. Turning back to Cassidy, he said, "Yes, that was a stellar sales job. But even better, was talking them into taking all of their money out of the banks and bringing it with them to invest in the new town."

Hughes leaned back in his chair, a big grin on his face. "I truly outdid myself."

Sabrina leaned down. "You did, Father. You truly did."

"Yes, I did, and taking the Cherokee Trail was even more genius. With all of the Indian tribes around, there will be more than enough to take the blame, when the whole wagon train is ambushed and burned." He shook his head. "Genius, just genius."

Cassidy thought he would be ill. Not from the thought of killing all the occupants of the wagon train, including women and children. He had done much worse than that during the war. His disgust came from the gloating of that pompous ass Hughes. *I was going to let Blake kill Hughes and his daughter, when the time comes,* he thought, *but maybe I'll save that privilege for myself.* He looked over to Flatnose. The boy was looking at him. He could swear, at that moment, they both wanted to blast Hughes. He allowed a small grin to cross his face and then turned back to Hughes.

"Colonel, I'll look for the right time. This is my kinda business. You don't want anyone to suspect us. It may happen before Little Rock, but it could be after. The right time, that's what's important."

Hughes thought for a moment. "Cassidy, as much as I would

like to see Logan done for as soon as possible, you make good sense. But I want it done as soon as the chance arises. Any questions?"

Cassidy shoved his chair back and started to rise. "No."

Flatnose had jumped up and was moving toward the door.

"Cassidy, you wait," Hughes said.

Cassidy slowly dropped back into his chair. Flatnose stopped and turned, a questioning look on his face.

"Jack," Cassidy said, "you go ahead. Gather the boys in my room. I'll be along shortly."

As Flatnose stepped into the hallway, the only sound that could be heard was the high-pitched squeal of air passing through his smashed nose.

After the door closed, the room was silent for a moment.

"Well?" Cassidy asked.

Hughes shook his head. "I don't like that boy's insolence. You've got to control him better. Sabrina doesn't need that kind of attention."

Cassidy looked at Sabrina, still standing beside her father. "She's never struck me as a girl that couldn't take care of herself. I figure she's more dangerous than Jack will ever be."

Sabrina gave Cassidy a cold smile.

"Just do as I say. That goes for all of your men. We're in this together to the end. One misstep, one wrong word said, and this whole plan could go up in smoke. I've got these simpletons believing every word I utter. They're a little uneasy about your crew, but I've got them convinced that all of you are experienced Westerners. Don't mess that up."

Inside, Cassidy was seething. People didn't talk to him like that and live. He'd find it a real pleasure to put a forty-four-sized chunk of lead in that pompous pig's belly. But outside, he was as calm as still water. He kept his eyes down as he rolled a smoke. Holding the edge up, he ran his tongue across it to seal, stuck a twisted end in his mouth, fished a match from his vest, and flipped the end across his holster. The tip flared. He held it to the end of his cigarette, pleased his hands weren't trembling with anger, and took a quick pull, then shook out the match and tossed it into the ashtray on the desk.

After a deep draw, Cassidy blew out the smoke and said, "Plan's still the same?"

"No change. I'm depending on you to have your men at a suitable place, far enough west of Fort Smith so that the remains of the wagons won't be found for a long time."

"I've already located the place. Them city folks'll never know what hit 'em. You're sure they'll all be carrying their money with them?"

Hughes gave a deep sigh, as if he found it trying to his soul to have to explain, again, to the hired help. "Yes, Cassidy, they will have all of their money with them. That's the only way they can take part in this train. That's why they're so excited. Every single one of them sees himself as opening his own business and getting rich selling to the needy pioneers traveling to Oregon. They've swallowed it hook, line, and sinker. Now all we have to do is reel them in."

Hughes leaned forward and pointed a big index finger at Cassidy. "You just keep control on your men, especially that boy."

Cassidy stood, now looking down on the big man behind the desk. "I'll do my part." He touched his hat to Sabrina, getting her cold stare, and turned for the door.

"You just see that you do," Hughes said to his back.

Lifting the latch, Cassidy stepped outside, feeling the cool breeze of the river across his hot forehead. He clamped his hands on the railing and looked downriver, where he could just make out the mouth of the Arkansas.

Finally relaxing his grip on the railing, he smiled across the muddy Mississippi. It was going to feel so good to kill Hughes. That would be almost as rewarding as the money.

"The boys are ready, Boss," Flatnose said from behind.

"Jack, don't slip up on me like that. I've killed men for less."

"Sorry, Boss. Just thought you'd like to know."

Cassidy nodded and headed down the stairs to his room on the lower level. As he walked he calmed down and began to think about how he would take care of Callum Logan.

## 18

Now that they were away from Little Rock, the night breeze, generated by the boat's slow movement upriver, flowed through the cabin, bringing the smell and sounds of the river. The city sounds had disappeared, replaced by thousands of frogs constantly croaking their nightly serenade. A great horned owl hooted to their tune, and occasionally, a splash from the strike of a feeding bass added the percussion section.

Callum rolled over and looked at the boys in the other bed. They were sound asleep. This trip had been good for them. After their rocky start, he had been worried there might be a rift between them, but now they were fast friends.

Colin had always been the youngest, but with Virgil, there was someone younger whom he could teach. Having lived on the streets for a while, Virgil was wise past his years. Every day, the two would take off on the riverboat, exploring. The captain had complete trust in Virgil. The boys were allowed total freedom, from bridge to engine room. Callum was amazed at how exploring had held their interest for so long. Captain and Mrs. Hill had already known Virgil and liked him, but they quickly adopted the pair.

Colin had excitedly told the story of how the captain allowed each boy the opportunity to steer the riverboat. He was now committed to becoming a riverboat captain. Hamish had taken the two under his tutelage and put them to work, while showing them the depths of the boat. Callum had been concerned the two would grow bored, but they seemed to find something new every day.

Callum's thoughts drifted to the ranch. How was everyone? They were deep in Ute country, and unlike many of the tribes, including the Cherokee and Shoshone, they had never been friendly toward the white man. Josh, his younger brother, was there with his family, Fianna and their new son, Matthew. Josh had proven his mettle during the war, even if he did fight for the North, and he brought his new wife, her brother, and a herd of cattle through Texas to Colorado. He did it through Comanche and Kiowa country.

He chuckled quietly to himself. They would be fine. Then he sobered. Of course, it would break Josh's heart to hear about Pa's death. The two of them were close. He understood. Though they had all worked together, felling trees, building barns, plowing, and all the other labor that goes with a horse farm, he and his older brother, Will, had always hung out together. Not that they ignored Josh, but they tended to go off on their own. As he had taught them, Pa taught Josh about the way of the woods and the animals that called it home. As Josh grew, he was more of a loner. *Enough,* he thought. He shook the thoughts from his head and rolled back over toward the door.

The tinny sound of the piano man's efforts in the lower deck lounge drifted up through the open windows. As sleep slowly overtook him, almost lost in the night sounds, a board squeaked outside the room.

Coming instantly awake but remaining motionless, Callum slowly thumbed the hammer of one his Remington forty-fours to full-cock. The metallic clicks of the hammer were muted by his hat as he held it over the handgun. He eased his weight to the floor and, in stocking feet, quietly drifted next to the door. He watched the latch string as it was pulled taut. Switching his revolver to his left hand, he waited. There was the rhythmic whoosh-splash of the big wheel on this side of the ship as it drove the riverboat up the Arkansas. The crickets' constant chirps tried unsuccessfully to drown out the frogs. When the latch released, the door was slowly pushed open.

As soon as he saw the man, Callum reached out and grabbed a handful of collar, including skin. There was an audible croak as his big fist closed off any passage of air into the unlucky would-be murderer's lungs. At the same time, Callum yanked hard, pulling the assassin almost off his feet and into the room. As the man stumbled past him, Callum stepped out the door, still holding the intruder's throat and collar. In the few moments the assassin had to react, he managed to pull the trigger on the gun in his hand, blowing a large hole in the floor. From the corner of his eye, Callum could see the boys leaping from the bed, pulling their weapons.

Never losing his grip on the man's throat, his arm extended its full length. Now he yanked hard in the opposite direction, spinning the man on his boot toes, and sending him stumbling, in a half-run, back out the door. Callum's shoulder and back muscles that had become like iron from all of the heavy lifting around the farm, now worked with his bicep and forearm, to thrust the man toward the railing. When his arm reached its full extension again, he released his hold on the man's collar, just as the burglar sailed over the second-floor railing into the darkness below. Having the restriction at his throat released, the man took a last deep breath and let out a chilling wail as he soared out and down toward the frothing water. The cry abruptly ended when he struck the river, just in front of the big side paddle wheel, which followed his flailing body down, and after striking the man's head, pushed him into the depths of the dark, murky water.

His two companions who had been along to assist had almost reached the bottom of the stairs when the man's falling body passed them. Callum watched their shadowy outlines disappear under the second-floor railing.

The gunshot and scream brought passengers out of their rooms and onto the walkway. Colin and Virgil stood by their door, handguns ready.

"What happened?" Colin asked.

"We had visitors. It's all over now. You two can go back to bed."

Colin and Virgil looked around, yawned, went back into the room, and were sound asleep before Hamish showed up, pushing past the folks standing along the walkway.

He looked around, saw Callum standing in his long johns, a gun in his hand, and looked back at the curious observers. "It's all over, folks. Best get to your beds."

All of the family was outside their rooms, anxiously watching Callum.

"Are you and the boys all right, son?" Ma asked.

"We're fine, Ma. Like Hamish said, it's all over. If it's all right with you, we'll see you in the morning and tell you all about it over breakfast."

She nodded, looked at the next room, where Frank and Bret were standing, armed, and headed back inside. After all of the observers had dispersed, Hamish asked, "What's goin' on?"

"Somebody tried to come into our room. Looks like he changed his mind in favor of taking a long swim."

Hamish looked at the water and at the big paddles of the side wheel constantly slicing by, pushing the Lone Star up the Arkansas. "A permanent one, I'd say. Is it the possibility that you recognized the blighter?"

"Matter of fact, I did. I saw him on the wharf in Little Rock. He was there with two other men, probably the two I saw running away. I'm surprised you didn't see them at the base of the stairs."

"I must've been a wee bit late. We'll do a search tomorrow. If they're on the boat we'll find 'em. Any idea you're having about why they did it?"

"I've got a suspicion, but right now, it's not worth talking about. Let's see if you can find those two tomorrow. I'm sure they'll be glad to clear up any questions we have."

"Aye, it's sure I am that they will. Now, get back to sleep, and I'll tell the captain."

"Thanks, Hamish. Tell him I'm sorry for the ruckus. I told him I wouldn't cause any problem for him."

"It's not to worry yourself, lad. There's nothing you could've done exceptin' what you did. See you in the morning." Without another word, Hamish turned and headed back to the ladderway that would take him to the next level and subsequently up to the pilot house, where the captain was steering the boat.

Callum watched him go, then turned to Frank and Bret. Both armed, they had remained outside to make sure Callum, Colin, and Virgil were all right.

"You heard?"

"Yeah," Frank said. "So you recognized the one you tossed over the side?"

"I did, but until I saw him in Little Rock, I'm sure I never saw him before. Neither he nor the two that were with him looked smart enough to come up with this on their own. They just looked like cheap thugs. I'm guessing somebody hired them."

Bret spoke up. "I know who comes at the top of my list."

Callum nodded. "Yeah, the only one that comes to mind is Hughes. Of course, he wouldn't have gotten his hands dirty, he would've had Cassidy do the hiring."

Frank said, "You didn't see Cassidy with those three?"

"No. They were all I saw."

"Well, we better stay sharp. Somebody wants you dead, and

they don't care how many they kill. You know Cassidy knows the boys are in the room with you. If they killed you, they'd have to kill the boys too."

"You're right, Frank. I'd like to have this over. I don't want anyone else getting hurt."

"Callum," Bret said, "you take care of yourself. We'll watch out for the family. That includes Virg and Ezra. In fact, I bet Ezra is dying of curiosity after hearing that shot."

"We'll go back there tomorrow and tell him. I'll check again to see if he wants to move up here and sleep in a bed."

"He won't," Frank said. "After Mrs. Mason died, he took to sleeping in the barn with his mules. He likes being outside. Darned if I don't think the mules like it too."

"I'll ask him again, anyway. Why don't you two get some sleep? They won't be trying that again tonight."

"Right," Frank said. "We'll see you in the morning." The men went back into their room, closing the door on the black night. Just a small sliver of moon sank toward the west.

Callum went to the rail and looked below one more time. His eyes searched every bale of cotton and every box, looking for a shadow or something indicating a man was hiding. Nothing. He turned and entered the room, closing the door. Glancing at the boys' bed, he could see they were both sound asleep. The sound of their steady breathing filled the room.

*Young folks are truly resilient,* he thought. Callum sat on the side of his bed, then lay down and stretched out. He hadn't said anything to anyone else, but tomorrow morning, he was going to pay a visit to Mr. Colonel Hughes. If he was behind it, he needed to know what he had at stake when Callum found out for sure. The forty-four located easily within his reach, he relaxed his tired body and was quickly asleep.

~

Light streamed into the large cabin Hughes and his daughter shared when Cassidy walked in. This was the first time he had seen Hughes since the unsuccessful attempt on Logan's life last night. The big man sat at his desk, while Sabrina, still in her nightgown, sat at the dresser, brushing her long brown hair. She gave a curt nod when Cassidy said good morning to her, straightened her back, and took a deep breath, her chest now pressed tighter against the light material of her morning robe.

Cassidy missed none of the display as he was again seated in the straight-backed, uncomfortable chair across the desk from Hughes. This morning, Hughes had a smile on his face, even looking pleased to see Cassidy.

"I heard the shot last night. I assume Callum Logan is now floating in the Arkansas?"

"Not exactly," Cassidy said.

The smile immediately disappeared, replaced with pursed lips and wrinkled forehead. "What do you mean?"

"I mean that Logan killed one of the men I hired, and the other two are having no part of trying to kill him after what they saw."

Sabrina spun around in the chair, not yet having put on her makeup. "What do you mean, not dead? Papa and I both heard the shot."

It's amazing how much war paint can help some women, Cassidy thought. But she's a real looker, even without it.

"What I mean, Miss Hughes, is that the gunshot you heard was from Jasper Kagel, one of the men I hired. He—"

"Blast it, Cassidy!" Hughes shouted, "I've told you I don't want to know names. I already know too many."

Cassidy turned cold eyes on his boss. "What would you like to know?"

Hughes, obviously confident in his own strength over Cassidy's, ignored the danger of the man, and continued, his voice dripping sarcasm, "What I want to know, Mr. Cassidy, is what happened—without any names."

Cassidy watched Hughes for another moment, then said slowly, "The man I hired fired the shot you heard." Then he continued normally. "Evidently, from the explanation of the other two, Logan was waiting for them. The first thing any of them knew, Ja—the man I hired, was jerked into the room by his throat. At that point, he fired, but hit nothing because he was being choked to death. Then Logan threw him out and over the railing. The other two said he disappeared into the water, in front of the paddle wheel."

Hughes, a disgusted look on his face, said, "Of course, the other two ran."

"Yes, the other two ran."

"Where are they now?"

"Where they belong, fish food. After they explained the situation, they were quickly and silently disposed of. I know Hill will be searching every nook and cranny on this boat. He'll never find them."

Hughes leaned back in his padded chair and sighed. "Well, finally a piece of good news. Well done on cleaning up after your mess."

"Thank you," Cassidy said, enjoying a fleeting picture of shooting Hughes.

"What are you smiling at?"

Cassidy hadn't realized he had smiled. *I'll have to be more careful. He's getting to me,* he thought. "Just thinking about the future."

"Yes, there will be plenty for all, if we can pull this off. Logan has been talking to some of the people on the train, particularly Avery Simpson. They are asking uncomfortable questions."

"I can have a couple of my men talk to Simpson and persuade him to keep his mouth shut."

Hughes shook his big head. "No, no, no. We don't want to cause any doubt in their mind. We want them to anxiously race toward their untimely future. If we give them reason to start doubting, there will be more questions. It could get so bad, we might lose this opportunity."

Sabrina had lost her patience. She stood and walked to the corner of the desk, where she rested one hand. Her long fingers looked enticing as they stretched along the side of the desk, cherry-red nails glistening. "Mr. Cassidy, why not just shoot him, or have you lost your nerve? Does he scare you that much?"

Cassidy had watched her rise in her swishing, pale pink robe, then stretch her hand on the table, but the sharp voice jerked him out of his fog. No person ever talked to Cassidy like that. If she were a man, he would kill him; a woman he would kill also, after he was through with her. Now, he sat in the uncomfortable straight-backed chair and stared up at this frightfully beautiful young woman. His hands, covered with gloves, were in his lap. He looked at them, stretched out his fingers wide, and then made them into hard fists.

He stood, towering over her, but she didn't budge. Stupid woman, he thought. Just as stupid as her father. He turned back to Hughes and leaned over the desk, resting on his knuckles.

"Hughes, I've taken a lot from you because we have a deal, and the potential to make big money. As much as I want that money, I will not put up with this kind of insult from your daughter. Put a muzzle on her, or find another gang to take care of Logan and your settlers."

Cassidy's eyes were locked on Hughes. He could see the man was taken aback. This was the response of a man who was used to being top dog. He had a reputation for never allowing his men to talk back to him, or talk about his daughter in this manner. But Cassidy could also see the slight doubt, a subtle loss of confidence, in the man's eyes, as if he was receiving a warning, a notion, slight, but still there.

Hughes took a deep breath and began his response. "Mr.

Cassidy"—this time there was no sarcasm—"I find myself in the unusual circumstance of having to apologize for my daughter."

Sabrina whirled to face her father, her chest heaving and her face red, cursing, using words that would embarrass a sailor. Finally, when she had gained some semblance of control, she said, "Father, don't apologize for me! How can you let this. . . this thug, talk about your own daughter like that? If you're not going to tell him what for, I—"

The sound of the slap rang throughout the room. Her father towered over her. Sabrina, her face frozen in shock, staggered to her right and immediately attempted to whip her well-manicured hand toward her father's face. He grabbed the small wrist in his large, beefy left hand and twisted to the left. She let out a yelp, stumbling and trying to pull her hand from her father's firm grip.

"Sabrina, stop!" Hughes demanded.

She jerked her arm from his grip and started rubbing her wrist. "You slapped me."

"Yes, I'm sorry I had to, but you were out of control. You must learn to control yourself. Cassidy had no influence on last night's outcome. You had no right to berate him. Now, apologize."

She glanced at Cassidy for a moment. "I will not!" Then her voice dropped lower. "Daddy, I love you, but don't ever slap me again. If you do, I swear I'll kill you." With that, she spun around, went into her bedroom, and slammed the door so hard that dust rose from the jamb.

Cassidy continued standing. "Mr. Hughes, Logan needs to die. You can depend on me. I'll take care of it—at the right time."

Both heads jerked toward the door as it flew open.

# 19

Callum Logan's broad shoulders filled the door. He saw Cassidy's eyes drop to his guns and register that both leather thongs were off. The man immediately relaxed and sat back down, placing both hands in his lap.

"What's the meaning of this?" Hughes said, as he, too, returned to his plush office chair. He leaned forward, both hands on the desk.

"Hughes," Callum said, "keep both hands on your desk. My patience has run out. You sent men to kill me. That now makes you fair game. All you need to do is twitch, and I'll kill you. Right here, right now."

Hughes looked nervously around his office for help. His panicked eyes settled on Cassidy. "Do something!"

Cassidy leaned back in his chair. "Not much I can do right now. Anyway, if we start shootin' in here, no tellin' who might git hit."

The bedroom door opened, and Sabrina re-entered the room. Hughes watched his daughter move to the vanity, sweat starting to bead on his forehead.

Once at the vanity, and seemingly ignoring Callum, she pulled open a drawer and started to reach inside.

"Ma'am," Callum said, "I ain't never shot a woman, but you pull a gun out of that drawer and I'm gonna be forced to put a big, nasty forty-four-caliber slug right between your eyes. My argument's with your pa, here, not with you, at least not at this moment. You best sit down and just relax yourself."

Callum watched the young woman play the possibilities over in her mind. He knew she was debating whether or not he would shoot her. He realized that he was debating the same thing.

"Don't do it," Cassidy said to Sabrina. "I know men. This man would shoot you, and trust me, you don't want to be shot. If it doesn't kill you, it hurts an almighty bunch."

Sabrina cursed Callum but moved her hand from the drawer and sat down.

Callum turned back to Hughes, who was still sitting, leaning forward in the chair, hands on the table. "You're a sorry excuse for a father, Hughes, to raise a daughter that cares about no one but herself and has a mouth that'd make an outhouse ashamed. But I'm not here to tell you something you already know." Callum stepped farther into the room and moved to one side of the door. Frank followed him in, the big fifty-six-caliber hole of the Spencer's muzzle centered on Hughes's gunman. Cassidy stayed relaxed, acting as if he hardly noticed.

"Hughes," Callum continued, "you hired men to kill me in my sleep. My nephew and Virgil Brogan were in that room."

"Logan," Hughes said, the beads of sweat now developing into small rivulets coursing down his forehead, "I'd never resort to murder."

"A man that would lie would resort to murder, and I say you're a liar, a bald-faced liar."

"No man calls me a liar. If you weren't standing there with a gun in your hand, I'd teach you more respect for your betters."

Callum smiled. "Is that an offer?"

"Don't smile at me. I've beaten better men than you into the dirt. You called me a liar and a murderer. I deserve satisfaction. You take off those guns, and I'll teach you a lesson you'll never forget."

"I'll do that. But first, I want you to understand that one of your men is dead. If there is another attempt on my life or on any of my family, I'll come for you, and the next time, I won't be talking. Meet me on the wharf after we've unloaded. I'll give you a chance to 'teach me a lesson.'"

With his last words, Callum motioned with his head toward the door, and Frank stepped out, keeping the Spencer trained on Cassidy. Callum slowly backed out of the door, leaving it open, then turned and, with Frank, headed toward the stern.

CALLUM LEANED against the railing at the stern of the Lone Star, Ma Logan next to him. He had been looking at the wagons.

"Son, are you really going to fight this man?"

"Yes, ma'am. He asked for it. I reckon I oughta give it to him."

"Callum, he's at least four inches taller than you and outweighs you by close to forty pounds, and, have you seen his hands? His knuckles are scarred. He's no stranger to fighting."

Callum grinned at his ma. "No, ma'am, I reckon not. He don't look like he's used to losing either. Maybe it's his time."

"You be careful."

"Yes, ma'am, I will. Ma," Callum said, changing the subject, "those bonnets on the wagons are way too white. When we get the wagons off the barge, I'd like for you and whoever you need, to finish stockin' supplies. I'll keep Frank here to keep any of Cassidy's henchmen off of me, and I'll be along shortly. After the wagons are stocked, move to the west side of town to make camp. If you wouldn't mind telling us what kind of bark you need to dye the tops, we'll get it for you."

"What color do you want, son?"

"Those bonnets'll be stickin' up high above the prairie. At a far distance, changing it to a natural color just might save our bacon. I'm thinking a light brownish-green. The important thing is to blend in. The prairie will be covered with grass, as far as you can see. We'll see mighty few trees, except along creeks and arroyos. That grass'll be anywhere from two to four-feet tall."

"All right. All we'll need is some oak bark, and we'll have it done by tonight."

"Thanks, Ma. That'll make me a lot more comfortable. The territory we'll be going through is claimed by a lot of tribes. This'll help."

Ma reached over and patted Callum on the forearm. "Son, after this fight, I don't think anything's going to make you comfortable."

"Mr. Logan."

Callum and Ma turned to see the captain approaching them. "Afternoon, Captain."

Captain Hill nodded to Callum and doffed his hat to Ma Logan. "Madam, what's this I hear about your son and Hughes?"

Ma sighed. "Yes, I suspect there'll be some doctoring for me to do this evening." She rested her hand on Callum's shoulder. "But I've always found that Callum and his brothers are much like my late husband. They don't pursue fights, but they do finish them. Now, I must go and make sure Kate and the boys are all packed and ready. Good day, Captain."

The captain made a slight bow. "And may you also have a good day, Mrs. Logan. It has been a pleasure having you and your family aboard the Lone Star. I wish you a safe journey."

Ma smiled at the man. "Thank you." Erect, looking at least ten years younger than her fifty-four years, she strode to her cabin.

"Your ma is quite a woman," the captain said to Callum.

"Yes, she is. Pa's death hit her hard, but you could never tell it." Callum turned from watching his ma walking up the stairs to the second deck.

"Captain, this has been a fast trip. Thank you."

"We've been very fortunate. Now, about this fight. You are aware that there have been rumors in Memphis that he was an enforcer for a New York gang?"

"Yes, Virg told me."

"Were you aware that there are also rumors that he has beaten several men to death with his fists?"

"Captain, when Virg heard about our fight, he told me all of that. It makes no matter. If it's true, those things are in the past. What counts is today."

"Well, thanks for keeping it off the Lone Star. I can't even begin to imagine how much damage a fight like this could cause on a boat."

Callum nodded. "I gave you my word."

"Thanks anyway. By the way, I'll be there, and I'll have some hands in the crowd. You won't have any trouble. I also have a man working for me that's good at fixing cuts. I'll send him to you."

Callum laughed. "Thank you, Captain. I imagine he will come in handy."

A whistle sounded from the Lone Star.

"Got to get back," the captain said. "Good luck to you."

"And you," Callum said. Now watching the captain hurry back to his duties, thoughts crowded his mind. *I've gone and got myself into another impossible situation,* he thought. *If I get hurt in this fight, what's the family going to do?* Then he chuckled. *They'll do exactly what all the other families do. They'll make their way.*

He knew worrying helped nothing. Pa always said that worrying was time poorly spent. Callum watched the Lone Star near the wharf, glanced back to the barge, and saw Ezra wave. Pushing the worry from his mind, he moved to the side of the boat where his family waited. Time to go to work.

EZRA HAD MOVED the stock toward the west side of the barge. When the gates opened, the animals trotted off, obviously happy to be on solid ground again. The wagons followed, with Ma and Bret driving. Kate, along with the boys and Ezra, were upset. They wanted to see the fight.

Callum spent some time with Shoshone. The horse, though glad to see him, wanted to stretch his long legs. Callum finally got him settled down. Reaching inside his saddlebags, he pulled out a pair of moccasins, removed his boots, and quickly slipped them on.

Frank nodded. "Good idea. Boots get hung on something, they could have you in trouble."

He and Frank tied their horses on the wharf and eyed the makeshift ring that had been hastily roped off. Frank had one Remington in his holster, the other thrust in his pants, with the grip facing to the right, and the Spencer in his left hand.

Callum eyed Frank for a moment. "You expectin' trouble?"

Frank shot a stream of tobacco juice at a rat scurrying across the wharf. "Nope. I figger this'll keep it calmed down, but if it don't, I'm ready."

The two men walked to the ring. There was a small man standing inside. He nodded to Frank and Callum.

"I'm Felix Tester. The captain sent me to help you with cuts, if you'll have me."

Callum shook hands with the man. "Glad to have you here." He bent and went under the stretched rope.

Felix looked up at Callum's hat, shirt, and vest. "That comes off."

Callum shrugged and handed Frank his hat. He put it on over his. After removing his vest, he handed it to Frank, who slipped the vest on over his, unbuttoned. He was about to take his shirt off, when Hughes came walking up with his entourage.

Hughes, ignoring Callum, walked directly to the opposite side of the ring. The man was big. He wore boxer's tights and no shirt, only a towel slung around his broad shoulders.

Bets were being taken around the ring, and the crowd was growing. In unison, the throng gasped as Hughes yanked the towel from his shoulders and flexed his back. Betting increased immediately. Callum could hear that the bets were heavily in favor of Hughes. Callum looked over the man's body. He was big, His arms at least three inches longer than Callum's. The only thing in Callum's favor, that he could see, was that good living had put a belly on the big man. But if one of those big hands connected early, it wouldn't matter how fat he had become.

The captain had assumed the role of referee. He had a Pocket Colt thrust into his waistband.

"The shirt," Felix said. While Callum was pulling off his shirt, Felix dragged a pair of wrinkled, thin leather gloves from his vest pockets. "Put these on."

Callum, his eyes remaining on his adversary, pulled his shirt over his head and handed it to Felix. Then looked at the gloves. The tips of the fingers were cutoff so that the outer portion of the fingers were exposed, but the knuckles and flat portion of the fingers, when a fist was made, was covered with the thin leather.

"They'll protect your hands."

Callum slid them on quickly, noticing that Hughes was also slipping on similar gloves and frowning when he saw his opponent do the same.

Felix tossed the shirt on the corner post. Callum's arms and shoulders had been disguised with his shirt on, but when he removed it, a second gasp came from the crowd, though not quite as loud as the first. He figured they were gasping at the healed bullet wound in his back and chest, which may have been partially true, but they were also seeing the results of hard work. The felling of trees, sawing, plowing, digging fence holes, all had contributed to what had now been revealed to the crowd. Thick wrists, large biceps, chiseled back and chest, with no evident fat. Giggles came from a group of ladies in the crowd. He looked over to see all smiling, and one winked at him.

Frank leaned over to Callum. "Looks like you got some lady admirers."

Callum shook his head. "Hope they enjoy the fight."

"You don't know women, boy. They'll enjoy it just fine."

Low, almost in a whisper, Callum said to Frank, "There's gold in that vest you're wearing. I like the odds I'm hearing. Bet five hundred dollars."

"My pleasure," Frank said.

"Fighters," the captain said, motioning for the two men to step to the center of the ring.

The men moved to the center, facing each other.

Hughes smiled. "You're in my bailiwick, boyo. You'll be lucky if you make it out of here alive."

"I'll hear none of that!" the captain said. "I'll have this fight fair. No biting and no stomping."

Hughes frowned at Captain Hill.

"You heard me, Hughes. Why do you think I have this pistol with me? If either man attempts to stomp the other, I'll shoot him. Trust me. I am not joking. Now, when a man goes down, move away from him. Each of you will go back to your corner before starting again." He looked at both fighters. "Clear?"

They both nodded. While Captain Hill had been talking, Callum surveyed the spectators. Most of the settlers were standing around the makeshift ring waiting to see the outcome of the fight. Some of them had become friends with the Logans. *Unfortunately,* Callum thought, *they still trust Hughes. I know he's up to something. I'd like to know what it is, but I've got my own family to think about.*

The captain jumped back, jerking Callum from his thoughts, and at the same time, shouted, "You may begin!"

Immediately, Hughes swung a powerful right cross. Callum,

distracted by his thoughts, barely had time to move his head. The blow, powered by all the concentrated effort in his opponent's body, struck his ear and side of his head a glancing blow. However, enough energy was transmitted to Callum's head that it did three things. It drove him back on his heels, causing him to stumble backwards, fighting to regain his balance. A myriad of lights went off in his eyes, causing a feeling of dizziness to wash over him, and the top of his ear split like it had been sliced with a skinning knife. Blood gushed down the side of his face and over his left shoulder and side. The crowd roared.

Callum suspected Hughes was a brawler, but had no idea he had been trained in the bars and backrooms of the roughest dives in the depths of New York City. Before Callum could protect himself, Hughes threw a roundhouse left, aimed again at the younger man's head. This one Callum saw coming and managed to move to his left, hearing the blow whip past. Now it was his turn. In his eagerness to finish the fight before it had barely started, Hughes misjudged Callum's ability to recover. Steady now, he saw an opening. While mentally thanking Pa for all the fight training he had received while a young man, he set his leading foot, and twisting his hips, he drove a left cross into the older man's pudgy midsection. He was surprised to feel hard muscle behind the fat. He moved away quickly after throwing the punch, getting out of the long reach of those arms.

"I'm going to smash you like a bug, Cowboy." Hughes's voice was normal. He wasn't even breathing hard, after Callum's blow to his midsection.

This could be a long fight, Callum thought.

The two men moved cautiously around the ring. Shouts for Hughes to finish him came from many of the movers. As if responding to their calls, Hughes stepped within his long reach of Callum and shot a hard left jab into Callum's forehead. His head snapped back. Hughes moved closer and drove a big, gloved fist into his belly.The power of the blow rocketed the air from Callum's lungs.

He moved quickly to get away from the fighter. As he backed away, he found himself near the rope. He turned slightly, and stepped back again, all the while watching Hughes. But this time, he had moved too close to the crowd. One of Cassidy's men stuck his leg into the ring just behind Callum's feet. His moccasin-encased right foot hit the boot, and, still gasping for air from the previous blow, he plummeted back onto the thick wooden wharf, knocking what little breath he had regained from his oxygen-depleted lungs.

Hughes wasted no time getting to Callum. Gasping for air, and attempting to regain his feet, he watched Hughes lift his heavy booted foot. The crowd was suddenly silent. In the quiet, the ratcheting clicks of a Colt Pocket revolver's hammer being pulled back split the air.

"Hughes, you drop that foot and you're a dead man," the captain said.

His face red with anger, Hughes lowered his foot to the wharf. With the delay, Callum had regained his breath and jumped to his feet. He had seen something. Hughes was wearing huge teamsters boots. There was only one reason to wear that type of boot if you weren't a teamster, to stomp the life out of someone. Unfortunately, they were heavy. Hughes was moving around the ring all right for now. But that weight on his legs would start tiring him sooner than normal.

Callum was a man of action. He had been his whole life. He could feel cold rage rising. Hughes had had it easy for the first few minutes, but that was going to end, and end right now.

He smiled at Hughes and moved toward him.

## 20

Callum saw the frown on his opponent's face when he smiled. This is gonna hurt, he thought. The two men traded blows, Hughes landing some hard punches, Callum used jabs to protect himself, waiting. His waiting paid off. Hughes must have seen an opening he thought he could exploit and threw a devastating right cross. If it had connected the fight would have been over, but Callum had figured out Hughes's tells by now. At his first move, Callum moved slightly to his right and threw a smashing jab to the older man's nose and mouth. The gloved hand smashing flesh, sounded like an over-ripe watermelon being slammed with a fence post. Blood showered both men. Lips lacerated, Hughes's nose was smashed to the right side of his face.

That, however, wasn't Callum's goal. The big man involuntarily brought both hands to his face. Immediately, Callum could see the man recognized his mistake, but it was too late. Callum moved inside the reach of those long arms, and delivered four fast and devastating blows, before he quickly stepped out of range. The first blow had all of his weight behind it, a right cross straight to the man's heart. Hughes had tried to kill him, and had probably been behind Virgil's family being burned alive. Now maybe he could deliver a little payback. The fist landed with perfect aim, right over the man's heart. It was delivered by muscle and sinew grown over years of backbreaking hard labor. Struck correctly, a blow with this kind of power could stop a heart permanently.

He didn't hesitate. The next three blows landed to the midsection. Muscled under the fat Hughes might be, but Callum knew that repeated blows to the belly could beat any man. Finished for now, he stepped back. Hughes was in pain, gasping for air. Callum caught a glimpse of the man's daughter, her face contorted astonishment and anguish. Hughes brought his hands back up and stepped toward Callum, hurting, but now carried by determination and pain, not yet willing to believe he could be beaten.

Don't get careless, Callum told himself.

He moved to his left, forcing Hughes to chase him. Hughes connected with his roundhouse right, but the steam wasn't there. It knocked Callum back to his right for a few steps, but caused no ear-ringing or seeing spots. The majority of the crowd cheered loudly. Their silence had been deafening since Callum's attack. The few Callum supporters were cheering cautiously, for as they cheered, they received threatening looks from Cassidy's men.

Callum spotted another opening and went in. He knew his best bet was working on the man's heart and belly, but he couldn't resist the temptation. Hughes was a vain and pompous man, Callum wanted to deliver a strong remembrance of what happened today. His first jab struck the taller man in almost the same place the previous one had hit, his nose and mouth. The bleeding had slowed, having covered his chest and a good part of his arms with blood. With this blow, Callum could see the pain flash through the man's eyes. He threw the next jab at his opponent's right eye, splitting the eyebrow, then dancing out of range.

Callum could tell that Hughes was just about done. The

bigger man was tired and in pain. He had his hands up and looked ready, but Callum knew it wouldn't be long. However, he could still get lucky. Callum thought he saw an opening, and moved in. It must have been painful, but Hughes actually smiled, as he released a devastating uppercut, catching Callum directly under the chin. His head snapped back. He staggered, almost out, but still on his feet. Fortunately, he was in his corner, and the blow drove him against the rope in front of Frank and Felix. Hughes lumbered toward him, hate in his eyes. Felix yanked a small glass vial from his vest pocket, jerked the top off, and thrust it under Callum's nose. Callum jerked his head away just as Hughes threw a roundhouse left. It missed Callum, but nailed Felix on the top of his head, knocking him out and into Frank, who caught him, and laid him down on the wharf, then went back to watching the fight.

Callum shook his head hard. It felt like whatever Felix had thrust under his nose had seared his sinuses, but it brought him back, and quickly. Now, Hughes had a grotesque grin on his face, obviously enjoying the thought of beating Callum to death. Callum faked grogginess, trying to stumble away from Hughes. The crowd was, again, in an uproar, their bloodlust high, awaiting the demise of Callum Logan.

Hughes moved in and swung a roundhouse right, leaving himself wide open. He clearly was no longer concerned about Callum's ability to respond with anything, and he was so wrong.

When the wide-ranging blow began, Callum stepped in close to his target. This time, all he was thinking about was putting the man down. He drove multiple blows to the man's heart and belly, until he felt rather than saw the big arms drop and hang useless. Callum kept pummeling. Slowly at first, then like a tall pine toppling, Hughes gained speed, falling straight back with his arms tossed out to his sides. A few cheers could be heard, but the large portion of the crowd was silent.

Callum stood, hands down at his sides, looking at the bloody and beaten man. It was done, and he hurt all over. He had never been hit with that kind of force before. *I'm amazed I'm still standing,* he thought. *If someone hadn't thrust that awful smellin' stuff under my nose, it might be me lying on my back.* He turned to find Felix and saw Frank helping the little man to his feet.

"You all right?" Frank asked Callum.

"It depends on the meaning of all right."

Frank laughed. "Yeah, I get yore meanin'. Wait here. I'll be right back."

Callum turned back to Felix. The man was now on his hands and knees, looking for something. He stood up and held out his hand. It was a tiny glass bottle that had broken when he dropped it. Felix held it out to him, and Callum leaned over to look. The smell hit him, causing him to jerk away.

"That's it! That's what I smelled."

"Yes, sir, that is smelling salts. At least, it was. That was the last I had."

Callum skinned off the gloves that Felix had given him and handed them back to his cornerman. "Thanks, Felix, these really helped. My hands hurt, but they don't feel near as bad as if I hadn't used your gloves."

Felix nodded in agreement. "Yes, just that little bit of protection can make a huge difference. I'm glad they worked for you." Felix looked around Callum at the returning Frank.

Frank had a big smile on his face. "This oughta help git rid of some of that pain."

He had another heavy pouch.

Callum looked at the pouch and then back at Frank. "Winnings?"

"Yep. They were giving ten to one odds on you. You should have seen the laughin' idgits when I placed that five-hundred-dollar bet. Weren't laughin' much when I went to collect. Had to grab that little weasel as he was sneakin' off in the crowd."

Felix had doctored Callum's cuts and wiped the blood from

his upper body and arms. Callum slipped his shirt on, over his head, put his hat on, and then his vest. Frank handed him his gunbelt. He swung the belt on and checked his guns.

"Here you go," Frank said as he handed the sack to Callum.

Callum opened it. "Felix, hold out your hand."

A puzzled look on his face, Felix held his hand out, while Callum counted out five hundred dollars.

"Will that buy you some more smelling salts?"

Felix grinned. "It'll buy more than that. It'll buy me a happy Blanche when I get home. Course, I doubt she'll ever believe me. She's always said that fighting ain't no way to make a living. That's why I went to work for Captain Hill, a fine man. Thank you, Mr. Callum."

"Thank you, Felix. If it hadn't been for those smellin' salts, it would've been me laying out there." He cast a glance across the ring. They had found a stool for Hughes to sit on as a doctor looked after him.

"I best be gettin' back to work." Felix bent down and picked up his bucket, containing some water and rags. He had no place else to put it, so he put the gold in the bucket and grinned. "Reckon this is the most expensive bucket I've ever had." He laughed out loud and headed back to the boat.

"What was Felix laughing about?"

Callum turned around at the new voice, his sore back protesting. "Captain Hill, thanks for stopping Hughes. He would've tried to stomp me for sure."

"I don't joke, Mr. Logan. If he'd done that, I'd a shot him right through the gizzard. How you feeling?"

Callum smiled and grimaced. "Like I've been beaten."

The captain laughed. "It was one hell of a fight. I sure thought he had you there for a second. It's a good thing you came out of it."

"I can thank Felix for that. I was close enough that he could reach me with his smelling salts. I swear that stuff almost took the top of my head off. Unfortunately, he was paid for it by getting slugged by Hughes, but he recovered all right. He'll be fine."

The captain laughed again. "I saw it happen. Poor Felix, Hughes cold-cocked him. Well, Callum, Frank, I've got to get back to the boat. We're pulling out for Little Rock as soon as we're loaded. The water's going down. This will definitely be our last run until the winter rains. You men take care of yourselves."

The men shook hands. Callum turned back to see Hughes getting to his feet. "Cover me, Frank," Callum said, and walked across the ring.

Several of Cassidy's crew were gathered around. One said something to Hughes that made the man look up to see Callum approaching.

Hughes looked bad. The doctor had attempted to straighten his broken nose, but was unable to align it accurately, and it skewed to the man's right. His lips were almost shredded. The cut over his left eye had started swelling, and the eye was almost totally closed.

Sabrina stepped in front of her father. "What do you want?"

"Nothing from you," Callum said, and stepped around her. "Hughes, I'll give you one thing, you're a fighter, but understand, what I told you in your office still stands. Stay away from my family. If anything happens to them, I'm coming for you."

Callum glanced at the settlers milling around the ring. "I don't know what you've planned for these folks, but I know it isn't good. So I'm going to extend my promise to them. Don't let anything happen to these families. Heed my word."

Without allowing Hughes the chance to speak, Callum turned and walked back to Frank. "Let's get out of here."

"I'm long past ready," Frank said. They walked to their horses.

"Mr. Logan, Mr. Logan, may I have a moment?"

Callum turned and saw Avery Simpson trotting toward them. "What can I do for you, Mr. Simpson?"

Nodding at Frank, Avery continued, "Mr. Logan, some of us are concerned about the upcoming trip. We thought maybe you might ride along."

Callum shook his head. "I'm sorry, that's just not possible. Your people still have to purchase and stock your wagons. We're ready. right now. Anyway, Hughes wouldn't hear of it."

"I just don't know what to do. I've my family to think about, and my instincts tell me not to trust Mr. Hughes."

"I'd say you're gettin' the right signals. He's an evil man, and I suspect that anything he is involved in will turn sour for everyone except him. You've got the money. Just open a store here. I'm sure this is as good a place as any."

"I can't. My family has their hearts set on going to Oregon."

"Then wait for the next wagon train, and go with them. This isn't the only one going to Oregon."

"I don't know how long we'll have to wait. I certainly don't want to wait too long and end up like those poor people in the Donner party."

Callum was hurting. He wanted to get to a stream and clean up. Soaking in cool water would certainly ease the aches. "Mr. Simpson, I can't help. I've got to think of my people. They're ready to go. We're leaving in the morning. I wish you luck."

He swung up onto Shoshone and eased the horse into the street. Frank rode next to him.

"You was mighty sharp with that feller, son."

"I know, Frank, but I can't help everybody. I've got to think about this family first. Hughes is going to be after blood as soon as he gets to feeling better. He might even send Cassidy out before then. We've got to get our wagons moving west, and soon."

"That's a fact."

Callum wondered why he didn't feel any better having had Frank agree with him. He could feel Frank's concern about those folks' involvement with Hughes.

*Dang it,* he thought. *I can't take care of 'em all. I've got to think of*

*Josh and his family back at the ranch. Those Utes are testy folks and don't abide strangers. Ma and the kids need me. Pa always said take care of your family. But he also said, don't dwell on how you can't do something, ask yourself how you can. I feel like my head's gonna burst, and not from Hughes's punches.*

They continued to ride down Main Street, Callum deep in thought. They had passed several saloons that he paid no mind to, since he didn't drink. He liked a sarsaparilla every once in a while, but not to—.

"I say Callum, you all right?" Frank said.

"What? Did you say something?"

"I danged shore did. About three times. I said, I'm thirsty. We done passed a bunch of saloons, and there's one coming up on our right. Let's make a quick stop, so I can wet my whistle."

Callum glanced to his right and pulled up Shoshone. He sat looking at the horses tied in front of the saloon—one in particular. He turned to Frank. "You recognize that buckskin with the star on his hip?"

Frank looked at the horse for the first time. His graying eyebrows raised, and his eyes opened wide. "You reckon it could be him?"

"I've never seen another horse marked like that in my life. It's either him, or the fellow that owns him is gonna have a heap of explainin' to do." The two men swung their horses up to the crowded rail, swung down, tied them, and headed toward the swinging doors.

"Took you boys long enough," a voice, easily recognized by both Callum and Frank, said from a gent in a chair leaning against the front of the saloon. He pushed his old, worn flop hat to the back of his head and stood.

Both men stopped in their tracks, grins breaking across their faces. Callum started to grin and the pain from the blows he had taken, made short work of it.

"Floyd," Frank said, "ain't you a sight for these old eyes."

"You too, Frank. It's been a while."

"Uncle," Callum said, as he looked over the man in front of him. He had last seen him when they left the ranch in Colorado. He was headed back to Tennessee to get his folks, and Uncle Floyd was escorting Sarah Radcliff and her son, Jimmy, to her Mormon relatives in Salt Lake City. He hadn't changed—tall, rangy, wide-shouldered, wearing his old slouch hat and buckskins. His gunbelt fastened around his long pale-yellow buckskin jacket, carrying a Colt snug in its holster, another shoved behind his gunbelt, and a big Bowie knife.

"Uncle, I'm almighty surprised. Why, I figgered you'd be hanging around that Salt Lake country, or moseying down to Arizona. You're about the last person I expected to see this far east, this soon."

"I hear what you're saying, boy, but after finishing up my business in Salt Lake, I got to thinking about you and the family. Thought I'd mosey over this way. You need to know, that there Sarah Radcliff and her son, Jimmy, arrived safe and sound. They're all settled in with their family."

"I'm glad to hear it," Callum said. "I'm just surprised to see you this far east."

"Well, I'll tell you, Callum. I ain't been there more'n a couple of days, and I just had this feelin'. So I loaded up and headed this way. Didn't know where I'd catch you, but figgered it'd be before you got to the ranch. Meetin' you here is right fine. We saw your ma, Kate, and the boys settin' up camp on the west side of town."

"We?" Callum said.

"When I hit Denver City, I ran into a couple of my old pards. We trapped plew together in the thirties, for them foreigners what wanted beaver pelts for their hats, until they started wearing them silk hats. They pitched in with me, said they had nothin' better to do, and here we are."

Callum nodded. "You're sure a welcome sight. If you saw Ma, then you know about Pa."

Floyd pulled his hat off and combed his thick gray hair back with his hand. He shook his head, stared at a dog sleeping at the bottom of the boardwalk, and said, "Yep, she told me. I always figgered he'd die behind a danged plow.

"Come on," he said, putting the beat-up hat back on his head. "Let's go inside, where we can talk. I'll meet you up with my pards."

# 21

The three men went into the saloon, Floyd leading. He walked straight to the bar, where two old and dirty mountain men stood arguing. The city patrons were giving them plenty of room.

The shorter man was shaking his finger in the face of the other one, who towered over him. The tall man stood at least six feet four inches in his moccasins.

"Boys," Floyd said as they walked up, "it don't matter when the last time was that you been to Fort Smith."

The short one turned to Floyd, while the taller man picked up his drink and knocked it back. "Floyd, Morg here insists on arguing with me. I know we ain't been to Fort Smith nigh on to ten years. He says different. One of these days, I'll get fed up and leave. Yessir, just flat leave."

"You ain't gonna leave," the tall man said. "Who'd listen to yore whiny voice?" He looked at the bartender, pointed at the empty bottle, and held up his glass. The bartender nodded and handed over another bottle. Morg slapped down a buck and two bits.

"All right, boys, settle down. I want you to meet another one of my nephews."

"Heaven help us, Floyd," the short one complained. "How many kin you have in this town?"

"Shorty, shut-up," Floyd said. He turned to Callum and Frank. "The tallest thing about the short one, is his name. Meet Archibald Leander Zebulon the third, but to save time, just call him Shorty. It's a whole lot easier. The tall one is Morgan James. He goes by Morg." Floyd placed his hand on Callum's shoulder. "This here is my nephew Callum, and the other gent is Frank.

"Now that's done. Morg, grab the bottle." Floyd made eye contact with the bartender. "We need four glasses, and this feller"—he indicated Callum—"needs a sarsaparilla."

The bartender nodded, and the five men walked to a table near the front door and sat.

Morg looked Callum over. "You're mighty handy with your fists."

Callum turned to Floyd. "You were at the fight?"

Floyd grinned. "Yep, and a mighty good fight it was—profitable, too."

"Danged sure was," Shorty said.

"Yep," added Morg.

Callum looked around the men. Even Frank was grinning. "You all bet on me?"

The four nodded, and Frank said, "I bet all of my stake, four hundred dollars. I ain't never had this much money."

Callum shook his head. "I could have lost."

"No, boy," Floyd said. "Yore pa ain't raised no loser. I done told these fellers about you gettin' shot at the ranch. They didn't figger on you losin' either. You done staked all of us mighty big."

"Now, let me tell you why we was there. Your ma told us what was happening, so we rode down there to make sure you had a fair fight. But it looked like Captain Hill and Frank, here, had everything under control."

"You know Hill?" Callum asked.

"Danged right we do," Shorty said. "He's been known to stake a man who's down on his luck."

Floyd nodded. "He helped us out a couple of times. Course, he made a bundle off our trapping, but he trusted us. He's a good man.

"So tell me what happened to my brother."

The banter between Shorty and Morg settled down as Callum began to tell the tale of his pa's death.

As he told it, Floyd's jaws clenched, and the muscles could be seen working under the sun-baked skin. When Callum finished, it was quiet around the table.

Finally, Floyd said, "So you killed 'em?"

"Yes, Bret and me. They'll not be harming anyone else."

"Did you kill their pa?"

Callum looked at the cold blue eyes of his uncle. "No. His badge was taken, and he lost his sons. I figured that was enough."

"It ain't. You done good, as far as you went. But if you want to kill a snake, you got to cut off the head. He spawned that brood, and he needs to die."

"Someone else'll have to take care of it," Callum said. "I don't see myself ever going back there."

"Mark my words," Floyd said, "you won't have to. You killed his boys. Even a worthless piece of trash like Pickering will find the nerve to come out here and try to kill you."

"He's got to make it across a lot of country," Callum said.

Avery Simpson walked through the doors of the saloon, stopped, spotted Callum, and came straight to his table. "I was told you were here. I didn't realize you drank." He looked uneasily at Floyd and his friends.

"What can I do for you, Mr. Simpson?" Callum asked.

Simpson looked around the table at the disheveled mountain men. "Could we have a few moments of privacy?"

Callum leaned back in his chair. He was getting fed up with

this holier-than-thou businessman. "Simpson, if you have something to say, then say it. Otherwise, leave us alone."

Simpson's discomfort was visible to anyone who took a moment to examine the nervous man. He paused and looked at each of them. "I think you were right. I believe that Hughes is up to something. I don't know what it is, but he is certainly going to do something, and it won't be good."

"Simpson," Callum said, "I've been telling you and your friends that for the whole trip, but you chose to ignore it. Now it's time to fish or cut bait, and it looks like you don't know what to do." Callum paused to take a drink of his sarsaparilla. Then he slowly returned the glass to the table. Looking up at the man, he said, "The answer is to elect someone else as wagon master."

"I don't think we have the votes."

"Then you have two choices. Stick with him, or form another company with those that agree with you."

"That's why I'm here. We have no one to lead us, and we have no earthly idea how to get to Oregon."

Callum looked at his uncle, who was watching him intently. He turned back to Simpson. This wasn't a bad man—a little pompous, maybe somewhat self-righteous—but not bad, and what he was doing took courage. If Hughes got wind of Simpson's continued pursuit of an answer, he might have him killed.

Callum let out a sigh, took another sip of his drink, and watched Simpson fidget. "All right, Avery, what did you have in mind?"

The words rushed from the man's mouth. "We want you to lead us. You are not afraid of Mr. Hughes. In fact, you have already beaten him and killed one of his men."

At the mention of a man being killed, Floyd looked at his nephew, and then his pardners. A silent glance passed between them.

Callum caught the look, turned to his uncle, and said, "One of his men tried to murder me in my room, with two of the boys sleeping in there. I threw him off the side of the boat—in front of the paddlewheel."

A smile tugged at the corner of Floyd's mouth, while the other two mountain men looked at each other and nodded.

"Avery," Callum began, "I am only going to Colorado, and—"

"Please, Mr. Logan. We have no other person to turn to. We have families that are dependent on us. We pulled up stakes, sold our homes, our businesses, we're committed, but now we're afraid that we will be robbed—or worse."

Callum shook his head. He was tired of being responsible for other people. He'd had too many of those he was responsible for die in the war. He didn't want another person who was depending on him to die.

After a long silence, Floyd said, "Maybe we can help." He looked at his pardners, and they at least showed an interest.

Callum looked at his uncle, sighed, and turned back to Simpson. "Sit down, Avery."

Simpson wasted no time in pulling a chair from another table and sliding it up to theirs. Floyd started to say something, and Callum held up his hand.

"Avery," Callum asked, "when can your group be ready?"

A look of hope settled on the beleaguered man. "We can be ready soon, maybe two weeks."

"Won't work," Morg chimed in. "You"re already too late. There'll be snow in the mountains in September. You get caught up there in the winter, and you'll all be just as dead as if this Hughes shot you."

Simpson looked stricken and leaned toward Callum. "Mr. Logan, is this true?"

"If any of these three men," he said as he nodded to the three mountain men, "say it's true, then you can bank it." Floyd and Shorty nodded.

"Then we're trapped in Fort Smith until next year."

"Mr. Simpson, my name is Floyd Logan. I'm Callum's uncle. We might be able to work something out, but you've got to get your wagons ready sooner than two weeks, and you must expect to winter on the eastern side of the mountains. That means Denver City, Colorado City, or Pueblo. Personally, I'd recommend Pueblo. Farther south, a little warmer."

Simpson looked at Floyd, growing more agitated. "Mr. Logan, first, I don't know how we can be ready sooner. We each need two wagons for all of our furniture and supplies. So if that's ten families, we're looking at twenty wagons. Second—"

"I'm gonna talk straight to you, Mr. Simpson," Floyd interrupted. "You're not gonna be taking furniture over those mountains. You ain't never seen mountains like you're gonna have to cross. There'll be places that we'll have to lower everything by rope—wagons, mules, horses, and people. The more stuff you have, the harder it'll be. You'll see the trail lined with other folks' furniture that they decided they could do without. Not only do you need to get rid of that heavy furniture, you got to cut your wagon requirements in half—"

"That's impossible! We have heirlooms that must be taken, and Mr. Hughes assured us, they would be no problem."

Floyd leaned back and crossed his arms. "Go with Hughes, then. I'm tellin' you how it can be done. If you think you can do it better, this conversation is over."

The businessman sat with his hands in his lap and his head down. His voice was almost a whisper. The other men around the table could hardly hear him. "Our wives will be devastated."

His voice hard, Floyd said, "Better devastated than dead."

Simpson looked across at Floyds sun-baked, wrinkled face. He looked at the long knife scar that ran along the man's jawline. Then his eyes traveled to the older man's big, brown hands covered with scars.

"Do you think we could make it, Mr. Logan?" Simpson asked.

Floyd looked to his pardners, who had ridden and trapped and survived freezing winters, blistering deserts, and Indian attacks with him for over thirty years. They shrugged their shoulders.

He turned back to Simpson. "We might make it, but it won't be this season. I won't sugarcoat this. It'll be hard. The winter ain't gonna be no cakewalk. Besides bringing too much weight, the big mistake you've made is leaving when you did. You should've been rolling out of here in April. Waiting this long guarantees you'll die if you try to start across those mountains this year."

Simpson turned back to Callum. "Will you go?"

"I've told you, no." Callum thought of wintering again at the ranch, but this year with almost all of the family in a warm house. It would be good to be back at the home he helped build, and with everyone inside, on those cold mountain nights. He was sure there was still much work to be done, and his strong back would be welcome. He knew, with Floyd, Morg, and Shorty, the wagon train would be in good hands. "It's still no. I've got to take care of my family, but you can't do better than with these three."

"Then it's settled," Floyd said. "Now all you've got to do is convince your people and your wife to give up a wagon's worth of goods, and do it now. Do you have your wagons and supplies purchased?"

Exasperated, Simpson said, "We just got here."

"Then you better get busy. One other thing, we ain't doing this out of the kindness of our hearts. You're gonna have to feed us, provide us extra mounts, and pay us five hundred U. S. dollars—a piece."

Simpson looked at Floyd in surprise. "But—"

"You didn't expect them to do this for free, did you?" Callum asked.

"Well, no, but that's a lot of money."

"Mister, if that's the way you look at it," Floyd said, "then you can find your own way to Oregon, or go with your Mr. Hughes."

"But we've already paid Hughes."

Callum stood. The others followed. "Avery, we're located west of town. We're heading out in three days. That'll be Friday. That's your deadline. If you're there, you've got the men you need to show you the way. If we don't see you, we'll know you decided against it." Callum picked up his hat, slapped it on his head, and marched out the door, followed by the others, Shorty bringing up the rear.

Floyd stopped as he came even with Simpson. "If you decide you want us, ride out and let us know. We'll help you get ready. If not, luck to you."

Callum was mounted when Floyd came through the door. "Uncle, you figgerin' on stayin' in town, or joinin' us at the wagons?"

"Lead the way, boy. We wouldn't know what to do with an inside bed. We been sleepin' under the stars for too long."

"I'd know," Shorty said.

Morg had swung up on the back of his big buckskin. "Stop your bellyachin', Shorty. Don't you want to eat somethin' besides my cookin'?"

Shorty almost leaped into the saddle. "Callum, your ma a good cook?"

Callum looked over at the short, wide-shouldered mountain man. "Only if you like biscuits that float right off your plate."

Frank swung up on his mount and pulled up next to Shorty. "I'll tell you something else. Rebecca makes the finest doughnuts I've ever tasted."

"Bear sign! All I need to know," Shorty said. "Who needs a city bed?" He shoved his left hand under his buckskin shirt, scratched for a moment, and pulled out a tiny insect, popping it between his thumb and forefinger. "Those beds probably got bedbugs, anyway."

Callum looked over at Floyd. He shrugged, and both men shook their heads as they all rode west out of Fort Smith.

An hour later, they came upon a clearing on the north side of the river. It was large enough for the wagons and a rope corral for the animals. Ma had led the wagons into the clearing, and when Callum arrived, smoke was rising from the cooking fire, where Kate was helping get supper together. Bret and Colin had dug a pit, similar to the one they had at home. Ma saw them coming and walked over to Callum.

"Well, son, you don't look good, but you look better than I expected. I take it you whipped Mr. Hughes."

Floyd spoke up. "Rebecca, you should have seen yore son. He whipped that big galoot something fierce. Course, there for a little bit, it were lookin' a little chancy."

"Good fight," Morg said.

"Well, you men get down. You're just in time to eat. I got some chickens in town, so we got a big pot of chicken and dumplings."

The five men climbed down from their horses and led them to the river. After the animals had had their fill, they were turned loose in the makeshift corral and given some oats.

"Callum," Ma called. "You come on over here and let me clean up that face."

He walked over to where she in her rocking chair, and knelt down beside her. She took his hat off, laid it on the ground, and ran her fingers through his brown, curly hair. Then she gently examined the deep cut just in front of his ear and below the hairline, and his split ear.

"Son, you always did have the thickest hair. If you're like your pa, you'll have it till you die. Now, lean over here and let me look at these."

After examining the cuts, she said, "It's going to take some stitching. When I saw them, I thought they might."

She had a bowl of water and a cloth of clean white muslin, along with needle and thread. She took her time cleaning the cuts. Callum rested his head on the arm of the chair and let his mind drift. *Her hands feel good. Makes me think I'm ten years old. It'll be good to have her at the ranch, where we can take care of her for a change. Just a little payback for all she's done.*

The sharp pinch of the needle caused him to wince and then he caught himself. Her hands moved deftly, having sewn up many a wound. She finished, cleaned the remaining scratches and bruises, and then spread some of her special ointment on them.

She smiled at Callum. "Now you go get something to eat," she urged, gently pushing him away.

He stood, looking down on the woman who had given him life, her hair graying and wrinkles starting to appear where once there had been smooth skin. Softly he said, "Thanks, Ma," before he turned and headed back to the fire.

Bret, Colin, and Virgil had dragged a couple of large logs near the wagons, providing enough sitting room for everyone. In between them, they had built another firepit.

"You look a sight," Kate said, handing Callum a bowl of chicken and dumplings, along with a couple of biscuits.

He grinned at his sister. "You're looking mighty fine, Kate."

She pushed a loose strand of blonde hair behind her ear and smiled at him.

"I told her," Floyd said, "if we have more folks join up, she's liable to be hitched fore we get to the ranch."

She turned to Floyd, her hand holding the big ladle propped against her right hip. "Uncle Floyd, I'm not interested in anything concerning marriage. I want to get to the ranch, see my new nephew, and start mixing these Morgans with something like that." She pointed to Shoshone standing in the corral.

Floyd nodded knowingly. "We'll see how important those horses are when some boy takes your eye."

Ma came walking back to the fire. "Floyd, quit teasing your

niece, or I'll take that ladle away from her and take after you with it."

He grinned at his sister-in-law and ducked his head. "Yes, ma'am. Anything you say."

Floyd leaned toward Callum, the humor on his face disappearing. "We've got to talk about what we saw west of here."

# 22

Silence fell upon the Logan encampment. The horses had settled in for the night, and only the sound of grass being ripped from the ground and chewed, drifted across the campsite.

"First," Floyd said, "I've got to tell you about the Indian problem. Seems almost every tribe west of the Verdigris River has blood in their eyes. We're gonna have a fight on our hands out West."

"Danged right," Shorty said. "Plenty of ammunition and gumption, that's what's gonna be needed. Without either, yore scalp'll be hanging on some big Injun's lance for sure."

"I wouldn't put it quite as colorfully as Shorty, but he's right. We want to make sure everyone has at least three hundred rounds for rifles and plenty of powder and ball for the handguns."

Callum stretched out his long legs and nodded. "Yep. We're covered there."

Morg turned to Floyd. "If those pilgrims go with us, we best make sure they understand powder and ball goes before their beloved furniture." Morg looked over at Ma Logan. "Thanky ma'am. This be mighty fine chicken and dumplings. Why, it's just plain scrumptious."

Ma ducked her head to Morg and smiled. "Thank you, Mr. James, I'm glad you like it. However, I suggest you save room for the peach cobbler that Kate cooked up. You don't want to miss that."

"No, ma'am, I sure don't, and I reckon calling me Mr. James is like calling a pig a gentleman. We ain't neither. So you just call me Morg, if you don't mind."

Ma smiled again at the man. "Why, I'm sure you are a gentlemen, Morg, and thank you."

Floyd looked impatiently at Morg. "If I can continue, the Injuns ain't the only problem."

Shorty's head bobbed up and down in agreement. "He ain't kiddin."

This time Shorty got the look from Floyd, but he was not the type to stay quiet. "You ain't got no call to put that stare on me. I got just as much right to say so as anybody."

"Yes," Floyd said, "and you exercise that right way too much."

Shorty snorted and turned to Morg. "Danged if he ain't got more crotchety in his old age."

Morg just kept on eating.

Floyd looked around the camp, to see everyone grinning. He winked at Kate. "See what I've got to put up with? He ain't changed for thirty years." Then he turned back to Callum. "About ten days west of here, along the Arkansas, we ran across a camp of about twenty white men. We seen their smoke quite a ways off and figured to ride in and get a taste of somebody else's cookin' and some coffee."

He stopped long enough to take a couple of bites of the dumplings, looked at Ma Logan, nodded, and winked. "Mighty good, Rebecca. Those folks weren't exactly tryin' to hide. Guess they figured there was enough of them that no Injuns would bother. They have no idea how wrong they are. I've seen them

Injuns gather up three, four hundred braves when they go on a warpath. Sometimes different villages join together, makin' them mighty threatening.

"So, like we always do, we pulled up on the backside of a hill, eased to the top, and looked 'em over. First thing we noticed, weren't no women in that bunch. They're plannin' something. What you've told me about this here Hughes feller, he could be the head man. It looks like he's put together a mess of well-to-do businessmen and convinced 'em the grass is greener in Oregon. But I'm bettin' he's plannin' on them not even making it out of Indian Territory.

"Morg's seen it done before in Kansas. Raiders leave sign like Injuns, kill everyone, and expect they ain't gonna be found out. Someone always talks or makes a mistake, and they do git found out. Makes for a right good necktie party. But I bet that's what this here Hughes has planned."

Callum finished his dumplings, cleaned his plate, and followed Bret to the cobbler. The aroma from the cooked peaches and cinnamon made his mouth water. He cut through the thick crust with the large spoon and dished himself a helping and returned to his seat on the log. After sitting, he took a bite of the dessert.

It was delicious, but his mind hardly registered the taste as it worked on the problem of the men and women under Hughes's leadership. The man was leading those folks to certain death. He looked first at Morg and Shorty, then turned back to his uncle. "So what do you think we should do?"

Floyd looked disgusted. "As much as I want nothing to do with those folks, someone has got to look after them, at least get them through this Hughes mess. I won't fault you if you take the family on to the ranch, but you've got to wonder if that bunch would even let you through without attackin'. Specially with only two wagons."

Callum thought on it for a moment. "I'm thinking the smart

thing is to join up with those folks and take everyone through. I'm still not going to Oregon, but you boys have already committed, so the rest is up to you."

Everyone had been sitting around listening to the conversation. Ma Logan spoke up. "I couldn't live with myself if we left those folks to be slaughtered when we could do something about it. That's just not the Christian thing to do."

Frank added, "I'm with your ma. Callum, we've already had a taste of what Hughes is capable of. They may not know it, but those folks need our help."

"Yep, me too," Ezra joined in.

Callum looked at the rest of his family and Virgil. Kate, Bret, and Colin nodded. Virg spoke up. "I reckon most folks here know my family was murdered by Hughes, at least by his men. Also, I've heard cowmen talking, and I know what riding for the brand means. I'm with you."

Callum glanced back down at his plate. The cobbler was gone. With all that was going on, he didn't even remember eating it. He looked up, his eyes moving to everyone, stopping for a moment and then moving on. Finally, he said, "Thanks, Ma. I think you voiced it for all of us. Virg, I appreciate your loyalty. So that's settled. Let's get some rest and start planning in the morning." He stood.

Everyone else stood and moved over to the big iron pot of water Ma had boiling over the fire, dropping their metal plates into the pot. Colin walked up to Callum. Just in the past couple of months since Callum had been home, Colin had grown taller and wider in the shoulders.

"Callum," Colin said, "will there be fighting?"

"I reckon."

Colin nodded. "Thanks." He turned and, with Frank, Kate, Ezra, and Bret, headed for the corral to get the animals watered. Callum watched Colin go, concern clouding his mind like an early morning fog. Did he see a glint of anticipation in Colin's eyes? After a moment, he decided it was only reflections from the fire.

The three mountain men were standing around Ma when he walked up. She was saying, "There's going to be fighting, isn't there?"

"Likely will be, Rebecca," Floyd said. "I ain't seein' no way they won't attack those carrying all that money."

"You can bet on it, ma'am," Shorty said. "You don't get that many gunmen together for a church social. I'm sure they ain't planning on leavin' nary a soul alive, be it man, woman, or child."

Morg, towering over everyone else, shook his head. "That's gospel, ma'am. All we or them settlers can do is be ready."

Callum stepped in. "And to get ready, we need to be rested. But first, I'm thinkin' we best start standing watch. Floyd, you take the first, then Shorty, and I'll take the last."

"You done been in a big fight, boy." Morg said. "I'll take one of those, so you can sleep."

"Morg," Callum said, not wanting to embarrass the old mountain man, "you've had a couple of drinks today. I just thought you might be tired."

"Him, tired?" Shorty piped up. "I've seen Morg down a bottle of rotgut and never slow down." He glanced at Ma Logan, and touched his hat, "Pardon, ma'am, I'm mostly used to bein' around men."

Ma placed a hand on Shorty's arm. "You needn't apologize to me, Mr. Zebulon. Though I and my late husband, Matthew, did not drink, we were around plenty of folks, including family, that did. I don't hold to it, but I don't condemn people for it either."

Callum grinned at Floyd. Shorty would spend days trying to figure out whether he had been forgiven or reprimanded. "Well then, Morg, you take the last watch, and I'll get some rest. I'll admit to being a little sore."

They all chuckled, and Morg said, "I'm just bettin' you are. Glad to do it."

"Goodnight, Ma," Callum said. He picked up his bedroll and spread it under the stars, twinkling down at him like diamonds. After taking off his guns and removing his boots, he leaned back against the saddle, placed his hat next to him, and made sure his guns were loose in the holsters. He rolled over on his side, winced from his bruised ribs, and was asleep before anyone else spread their blankets.

THE SOUND of running hooves jarred Callum from his sleep. Automatically, he reached for a Remington. In the false dawn of the morning, a horseman could be seen against the lightening sky in the east. He was riding hard out, straight for the camp. Callum glanced around to see Morg standing, waiting, a rifle in the crook of his arm. The other men were in varied states of dress, all with guns in their hands.

He took a moment to pull his boots on, forgetting to check them. Quickly, he reached down for his hat, and then swung the gunbelt around his waist. By this time, the rider was arriving in camp. It was Avery Simpson.

The merchant jumped from his horse. He stopped for a moment, looking around. Recognizing Callum, he ran to him. "Kelly Thompson has been murdered!"

Everyone was now up and gathering around.

"Do you know how it happened?" Callum said.

"Yes, it was in public. In the Arkansas Saloon. One of Cassidy's men killed Mr. Thompson in cold blood."

"Slow down, Avery." Callum turned to Virg, who, along with everyone, else was hanging on every word. "Virg, would you take care of Mr. Simpson's horse?"

"Yes, sir." Virg stepped up and took the reins from Simpson.

"I'll help," Colin said.

As the boys walked away with the horse, Kate came up with a

cup of coffee, handing it to Simpson. He took it from her, his hands shaking. “Thank you. I need this.”

“Now, Avery,” Callum said, “relax, take a deep breath, and tell us what happened.”

“Yes, you’re right.” Simpson took a couple of deep breaths, sipped his coffee for a moment, and began. “Kelly Thompson is the son of a very prominent citizen of Memphis. He came back from school to join his father in running their large department store. Kelly was a privileged individual, if you know what I mean.” At this point Simpson looked around at his audience, but only Ma was nodding.

He went on. “He was spoiled. His mother died when he was born, and his father doted on him. He always got everything he wanted. As a man, he was almost insufferably prideful. He would brook no disagreement and always said exactly what he was thinking. He could be quite rude.”

Simpson had seated himself on one of the logs. He looked up at Kate, who was standing. “This coffee is quite good, thank you.”

She smiled back at him.

He continued. “Kelly wanted to go West. His father is a very dignified man and looked up to in Memphis. I’m sure the boy wanted to prove himself on his own. His father not only allowed, but encouraged him to strike out on his own, and to hear Kelly tell it, gave him quite a bit of cash to start with.

“He decided to join our group, and has been speaking harshly of Mr. Hughes and Mr. Cassidy. Though his wife was against it, he accompanied Nathan Priest to the saloon. He and the bartender told me everything. From what he said, Kelly was very loud with his harsh comments. They came to the attention of Cassidy’s man. I think they call him Flatnose, for the obvious reason. Anyway, there were words exchanged. When we boarded the riverboat in Memphis, Kelly put on a beautifully tooled gunbelt made for him in Memphis, along with a specially made silver Colt with ivory handles. He was very proud of it.”

Shorty grew impatient, turned away from the group, and spit a long brown stream of tobacco juice, wiped his mouth on his sleeve, and cleared his throat. Simpson stopped talking and looked up at the old mountain man.

"Mister," Shorty said, "I ain't meaning to be disrespectful of the dead, but could you just get to the point? How'd this feller git shot?"

Simpson looked around at the group and back to Callum. "Sorry, I guess I got carried away. This Flatnose was standing at the other end of the bar from Kelly. The man, just in a normal tone, said, 'You're a liar.' From what I heard, Kelly turned and asked him what he said, and Flatnose said it again and called him a yellow-livered coward. Then he told Kelly to draw or apologize. The bartender said that Kelly had turned white as a new sheet. Then he started fumbling for his silver gun. He had to take the leather thong off that keeps it in the holster, but he finally got it out. All this time, Flatnose was just standing there, smiling and waiting. He hadn't even drawn his gun.

"Nathan said it wasn't until Kelly started to bring his gun up that Flatnose drew. His speed was disquieting. He shot Kelly four times. The poor boy was shot in the chest, a leg, and both arms. Flatnose laid his gun on the bar and told the bartender to get him another drink and get the sheriff. He then turned to Nathan and said, 'A tenderfoot would be smart to keep his mouth shut.'"

"That's gospel," Morg said. Everybody looked up at him. He continued. "Makes no sense for any man to be talkin' out of turn unless he's ready to back it up. Looks like your Mr. Thompson ain't had the sense the good Lord gave a buffalo calf. What'd the sheriff say?"

"Mr. Morg," Simpson said, "Kelly was a brash and arrogant young man, but he didn't deserve to die."

"Lots of folks don't deserve to die, Mr. Merchant Man, but they do. Out here, it hastens death along if you're loose-lipped. Now, what did the sheriff say?"

Simpson turned back to Callum. "He ruled the murder was self-defense."

Callum nodded. "What would you have us do, Avery? Certainly it was a murder, but a murder condoned by the law, since Flatnose didn't shoot until Thompson had his gun out. Like Morg said, this is a hard country, and you must be cautious about what you do or say, unless you are prepared to back it up."

"But, Mr. Logan, that is so unfair. This was obviously murder. The taking of a life, a man with a wife and a future. The law should do something about it."

Callum stood and Simpson followed. "The law's hands are tied, but I'm surprised he didn't post Flatnose out of town."

"Oh, yes, he did that. He told the man to be out of Fort Smith by this morning."

"That's all he could do," Callum said. "It was a fair fight. Do you know if he left?"

"I didn't see him around town when I came out here, so he may have."

"All right, again, Avery, what would you have us do?"

The storekeeper looked around the group, his frustration obvious. Finally, he held his hands out to Callum, palms up, and in desperation, said, "I don't know, something."

Callum looked at the empty, imploring hands, then turned his hard eyes to Simpson. "The question is, what are your people going to do?"

Surprised, Simpson said, "Us? We're not gunfighters."

"Neither are we," Callum said. "We just know how and when to defend ourselves. Didn't you say you were in the war? Aren't there others of you that fought?"

"Well, yes, but that was the war. It's peacetime now."

"It's not peacetime out here. When you leave Fort Smith, the defense of you and your family from Indians, raiders, and gunfighters, ain't gonna come from a policeman or sheriff. It's gonna come from you. If you and your people can't handle that, now's the time to head back to Memphis and live a nice, quiet life, 'cause you won't find it out West. If that's what you're looking for out here, you'll have to build it and fight for it. It's up to you."

Callum watched the man process what he had been told. It was a lot to digest. Hughes had probably filled them all with the idea of how easy this was going to be. Most of them probably knew better, but clung to that hope. It was human nature. Now Simpson and his group had a decision to make, and he didn't much care which way they went. His family came first. They were loaded and ready to roll. It would be safer with a larger group against the raiders who waited out to the west, but if necessary, they could take the southern route, though when they turned north it would put them in Comanche country for a longer time. He waited for Simpson to make up his mind.

# 23

Virg and Colin returned with Simpson's horse. He looked over at the boys. "Thank you."

They nodded, sensing the tension around the camp, looked at each other, shrugged, and headed over to see what Ma Logan had prepared for breakfast. She saw their movement.

"Boys, I need some more water."

They picked up the buckets, one in each hand, and headed back to the river.

"Mr. Simpson," she said, "why don't you stay for breakfast?"

Simpson had been deep in thought, but he responded quickly to Ma. "Thank you, ma'am, but I've got to get back. We have a lot to do if we're leaving tomorrow." He looked at Callum, then, turning, at Floyd, Morg, and Shorty. "If we're going with you."

He thrust out his hand to Callum. "Thank you. You cleared things up for me. Though we lost, we fought that war for our freedom and can do no less now. I'll speak with the others. I believe the majority will be deciding to accompany you. Hughes is going to be mightily upset. I doubt that we'll get the money back we've already paid him."

Floyd spoke up. "At least you'll have a chance of keeping the rest of your possessions and your lives. You'll need to elect a wagon master. Here's a list of goods you'll need. These are the basics for one person, but with everything, you don't want those wagons weighing over two thousand pounds."

Simpson looked at the list. One hundred eighty pounds of flour, one hundred pounds of bacon, twenty pounds of salt, three pounds of soap, and three hundred rounds for rifles, fifty pounds of gunpowder and twenty pounds of lead.

"That's per person. The rifle ammunition is per rifle, and I'd recommend you have at least two repeating rifles per wagon and one handgun. If you want more, just stay below the weight limit."

Simpson nodded as he read. "Yes, this is about what we figured for our basic food needs. We'll add the weapons. I imagine there will be more than one handgun per wagon."

"Then adjust your powder and lead accordingly. Include at least one, and if you've got the weight, two water barrels. Sometimes it can get mighty dry on the prairie. Have you got your wagons yet?"

"Yes, we bought them yesterday, built in Fort Smith. They seem to be quite sturdy. My wife, along with many of the others, is buying the supplies. Hopefully she will be able to barter some of the furniture we're leaving behind."

Simpson looked up from the list. "They weren't very happy about doing away with one wagon. They're all saying that your family has two."

"I understand," Floyd said, "but be sure and tell them these wagons ain't going over all those mountain ranges. If they was, we'd have one."

"Yes, I see what you mean. That point will certainly help."

"One more question," Floyd said. "Who do you think they'll elect for wagon master?"

At the question, Simpson looked down at the ground and back up at Floyd. "It looks like they may elect me. I've told them I know nothing about being a wagon master, but many are insisting. They say I can learn from you and the others."

Callum spoke up. "They're right. You couldn't have better teachers than Floyd, Morg, and Shorty. By the time you get to Oregon, you'll be a seasoned veteran. Do you need any help from us?"

Simpson thought for a moment. "I think it would be a big help if you came to town, all of you, if you can." He looked at the mountain men and Callum. "I feel sure we will have some problem with Cassidy's men. We'll stand up for ourselves, but I think your presence would help."

"We'll be there," Callum said. "You head on back, and we'll be in as soon as we eat. Don't confront Hughes or any of his men."

HUGHES WAS SITTING at his desk in the suite he and Sabrina occupied. His eyes were wide, and his face was red. His big, bruised hands gripped the carved edge of the desk so hard it looked like he would leave indentations.

"What the hell do you mean? You had to do it? Why did you have to do it? He was just shooting off his mouth. I could have handled that! You have no idea how badly you have messed up this deal."

Jack "Flatnose" Blake and George Cassidy were on their feet on the opposite side of the desk. The only indication of emotion from Cassidy was the corner of his left eye that had a tic popping every few seconds. That only happened to the gunfighter when he was seething. Right now, he felt like sticking the muzzle of one of his Colt revolvers in Jack's ear and pulling the trigger. This plan had taken a long time to pull together, and as much as he hated Hughes and the man's daughter, it was a good plan, and his cut would go a long way to getting out of this business. With the Hughes' cut added to his, he could retire for sure, and that had been the plan. But now this young pup had riled all of those settlers, and maybe muddied up the whole deal.

"What are we going to do, Papa?" Sabrina said. "This itchy-fingered idiot has messed up everything!"

Flatnose turned a cold, cruel gaze on Sabrina. "You've got a nasty mouth, missy. You best be careful, or someone might slap it shut for you."

Cassidy started to tell Hughes to put a rein on his daughter, when she shoved her dainty little hand into her reticule and yanked a single-barrel, forty-one-caliber, Philadelphia Deringer out. "Wait!" Cassidy yelled.

Unfortunately, she gave no sign of hearing anything. Her rage focused on the young gunfighter, Flatnose.

It was obvious the girl had always had her way, her father and other men deferring to her every whim. Though she had been around the eastern criminal element, her father had always kept her away from the killers he dealt with, until they came out West. From her determined, angry stare, it was obvious she was intent on putting a forty-one-caliber lead pill into Flatnose.

Cassidy knew the younger man. He was bloodthirsty. He had been that way since he was young. As a boy, he had delighted in torturing cats or dogs, or any small wild animal he might catch.

There was the time Cassidy returned home from a robbery and Jack, about eleven years old at the time, was sitting on the porch of the old rundown shack that doubled as a hideout. Every once in a while he would look around the corner of the house and giggle, then go back to whittling. Cassidy had walked around to the back, with Jack following. There, in the hot Kansas sun, a great horned owl was staked to the ground with a cord around one of its legs. The bird's body was red as a painted woman's lips, as it stood there blinking, staring up at him. The boy had plucked every feather from the owl's body. As tough and mean as he was, it made him sick. He whipped out his revolver and put the bird out of its misery. The kid wouldn't talk to him for a week. Now,

Sabrina was drawing a gun on him. The thought dashed through his mind, *He's gonna kill her. She'll never get that gun up in time.*

He watched everything play out in slow motion. The Deringer coming out of her reticule, gripped in her small, white hand, the young skin pulled tight around her tiny knuckles. Jack's face, a smile on it, as his hand smoothly dropped to the butt of his revolver, gripping it. It slipped from the holster easy like and started tilting up, the angle of his barrel decreasing quickly, while the girl's was still pointing toward the floor. Cassidy saw the kid's thumb pull the hammer back as the gun rose in a practiced motion.

A high-pitched yell, almost a scream, came from Hughes. "No!"

But nothing was stopping this dance the two young people were locked in. The woman, moments before, had had her whole life ahead of her, but now, from the shock on her face, it was clear she recognized that life was only ticks-of-the-clock away from an abrupt end. Her left hand thrust out in front of her, as if to stop the bullet that was surely coming, and before her gun ever came to bear on Flatnose, in desperation, she pulled the trigger, only a moment before Flatnose pulled his. The bullet she fired hurt nothing except the oak floor of the hotel, where it plowed a furrow between the legs of the kid.

Before the explosion of the Deringer had subsided, Flatnose's revolver blasted. Smoke leaped from the barrel and around the gun, momentarily hiding the damage the bullet caused to Sabrina's left breast, where it entered just above the bustline of her dress.

Her hand released the Deringer, and she whispered, "Papa."

Cassidy caught movement from Hughes. He looked over just in time to see the explosion from the pocket pistol in the man's hand. It was pointed at Flatnose, but it was time for Cassidy to stop observing and start thinking about himself. He drove his hand to his forty-four and whipped it from the holster. The corner of his eye saw Jack's head explode. Bits of brain, blood, and bone were thrown on the light blue wallpaper behind him. It appeared Hughes was turning the gun toward him, but Cassidy knew the big man was too late. He pulled the trigger three times in close succession, all three rounds slamming into the man's chest.

Hughes, his face brutally beaten and smashed from the match with Logan, relaxed in the big chair, his eyes on Cassidy. "I wasn't going to shoot you. We need each other."

Cassidy shook his head in regret over losing his partner before the deal was done. "I couldn't take the chance."

Hughes laid the gun on the desk. His breath rattled now. Cassidy could hear the wheezing coming from the holes in the man's lungs. Blood started to froth around his lips. He looked up at Cassidy one last time. "We would've been set for life." The last word hissed softly from the man's mouth and as head dropped to his chest, the door burst open.

The sheriff was in the lead. "Drop your gun, Cassidy!"

Cassidy leaned forward and laid his forty-four on the desk, careful to keep it out of the spreading pool of blood.

The sheriff looked around the smoke-filled room, taking in the carnage. "I've seen a lot, but I ain't never seen such in all my life."

The room had filled behind the lawman. There were gasps from the observers. One woman fainted and had to be carried out.

Moments later, racing steps could be heard on the stairs, then, "Let me through, blast it. Get out of my way."

The town doctor burst into the room and came to a sudden halt. He took in the sight and stood frozen. "Oh my heaven," he said, when his eyes fell on Sabrina. Breaking out of his spell, he first went to the girl, checked her, moved to Hughes, and finally, he looked at Flatnose. The top of the boy's head was missing. He turned abruptly to the sheriff. "You don't need me. They're all dead. I don't know what happened, but I'm glad I wasn't here." He turned abruptly and headed for the door.

"Doc," the sheriff called as the man was almost out of the room, "would you tell the undertaker I need him up here?"

"Be glad to. I think he likes dead bodies better than he does pulling teeth. I guess it pays better." The doctor's boots echoed as he went down the stairs, much slower than when he arrived.

The hotel manager had been standing just inside the door. "Sheriff, how long before these bodies are removed? I need to get this room cleaned up. There's a lot of people in town."

The sheriff shook his head, and with sarcasm dripping from his voice, said, "Well, George, I'm right sorry that you're put out, but you ain't gonna be rentin' no room until we get these bodies outta here. Now, if you want to hire some men to carry 'em down to the undertaker's place, then you go right ahead, but you make sure you respect this young lady, when you do."

George looked at the three bodies and thought for a moment. "No, Sheriff. I'll wait. They just need to be out of here before they start smelling."

The sheriff gave a curt nod, then turned to Cassidy. "Step back from that gun, and give me the one in your holster, also that derringer in your vest. Careful like."

Cassidy handed him the remaining Colt from his holster, along with the derringer he fished out of his front vest pocket.

"Turn around. You know where the jail is. You can head that way."

"Sheriff, I was just defending myself."

"Shut up, Cassidy. I know all about you. If you ain't got the most perfect story, your neck is gonna get stretched. Course, that'll be after the good people of Fort Smith find you guilty. Git along."

Walking out, the sheriff stooped and picked up the remaining Colt from the floor and thrust it behind his waistband next to the other two weapons.

"George," he said, "git these folks out of here, and keep the door closed until someone arrives for those bodies." After getting a nod from the manager, the sheriff disappeared down the stairs behind Cassidy.

"Is that Flatnose Blake those gents are carryin'?" Shorty pointed at the body being carried past them.

"Hat's sittin' a little low, but I reckon that's him," Morg replied.

Floyd and Callum looked at each other. "Wonder what happened here," Floyd said. "You figger our boy did that?"

Callum shook his head. "I doubt it. It looked like his head was darn near blown off. I can't picture Avery getting in a shot like that. I imagine it'd be just the opposite. Wait, look at the hotel. They're coming out with two more bodies."

The four men stopped. All around them people had moved closer, where they could see the procession of dead bodies.

Floyd watched the six men carrying Hughes. They had gotten an old door to lay him on. "Ain't that the feller you had the fight with?"

Callum shook his head. "Yep, it sure is. I wonder what went on."

The third body was also on a door, but this one was respectfully covered with a blanket. Her dress fell out each side of the blanket and off the door.

Shorty took off his hat, as the other men did when the body went by. "Somebody killed the girl too. That must have been a mighty wild gunfight."

The men moved their horses past the procession and gawking people to one of the general stores where the settlers were being outfitted. A lady walked from one of the wagons toward the store. "Pardon me, ma'am," Callum said. "Can you tell us where we could find Mr. Simpson?"

She looked the four men over and, recognizing Callum, said, "Yes, Mr. Callum. You will find Mr. Simpson inside the store."

"Thank you, ma'am," He said, swinging down from Shoshone.

The others followed and they made their way to a hitching post. The street was crowded with wagons waiting their turn for loading. Inside, the store was abuzz with conversation. People were gathered in small groups, animatedly discussing the killings.

Callum spotted Simpson in the back of the store surrounded by people. Simpson caught his eye and, obviously relieved, motioned him over. "Have you heard? Hughes, Sabrina, and Flatnose have all been killed. The only survivor is Cassidy. Can you believe that? We have no idea what happened, but all those who had decided to stay with Hughes are now wondering what they're going to do. They have no guides. They have nothing."

Floyd looked at his partners, and they both nodded. "Well, Mr. Simpson, if they'd like to go with us, they'll be welcome, if it's all right with you. Won't cost any more, cause we're goin' there anyway."

Simpson breathed a deep sigh of relief. "Thank goodness. I was hoping you would say that. I've talked to several of them, and they're all for joining up and us continuing together."

Callum was listening to the conversation. This was about him no more. Yes, his family would be with them, and he would work with Floyd and the other mountain men, but upon reaching Pueblo, he'd veer off and head to the ranch. He definitely wasn't going to Oregon, although he hadn't seen that country yet.

"Callum, I have a question for you," Simpson said. "Most of those folks that were going with Hughes, were figuring on leaving in a couple of weeks. Would you mind waiting a few more days?"

Floyd said nothing. He just stood watching Callum as he thought about it. They needed to get moving West. If they got caught in the early rains, the plains would be a quagmire. Mules couldn't drag a wagon far in that mess, and it would become impossible to even move. What if the snow started early? Granted, they weren't crossing the mountains, but the plains could get heavy snows and deadly blizzards. He'd heard Floyd talk about it, but these folks would need some time to put things together.

"How many days?"

Simpson gave him a pleading look. "A week?"

"No. We ain't waiting a week. I gave your bunch three days. I'll give the second group three days. We'll pull out Monday morning.

"How's that sound, Floyd?"

"Sounds fine." He turned back to Simpson. "I'm gonna call you Avery, and you call me Floyd. I ain't much with misters. I'd recommend that all your wagons be on the west side of town, lined up and ready to go Sunday afternoon. Then, when Monday morning gets here, we can just push off, nice and easy."

Shorty rolled his eyes at the "nice and easy" comment.

"All right. We'll try to be ready. By the way, Hughes had scheduled a meeting of everyone at the Fort Smith Civic Center for this afternoon at three. That might be a good time for everyone to meet you," Simpson looked at them hopefully.

"Floyd, I think that's actually a good idea," Callum said. "These folks need to hear some difficult words. They need to understand this is not going to be a picnic."

"You're right," Floyd said. "Be a good time, too, for election of officers. You need to get organized. Also, you got to do some paperwork before you leave Fort Smith. You'll need to draw up a constitution, rules for camping and traveling, drinking and gambling. I'd suggest no drinking or gambling when you're traveling."

Morg rolled his eyes.

Floyd ignored him. "You think they still want you for wagon master, Avery?"

"I think none of the other men want that position, so they'll be glad for me to undertake it."

"Yep, I know how that works," Floyd said. "Well, there's been quite a few trains leave from here. You might check with the sheriff or find an attorney around here. They may have a set of rules you could use for a guideline." Floyd looked around, then angled for the door. "I've got some things I need before we head out. See you this afternoon."

Morg, a glint in his eyes, smacked his lips and said, "Yeah, me too."

Callum followed the older men out of the store, knowing they were headed for the saloon.

# 24

At three o'clock, Callum walked into the civic center with all of the family, including the mountain men. Frank and Ezra had volunteered to stay with the wagons.

The center was packed. Surprised, he looked around. He figured there must be close to two hundred people, counting the kids, so that meant at least twenty wagons. It wouldn't be a big wagon train, but maybe big enough to keep the Indians away.

The noise was deafening. To think that these were all successful businessmen from Memphis and the outlying towns. Hughes must have been one heck of a salesman.

Avery Simpson was standing on a large crate at the front of the gathering. The few chairs and boxes available for sitting were being used by the older folks up front. The rest of the movers were standing. Callum saw him wave when they came in. "Avery's motioning us to the front," Callum said.

"Just what I wanted to do today," Shorty said, "talk to a bunch of sodbusters."

Morg looked down at Shorty. "For one thing, they ain't sodbusters, they're businessmen."

"Even worse."

"For the other, you ain't gonna be talking. We leave that up to Floyd and Callum."

Shorty looked like he was about to break out in an argument, then decided to say nothing, continuing toward Simpson.

Arriving at the front, Callum noticed several of the older women were sitting on crates. He turned to Bret. "Find Ma something to sit on."

Ma Logan took Bret's arm, while speaking to Callum. "I'm fine, boys. I'm perfectly capable of standing for a few hours."

Bret nodded to his ma and Callum smiled at her. "I reckon you are, Ma. No disrespect meant."

Her deep blue eyes crinkled at the corners as she returned her son's smile. "None taken, son."

Simpson motioned Callum and Floyd up next to the box he was standing on. He knelt down. "We were lucky. The sheriff had a constitution and set of by-laws with the number of recommended officials. We've already had the elections. These men standing to my left are the ones elected, two lieutenants, two sub-lieutenants, a constable, and a magistrate. The magistrate's a lawyer. I'll introduce you to them later."

Simpson stood and started waving his arms. The bedlam ended quickly and even the kids quieted down. "All right, folks. You've elected me wagon master and captain of this train. I've been honest with you and let you know that I have no experience, but will do my best. Most of you know Callum Logan, his mother and their family. The other gentleman standing next to me is Floyd Logan, Callum's uncle. He, along with his two friends will be our guides to Oregon."

A cheer lasting over a minute went up from the crowd. Simpson finally got them calmed down. Shorty basked in the shared spotlight.

"We'll see how much they're cheering," Floyd said to Callum, "after a few hundred miles on the trail."

"Floyd Logan," Simpson continued, "was the one that suggested drawing up the by-laws and the constitution. He has a few words for us. These men are highly experienced mountain men, so please listen to what he has to say."

Simpson turned and extended his hand to Floyd. The older man looked at it and, from a flat-footed position, jumped on top of the box, which stood at least two feet above the ground. A surprised murmur erupted from the people who could see what he had done. Once he was up, Simpson stepped down from the makeshift podium.

Floyd looked around the center, making eye contact with many of the people. A number of them held his gaze, while a few looked away. Callum knew his uncle was evaluating the people in the train. He didn't know their names, but now was the time to start learning their character. Floyd took another minute, then his voice boomed out to the people.

"My name's Floyd Logan. I been all over those mountains for the past thirty years. I don't know everything there is to know about that country, but what I don't know, my pards do. You'll get to know each of us. The tall feller is Morgan James. He answers to Morg. The not so tall, but wide-shouldered one is Shorty Zebulon."

A ripple of laughter flowed through the room. Shorty's jaw muscles worked a couple of times and then he was still.

"Let me address this right now to save some of you folks from gettin' hurt. If you're a bigger feller than Shorty, don't make the mistake of thinking you can take him on. There's Injuns and white men danged near twice his size who made that mistake. Their bones have been long past cleaned by the varmints."

The laughter ended like it had fallen off a cliff. People strained to see the short man.

Floyd waited for a moment and then continued. "Now, I ain't here to spin you no fairy tale. This trip you've decided to take ain't gonna be no picnic. I want you to look around at your neighbors.

If you're lucky, no more than about ten percent of you folks, that's about twenty people, I guesstimate, ain't gonna be around when you reach Oregon."

Another murmur traveled through the group. This one much more hushed. Men and women alike pulled their children closer.

"People die from all sorts of things on the trail, much like they do at home. You just have more opportunity to meet up with the Reaper out here."

Floyd went on for about twenty minutes then he stopped and looked around. "I reckon that's all I've got for now."

He turned and started to jump down. Someone in the crowd said, "Don't we get to ask some questions?"

Floyd stopped, looked for the speaker, and said, "Shore, say your piece." He found the speaker near the front, a tall man with hawkish features wearing a bowler hat.

"Are you worth five hundred dollars apiece?"

"What's your name, Mister?" Floyd said.

"I am Horace Bilington, with one L. I have been elected as lieutenant and first assistant to Captain Simpson."

"Well, Mr. Bilington, with one L," Floyd said, and several chuckles were heard throughout the large room, "do you know Indian sign language?"

Bilington stiffened at the laughter but shook his head, no.

"You ever fought an Indian or bandit?"

Again, the man shook his head.

"You know how to cross a river with your wagon?"

Again the head shake.

"Well, you may be a smart man when it comes to business, but it sounds like you don't know squat out here. So, yeah, I reckon I'm worth five hundred dollars, and if I hear much more of that kind of talk, I'm changing it to a thousand dollars a piece." He looked into the audience again, making eye contact with as many of the men as possible.

"We ain't planned to be guiding a bunch of greenhorns into

God's country. We're doing it to help you. As I've told Captain Simpson, if'n you're unhappy with us, just say the word, but say it now. 'Cause once we get started, you done committed and whether we ride one day or all the way to Oregon, you owe us our due.

"If there ain't no more questions, you men need to get to work with your wagons. We leave at seven—"

"I'm unhappy!" a harsh voice called from near the door in back of the room.

Floyd looked to the back, and people turned to see who the man was as boots echoed on the wooden floor. There were gasps from the surrounding people as they recognized the man, and his name was whispered among the people. "Cassidy."

Cassidy strolled up to Floyd, where he stood on the speaker's box, stared up at him, hooked his thumbs in his gunbelt, and said, "You must be the old, used-up mountain man I've been hearing about."

Floyd, while eyeing the gunfighter, saw Shorty drop his hand to his Bowie knife. He gave a small shake of his head and said, "Mister, your ma sure ain't taught you no manners, but that can be arranged anytime."

A slow smile spread across Cassidy's face. "I don't think there's much you can teach me, but I'm not here for you. I'm here to offer these folks salvation. Let me up there."

"You got something to say, Cassidy, you can speak your piece from down there," Floyd said.

Upon recognizing who had entered, Callum flipped the thongs from both of his guns and relaxed. He felt confident his uncle would need no help, but better to be safe.

Cassidy frowned for a moment, then turned to the settlers. "I think many of you know me. I was hired by the late Mr. Hughes to guide you to Oregon. He has already paid me, therefore I am duty bound and willing to fulfill my obligation."

"What about the killings?" someone yelled from the crowd.

Cassidy nodded. "That is for sure a fair question. I'll give it to you straight, just like I told the sheriff."

Shorty snorted.

Cassidy turned around, focusing his cold gray eyes on Shorty. The wide stump of a man locked and held the gunfighter's glare until the killer turned back around.

"As I was tryin' to say'," Cassidy continued, "the good sheriff turned me loose when he realized I only fired in self-defense. It was a horrible sight." He shook his head. "Poor Miss Hughes, just a sweet, innocent woman."

The gunfighter lowered his head and was quiet for a few moments. Then he looked up and said, "We all need to follow Mr. Hughes's plan, and that is to be leaving for Oregon soon, so we can beat the snow. He planned this with your safety in mind. He wanted you all to be happy and successful." Cassidy dusted his hands off as if the killings were behind them. "Since you're getting all loaded up, why don't we plan on meetin' up Monday, before noon? We can head out then."

"You gonna take us all the way?" someone shouted.

Cassidy looked across the crowd, trying to locate the speaker. "I plan to. I've got the maps, so I know the way Mr. Hughes planned to take you."

"You mentioned it," Floyd said, looking down on the man from the podium. "When you think the snow's a-comin'?"

Callum watched the man thinking for a moment, noticing a small tic in the gunfighter's left eye. About every ten seconds it jerked. He had noticed it when Cassidy had tried to drive the mules onto the barge, and he could tell Cassidy hated having to look up to Floyd.

"I reckon we can make it if we get started now."

Floyd looked out over the crowd, his eyes stopping on the children. "Folks, I'm tellin' you gospel. You start across those mountains in September, you'll never reach the other side. Right now, today, if we was sitting at Independence Rock, in Wyoming

Territory, we might make it. From here, we don't stand a chance. Every living one of you will stay in them mountain passes. The first folks through in the spring will find your bodies frozen solid, yes, your bodies, your wives' bodies, and your kids' bodies."

Captain Simpson stepped forward and extended his hand to Floyd, who took it and pulled the smaller man up next to him.

Simpson addressed the crowd. "Is there anyone here that thinks we should have a vote on using Cassidy as a guide?"

From the group of lieutenants to the left of the podium, a hand went up.

"Yes, Mr. Bilington?" Captain Simpson said.

Before he started talking, Bilington pulled back his shoulders and cleared his throat. "In my estimation, Mr. Cassidy has already been paid. We could save fifteen hundred dollars if we used him as guide."

Simpson stared at Bilington in disbelief, then turned back to the crowd.

"I think you all remember my question? Do we need a vote?"

This time his question was met by a resounding no from the crowd.

Cassidy turned to Simpson, and, just loud enough for those around the podium to hear, he said, "You'll remember and regret this day." Then Cassidy moved closer to Shorty.

Callum would normally not eavesdrop in any conversation, but Cassidy was violent, and Callum regretted not having killed him when he had the chance. In this case, he moved closer to Shorty. He could just make out Cassidy's threat, whispered low.

Leaning close to Shorty, Cassidy said, "You're gonna find yourself poking up daisies, old man."

Never having met anything or anyone he feared, Shorty moved forward, where his chest was almost touching Cassidy. "Why don't you bend over here, young feller, and kiss an old mountain man where he meets the saddle?" He then slowly winked his left eye. He had also caught Cassidy's tic.

The gunman was dangerous. Callum knew that, but he only barely controlled the laugh that threatened to burst from his throat, however, he couldn't keep from grinning. Cassidy looked over Shorty's shoulder and into Callum's wide.

He glared at him, hate emanating from his hard gray eyes. Leaning closer to Callum, his whisper was only audible to Callum and Shorty. "You're a dead man, Logan, and it won't be pretty."

Callum's grin disappeared, and his hard eyes locked Cassidy's. "Now's the time, gunfighter. Let's find out if you're as bad as you think."

The two men held the gaze for a moment more. "Not now, but soon," he said and spun around to the settlers. "You'll regret this," he said to them all, and marched out of the building.

"Whoo-ee," Shorty shouted to the man's disappearing back. "I'm plumb scared."

That broke the ice, and everyone in the building started laughing. Callum even saw his uncle grinning.

"All right," Floyd continued, "as I was saying, we'll be pulling out at seven o'clock sharp on Monday morning, from the west side of Fort Smith. You need to be there early, and ready to go."

He started to get down again. "Mister Logan, may I ask you another question?" The feminine voice came from near the front.

He straightened up again. Finding the lady who had raised her hand, Floyd nodded.

"You didn't talk about the Indians. Should we expect trouble from them?"

Floyd couldn't help but look at the woman like she was crazy. "Ma'am, you're gonna be traveling through the hunting grounds of a bunch of different tribes. They've seen the white man travel through their land by the thousands, leaving piles of waste across the prairies and killing their buffalo, which, by the way, they're dependent on for food, clothing, housing, and medicine. They don't throw any part of an animal away. They respect it, and if they have to kill it, they use all of it.

"The white man has also brought disease and pestilence to the Injun—smallpox, cholera, typhoid, and syphilis, just to name a few."

At the mention of syphilis there was a gasp from the crowd, and the murmur started up again. Floyd stood tall, waiting for them to quiet down. When the noise subsided, he continued.

"On top of that, there are some white men that make their living by takin' scalps and sellin' 'em. So, yes, I do expect trouble from the Injuns.

"I'll tell you this, they respect strength. You can't bribe 'em. They'll figure you're just scared, kill you at the first chance, and take your scalp. Also, they's good and bad ones, just like the white man. Don't judge 'em all based on what a few might do."

A small boy dropped his carved wooden horse. It clunked loudly on the floor. People jumped, and a nervous laugh could be heard throughout the room.

"Right now, there's an Indian uprising taking place out there." Floyd flung his arm out to the west. It could be settled by the time we get there. But all of you should be able to shoot. Don't depend on your neighbor to protect you. When that's needed, he'll be too busy protectin' his own family." He looked around again. "Now, are you people through with me?"

The audience was quiet. Simpson held out his hand to Floyd, who helped him up, and then stepped down from the podium.

Ma Logan leaned over to Floyd. "You never were very good at soothing peoples' feelings."

"I tell the truth, Rebecca. With the Indians the way they are right now, and the bandits, I reckon this bunch will be lucky to get to Denver without losing a lot more folks than I said. I ain't much for people, but I sure don't won't all these women and children left to die on the plains or in the mountains."

She patted him on the arm. "You're a good man, Floyd. Your brother always spoke highly of you."

He looked up, as if looking for Matthew. "He was a fine brother. Smarter than all of us. A fine, upstanding man." Then his serious face broke into a grin. "And he got himself a mighty pretty gal."

Ma Logan slapped Floyd on the arm. "You always were a big tease."

Simpson was listing a few things the people needed to include in their supplies. Shorty leaned over to Floyd and said, "That there Bilington is gonna be trouble. You mark my word."

Morg nodded to Floyd. "He ain't right often, but he's right now. I can't figger why Simpson let that feller be appointed as lootenant."

"He might be trouble," Floyd replied, "but it won't be to us, and he wasn't appointed, he was elected. Simpson had nothing to do with it. The man's friends voted for him."

"Humph," Shorty said, "I'm surprised he's got any."

Simpson brought the meeting to a close, urging everyone to work quickly. He jumped down and moved over to the Logan group. "Sorry about Bilington. I did all I could to make sure he wasn't elected to anything. The man loves intrigue. Unfortunately, his friends outnumbered us. He was part of the group that was still planning on going with Hughes."

People were emptying the building. Callum moved to get out of the crush of folks who were surrounding Ma and the mountain men. Many of the women were talking to Ma, while the men were introducing themselves to the guides. Callum watched Bilington, followed by his entourage of men. Callum had overheard Shorty's remark, and he agreed with him. He'd found in the military that it took only one malcontent to rile up a lot of people.

Bilington was obviously in a hurry, pushing several people out of his way. Callum's eyes traveled ahead of the man and stopped. There, dressed in black, was a striking young woman. She was tall, almost five and a half feet, near the height of an average man. High cheekbones and wide-set brown eyes contributed to her stunning face, softened by a wide mouth and full lips. She stood erect, emphasizing her rare height. This had to be the widow of Kelly Thompson. He hadn't heard of anyone else dying.

Bilington neared her, slowed, and reached out to grasp her hand. The ladies around her moved aside, allowing them some privacy. From this distance, he couldn't hear the conversation, especially over the din of conversations in the big room. She shook her head, and Callum could see a frown wrinkling her forehead. She said something and tried to pull her hand from his, but Bilington held on. She finally jerked her hand from his grip, and the man reached out for her arm. The women she had been conversing with stopped talking and turned to watch.

Callum was almost halfway there when the woman looked from Bilington's face and saw Callum moving toward her. He felt something. Something he hadn't felt since Charlotte. Quickly, he tamped it down. *This is no time to get involved with anyone,* he thought. *I just need to help this lady.* He reached the two, coming up on Bilington's right side.

"Afternoon, ma'am," he said, a little louder than normal. Bilington jumped, surprised at a man's voice so near.

He released her arm and turned to Callum. "You're intruding on a private conversation."

Callum tipped his hat to the lady, ignoring Bilington. "I'm Callum Logan, ma'am. If I'm intruding, please accept my apology, and I'll be on my way."

"Why, no, Mr. Logan, you certainly aren't. I am Annie Grace Thompson."

She extended her hand, which he took in his firm but careful grip. Her hand felt cool, dry, and blistered from the work she had been doing. She returned his grip for a moment, then released it with a smile.

"I am sorry about your loss, Mrs. Thompson," Callum said.

"Thank you, Mr. Logan. Life will definitely be different."

Bilington cleared his throat, his face flushed in anger. His brows were pulled down in a stare that must have been intimidating to those who worked for him. Callum almost laughed in the man's face, then smiled at Mrs. Thompson.

"Is there anything I can do for you, ma'am?"

"Why, yes, Mr. Callum, would you mind escorting me to my wagon? It's parked over by the general store."

"I'd be glad to."

"Good day, Mr. Bilington," Mrs. Thompson said, starting to turn away.

Bilington immediately shot his hand out to grasp the young woman by her upper arm. But it was his hand that stopped short when he found his wrist clenched in Callum Logan's hard grip. Affronted and confused, Bilington looked first at Mrs. Thompson and then at Callum.

# 25

"Mister," Callum said, "Westerners respect women. I've been in Memphis, and I know they respect 'em there, too. It's time you learned some respect." Callum tightened down hard on the man's wrist. Bilington winced. Callum held it for a moment longer, then tossed the wrist away like he was throwing a piece of slop to pigs. He turned to the young lady and offered her his arm. "Ma'am?"

The talk had quieted down, as people noticed something going on with the new widow. Soon everyone was watching. Across the room, Callum could see Floyd. His uncle was grinning. *I'm in trouble now,* he thought. *All I'm doing is helping a lady, and those three old goats, and Ma will have me married before I get back to the wagons.* He shook his head as they continued out the building.

Mrs. Thompson noticed the head shake. "Anything wrong, Mr. Logan?"

"No ma'am, nothing at all."

"You were quite gallant, and I thank you for that. If you like, you may call me Annie. Sometimes I can be a blunt woman, and I fear this is one of those times. As you know, my husband has just been murdered. It will be a long time before I shall allow myself to be interested in another man."

"Yes, ma'am, Annie. I understand, and I meant no offense."

"It is I who must apologize, Mr. Logan. You have saved me from a frightfully rude man, for which I shall be eternally grateful. Thank you . . . ."

"Callum, ma'am."

"You seem more of a Cal than a Callum," she said, looking up at him. "May I call you Cal?"

Callum had never liked the shortened version of his name. Only his brother used it. It was all right coming from Josh, but no one else, however, when he heard it roll off the tongue of Annie Grace Thompson, it sounded like a note of sweet music. "Yes, ma'am, I reckon you can."

The two walked along the dusty street to the general store, where her wagon was being loaded. The day was hot, and dust boiled up under the hooves of horses passing and the wheels of wagons. Little wind was available to cool the late summer day. The men loading the wagon were drenched in sweat and covered with the fine Arkansas dust.

Callum and Annie stopped at her wagon. He glanced into the back, where they were throwing her supplies. One of the men had just tossed a sack of flour into the wagon. The supplies were strewn haphazardly across the narrow space, making it difficult to get to anything, and taking up more room than necessary.

"Hey!" Callum said to the man who was entering the general store for more of Annie's supplies.

The large man turned, his face and upper body covered with sweat and dust, a belligerent frown on his face. "What?" he snapped back at Callum.

"You need to stack these supplies in this lady's wagon. You can't expect her to try to move these ninety-eight-pound bags of flour."

The man walked back to the edge of the boardwalk and

placed his hands on his hips. "You want it stacked, Cowboy, you stack it."

The man's partner had stuck his head out the door and saw what was happening. He moved quickly to his friend's side and whispered something in the man's ear. Instantly, the man calmed down.

"Sorry, Mr. Logan. I didn't realize it was you. We'll be glad to stack it a little more neatly for the lady. We thought her husband would set it up like he wanted."

"Her husband was shot in the Arkansas Saloon," Callum said.

Now the man was sincerely apologetic. He touched the visor of the cap he was wearing and nodded to Annie. "I'm right sorry for your loss, ma'am. I know it must be hard. My Susan and I lost our son Ronnie to cholera two years ago."

"I am sorry for your loss, sir," Annie said. "Thank you for your consideration."

The two men moved quickly with the supplies, stopping occasionally to follow her directions.

The loading was soon finished. As the men moved to the next wagon, she said to Callum, "Thank you for walking over here and helping me with the loading. I must move the wagon to allow the next one into position. Mr. Simpson has arranged parking space near the hotel. I suppose I'll see you Monday morning?"

Callum was looking at the mules attached to Annie's wagon. "Can you handle those animals, Annie? They can be a handful."

"Yes, they can, Cal. I've already found that out, but I did manage to get them and the wagon here from the wagon builder. It is quite a challenge, but the only way to learn is to do it."

"You sure you don't want me to help?"

"Thank you, but I must do this myself." She quickly looked away, and Callum could make out a single tear glistening in the corner of her left eye.

"Ma'am, I sure believe you can do it yourself, but it's a long way to Oregon. You ought to hire yourself a driver, that way he could do a lot of the man's work around your wagon."

"I know you mean well, but I can't hire a driver. I just barely have enough money to get me to Oregon."

Callum was incredulous. "I don't understand. I thought your husband had been given plenty of money by his pa. Sorry, ma'am, but that's pretty much what everyone is saying."

She balled up her little fist and slammed it on the back of her wagon. "Yes, he was given a large sum of money, but by the time we arrived in Fort Smith, he had lost a sizable amount gambling. I tried to get him to stop, but to no avail. Fortunately, I think I have enough to get to our destination and open a store, but I cannot be frivolous with the remaining funds. That includes not hiring a driver."

Callum heard some horses near and looked around. It was the family.

"Brought your horse," Shorty said, a gleam in his eyes. "Thought you might need him."

"Thanks," Callum replied. He looked to his brother Bret. "Do you want to do this lady a favor?"

Bret was riding next to Ma Logan. "Shoot yeah, Callum, I'd be glad to."

Callum nodded and introduced Annie Thompson to his ma first, and then the others. Everyone seemed to hit it off. Callum quickly explained Annie's difficulty. It was obvious she had no idea what was happening until Callum said to Bret, "You drive her back to the spot Captain Simpson has designated for parking. Give her some pointers, and then unhitch and water her team. You can help her hitch up and pull out Monday morning."

"Be glad to." Bret jumped off his horse and tied it to the back of the wagon, looked inside, then walked around front to check the harness on the mules.

Annie was looking around, surprise on her face. "But, wait, he can't do all of that. I don't have the funds to pay him."

Ma Logan guided her Morgan close to Annie, where she could reach down and take the young woman's hand. "Annie, my boys don't need money to help a lady in need. Why don't you figure on camping with us Sunday night? We'll get to know each other, and then we'll travel together. There's enough men in our group to make sure you are well taken care of."

Annie Thompson's eyes filled, and she blinked quickly, trying to keep the tears away. "Thank you. All I need is some time to learn my duties. Mrs. Logan, you and your family must be sent from God."

"Well, knowing some of my family," she said, as she looked around at Floyd and his partners, "I'm not real sure about that." Then she laughed and said, "Honey, you come on out Sunday. You'll be welcome."

"Thank you. I shall."

"You comin'?" Floyd asked Callum.

"Course I am," Callum said gruffly, then turned to Annie. "Ma'am, Bret will help you with anything you need. He'll get your stock settled down for the night, then be back to take care of them tomorrow. He'll also bring you out Sunday. If you need anything, you let Captain Simpson know, and tell him what we said. Now I've got to be gittin' along."

Callum swung up on Shoshone, and, leaving a dismayed but relieved Annie Thompson with Bret, he rode off to the Logans' camp.

Ma swung her horse next to Callum's as they walked the animals out of town. "She seems like a nice lady."

Callum turned his head to closely examine his ma's expression. He could glean nothing. "I guess she does."

Kate, who was following behind them alongside Colin, spoke up. "I think she's pretty. Don't you, Callum?"

Callum ignored her, which he knew never worked.

"Well, don't you?"

He knew if he didn't answer his sister's question she would only become more insistent, and louder.

He turned in the saddle to look at Kate. She was smiling at him with the most innocent smile she could fabricate.

"Yeah," he spit out, and turned back around.

"See," she said, "that wasn't so hard."

"I STILL DON'T SEE the necessity of having him in our meetings?" Bilington said, pointing at Callum.

Callum sat silent on the log, promising himself he would contain his temper. The meeting had gone fairly well. Simpson, at the beginning, divided the wagon assignments among the two lieutenants.

He pulled out his Bowie, picked up a small stick, and started whittling.

"I said, why is that man here?"

Joseph Lang was the lieutenant in charge of the lead company. In Callum's estimation, he was probably the sharpest of the elected group, including Simpson. He tossed Bilington a disgusted look from his seat on the log next to Callum, held it for a moment, and said, "Because this is his camp?"

"Lang, why don't you mind your own business?" Bilington said.

At that comment, it was obvious Lang had had enough of Bilington's constant carping and smart mouth. He thrust himself from the log and started for the man. Simpson stepped in between the two men, holding his palm toward Lang. "Joseph, cool down. What kind of example will we be to the folks if we start fighting amongst ourselves?"

Lang nodded, but kept looking at Bilington, who had stepped back several steps. He turned around and returned to his seat.

Simpson spoke quickly to Bilington. "You know he's important to our protection. He's another Logan with experience. He knows how to use a gun. He's familiar with this country. Is that enough reasons for you? Now, leave it be."

Bilington immediately changed the subject. "My group should be leading this train, not Lang's, and why is Annie Thompson not with me, so I can look after her?"

Callum could stand it no more. "We saw yesterday how you 'look after' her. Now button your lip, or I'm comin' over there and buttonin' it for you."

Callum had never heard so many petty complaints as had come from Bilington this evening. Simpson had his hands full for at least the next year, but that was his problem. He stood, brushed his hands off on his trousers, and said to Floyd, "You work this mess out, and let me know what you want me to do." He turned and walked back over to the Logan fire, where the family, with Annie Thompson, were gathered around.

Bret had brought her in earlier in the afternoon. She was one of the first wagons that had made it out from Fort Smith. They wanted to get an early start tomorrow, and not one of Bilington's party had made it out today.

He walked over to Ezra. "How's the stock doing?"

Ezra looked up at him from his seat on a stump he had found and brought near the fire. He was sitting with his back to the fire. "Fine. I 'spect they're about as anxious as us to get on the move." His glance turned to Annie. "Single female could be a problem."

Callum shifted the guns around on his waist. Once they were settled, he nodded. "Could be, but I got a feeling she'll be fine."

"Hope so. Trouble on the trail can affect everyone."

Callum nodded again.

"Callum?" Ma Logan called.

"I'll be back shortly," he told Ezra as he headed over to his ma. He thought about how much better she was looking. She still missed Pa, and would for the rest of her life, but being busy and involved with others helped pull her from the doldrums.

Nearing, he saw she was showing Annie how to mix special herbs for a hand poultice.

"This will feel very good on your hands. You leave them wrapped overnight. You'll find they'll not be as stiff and sore in the morning."

Kate sat next to them, paring down her fingernails with her Barlow knife. She turned her hands over and looked at the calluses on her palms, rubbing the hard spots with her fingers. "Ma, what's it like to have soft hands?"

Ma Logan turned to her pensive, seventeen-year-old daughter. The young girl's lovely face glowed, and her flaxen hair was glistened like spun gold in the warmth of the fire.

Before she could respond, Annie spoke up, "It means you are spoiled, just like I was before coming West. Kate, may God forgive me, but even with my husband gone, I haven't felt this alive in all of my twenty-two years. I envy you, your callouses, your ability to ride and shoot and work right along with your brothers. Don't you ever think that because your hands aren't smooth you're not beautiful. You are one of the most beautiful girls—no, women—I have ever seen. Any man would be lucky to have you so much as smile at him."

Callum sat down next to his sister, put his big arm around her slim shoulders, and gave her a squeeze. Then he looked down into those clear blue eyes. "Any man best be on his good behavior, or I know a brother that might have to whip me a beau—or two."

Kate laughed and hit Callum in his bruised ribs with her small fist. A short, involuntary grunt escaped his lips. Kate's laughter immediately turned to concern.

Shocked, she said, "Oh! I'm sorry. I forgot about your ribs."

Callum grinned at her. "Reckon I don't have to worry about defending you. Looks to me like you can take care of yourself."

All three women's faces cleared from concern for Callum, and they broke into laughter. They were joined by the boys, who had been watching. Frank and Ezra just shook their heads.

Floyd and Captain Simpson came walking up to the fire.

"Meeting over?" Callum asked.

"Callum," Simpson said, "I'm sorry about Bilington. I fear he is going to be difficult."

"More your problem than mine," Callum replied.

Kate had jumped up. "Would you like some coffee, Mr. Simpson?"

"No, thank you, Kate. I must be getting on to my family."

Floyd walked over and poured himself a cup. He was joined by Morg and Shorty. All three men remained standing.

Simpson, his face stark from the fire's reflection, said, "Callum, Floyd told me it was no use, but I sincerely request that you accompany us to Oregon."

As Callum started to reply, Simpson held his hand up. "Don't answer now. We've plenty of time. But, I want you to know, I've talked it over with the other members, and they are enthusiastically behind you going with us as an additional guide, and we will pay you just as the other guides, five hundred dollars."

*What do I have to do to convince these people?* Callum thought. *I ain't goin' to Oregon.* "Avery, I don't know how many times I'm goin' to have to tell you this, but it ain't goin' to happen. That's final."

Simpson nodded, obviously not convinced. "Well, be that as it may. We have a long time on the trail till Colorado." He turned to the ladies and touched his hat. "Good night."

"Mr. Simpson," Annie said, "would you kindly walk me to my wagon?"

"Certainly, Mrs. Thompson."

She smiled at everyone, then looked at Ma Logan. "Thank you so much for helping me, and for this wonderful poultice. My hands are feeling better already. Good night."

Bret spoke up. "I'll be around in the morning to take care of your mules, ma'am."

"Thank you, Bret."

She joined Simpson, and they walked into the night.

"This is so hard on a single woman," Ma said. She leaned forward to look around her daughter at Callum. "You should have seen her face, son, when you told Captain Simpson you weren't going on to Oregon. That poor girl is all alone."

"Ma, her husband was just killed. Of course she's sad."

"I hate meddling gossips, but you've got to know her husband was not good to her. One of the ladies from Memphis said that his being shot was the best thing that could have happened to Annie. He was gambling their money away so fast they would have had nothing by the time they reached Denver."

"Rebecca," Floyd chimed in, "I reckon I ain't never knowed you to be a gossip."

Ma Logan whipped around to glare at Floyd in the firelight, her eyes flashing. "Floyd Logan, don't you dare call me a gossip. That young woman has been dealt a hard life, and she's stepping up to it with courage. I admire her, and I think she's developing feelings for Callum."

Floyd ducked his head at the fusillade. "Sorry, Rebecca. Reckon I'll be gettin' some sleep." He withdrew from the encounter intact.

"I'll join you. Frank, you got first watch?"

"Yep, then Bret, and Ezra. Get some sleep. We need you well mended for this trip."

"Wait a moment, Callum," his ma said.

He remained standing, now center of the family audience. "Ma, I best get to bed."

"What are you going to do about that girl?"

"Ma, that ain't no girl, and I'm not going to do anything about her."

"Son, it's time you found someone to settle down with, and I think she is perfect for you."

Everyone was entranced with the conversation. Kate's head turned back and forth between the two of them.

A coyote howled, followed by another. They were singing to the moon, now just creeping above the eastern tree line. Soon, they were joined by the deeper howl of a gray wolf. At the sound of the wolf, the horses and mules stomped their feet and snorted, restless with a wolf so near.

Callum looked over to Frank. The man nodded, assuring him they would keep an eye out should any wolves come slinking around.

He turned back to his ma. "Ma, I'm not ready to settle down. Maybe one day, but not now. Anyway, she's a new widow. It'll be at least a year before she's ready to start lookin' for another man. By then she'll be in Oregon, where there'll be plenty of good men to choose from."

"I think she's found a good man."

An awkward silence followed.

"I'm gettin' some sleep. Night, Ma." Callum said, his voice final.

He joined his uncle and the two of them moved toward their bedrolls.

"Your pa knew," Floyd said.

"Knew what?" Callum snapped.

"Knew not to get into an argument with your ma. Course, he had to learn it the hard way."

# 26

The fat man's body lay on the backside of a hill, his head and shoulders beneath a scrub oak on the crest. Relaxed, he lay watching the slow-moving wagon train. It had taken him a while to get his boys buried and take out after the Logans. He'd to sell his farm. It was a shame he was going to lose all that money from the farms he had confiscated.

But Arlo Pickering had lost his interest in profit the day his boys had been murdered by Old Man Logan and his boy. Fortunately, the old man met a well-deserved, bloody death on the boardwalk in Limerick—too bad his two nits hadn't gone with him. *Oh well,* he thought, *I will surely fix that mistake.*

It was a good thing they were traveling by wagon. He had managed to get to Memphis just ahead of 'em. Course, they stayed in one of them fancy hotels. Somebody told him that Callum Logan was carrying a bunch of gold. He'd love to lighten the boy's load. At that thought, Arlo giggled.

His high-pitched laughter startled a jackrabbit that had been eating on a wild sunflower it had cut. The rabbit jumped, ran four paces, and waited. When it realized there was no threat, it hopped back in its ungainly, high-hip stride.

Arlo watched the rabbit for a moment, thinking if these danged rabbits had any meat on their bones they'd make a decent meal. After staring at it for a moment, he moved his gaze back to the wagon train. It looked like they had grown no closer —they sure moved slow.

Gettin' on the riverboat weren't no problem either. Nobody but the Logans knew him, and he just stayed out of their way. That was a right nice trip, even though he was sleeping on the deck with the other folks that ain't had the money to rent a cabin. Sure, he had money, after sellin' the farm, and with what he'd already made marshaling, but he'd be danged if he was goin' to spend it on a roof over his head. He still got to Fort Smith just as quick as the Logans.

He wasn't worried. His plans were to wait until the Logans were almost home, when they'd separated from the rest of the train, and then kill the men. At least Callum and Bret. He'd like to kill them all, except for the women, of course. That Rebecca Logan was still a looker, and her daughter, Kate, my, my, my, that girl could bring him some big money. He'd wait. If his pa, that good-for-nothing piece of pig slop, had taught him anything, it was patience. He'd waited many a year until he got big enough to shove that pitchfork clean through the old devil. My, that sure had felt good.

After watching the slow progress of the wagon train for a while longer, he backed down the hill until he was far enough to stand without being seen. Then he got up and continued to the bottom. It wasn't as easy as when he was younger. He'd put on a mite of weight. Course, he felt like he'd lost a few of those pounds over the past couple of months. Taking his time, he made it to his horse, only breathing a little hard. Then he slid his Spencer into the scabbard, and rode off to look for a campsite.

~

Callum rode next to Floyd, well ahead of the train. They both caught movement on a hillside several hundred yards away. Watching, they saw a jackrabbit hop back and pick up something and start eating again. Though the hills were covered with yellow sunflowers, the jackrabbit was sitting in an opening just below a bush on the crest of the hill. The two men watched the area surrounding the rabbit for a time and continued riding.

Two weeks had passed. The members of the train were falling into the routine. *Falling is right,* Callum thought. Every night folks were falling into their beds. At the beginning, it was hard to get some of them to stay up long enough to eat or take care of their animals. Everyone walked, except for the wagon driver, and maybe one or two others who sat on the wagon seat. That was the only thing that had a spring on it. If you were in the back of the wagon, you'd be beat to death.

They had been lucky on their first river crossing. The river banks had already been cut down from previous travelers, which saved them time. Every wagon had made it safely across the Verdigris River. A couple of the wagons were almost washed away, but thanks to Floyd and Morg, and their fast ropes, the three of them were able to keep the wagons upright. Some of the goods in the wagon had gotten wet, but it could have been a lot worse. Friends had chipped in and helped the family replace their lost flour and cornmeal.

Floyd studied Callum for a moment. "Yore mighty thoughtful."

Callum snapped out of it. "Just thinking about these folks. They came together pretty good at the river."

"Yep, most are like that. Like your pa. He was always a helpin' neighbors. He was even like that as a boy. Always helpin'. But, son, I been seein' you gettin' pretty thinky. You gotta keep your eyes on the trail, or some brave's liable to lift that fine head of hair you're sporting. Morg and Shorty both have noticed."

"You're right. I find my mind's been drifting more than I'd like."

"Ain't aimin' to pry, but anything I could be helpin' with?"

Callum shook his head. "No. At least, not right now."

The two men rode on in silence for a few more miles, keeping their eyes peeled for any movement or anything out of place. The trees had mostly disappeared, replaced by grass, high grass, some of it up to the horses' bellies. In the distance, to the left, a dim tree line could be seen, paralleling the wagon train's progress. It was the Arkansas River. Floyd had insisted they not travel any closer to it than necessary. He received substantial arguments from many of the settlers. The loudest, of course, had been Bilington.

Callum had hoped the man would settle down once they were on their way, but if anything, he had gotten worse. Once told that they would not be traveling next to the Arkansas, he launched a vicious campaign. He accused Floyd and others, meaning the rest of the Logans, as well as Morg and Shorty, of planning on leading them away from water and robbing them.

It was a stupid claim, but there were a few people who grabbed on to it. Bilington had managed to keep the settlers split and agitated. As if that wasn't enough, he couldn't get it through his head that Annie wanted to have nothing to do with him. He was constantly stopping by her wagon and bothering her. It was all Callum could do to keep from beating the man to a bloody pulp, but as Ma explained, that would accomplish nothing other than drive a deeper rift in the train. So, he held his peace.

Callum scanned close, and then, with each sweep, moved his target distance farther out. He realized his mind had been drifting enough to interfere with his concentration. He had to change that. Swinging his visual sweep over to Floyd's side, he saw nothing more than waves of grass in the wind.

Once during the war, he had made it to the eastern shore. There, he had watched the endless waves and indistinct horizon. Crossing the vast plains, he was reminded again of that ocean.

The wind flowed across the tops of the tall grasses, looking like waves glistening in the sun. This horizon was as indistinct as the ocean, promising new sights, yet upon reaching that far point, there was nothing but the same infinite distance. He loved this big country. Open to the eye, yet hiding surprises in the hidden draws, cuts, and canyons. Falsely peaceful to the untrained eye.

Callum pulled Shoshone up. Floyd stopped next to him, watching the open country.

"See something?"

Callum pointed to an almost indiscernible change in the color of the hot, brassy sky at a point where it melded with the faded green of the grass. Floyd watched it for a moment.

"Yep, dust. Ain't much. Only a couple of riders." Glancing at Callum, he nudged his horse back into a walk.

*Yeah, Uncle,* Callum thought, *I reckon I'm back. Been thinkin' too much.*

Callum turned in the saddle to check the wagon train. No change.

The two men rode on. As the dust became more distinct, they checked to make sure their weapons were ready. Rather than pull out his watch, Callum checked the position of the sun. It had been almost an hour since he had first seen the dust.

They relaxed as Morg and Shorty became distinct in the waving grass. The four men met at a shallow stream crossing and dismounted.

Shorty had a big, wolfish grin on his face. "Found 'em," he said, as he pulled a pot and coffee makings from his saddlebag, squatted, and started building a fire.

"Yep," Morg said. "They're all bunched up about twenty-five miles northwest of here. Cassidy's there too."

Shorty quickly had the fire started, using a Lucifer pulled from a small oilskin-wrapped package he kept in his bulging vest pocket. "Yessir, it was mighty tempting not to part that boyo's hair with this here ole Sharps. He and them other fellers were just sittin' around like they had nowhere to go and plenty of time to git there."

Callum looked at Floyd. "I've been wondering why they haven't hit us yet. Sounds like they're waiting on someone."

Floyd gave a slow nod. "We know they want the money these folks are carrying. We also know that they don't want the blame. What if they're waiting to be joined by another group? Maybe"—he paused and thought for a moment—"Injuns."

While Shorty was starting the fire, Morg had taken the pot to the stream, only a few feet away, and was filling it. "That's what we figure, Floyd. If'n Cassidy's got some real live Injuns with him, they'll make enough of a mess, where his bunch might just get away unnoticed."

It didn't take long for the water to start boiling. Shorty pulled out his bag of coffee and tossed half a handful in the pot. Carefully grabbing the pot with part of the loose portion of his buckskin jacket, he set it to the side of the fire. "That's what we come up with, and here's somethin' else. We scouted out quite a ways. There ain't no sign of Injuns anywhere. So those boys still have a while to wait." Shorty looked up at Floyd expectantly.

The thought came to Callum at the same time it registered on his uncle.

"We hit them first!" Floyd said.

"Hit 'em now," Morg said. The tall man straightened to his full height. His face was grim and eyes hard as flint. "They're planning on killing all these women and kids. I say we don't leave a one of 'em breathin'. The ones we don't kill right out, we hang. That'll send a message that'll be heard loud and clear."

Shorty had thrown some cold water in the pot to settle the grounds. Each man pulled a cup from his saddlebags and filled it from the pot.

"I swear, Shorty, you make a fine cup," Floyd said.

The stocky old man, squatting next to the fire, nodded. "Yep,

I'm known for it. Trappers used to come from miles around to get a taste of my coffee."

Morg shook his head. "Modest too."

Shorty shot a squint-eyed look at Morg. "Don't start nothin' you ain't big enough to finish."

Callum chuckled inside. He drained the last tasty drop and rinsed his cup in the stream. "We best be getting back. We've still got to persuade Simpson and those folks that this is the right thing to do."

Shorty poured the remaining coffee over the fire, then refilled the pot twice, pouring it over the dying embers. The last thing they wanted on this prairie was a fire. The four men mounted and galloped back to the train.

"I'M AGAINST THIS BRUTALITY," Bilington said. "We can't just go riding into someone's camp and murder everyone. That's completely uncivilized."

Shorty shook his head in disgust. "We ain't talkin' about ridin' in like some idgit. We're talkin' about slippin' up and blastin' 'em 'fore they know we're anywhere around."

Muted laughter accompanied by some gasps followed Shorty's comment.

When the mountain men and Callum had brought the news to Simpson, he had the wagon train halt for the day. They formed a circle, releasing the stock into a rope corral inside that protective circle.

The men and women had gathered for a meeting.

"We've been meeting for over an hour," Simpson said to the travelers. "I want Floyd to go over his plan once more, to ensure we all understand it."

Floyd stood again obviously frustrated with the people taking so long to make a decision. "I've told you what I think. If we don't stop these men, they are going to strengthen their numbers with Indians, and they will attempt to kill every living person on this wagon train. It will be brutal and gruesome. We have an opportunity to stop that from happening." He indicated himself, Shorty and Morgan. "We know many of these men that are in this bunch, including Cassidy. They are most all killers."

Callum assessed the settlers. Many folks from the East might mistake these businessmen for pushovers, but there was hardly a man who hadn't fought in the war. For the most part, they were familiar with weapons, and many of them had grown up on farms, their fathers and themselves hunting and fishing for survival. They weren't killers, but he felt sure they would do what was needed.

Floyd continued. "We've got enough men. We can take half with us. That'll leave about thirty men here. I know the numbers are close, but our hole card is surprise." Floyd looked at the wagon train constable. "If we're going to do this, we need to make it as legal as possible."

Bilington gave a snort, but said nothing.

"I'd like to have the constable along with us." At this statement, everyone else looked to Constable Herman. He nodded.

"Good, the plan is to circle well away from their camp and come in from the northwest. Wind's blowing from the southeast, and I expect it to continue. By circling their camp, their animals won't smell us. Grass is high, so we'll slip within about fifty yards of the camp and wait. I'll open the party."

Simpson spoke up. "I appreciate your plan, but I believe we should at least give them the opportunity to surrender."

Several of the crowd agreed.

Floyd looked at Callum. Callum waited for a moment and stepped forward. "Folks, you come from civilization. You have police in your city to take care of the criminals. The only police out here are you."

He started taking off his vest. He handed it to Annie, who was standing next to him. "I want you to see what giving this kind of vermin a chance will get you." He pulled his shirt over his head, exposing his chest. This time gasps of shock rose from the crowd. He turned, exposing the entry wounds of the bullets. He waited a moment, then started putting his shirt back on.

"I know that many of you carry wounds from the war. This may seem no different, other than the location. What is different, is that I was shot and left for dead, and a friend of mine was murdered simply because we gave a gang like this one a chance."

He buttoned his vest, leaving the bottom button loose.

"You are good, God-fearing folks. I appreciate that. You want to bring civilization to this country. That's good too. Unfortunately, it isn't here yet. So, you are, if not the point of the spear, at least the blade. If you give these animals a chance, they'll answer with their guns, and some of you will not return."

"Be that as it may, Callum," Simpson said, "I don't think any of us can shoot down unsuspecting men."

Morg shook his head, and Shorty spit.

"All right," Floyd said. "Constable Herman will yell 'drop your guns, this is the law,' or something like that." Floyd looked over at Herman. "Does that work for you?"

"It does."

"Good," Floyd pointed his finger at the constable. "You make sure you've got some cover when you say that, because lead will be flying as soon as you speak. They don't respect law—in fact, they respect nothing."

Herman nodded back to Floyd.

Simpson started speaking again. "Here's how we'll choose. I want no man along under seventeen. Those that qualify will take part in a drawing. There will be thirty short straws. Whoever draws the short straw stays. Constable Herman, would you see to the preparation of the drawing?"

Again, the constable nodded and went to work. Wives and

children clung to their husbands, fathers, and brothers, in deep concern for their safety. Tears flowed from many.

Annie looked up at Callum. "You're not drawing?"

"We don't count," Callum said, indicating the mountain men and himself.

"You count to me."

Callum looked down at the strong-featured girl, strands of her long, soft brown hair escaping from under her Calico bonnet. He felt a twinge in his heart. Maybe . . . no! He had much to do before he could think about settling down.

"Thank you, ma'am. I best start getting ready."

He looked over Annie's head to see his ma looking at him with sadness in her eyes. "You'll excuse me." He grasped Shoshone's reins and led the horse to the makeshift corral, where he started stripping off the tack.

Kate walked up, leaned near his ear and whispered, "You can be so mean!"

He looked at her in surprise. "What?"

She gazed into his face for a moment. "You really don't know, do you? I take that back. You can be so stupid."

Callum was astonished. *What have I done?* he thought.

She yanked Shoshone's bridle from his head and walked up to the Morgans as they gathered about her. Picking a big chestnut gelding with three white stockings, she slipped it over his head, and brought him back to Callum. "Here, take care of Rebel. He's solid, fast, and won't let you down." She walked off, muttering something about "dumb" and "stump."

Callum watched her, thinking she must really be growing up, because she was becoming just as confusing as other women. He saddled Rebel and led him back to the cooking fire where Ma, Kate, and Annie were preparing supper. The drawing had been finished, and the same scene was being repeated at other fires throughout the camp.

Floyd joined Callum, watching the camp activity. "Hope this works. If it don't, these folks are gonna be in deep trouble."

"It'll work," Callum said. "You talked to those that are staying?"

"Yep, all set up. We've got seventy men staying back. That counts the younger boys, like Virg and Colin. I swear, I think Colin is itchin' for a gunfight. That boy worries me."

"I've noticed the same thing. As much as we can, we need to keep an eye on him. I don't want him going off half-cocked and shooting someone."

Floyd nodded as Frank walked up. "Looks like I'm staying."

"Good," Callum said. "We need good men back here with these folks."

"Hopefully, we'll have as few do-gooders as possible," Floyd said.

"They've just got to learn, Uncle."

"Hope they live long enough."

# 27

The trip had gone without a hitch. Even Shorty was pleased. The men had been positioned in a half-moon formation, leaving it open on the southeast side. With any luck, this should prevent any of the settlers shooting each other. Nothing else was left to do but wait.

Callum lay at the east end of the half-circle, watching daylight gradually chasing the stars away. He liked this time of day, the changing of the guard, the bringing of light. The camp started coming to life.

It wasn't light enough to make out faces yet, even though he strained to find Cassidy. He wanted that man. He felt sure it was Cassidy who had set up the ambush of his cabin on the riverboat. He owed the man, and wanted to settle his debt.

Daylight stalked into camp, chasing away the lingering shadows and lighting the gunmen's faces. It was nearing time for Herman to speak up, but still no Cassidy.

A shout rose from his right. "You men throw down your guns! This is Constable Herman. You are surrounded."

Herman barely got the first word out, before his location was hammered with lead. Callum picked a broad-chested man with crossed bandoliers, who was firing indiscriminately into the tall grass. He settled the front sight of his Spencer into the notch of his rear sight, focused on the man's chest, and squeezed the trigger. It wasn't necessary to watch, for he knew the man was dead. He worked the action, throwing in another load, pulled back the hammer, and squeezed the trigger, ending another of the killers.

He had learned in the war to operate automatically. You couldn't think of what you were doing, you just did it. Round after round fired from his rifle. A cacophony of shooting and yelling echoed around the camp. He looked for another target. There was none. Thanks to the wind, smoke from the short-lived battle drifted speedily away, showing the carnage remaining. Three or four men stood with their hands in the air.

Captain Simpson yelled, "Hold your fire."

Once the firing had stopped, Callum stood. He looked around to see who might be hurt. It seemed they might have gotten lucky, then he heard someone shout, "Constable Herman!"

He moved through the tall grass toward the voice. Upon arriving, his eyes found the riddled body of the late constable.

Simpson stood next to him, looking down on the bloody body. "I didn't realize they would shoot that quick." The man looked up at Callum. "I condemned this man to death."

Callum turned a stern face on Simpson. "Maybe next time you'll listen to Floyd. You folks wanted fair. There lies fair. There's a time for it, but this wasn't it. However, he wanted the same thing. So you can't blame yourself. Anybody else shot?"

Simpson shook his head. "I don't know." He looked up and down the line. "Anybody hit?" he called.

All the other men were shook their heads. Several of them had rushed into the camp and were manhandling the captives. Floyd and Shorty walked over.

"Anybody see Cassidy?" Floyd asked.

Everyone shook their head.

Callum looked the bloody scene over. "He's either dead in a

tent, or he isn't here. If he isn't here, that means he left for some reason. Maybe to go get the rest of his gang, or the Indians."

"You're right," Floyd said. He turned to Shorty and Morg. "Cast about. See if you can find some sign of *anyone* leaving."

The two men hurried to their horses to start the search.

Now it was time for clean-up. As unpleasant as the ambush was, this would be worse.

Floyd spoke to Simpson. "Have the men search the tents, and see if there are any of the men wounded or hiding there. Also, send a detail along the river. It's possible some of them may have made it to the trees. Put a couple of men on watch to make sure we don't have the same thing happen to us."

Callum walked off to look around the camp. As he walked through it, he wondered how men could live in such filth. No means of disposal, no slit trenches. The men just threw their garbage on the ground next to their bedroll or outside their tent, if they had one. They had to have been camped here for a while —the stench was almost overpowering. He found he had to watch where he stepped, since they relieved themselves wherever they wanted. Sometimes, adjacent to their bedrolls.

He jerked up at the scream. Spinning around, without thinking, he raced to the sound. One of the men was pulling a young girl from a larger tent. Her clothes were torn, and there was blood on her arm, probably from a bullet.

"Turn her loose!" Callum shouted, running up to the two men who held her.

Still showing the bloodlust they had felt during the battle, they spun around, leveling their rifles at Callum.

He slid to a halt. He had seen this many times on the battlefield. Some people went momentarily crazy from the killing. "Hold on, boys," he said calmly. "It's over. Turn the girl loose."

They looked at him for a moment. Then one of them looked at his own hand, gripping the girl's bare arm. Repulsed at himself, he jerked his hand free. Staring now at Callum, he said, "I don't know what happened. I don't understand."

Callum stepped closer, pushing the muzzle of the rifle down and away. "I know, it happens. Why don't you go down to the river and wash your face? Sometimes cold water helps."

The businessman, family man, father of four, started walking toward the river, then broke into a run.

The other man lowered his weapon and looked at Callum. "It was like being back in the war. I thought I had put that behind me."

"We'll never be able to leave it," Callum said. "Our job is to control it, and make a life."

"Miss," Callum said to the girl. "Miss, can you hear me?"

The young girl raised her eyes to his. They were red, and her face was bruised.

Callum started to take her arm to guide her to a log where they might sit. She jerked violently away from him. He motioned her toward the log. "We can sit. Would that be all right?"

She looked into his face, and something must have reassured her. She moved over and sat, folding her hands and placing them in her lap.

"Miss, you're all right, now. You won't be bothered again. We're from a wagon train that's east of here, and we're headed for Pueblo."

At the mention of Pueblo, her face brightened for a moment, then she brought her hands to her face and started crying. Callum felt totally out of his depth. He motioned Simpson over. "You need to find someone that might be able to get her talking. This poor girl has been treated terrible. I'm guessing she can't be more than fifteen or sixteen."

She sniffed, and wiped her nose on her dirty bare arm, streaking the dirt. "Fifteen," she whimpered. "I just turned fifteen before those men grabbed me."

Simpson nodded. "What's your name, ma'am?"

She looked up at the wagon master. "Minnie. Minnie Parker."

"It's nice to meet you, Miss Parker. I've got someone I'd like you to meet. He's a really nice man. He and his wife have six daughters. His name is Jerome Daggett." Simpson turned and called to a tall man, one of several guarding the prisoners. "Jerome, could you come over here?"

Callum turned to the young girl. "Mr. and Mrs. Daggett will treat you fine, Minnie. All these bad men are either dead or soon will be. Trust Mr. Daggett. He'll take you back to the wagon train, and he and his wife will help you." As Daggett moved near, Callum stood and walked over to Floyd, with the prisoners.

The three mountain men were gathered around a man almost as tall as Morg. His gray, scraggly beard darkened the already-grim appearance of his deep-set eyes. The other three men were held by the settlers.

"I want you to meet one of our old pards," Floyd said to Callum.

"Ain't no pard of mine," Shorty spit out, his knuckles white, gripping the hilt of the big knife in his scabbard.

The tall man grinned at Shorty, his black and broken teeth turning his bearded face into its own caricature. "Never seen a short man grow such a fine head of hair. That'd match up mighty well with some of those Shoshone scalps I've got hanging from my saddle."

Shorty's hand moved quick as a mountain rattler. The knife slid from his scabbard and drove toward the man's belly. Morg grabbed Shorty's thick wrist just in time to pull the blade off target, slicing the scalper's greasy, buckskin jacket.

Shorty tried to twist out of Morg's grip, but found his wrist locked in the big hand.

He stopped struggling. "I'm all right," he said. Once released, he slid his knife back into the scabbard.

"Yep," the scalper said, "mighty fine hair."

Floyd watched Shorty, then turned back to the prisoner. "This smelly excuse for a man," he said to Callum, "is known, in the mountains, as Scalper John."

Scalper John flashed his broken teeth at Callum in another excuse for a grin. "That's some mighty curly hair you got there, boy. Be careful some Injun don't lift it."

Callum looked into the man's dead eyes, saying nothing.

The two big men stared at each other in silence. Then Scalper John looked back at Floyd. "You got a cold one here, Floyd. Almost makes me scared." He threw back his head and laughed, causing several of the settlers to turn and look.

"Where do you know him from, Uncle?"

"Uncle?" Scalper John spit. "Yep, that makes sense. Floyd, he looks almost as mean as you."

"This man," Floyd said, contempt dripping from his words, "makes his living scalping innocent women and children. Some say he's scalped over a hundred people, mostly those who couldn't fight back."

Shorty's eyes were dark with rage.

Floyd shook his head. "This animal killed Shorty's wife and son. We've been looking for him for years. Who'd ever think we'd find him this far east."

"Ain't you lucky," the scalper said. There was no fear in the evil man's eyes. In fact, there was no emotion at all.

"Watch him, boys," Floyd said to the settlers, turning back to the other three prisoners.

"Where's Cassidy?"

A younger man, slim and clean-cut, with a bullet in his shoulder, said, "He left yesterday morning."

"Shut-up, kid!" Scalper John snapped.

Floyd turned cold eyes on the scalper. "Now's the time for you to keep your filthy hole shut."

The man looked Floyd up and down, and then, a sardonic grin on his sun-baked face, said, "Floyd, I ain't never liked any of you Injun lovers. I'll see you in hell."

"I reckon you will, but you'll be stoking the furnaces long before I get there."

Morg was standing next to Floyd. Without uttering a word, he stepped over to one of the saddled horses, removed the lariat tied to the saddle, and draped it over the man's neck. Pulling the tall man along, he walked below a big oak and tossed the opposite end of the rope over a hefty limb. Shorty stepped up, grabbed the loose end, and started pulling out the slack.

"Now, wait!" Scalper John said as the rope started to tighten around his neck. "I got sumthin to say."

Shorty didn't slow down. He just kept pulling the rope. "Whatever you got to say, you can say it to the devil, face-to-face."

Once the slack was taken up, the noose tightened around Scalper John's neck. Gagging now, following the pressure of the rope, he scrambled into the saddle. Shorty snubbed the rope off on another oak. He walked over and slapped the horse on the rump. It leaped forward, Morg still hanging on to the reins. The man was jerked out of the saddle, where he hung from the oak—kicking—until he wasn't.

Callum saw a look pass between the two men, and a quick nod from Shorty. Still, without saying a word, they walked back to Floyd and the remaining three desperadoes.

While Floyd continued to question the three men, Callum noticed that some of the settlers were starting to dig graves.

He called to them. "No graves. Let the coyotes clean 'em up." The men looked at each other, shrugged, and stopped digging. "Start checking supplies. See if there's anything in this filth we can use. We want to be getting out of here pretty quick.

"Also, go through their pockets. We'll put whatever money is found together and give it to Mrs. Herman and the girl. It won't mend their grief, but maybe it will help." After a pause, he said, "Get all the guns and ammunition. We can use it all."

Callum walked around the camp area, being careful where he stepped. Then he strode over to the horses. There was some beautiful horseflesh here. That's the way it always went, the working man couldn't afford an expensive horse, and the outlaw couldn't afford not to have one. He'd never known an outlaw to outrun or outlast a posse on a nag.

Before long Floyd came walking over. "Found out where Cassidy went."

Callum waited.

"He headed north to find his renegades, whites and Indians. The boy said there was about seventy-five of them."

"I don't like those numbers. With that many, we could lose people."

"We will lose people," Floyd corrected. "But the good thing is, there ain't more. They haven't tied up with any of the tribes. So I figure we can handle this bunch, especially since we slimmed their numbers down."

The two men were looking at the girl. "They find out anything?" Floyd asked.

"No, she's so traumatized she ain't talking. Why, she's younger than Kate." Callum felt his blood boil within him. He could easily understand why it was so easy for Morg and Shorty to hang the other outlaw. This bunch was lower than animals. At least animals killed to live. This bunch enjoyed killing.

Floyd looked around and then up at the sun. "Near ten o'clock. We need to be heading back."

They walked over to Simpson, who was listening to the questioning of the girl.

"We best be on our way. If Cassidy's bunch showed up, we'd be sorely outnumbered. Those Indians he has with him would be riding around with our scalps on their belts."

Simpson nodded. He saw that anything worth keeping was packed on the horses, and everything was ready to go. "Mount up, everyone," he called. "Let's head back to the wagons."

One of the men had found some of the girl's clothes, and she had been able to wash in the creek and change. Simpson had semi-bandaged her arm. Clean, and anxious to leave this bed of horror, she quickly mounted a horse and anxiously waited.

Callum looked at the three remaining outlaws. "What about these?"

Floyd looked at them, all three shot, one probably dying, maybe all three. "I don't know about you, Callum, but I'm almighty tired of killing. If you sit well with it, I know Simpson will."

Callum didn't hesitate. "Cut 'em loose. I got no more stomach for it."

Floyd called to the men wrangling the outlaws' horses. "Cut out three of the worst you got there, and leave 'em." Then he looked down at the three wounded bandits. "I'm giving you boys a chance. If you're smart, you'll ride back to the south, find yourself a town, and give up the outlaw trail. If you're not, I may be lookin' at you over my front sight." He didn't wait for an answer, just bumped his horse in the ribs and headed after the body of men who were headed back to the wagon train. He called Shorty and Morg. "You fine fellers feel like doing some more scouting?"

Shorty nodded. "You want we should cover our rear?"

"That's exactly what I want. We'll all have a good rest when we get back to the wagon train."

"Got you covered, ole hoss," Shorty said. "This has been a right satisfying day." The two of them peeled off and headed back northwest, spreading out as they did.

"Uncle, how about if I get out front, to make sure we don't run us over a mess of Comanches."

"You do that, boy. We oughta be back at them wagons before dark. Keep a sharp eye out, and don't do any of that daydreamin'."

Callum touched his hat to Floyd and let Rebel run. Cutting through the hot wind felt cooling against his sweaty body. He was tired of fighting, tired of killing, but in this land, someone had to do it. For a moment, he just wished it wasn't him. Then he put it out of his mind, slowed Rebel, scanned the countryside for trouble, and rode for the wagons.

~

SMOKE WAS his first indication of trouble, much more than normal. He pulled Rebel to a stop. Gunfire touched his ears for the first time. Putting Rebel into a trot, he kept his eyes moving, checking every bush and shrub.

Every fiber in his body drove him to race forward to the rescue, but experience kept him examining each possible hiding place along his route. He would do them no good if he was killed or injured before he could help. Turning, he pulled his binoculars from the saddlebags. At the next hill, Callum leaped off Rebel, leaving him ground hitched, and hung his hat on the saddle horn, then jogged up the hill, slowing as he neared the top.

He dropped to the ground and crawled to the last few feet, pushing grass aside so that he could look down on the wagon train. A few of the Indians circled on one side of the train, hanging down on the opposite side of their horses. They presented small targets, and it appeared the settlers were hesitant to shoot the horses.

A larger contingent sat on horseback, on either side of one man, who must be their leader. Next to him was a white man! Callum refocused the binoculars, took them away from his eyes for a moment, then looked again.

"Cassidy," he said. "Now, how the blue blazes did you get over here. He thought for a moment. "Unless, your Indians were back in this direction. But why did you attack now?"

Even while Callum watched through his binoculars, the leader raised a lance and waved it to the men on his right, finally dropping the point toward the wagons. At least fifty braves kicked their horses in the ribs, and raced to join the fray.

Firing picked up, and Callum saw at least three of the Indians fall from their horses. He tore his eyes from the charge and searched around the wagons. Men from the opposite side had left their posts to help repel the charge. In the grass, about a hundred yards from the unguarded wagons, he caught a glimpse of an Indian. He strained to pick out any other movement in the high grass.

# 28

His heart leaped. That side was completely undefended. The Indians would be inside the perimeter in only a few more minutes. He slid down the hill and jumped on Rebel's back. Freeing both of the Remington forty-fours, he slammed his heels into Rebel's flanks. The horse, unfamiliar with that kind of treatment, leaped forward in a hard run.

*Two can play at the same game,* Callum thought. Bent low over Rebel's back, he guided him toward the Arkansas, then, when he knew he was behind the Indians, he turned and raced for their position. He was in the open. Immediately, the Indians on the opposite side of the wagons spotted him. Through the sound of the battle, he could hear additional yells as the massed warriors tried to get the attention of their cohorts in the grass. But the crawling attackers stayed low, unaware of his approach. If he killed a couple, that would be icing on the cake, but his goal was to warn the settlers.

His first indication that he was among them was when Rebel stepped in the middle of one of the prostrate Indian's back, and stumbled. Simultaneously, the other's leaped up. Rebel regained his balance and raced forward.

Though the Indians had been surprised, they recovered quickly, the nearest sprang toward Rebel. Callum fired the forty-four directly into the man's face, eared the hammer back, and fired at another leaping from the other side. Now all of the Indians were on their feet and charging toward him. The settlers were also racing back to fill the abandoned positions and firing at the now-exposed men. Callum only had time to level the Remington at a big, muscular man with a raised tomahawk. He pulled the trigger and saw a red blossom appear on the man's bare chest, then he leaped Rebel over the tongue of a wagon and was inside the compound.

He yanked his Spencer from the scabbard, spun around, dropped to one knee, and fired, striking an Indian, in midair, as he leaped over the wagon tongue Rebel had just jumped. The man fell dead at his feet. The remainder of those who had been on this side of the wagon train disappeared back into the tall grass.

Callum stood to look around, just as Annie threw herself into his arms.

"I knew you would come," she said into his chest. "I just knew it."

In the noise and confusion of the battle, he felt her warmth, her nearness. In that moment, her hair, fresh from being washed that morning, smelled sweet and enticing.

He grasped her arms, pushed her gently back, and cleared his throat. "Just in time, it appears."

She looked up at him, and, to his surprise, he thought he could see hurt and sadness on her face. Then he put it aside and started looking for Frank. He spotted him with their wagons toward the front of the train.

"Annie, is the family all right?"

"Yes, everyone is fine."

"Good. Would you take my horse?"

She picked up the reins as he turned and dashed off toward Frank.

The Indians were still milling outside the wagons, but the assault had slowed. Frank heard Callum running up and turned.

"That was good timing. Where's the others?"

"They're coming. Where's your Harper's Ferry rifle?"

"In the wagon, why?"

"You think you could hit that feller out there in the middle of that Indian bunch? The one directin' 'em."

Frank squinted his eyes toward the Indian. "That's a mite far, but I've hit things farther. Course, these eyes was younger too."

"You feel like tryin' it?"

Frank looked again. "Blamed right I do. I'll get it."

He ran over to the wagon, stepped up on the wheel, bent over and picked up the powder horn he had personally made and a bag of round lead balls. Then he grasped the forearm of the nine-pound, fifty-four-caliber rifle and carefully lifted it from the wagon. Before he stepped down, he leaned behind the seat and picked up a long metal rod, with a half-moon rest in the end of it.

He walked back to Callum, and began loading his rifle. "This here shooter's been with me since forty-two. It's brought down a lot of game and a few men." While he talked, he jammed the rod into the hard ground, pulled the ramrod from its retainer beneath the barrel, and swabbed out the barrel with a dry patch. Then he opened his powder horn and poured powder down the barrel until he was satisfied.

Callum watched Frank, occasionally scanning all around the wagon train. "You don't measure your powder?"

"Son, I've been doing this for so long, I know exactly how much it takes. The only time I've messed up is when I forget I'd powdered it and put in a double load." Frank laughed. "I'll tell you, boy, that'll tickle your shoulder."

Next, he stuck a small, square piece of pillow ticking in his mouth, chewed it for a moment, and placed it across the muzzle. Frank reached into his bag of round lead balls and pulled one out. He examined it and set it on top of the patch, then drove it in with the ball starter. With the ramrod, he shoved the ball and ticking down until it rested against the powder he had just poured into the barrel. After stowing the ramrod beneath the barrel, he pulled a percussion cap from a round snuff box, pulled the hammer to half-cock, and gently pushed the cap on the nipple.

"Watch him," Frank said, as he sat on the ground, and placed the forearm of the rifle in the half-moon cutout on the rod that had been shoved into the ground. He took a couple of deep breaths, let the air out and took a normal breath, leaning into the butt of the rifle.

Callum pulled the binoculars up from around his neck and focused on the chief and Cassidy. He would have preferred to have Cassidy in Frank's sights, but they needed to get this attack stopped. While he watched, Frank smoothly squeezed the trigger, releasing the hammer to strike the cap, which exploded. Fire ran down the ignition channel to the waiting black powder, which burned so fast it was like an explosion, building up gasses and massive pressure. The pressure built until it started moving the ball down the barrel, the grooves of the barrel biting into the soft lead causing the ball to start spinning, so that it would stabilize upon leaving the muzzle. By the time it reached the end of the almost-three-foot-long barrel, it had accelerated to its maximum velocity.

Callum kept the binoculars on the chief.

The bullet didn't travel in a straight line. But Frank knew his rifle. He had adjusted the sights so that the muzzle was actually pointing above the chief. When the bullet left the barrel it was climbing, working against the effects of gravity and drag. At a certain point, as the velocity decreased, the relentless effect of gravity and drag began to win the struggle, and the projectile began a gradual descent to its target.

The noise of the blast from Frank's rifle had completely dissipated and the smoke had blown from Callum's vision. He began to think that Frank might have missed. He was getting older. Eyes lost their clarity. Then he saw the chief jerk, wobble from side to side in the saddle. He could make out the astonishment on the faces of the surrounding Indians as the chief fell from his saddle and lay still at his horses feet.

Almost at the same moment, a roar of shots erupted from the west. He watched Cassidy wheel, kick his horse, and disappear over the hill, quickly followed by the remainder of the Indians, after they picked up their chief.

Callum helped Frank to his feet.

"These old bones don't get off the ground the way they used to."

"They may not," Callum said, slapping him on the back, "but those eyes make up for 'em. That was about the finest shooting I've seen in a long time."

The older man chuckled at the praise. Other men were gathered around Frank, exclaiming about the rifle and the long shot.

Before he moved away, Callum leaned over to him and said, "I saw the shot. You hit him square in the chest. He was dead before he hit the ground."

Frank patted the rifle, as he gathered up his paraphernalia. "This old rifle has been mighty good, and still is." Surrounded by grateful and excited men, Frank walked back to the wagon, climbed up on the wheel, and stowed his gear.

The Indians had disappeared. The only sign they had been there was the wounded and dead horses the settlers had shot to get at their antagonists. Kate came running over to him, followed by the rest of the family. He wrapped his arms around her and gave her a big hug, thankful his family was safe.

"You got here just in time," she said.

"Glad I did. Looks like you're all right." He shot a questioning look over her head to Ma Logan.

"Everyone is fine, son," Ma said. "Several people have been shot, including Mr. Bilington." She tilted her head and raised her dark eyebrows. "Annie has gone to his wagon to help him."

It passed right over Callum's head. "Well, I imagine he needs help. I'm glad all of you are fine."

Colin, excited, stepped up to Callum, his hand resting on the butt of his Colt. "I killed me an Indian, Callum."

The man looked at the boy. There was too much pleasure in those eyes for taking another man's life. But maybe it was just excitement.

"Bret did too," Colin said, sensing Callum's displeasure.

Callum looked over at Bret. That brother looked neither happy nor sad. He looked back at Callum. "It was us or them."

"Yes," Callum said. "It was." He placed his hand on Colin's shoulder. "I'm glad you helped protect the folks, Colin, but never take pleasure from killing another man."

Colin's face turned grim, and he tried to shrug Callum's hand from his shoulder. "He was just an Indian."

Callum heard his mother's gasp. "Colin, that Indian probably has a family just like you do. He's different, but he's still a man. There's a wife or mother, maybe a daughter or son your age, that won't see their pa tonight, or ever again."

Colin tried to turn away. Callum's grip tightened until Colin winced. "Listen to me, brother. Every man you kill will come back to haunt you, even the bad ones. You ever make a mistake and kill an innocent man, he'll ride your shoulders for the rest of your life."

Callum released the pressure, and Colin spun away, dashing toward one of the wagons where several boys his age were standing around waiting for his return. Callum watched him go, a dark feeling of fear for the boy drifting over him. He looked at

Virgil, obviously torn between comforting his friend, and staying with the family. The family won out.

Ezra broke the spell. "They ain't got none of the animals. We kept 'em herded up inside the wagon circle. They're all fine, maybe a little skittish, but fine."

"Good," Callum said. "Looks like we came off mighty good. Could've been a lot worse."

Ma Logan was still watching her youngest son. "Yes, it could."

THE GRASSES HAD CHANGED from the long bluestem to the shorter bunch grass and was more sparse. The mountains had come into view six days ago, and as the wagons drew closer, the majesty of the lofty peaks became clearer, more awe-inspiring.

Callum and Floyd rode well ahead of the wagon train.

Callum chuckled.

Floyd turned and looked at his nephew. "What's funny?"

"I can't believe we're almost done."

"You're almost done, you mean. Morg, Shorty, and I still have a long road ahead of us. You oughta come with us."

Callum looked at the snow on the distant mountains and thought of the valley he'd christened with his blood and his friend's, the home he'd help build with his own hands.

"Floyd, I'm tired. Tell you the truth, I've seen too much killing, too much dying. I don't want to be in charge of anyone or anything but myself, and I'm worried about Colin. Hopefully we can get him on the ranch and away from those other boys that constantly brag on him for killing an Indian."

Floyd looked at his nephew again. "Reckon I understand what you're saying. Sometimes a man's soul just plain gets worn out. Sounds to me like you need a dose of the mountains. They're good for what ails you. You spend a few months workin' cattle and helpin' around the ranch, I imagine you'll git to feelin' chipper again. Maybe that'll help Colin, too."

"I hope so."

At the sound of a horse coming up behind them, the men turned to see Avery Simpson. He pulled in to the left of Callum. "You folks ready for the wedding?"

Floyd winked at Callum and said, "I'm always ready for a wedding, as long as it ain't mine."

"Yep," Callum said, not knowing what else to say.

"The trip has gone quite nicely since the Indian attack," Simpson said. "Hopefully the winter and the remainder of the trip to Oregon will be equally as placid."

Floyd rubbed his arthritic knee. Looking around Callum, he said, "I've got to say Simpson, don't think I've ever seen a wagon train go this far so unscathed. But having said that, we ain't been in those mountains. I promise you, not even counting the Indians, people are gonna die. It could be from falling off a cliff, a wagon rolling over on-a-body, or one of them giant bears. It'll happen. You won't get to Oregon with all your people."

Simpson gazed toward the mountains. "They are big, aren't they?"

Floyd nodded. "You're right as rain. And treacherous. But see here, you've done a right good job. I didn't expect as much, but you taken hold. Your people respect you."

"Well," Simpson said, somewhat flustered at the compliment, "thank you. I'm glad it has worked out." To change the subject, he addressed Callum. "I still can't talk you into going on to Oregon?"

Callum shook his head. "Not a chance. I'm going to rest up this winter, and consider my choices."

"Annie was a real surprise, wasn't she?"

Callum looked at Simpson as if he didn't know what he was talking about. "I don't get your meaning."

"Her and Bilington. I sure don't understand that."

"She took care of him when he was shot," Callum said. "I

reckon they got close during that time. Looks like he's treating her better."

Simpson shook his head. "I sure thought she was sweet on you."

Callum looked at the man like he was crazy. "On me? Never. We was good friends, and I reckon we still are."

It was Floyd's turn to shake his head. "Boy, sometimes you're blinder than those deep cave bats."

"I don't need to listen to this," Callum said, and nudged Shoshone into a ground-covering lope. He pulled ahead of the other two men. Cresting the next rise, there was Pueblo. He pulled his horse to a stop, crossed his leg over the saddle, and took in the view. It was about this same time, last year, when he first saw Pueblo. It was good to be this close to home. He sat there going over the past year in his mind.

A lot had happened during that time. He'd been shot, Josh was at the ranch with his wife and son, Pa had been murdered, Ma and the family were almost to the ranch, and he had a younger brother who was crazy to be a gunfighter. Who would've thought?

He swung his leg back down to the stirrup just as Morg and Shorty came up out of a draw. They saw him and galloped toward him.

Shorty was the first to speak. "Guess who's in Pueblo."

"Just tell him, Shorty," Morg said.

Shorty gave his friend a disgusted look. "Cassidy. Said to tell you he's waitin' for you."

"Tell Floyd about it. I'm headed for Pueblo. It's time his luck ran out."

"Hold on," Shorty said. "We're going with you."

As Shorty spoke, Floyd and Simpson crested the hill.

Callum started to urge Shoshone forward.

"Hold on, Callum," Morg said. "We ain't lettin' you go in by yourself. Cassidy's got men with him."

"If you're goin' with me, you'd better make it fast." With that, he bumped Shoshone in the flanks and was off at a hard run, the appaloosa flying across the prairie.

His friends' dust was settling as Callum dashed to Pueblo. But he could see thicker dust rising, approaching him. He never slowed Shoshone's gait but eased him over to the side of the road. Topping a rise, a buckboard with a man and woman, loaded with kids raced past him, toward the wagon train, narrowly missing him. As big a hurry as those folks were in, Callum figured they were Minnie's family. Morg and Shorty must have gotten the message about Minnie to them.

For now, he put Minnie out of his mind and pushed Shoshone harder toward the small town, its buildings growing in the distance. Leaning over the big horse's neck, he said, "Come on, boy. It's time to settle a score."

SHOSHONE, sides heaving and covered with sweat, squatted and slid to a halt at the saloon's front. The big man leaped off, and looped the horse's reins in the tie ring on the hitching post. He stopped his forward momentum just long enough to slip both leather thongs from the Remingtons and make sure they were free in their holsters. Then he pushed through the saloon's batwing doors.

# 29

Stepping inside from the bright afternoon sun, Callum paused to let his eyes adjust to the saloon's semi-darkness. Once adjusted, he scanned the room. It was still the same. The bar was to the right, long enough for a squad of men to belly up to. The brass footrest, dull and unpolished, extended the length of the bar. Tables and chairs filled the left side, past the bar, to the back of the room. It was at the far back table that Cassidy, and four other men, sat playing cards.

He was watching Callum. "My, my, that didn't take long," he said, his voice calm and friendly. "I told those two old geezers to fetch you to me, and they didn't waste any time. How are you, Logan?"

Callum assessed the room. The two men at the bar looked like cowpunchers. One other table was occupied near the front. Town folks, having a beer and a hand of cards. Other than possibly the two at the bar, his only threat came from the back table. Cassidy sat on the far side of the table, facing him.

"Good, Cassidy. Now that I've found you, very good."

"Well now, that's funny. I was going to say the same thing.

"Logan, you know you've caused me a lot of trouble."

"Too bad. You been riding with any Indians lately?"

Cassidy had a toothpick in his mouth. He picked at a tooth for a moment, stopped, and laid the slender piece of wood on the table."I wondered if you recognized me. Now I know." He pushed his chair back across the rough-cut floor, the scrape loud and abrasive. In one easy motion, he came to his feet.

Callum heard a horse running, come to a stop, and then a man's footsteps on the boardwalk behind him. "Morg, is that you?"

Morg stepped through the swinging doors, his Spencer in his hands. "That would be me. Floyd and Shorty are behind me."

Cassidy motioned for the other men to stand. The four of them stood as one, turning to face Morg and Callum.

*"If they go for their guns now,* Callum thought, *Morg and I are dead. We can't get 'em all.*

Cassidy slowly pointed. "Boys, you go stand by the bar. This is between me and Logan, here." Cassidy's men moved as one toward the bar, none of them appearing anxious to be caught in a crossfire. "That all right with you, Logan?"

Callum motioned Morg toward the bar. "You don't need to be involved in this, Morg."

"I don't need to, but I want to."

"Go on, Morg."

Cassidy laughed. "You can stay if you want, old man. I can put a hole in that dirty buckskin before you can move that Spencer."

The tall mountain man held his ground. His desire to blast Cassidy was written all over his face.

"Stay out of it, Morg. This is my fight."

Finally, the mountain man moved reluctantly to the bar.

"Good thinking, old man," Cassidy said. The man's confidence was thick in the room.

The two cow punchers looked around at Callum, then at

Cassidy. They both reached in a vest pocket, slapped money on the bar, eased past Callum, and disappeared out the door.

*He's enjoying himself,* Callum thought. *No matter what, I've got to make this first shot count.* He could feel the cold anger settle over him. He flexed his hands.

Cassidy grinned, looking like a wolf about to take down a fawn, having taken Callum's movement for fear. "I've been looking forward to this since the dock at Memphis. I wanted to blast you then, but it was too civilized back there."

Two more horses pulled up out front, and the doors swung open. Floyd and Shorty stood on each side of him.

"Well, well," Cassidy said, "two more of the over-the-hill bunch."

Without taking his eyes from Cassidy, Callum said, "Floyd, you and Shorty move over to the bar with Morg. Those four at the end are Cassidy's men."

Floyd shook his head. "We're in this with you, boy."

"No. This is my fight. Just keep those four off me."

Floyd and Shorty sidled over to Morg.

The tension in the room was as tight as one of the strings on the saloon's weather-beaten, old upright piano. Cassidy waited, then he reached down, picked up the toothpick from off the table and placed it between his lips.

Outside, life in Pueblo moved at a normal pace. People were going about their business, none knowing about the long overdue, life-and-death, scene playing out inside the saloon. A rooster outside the back door crowed, the sound of his wings flapping coming through the thin walls. A conversation between two ladies moved in front of and past the swinging doors. One of them sniffed as the smell of stale beer drifted above the doors and out to the boardwalk.

Cassidy had moved forward. They were no more than forty feet apart. Callum could see the man's left eye start to tic. He waited.

Now the gunfighter was dead serious. "I'm gonna enjoy killing you, Logan."

Callum felt relaxed. He was as ready as he would ever be. He knew Cassidy's reputation, but none of that mattered now, only the first bullet.

The gunfighter's hand was a blur as he went for his gun.

Callum's hand flashed down, and he felt the solid weight of the Remington. It cleared his holster and the barrel started to tilt up toward Cassidy.

But Cassidy was faster! The man's Colt was coming level. Callum could see Cassidy's thumb releasing the hammer spur. A thought flashed through his mind. *Don't worry about him, you've been shot before.* He saw the hammer falling. It seemed like it took forever. It was down, but almost no flash, just a pop, a little smoke, followed by the bullet barely making it out of the barrel, then skittering across the floor.

Cassidy's face reflected shock. His life had always been predicated on the loving care of his guns. They had never failed him—until now. But he was a professional killer. Even as the Colt popped, he was smoothly pulling the hammer back for his next shot. Unfortunately for him, the edge his speed gave him was gone.

Callum pulled the trigger. His gun roared, belching smoke and a one-hundred-forty-one-grain slug. He watched Cassidy slammed in the chest, driven back, but the gunman, trained throughout his life, continued to ear back the hammer, and his finger pulled the trigger. This time his Colt fired, tearing a large hole in the saloon's batwing doors, accompanied by the screams of the two women who had just passed.

But Callum wasn't through. His second shot hammered into the back-stepping gunman, who came up against the edge of the table where he had been sitting. He stopped, and his gun drooped toward the floor. He looked down at it like he was surprised it wasn't pointing at Callum. Then, with massive determination, he brought the unsteady gun to bear again on his opponent.

Callum fired his third shot. This time, he had lifted the Remington into a classic firing position and taken aim. The front and rear sight lined up perfectly on Cassidy's forehead. When he pulled the trigger, the bullet ended the last thoughts, the plans, the hopes of the notorious killer and gunfighter. The outlaw's gun clattered to the saloon floor, followed by his limp body careening off the table, then a chair, before it came to rest, crumpled in a heap on the cold wooden planks.

Deafening silence assaulted the smoke-filled room. Callum mentally examined himself for pain, finding none. He turned his gun toward Cassidy's gang, but they all had their hands high in the air, more concerned about the rifles pointing at them than Callum.

A misfire! He couldn't believe it. Examining the floor, Callum walked toward the dead gunman, stopped, bent over, and picked up the round lead ball. He studied it for a moment, and dropped it into his vest pocket. Cassidy had him dead to rights. At best, he should be shot. He didn't care to think about the worst.

The bartender was the first to speak. "I wouldn't of believed it if I hadn't seen it with my own eyes. That was one of the fastest draws I've ever seen—and his gun misfired!" He stared at Callum. "You've got the bullet, don't you?"

"If you're done gawking," Floyd said to the men still staring at their boss, "you best not let the dust settle on you."

The four of them, moving as one, rushed past the tough old mountain men and slammed into the batwing doors. Moments later, the sound of their horses racing out of Pueblo was accompanied by the smell of dust drifting into the saloon.

"Bartender, set 'em up, three rye and one sarsaparilla," Shorty shouted through the dust and smoke.

Callum moved to the bar. He reached into his vest pocket, pulled the bullet out, laid it on the bar, and turned to the door.

Running steps on the boardwalk had stopped, and faces peered cautiously over the batwing doors, followed by bodies bursting into the room, the sheriff in the lead. He looked at Cassidy, dead in a pool of blood, and then at the bar. Recognition flooded his face when he saw Callum and Floyd.

He walked over and extended his hand. "You're gonna tell me what happened here, aren't you, Callum?"

The men first shook the sheriff's hand, then Floyd picked up the bullet, held it between his thumb and forefinger, and, looking at it, said, "You ain't gonna believe it, Sheriff, but we'll tell you. First, you better have a drink."

The sheriff shoved his hat to the back of his head. "I've never been known to turn down a free drink," he said, and bellied up to the bar.

WHEN THE MAYOR of Pueblo found out this wagon train was filled with prosperous merchants, he rode out to their camp, along the river, east of town. He also brought with him a sizable welcoming committee of citizens. Pueblo was growing, and the city fathers were on a mission. They hoped they could persuade the prosperous businessmen to join their community, instead of moving on to Oregon. Plus, there was going to be a wedding, and everyone was invited. No one turned down the opportunity to attend a party.

Callum and the others were busy saying their goodbyes. "Avery, you've done an excellent job. The people of this train are lucky to have you."

"Thank you, Callum. All of you made it possible." He looked around at the three mountain men. "If it hadn't been for you, we'd never have made it this far."

"That's for danged sure," Shorty said. Then he grinned at Simpson. "But you learned fast, Captain."

Simpson nodded his head. "Thank you. I'm just glad that Minnie Parker adjusted so well. I can't imagine what that poor girl went through, but by the time we got here, Priscilla Daggett and her girls had Minnie almost back to normal. Her family sure was sure were happy to see her."

"The Parkers' had quite a family. At least what I got to see of them. They had that buckboard stuffed with kids when I saw 'em headed for the train. They must not have waited long either. By the time I got back they all were gone."

"Yes, they didn't wait around long," Simpson said, "but they were mighty grateful. I think they just wanted to get Minnie home. She's made some fast friends with the Daggett girls, and some of the boys around. Who knows, if we stay in Pueblo, they might become lifelong friends."

"Well," Callum said, "that sounds like you might be thinking about staying in Pueblo."

"We're talking about it. There seems to be a lot of potential here, and the mayor said, with all of the gold strikes and movers, business is booming."

Callum shook his head. "I'll have to say, I'm surprised, but in a good way. This country needs your type of folks." He glanced around and saw Annie Thompson walking slowly toward them. "Excuse me," he said to the wagon master, and walked to meet her. He took his hat off and said, "Morning, ma'am."

"Callum, for goodness sakes, must you be so formal? It's Annie."

"Yes, ma'am," he said, and then grinned. "Annie."

"I wanted to thank you."

He almost stepped back in surprise. "Thank me? I can't think of a thing you should be thanking me for."

"Yes, thank you. I was very vulnerable when"—she paused for a moment before continuing—"my husband was killed, and you were such a gentleman. I'm afraid I all but threw myself at you. Thank you for not taking advantage."

Callum frowned. "Reckon I can't think of a time you threw yourself at me."

Annie frowned for a moment, then laughed. "Callum, you are such a . . . you are such a man!"

Now he was really confused. Of course he was a man. "Annie, I've got to give you a word of caution, and I don't mean to pry, but be sure about Bilington. No man should grab a woman like he did you. I didn't trust him then, and I don't trust him now."

A serious frown creased her face. "Callum Logan, Horace has changed. Getting shot has made him a different man, a kind man. I'll not have you talk mean about him, and this is the last time we'll see each other. Can't you be kind?"

*Ma's right. I'll never understand women,* Callum thought.

"Annie, I'm just telling it the way I see it. I best be going, but good luck. I do hope things work out for you."

She quickly stood on her tiptoes and kissed him on his cheek.

He grinned at her again, slapped his hat on his head, and headed for Shoshone. His horse was tied next to Ma's wagon. She sat on the seat next to Bret. As he looked at her, across the bunch grass, he caught her watching him and shaking her head. She stopped the moment she saw him looking at her and gave him a sad smile. He didn't know what that was about, but he figured she was sad leaving all these friends she had made.

Callum looked at the big, beautiful mountains reaching for the sky. At one time, he thought he would live and die in Tennessee, but he had found another love, the wide, open spaces, the tall, serene pines, and the quaking aspen. They were waiting for him. This was really his country.

He watched Stanley Simpson and Virgil saying goodbye. These past months had been good for Virgil. He'd put back on the muscle he had lost, plus more. He learned about horses quickly from Kate, and was growing to be a top wrangler, and it looked like he loved his life. Plus, he was a stabilizing influence on Colin.

With goodbyes completed, he swung up onto Shoshone and felt the big appaloosa quiver beneath him. Yep, it was good to be home, for both of them. Floyd had mounted, and was talking to Shorty and Morg.

"I'll see you boys in the spring. Who knows, I may drift back early, if'n I get bored in them mountains."

Shorty spit. "Get bored in them mountains? Whoever heard of such? Don't worry about us. We'll be fine over here sittin' on our rears gittin' fat. Course, with Morg this close to a saloon, the Bible-thumpers might run us off."

Morg looked down at his companion. "Shorty, did I ever tell you, you talk too much?"

"All the time."

Callum leaned in the saddle and extended his hand to the two men. "Been a pleasure. You ever want a break, you know where the valley is. Come see us." He looked at Morg and winked. "We might even be able to find a stray jug."

Shorty shook his head. "Oh, no. You gone and done it now. I'm gonna have to keep an eye on Morg all the time to keep him from slippin' off to yore valley."

Everyone laughed. Callum sat back up in the saddle and said, "Let's move 'em out."

Frank pulled the lead wagon out, followed by Bret and Ma. Kate, Ezra and the boys started pushing the remuda of horses, mules, and donkeys, plus two cows and a blue tick hound, behind the two wagons.

Callum rode along beside Ma for a ways. "We're almost home, Ma."

She looked over at him, her face brilliant in the morning sun, tinged with a touch of mature sadness. "Yes. I can't wait to see it. I have to say, I love this Western country, son." She looked over at Floyd, riding alongside her son. "Thank you, Floyd. Thank you for all you've done, and thank you for your valley."

"You ain't seen it yet, Rebecca. This country is mighty pretty, but it ain't nothin' compared with what your eyes are gonna feast on."

She smiled at her brother-in-law, who looked so much like Matthew. "I'm sure it will be grand."

The two men urged their horses into a lope. When they had pulled about a mile ahead of the wagons, they slowed to a walk, and rode in silence. Each man alert, searching for possible danger, but locked in his own thoughts.

Finally, Floyd spoke up. "You might think I'm crazy, boy, but I'm startin' to believe it."

Callum, puzzled, looked over at his uncle. "Believe what?"

"That medicine man."

Callum nodded. "You know, Uncle, I have to admit, I've thought about it once or twice."

Floyd shook his head. "I've lived with those folks off and on for quite a few years. They believe different than we do, but that don't mean all of what they believe is wrong. Mostly, it's just different. Sometimes they can be downright mystical, but that don't mean that's wrong either.

"When them Shoshones gave you that horse you're riding, that old medicine man said a bullet would never again touch your hide. Now, I was a mite skeptical, but over the past year, too much has happened to be a coincidence. Especially this last one. Cassidy's gun misfirin'? Now, I'm a logical man, and I know there are misfires. I've had 'em. But that one happened at the all-fired right moment."

Callum watched Shoshone step gingerly around a large rock in the trail and scanned the hills to the south. Floyd was right, too much had happened. Maybe there was something to the medicine man's spell. He shook his head. Coincidence, that's all it was. "I don't know, Uncle. That's pretty hard to get my mind around."

Floyd continued. "I know, son. I think it's easier for me. I've spent a lot of years in these mountains. I've seen a lot that can't be explained with logic, but that misfire takes it all. He had you beat, dead to rights. Why, he was even smilin'. That smile sure disappeared when that powder popped. How does only one load get wet, or whatever it was?" The old mountain man shook his head in wonder. "Guess we'll never know." The two big men rode west toward the towering mountains, both thankful for one misfire.

# 30

Thanks to the helpful folks in Pueblo, Arlo Pickering had no trouble finding the ranch. He had managed to stay out of sight and found a perfect ambush point that gave him a good line of sight to the wide headquarters veranda. He had seen Josh Logan and a woman, he guessed Logan's wife, and a little boy. The sight infuriated him. His little boys deserved to be happy, not them. He enjoyed lying on the ridgeline imagining what it would be like to put one big ole hole through the woman and her boy. That would hurt the Logans more than killing Callum or Josh.

Pickering lay in the soft spread of pine needles, letting his mind wander to the many possibilities. He looked across the small valley that ran at almost a right angle into the main basin. Cattle and horses grazed in the high grass. Across the north ridge, where it joined the open land of the big valley, he could see a few buffalo and elk mixed with the ranch stock.

Anger filled the vengeful man as he gazed at the pastoral scene. These people didn't deserve any of this. What had they done? So Josh Logan knew someone and became a major in the war—that didn't make him any better than his own son, Philo.

And what about Callum Logan? He should be dead. If it wasn't for Old Man Logan, he would be.

The sound of the ranch house door closing drew his eyes back. There, in all of his finery, stood Josh Logan, holding his son. Pickering was almost shaking with anticipation as he moved the muzzle of his Spencer to cover Josh. He started tightening the pressure on the trigger, then jerked his hand away—and froze. His movement had caught Josh's eye. Pickering lay dead still, fearing even to breath. He watched Logan closely examine the hillside. Then, a black-and-white carrion-eating magpie flew, just a few yards away, and sailed toward the house. Josh watched the magpie, shrugged, turned, and reentered their home.

Sweat drenched the fat man's body. It was cool here in the mountains, and the sweat made him cold. He had to control himself. He'd already made up his mind. The first person he was going to shoot was Ma Logan. She birthed that brood from hell, and it would be her he would send there. Not that he had anything against her. In fact, she had always been nice to him, but by killing her, he'd be driving a knife into the heart of every single Logan. He had been dreaming about her arrival, everyone happy and hugging each other. Then, when she stepped up on the porch, he'd blow a hole through all that happiness.

He waited until he was sure he was safe, and backed away from his hide. He slipped down the hill to his horse, and rode back to camp. Crossing the small, clear stream that came out of the mountains, he dismounted and got himself a drink. This was about the best water he'd ever tasted. Standing up again, he looked around. Other than a small buck feeding about fifty yards away, there was nothing in sight. Satisfied, he remounted and rode on to his hidden camp. After he ate, he'd ride to his other hide that overlooked the entrance to the valley. Once he spotted Callum and his bunch, he'd have plenty of time to ride back and get positioned for the kill. He couldn't help grinning in anticipation. He'd give 'em payback. He'd show that Callum Logan.

~

"WHAT YOU'RE LOOKIN' at, Rebecca," Floyd was saying, "here on our right, is the Greenhorn Mountains. So the story goes, the Spanish named them after a Comanche Chief. They're mighty impressive, but don't hold a candle to those big ones ahead of us. Those are the Sangre de Cristos."

Everyone except Callum hung on each word from Floyd, and he was enjoying being the tour guide. They were about to turn into the mouth of the valley, and in a few miles they would break out of the canyon to the vistas of the long valley and the massive mountains. While they were all under Floyd's and the mountains' spells, Callum kept a close watch.

This was Ute country, and they weren't known for being friendly to the white man. The sun had just come over the Greenhorns and was behind him and to his right. As his eyes covered the close timber and then moved up to the far rising mountains, he thought he caught a glint of something. A flash? A mirror? Maybe a signal, or the reflection off binocular lenses? He turned to Floyd, but the old mountain man was in his element, regaling his audience on the beauty and mystery of these mountains.

Callum reached into his saddlebags and drew out his binoculars. Halting Shoshone, he scanned the far mountain slopes. Nothing. While he had the glasses out, he shortened his range and checked the nearer trees. The aspen had turned a brilliant gold and flashed in the morning breeze. Ma had loved her first sight of them, and the tall ponderosa pine. *She's gonna like it here,* he thought.

He continued looking.

"See something?" Kate called as the remuda pushed up past him, the wagons already entering the canyon.

"Thought I did," Callum said. "Guess not. So, how do you like it?"

Her blue eyes, matching the deep blue of the sky, sparkled

with excitement. "Oh, Callum. This is beautiful country. I just can't get over the aspen. They are beautiful, and the animals, I've seen antelope, buffalo, deer, and what did you call the big deer?"

"Elk. The Indians call them Wapiti."

"Yes, everything is beautiful, and the snow on those mountains. It is so white. It's just beautiful."

Callum couldn't help laughing. "Sounds like you think everything out here is beautiful. Wait till you see Josh. He'll change your mind."

She shot him a mock frown. "Don't make fun of me, or I'll tell Ma you're teasing again."

"I wouldn't want you to do that. I sure don't aim to be on the wrong side of Ma. Seriously, little sister, I'm glad you like it out here. Some folks can't stand the solitude, but I find it refreshing."

"You would," she teased back. "When do we get to the ranch?"

"Soon. Won't be long before we break out of this canyon. Then you'll see the valley. Get ready to have your breath taken away."

"I don't know if I can stand anymore."

Colin yelled, "Come on, Kate. Quit jawin' with Callum, and help with these horses."

She spun her horse around and raced after the others.

Callum waited for a few more minutes after everyone passed. He was feeling better. It was good to see Colin loosen up. These last few days, since they had left the wagon train, had done the boy a sight of good. Being away from the other boys seemed to change his outlook. He and Virg were working like a real team with the horses, and he wasn't messin' with that gun.

*Speaking of Virg,* he thought, *that boy has really taken hold. He works like a man. No job's too big for him to tackle, and he takes to horses like he was born with them. This move looks like it will be good for everyone.*

He spun Shoshone around and galloped past the horses and

wagons, toward the mouth of the valley, where, breaking out, he stopped and waited.

The wagons rolled into the long valley and stopped alongside Callum, while the wranglers brought the horses up. Everyone was quiet.

Finally, Ma spoke. "Floyd, Callum, I could never have imagined anything so beautiful."

The day was still cool and a breeze blew down the slopes of the Sangre de Cristos and across the valley. Standing in the shimmering, chest-high grass, were longhorns, the sun occasionally glinting off the wide horns. A few buffalo fed along with the cattle. As far as the eye could see there was valley.

Ma turned to Floyd. "We don't need much, Floyd, but I'm curious. How much is ours?"

The happiness in the eyes of his brother's wife, brought moisture to the eyes of a man who seldom shed a tear. He took off his hat and using it as he would a paintbrush, wiped it across the Sangre de Cristos, the wide, deep valley, and the Greenhorns. "Rebecca, as far as those lovely eyes of yours can see, is Logan land."

It took a moment for her mind to comprehend. Then her Irish blood took over, and a frown crossed her face. "And tell me, Mr. Mountain Man, what will we be doing with this much land?"

Floyd threw back his head and laughed. When he stopped, he smiled at his sister-in-law. "Whatever we want, Rebecca, whatever we want."

Callum noticed riders coming out of the ranch house valley. He stood up in his saddle, took off his hat, and waved back and forth. He could see Josh, riding in his upright cavalry manner, rip off his hat and wave back. Fianna, unmistakable with her long, red hair flying in the wind, rode alongside her husband. He turned to the wagons. "Ma, here comes Josh."

Her head snapped to the left and her hand went to her mouth. Tears filled her eyes as she stepped down from the wagon and walked to the other side, waiting for the son she hadn't seen in over a year. She stood there, hands clasped.

Josh pulled Chancy up in a sliding stop and leaped from his back. Without breaking a stride, he rushed to his ma. She disappeared in his big arms. Finally, she shoved him back, pushing an escaped strand of auburn hair back under her bonnet.

"You are looking healthy, son. And who is responsible for that?"

With that question, she turned to Fianna.

Callum had dismounted, moved to Fianna, and helped her and little Matthew down. He gave her a hug, and then lifted the boy from her arms. "How's my nephew doing?"

Matthew looked up at Callum and grinned, which brought laughter from everyone.

Fianna moved up beside Josh. "Mother Logan, 'tis a true pleasure to be meeting you."

Ma cocked her head. "Why, I believe I'm detecting a bit of the Irish."

"Proud I am to be using it, ma'am."

Then they both laughed and grasped each other in a sincere hug.

Callum noticed Josh looking around.

"Cal, where's Pa?"

Quiet settled over the family.

Floyd spoke up. "He's dead, Josh."

"How?"

"He was gunned down," Floyd said, "by the Pickering boys."

Josh immediately turned to Callum. "Did you do something about that?"

Callum nodded. "Yes. They're both dead."

"What about Old Man Pickering. He was worse than any of the boys."

"He was the marshal of Limerick," Callum said.

In disbelief, Josh said, "You are kidding."

Ma spoke up. "It's a crazy time back there, son. He wangled his way in and was using his position to confiscate folks' property. We were about to lose the farm when Callum showed up. Good thing you thought to write that letter." She stopped, reached out, and took her son by the shoulders, and said, "I'm tired. How about we go up to the house? We'll tell you all about it, and I can hold my grandson."

"Sorry, Ma. I forgot myself. Let's head on up." He turned to Callum. "I think you're gonna like the changes."

"Don't forget us," Kate said.

Josh looked around at his sister and brothers. He walked back, threw his arms around Kate, and pulled her off her horse in a big bear hug. After almost squeezing the life out of her, he held her away from him, then looked down the trail where they had come. "My, my, girl. You're getting to be a mighty pretty thing. I'm surprised there aren't a bunch of suitors dogging your trail."

She slapped him on the arm. "You're as bad as Callum." She turned and jumped back on her horse, her even, white teeth exposed in a big grin.

Josh quickly said hi to Bret and Colin, and paused when he saw Ezra Mason. He shook hands with the man and reached up to scratch Blue behind the ears.

"Mr. Mason? I'm surprised to see you, but glad you're here. I see Blue made the trip."

"Good to see you, Josh, but drop that Mr. Mason. Just call me Ezra. Yep, Blue's walked just about all the way. He started gettin' a little tired back there, so I figured I'd give him a little ride-a-long. The rascal's earned it."

When Josh stopped scratching Blue, the hound stretched his head out for more. When no more scratching was forthcoming, he laid his head back on Ezra's leg.

Josh nodded, and, walking back to the horses, gave Fianna a hand up. He looked over at his ma. She was on the wagon, with Matt sitting in her lap laughing.

He swung up onto Chancy and rode over to Frank's wagon, extending his hand. "Didn't mean to ignore you, Frank. It's good to see you here."

"Ain't no problem, boy. Glad to see you." Josh turned Chancy toward the ranch. "All right, folks. Let's go see your new home."

The laughter had returned, and everyone was talking, including baby Matt to his grandmother.

When they arrived, Josh waved the horses and mules toward the corral. One of the ranch hands opened the corral gate, and the wranglers drove them in. Once inside, the three of them dismounted and started unsaddling their horses.

Several of the ranch hands slipped between the bars and walked over to them. "You folks go on in the house. We'll take good care of your animals. You've got a lot of catching up to do."

Kate's eye caught the younger one. He grinned and ducked his head, then took her reins. "I'll take good care of your horse, ma'am."

"Thank you," she said, her face flushed, and she quickly climbed through the fence.

Everyone had gathered on the veranda. Frank, Ezra, and Virgil had hung back, but the family was having none of that.

Colin grabbed Virgil by the arm and pulled him up on the porch. Josh was showing Ma Logan the vista from there. He stopped and stuck out his hand. "You must be Virgil."

"Yes, sir," Virgil said, as he took Josh's hand, "but everybody calls me Virg."

"Well, Virg, Callum has been telling me about you. Sounds like you are going to be a great addition to this ranch, if that's all right with you?"

Virgil beamed in the fading light. "Yes, sir, that's fine with me."

"Good, you come on in. You're family now, and I'll be expecting a lot from you."

"I'll do whatever you ask, Mr. Logan."

"The first thing I'll ask is to drop the Mr. Logan. I expect you to call me Josh, just like Colin does." Josh turned to Colin. "Is that all right with you, brother?"

Colin grinned up at his big brother. "It sure is."

"Fine," Josh said, and turned back to Ma.

She was looking down the ranch valley, into the wide expanse of the big basin, and across to the pines and aspen faintly visible on the ragged slopes of the Greenhorn Mountains.

"Josh," she said, "it takes my breath away. I never expected to see our side of the Logans with this much land, and every inch beautiful."

"I know, Ma. We can thank Floyd for that."

Floyd ducked his head. "Glad it worked out."

Josh took a sidelong look at Callum's left ear, where it had been split by Hughes. "Brother, it looks like you got into a pretty mean tussle."

Callum grinned. "That's another story." Then he looked up and down the veranda. "Josh, you and the hands have been working. This place is four times the size it was when we left."

Josh pulled Fianna close, his big arm wrapped around her shoulders, and looked at the house with satisfaction. "I wanted to make sure there was plenty of room for Ma and P—well, plenty of room." He brightened. "Cal, you said you'd bring the family out, and you danged sure did. I'm proud of you."

The two brothers clasped hands and stood for a moment longer. It was time. Josh turned to his ma. "Come in and see your new home."

She beamed. Squeezing little Matt to her breasts, she turned to stare out at the opposite ridgeline of the valley. For a moment, she stood stationary, taking in the conifer smell and the golden aspen. Facing the ridgeline, her body outlined by the large veranda and all of her family near, she glowed with happiness. The loss of her husband still weighed heavily on her, but having almost all of her children with her was certainly a balm. If only her oldest, Will, could be here, with the family, in these high, beautiful mountains. She waited a few more seconds, feeling the deep peace, the happiness mixed with sadness—life. Then the moment passed. She turned back to the door, stepping into a warm, inviting room with a roaring fireplace.

After the others had gone inside, Callum remained standing on the porch. He had been physically and spiritually drained, but these mountains were already invigorating him. He took a deep breath of the cold, pine-scented mountain air, and glanced over at old Blue. The hound had already staked out his spot on the veranda, where he could see down into the valley.

Callum gazed across to the distant Greenhorns. Behind him, the sun had started to drop below the peaks of the Sangre de Cristo, drawing shadows along the base of the Greenhorn mountains. The impending darkness marched up the slopes, darkening the golden aspen and the tall, somber ponderosa pines, until finally, only the snow-capped peaks of the Greenhorns remained. For a few instants of time, they glistened golden in the evening light, then the light was gone, and they, too, turned dull, covered in the shadows.

Callum watched for a minute more, then turned, pulled the latch, and stepped into the house he had helped build. Laughter and warmth welcomed him. He felt Blue slip by his leg and amble to the fire near Ezra. The blazing fireplace lit the happy faces of three generations of Logans. A quick thought of his older brother passed through his mind. *I wish Will was here.* He closed the door, leaving the darkness outside.

# EPILOGUE

Arlo Pickering rushed now. He had watched the Logans and their sickening display of happiness far too long. Their joy was at his expense, and he could feel hate boiling inside. He hadn't traveled over a thousand miles to watch the Logans hug each other. He wanted to kill them, to mutilate them, to rip their hearts out. But he would be satisfied just to kill the old woman, and then watch them wail.

He had to stop at his camp first. He was hungry. This mountain air seemed to increase his appetite, which was pretty big already. In rushing to his horse, he slipped on the loose rocks of the ridgeline and sat down hard. Starting slowly, he began sliding down the steep hillside, attempting, unsuccessfully, to stop himself with the palms of his hands against the sharp loose rocks. He finally came to a stop in a blueberry patch along a shallow draw.

Arlo's legs, extending into the draw, had come up against something soft. He pushed off from it to stand up and, to his horror, it moved. The animal started to rise up, and up, until it towered over him.

The grizzly had been preparing for winter, minding her own

business while she stuffed herself with wild blueberries. Pickering had disturbed her. The enormous bear leaned toward the fat man, opened its huge mouth, and roared. Pickering frantically tried to pull himself up the hill, but even if he made it, his horse was gone. At first sight of the grizzly, the horse had ripped the reins free from the sapling where it was tied, and raced over the hill.

The bear still did not attack the man, but stood towering above him.

Through his paralyzing fear, Pickering finally remembered his revolver. His hands shook so badly he could grasp almost nothing. They fluttered like a butterfly's wings in his attempt to release the leather thong holding the weapon in its holster. Still glaring down at him, the grizzly had stopped roaring and was sniffing.

At last, he managed to pull the revolver from its holster. Carefully, he leveled it at the bear's head, and, just as the grizzly began to drop to all fours to continue her blueberry treat, Pickering pulled the trigger.

The grizzly bawled in agony. The bullet had hit the animal at the top of its brown nose, carrying away a portion of that sensitive instrument. The hunk of lead continued its destruction just under the thick skin, gouging flesh and hide, ultimately reaching the grizzly's skull. However, because of the thickness and angle of the bone, the bullet didn't penetrate. It followed the sloping front of the skull, finally exiting above and between the little, beady eyes, now inflamed with fury.

Swinging her huge head from side to side, in an attempt to lessen the pain, she again spotted Pickering. He had struggled to his feet and was scrambling back up the hill.

With a roar, she was on top of the man in three leaps. One swipe of those long, four-inch claws, laid Pickering's back open. The blow turned him over. His puny kicks positioned his leg perfectly. Sharp, strong teeth clamped down on his knee. The tall pines and golden aspen muffled his scream.

He had dropped his revolver. If he could get the gun, he could still protect himself. Pain descended over him like a red cloak. He couldn't get away from it. He slammed his raw and bloody hand on the ground, time and again, reaching, feeling, searching for the gun. He couldn't find it, but he was successful in getting the bear's attention. The grizzly turned loose of the man's leg and grabbed his arm, shaking him like a dog shakes a rat. Every inch, every hair on his body screamed with pain.

Finally, the shaking stopped. He lay still, eyes closed. He welcomed the peaceful quiet, except for the roaring in his ears. He listened. It wasn't the bear. It was the pain. He had no idea how long the mauling had gone on, but now there was only silence. Pickering lay motionless for another minute, afraid to move, yet hoping the bear had gone. He took a deep breath and opened his eyes.

Staring directly into his face was a picture more awful than he could conjure up even in his most terrible nightmares. The bear waited no more than a foot away, blood dripping out of the channel wound along its nose and head. The instant his eyes opened, the bear spread her gaping mouth and roared, blowing spittle and stench into his face, huge teeth only inches away. The mouth descended, blocking all vision, until his eyes beheld only the inside of the terrible maw.

A single, last thought screamed through Arlo Pickering's mind. *Why didn't I stay in Limerick!*

# AUTHOR'S NOTE

I hope you enjoyed Callum's Mission. This is the third book in the Logan Family Series. The Logan family is unique only in that they are fictionalized. Thousands of pioneers pushed West, many to build a new life, some for the riches of gold and silver, others for freedom and independence, and finally those trying to escape the law.

Whatever their intention, those independent, searching men and women are the stock that many here sprang from. Their stories, the hard, dirty, day-to-day labor, the battle to survive, inspire us today to strive for our best. I certainly hope you enjoyed reading Callum's Mission as much as I enjoyed bringing it to you.

If there are errors they are mine alone. Those of you who are history buffs will find that Limerick, Tennessee, is a fictional town near Short Mountain, which is real.

You'll find missing, in all of my novels, crude language and overt sexual situations. There may be an occasional damn or hell, but even those will be few.

I'd love to from hear from from you. My email address is: Don@DonaldLRobertson.com, or fill in the contact form at:

<u>www.DonaldLRobertson.com.</u>

**Logan Family Series**

*LOGAN'S WORD*

*THE SAVAGE VALLEY*

*CALLUM'S MISSION*

*FORGOTTEN SEASON*

*SOUL OF A MOUNTAIN MAN*

**Clay Barlow - Texas Ranger Justice Series**

*FORTY-FOUR CALIBER JUSTICE*

*LAW AND JUSTICE*

*LONESOME JUSTICE*

**NOVELLAS AND SHORT STORIES**

*BECAUSE OF A DOG*

*RUSTLERS IN THE SAGE*

*THE OLD RANGER*